SARABAND
FOR
TWO SISTERS

❖ ❖ ❖

Philippa Carr

A FAWCETT CREST BOOK

Fawcett Publications, Inc., Greenwich, Connecticut

SARABAND FOR TWO SISTERS

THIS BOOK CONTAINS THE COMPLETE TEXT OF THE
ORIGINAL HARDCOVER EDITION.

A Fawcett Crest Book reprinted by arrangement with
G.P. Putnam's Sons

ISBN 0-449-23207-7

Alternate Selection of the Literary Guild, Summer 1976
Selection of the Doubleday Book Club, December 1976
Selection of Contempo Book Club, August 1976

Printed in the United States of America

10 9 8 7 6 5 4 3 2 1

ANGELET .

❖ ❖ ❖

Visitors from the Past

YESTERDAY, the twelfth day of June in the year sixteen hundred and thirty-nine, was our seventeenth birthday—mine and Bersaba's. It was fitting that we should be born in June, the birth sign of which is Gemini, for we are twins. In our family birthdays are always celebrated as joyous occasions. Our mother is responsible for that. There are certain women in our family who are born to be mothers and she is one of them. I don't think I am; I'm certain Bersaba isn't. But perhaps I am mistaken because it can be a quality which is only discovered when one reaches the state of motherhood, and one thing I have learned is that one can be mistaken about a great deal, which is one of the less gratifying experiences of growing up. I once remarked to Bersaba that every birthday our mother thanked God for giving us to her and Bersaba answered that she did it every day. My mother, Tamsyn Landor, was married five years before our brother Fennimore was born and then another seven years elapsed before she gave birth to us—her twins. I believe she had wanted a large family, but now she would say she had just what she wanted, for she

5

is a woman who can adjust existing conditions to her dreams of contentment, which I am old enough to know is a rare gift.

We had the usual birthday celebrations. June is a lovely month for a birthday because so much of it can be celebrated out of doors. On our birthday it became a ritual that if the day was fine we rode out into the meadows and there we would feast off cold poultry and what we called West Country Tarts, pastry cases with the fruit of the season—strawberries for our birthday—in them and custard or clouted cream on the top, which were a very special delicacy. Of course there had been rainy birthdays, and on these occasions the friends and neighbors who joined us would come to the house, where we would play games such as blindman's buff or hunt the slipper, and then we would dress up and act charades or produce the plays which we had seen the mummers do at Christmastime. Whatever the weather, birthdays were days to be looked forward to, and I had said every year to Bersaba that as ours was two in one it should be extra special.

On this particular birthday the weather had been fine and we had been out into the meadows and the young people from Kroll Manor and Trent Park had joined us. We had played ball games and kayles—which consisted of knocking down pins with a stick or a ball—and after that hide-and-seek, during which Bersaba had not been found and caused a certain anxiety because our mother was always afraid that something terrible would happen to us. We were an hour searching for Bersaba, and finally she gave herself up. She looked hurt when she saw how worried our mother had been, but I, who knew her so well, guessed that she was gratified to be so worried about. Bersaba often seemed as though she wanted to assure herself that she was important to us.

We all went back to Trystan Priory, our home, and there were more games and feasting and just before dark servants came from Kroll Manor and Trent Park to take our friends home and that was the end of another birthday we thought. But it was not so.

Our mother came to our room. We had always shared a room. Sometimes I thought that now we were growing up we should have separate apartments—there were plenty of rooms in the Priory—but I waited for Bersaba to suggest it, and I think perhaps she was waiting for me to do so, and as neither of us did we went on in the old way.

Our mother looked rather solemn.

She sat down on the big carved chair which Bersaba and I used to fight over when we were young. It was a wonderful chair with griffins at the end of the arms. I always felt I had the advantage when I sat in that chair, and as Bersaba felt the same there was competition to get there first. Now our mother sat there and looked at us with that benign affection which I took for granted then and remembered with nostalgia later on.

"Seventeen," she said. "It's a turning point. You're no longer children, you know."

Bersaba sat quietly, her hands in her lap. Bersaba was a quiet person. I was scarcely that. I often wondered why people said they couldn't tell us apart. Although we looked identical, our natures were so different that that should have been an indication.

"Next year," went on our mother, "you'll be eighteen. There'll be a different birthday party for you. It will be more grown up and there won't be games such as you've been playing today."

"I suppose we shall have a ball," I said, and I could not keep the excitement out of my voice, for I loved dancing and I excelled at it.

"Yes, and you will be meeting more people. I was talking to your father about it last time he was home, and he agreed with me."

I wondered idly if they had ever disagreed about anything. I couldn't believe they ever had.

"But that is a year ahead," she went on, as though she were pleased that it could be postponed. "There is something else. It's a tradition in our family that the women of the household keep journals. It's a strange one, because it had been carried on in an unbroken line since your great-great-grandmother Damask Farland began it. It is possible to follow our family history in these journals. Now that your are growing up you may read that of Damask and of your great-grandmother Catherine. You will find it of the utmost interest."

"And Grandmother Linnet's and yours?" asked Bersaba.

"They are not yet for reading."

"Oh, what a pity," I cried, but Bersaba was looking thoughtful, and she said gravely, "If people knew that what they wrote would be read by those living round them they wouldn't tell the truth . . . not the whole truth."

Our mother nodded, slowly smiling at Bersaba. Bersaba had a certain wisdom which I lacked. I said whatever came into my head, just allowing it to flow out without thinking very much about it. Bersaba often thought carefully before she spoke.

7

"Why should they not?" I demanded. "What is the point of keeping a diary if you don't tell the truth?"

"Some people see the truth as they want to," said Bersaba.

"Then how can it be the truth?"

"It's truth to them because that's what they believe, and if they are writing for people to read who might have been there when whatever they are writing about was happening, they would tell their version of it."

"There's some truth in that," said my mother. "So, your journal is your own secret. It must be so. It is only years later that it becomes the property of the family."

"When we are dead," I said with a shiver, but I was fascinated by it. I thought of the generations to come reading all about my life. I hoped it would be worth reading.

My mother went on: "So now that you are growing up I am going to suggest that you keep your journals. I am giving you one each tomorrow and a desk in which you can lock them up when you have written in them. They will be your very own private property."

"Do you still write in yours, Mother?" asked Bersaba.

She smiled gently. "I still write now and then. Once I wrote a good deal. That was in the days before I married your father. I had a great deal to write about then." Her expression clouded. I knew she was thinking of the dreadful mystery of her mother's death. "Now," she said, "I hardly ever write. There is nothing dramatic to record. Life has been happy and peaceful for these last years, and happiness and a peaceful existence have one failing only—they give little to write about. I hope, my darlings, that you will find only happy events to record in your books. But write all the same . . . write of the ordinary happy things of life."

I cried: "I'm longing to begin. I shall start tomorrow. I shall tell about today . . . our seventeenth birthday."

"And what of you, Bersaba?" asked my mother.

"I shall write when I have something interesting to write about," answered my sister.

My mother nodded. "Oh, and by the way, I think it is time we visited your grandfather. We shall leave next week. You'll have plenty of time to prepare."

Then she kissed us and left us.

And then next day we received our desks and journals, and I started mine by writing the above.

There was nothing unusual about visiting our grandfather in Castle Paling. We did it several times a year. The Castle is not far from us—a few miles along the coast only, but going there always excited me. Castle Paling was in itself a ghostly place; terrible things had happened there not so very long ago. My mother had hinted at them and she should know for she had spent her childhood there. Her mother—our grandmother Linnet Casvellyn—had died there in a mysterious fashion (she had, I believed, been murdered although this had never been admitted), and now our grandfather Colum Casvellyn lived a strange and solitary life in the Seaward Tower, a trial to all around him and especially to himself. My Uncle Connell and Aunt Melanie lived in another part of the castle with their four children. They were a very normal family, but extreme contrasts like the placidity of my Aunt Melanie and the wildness of my grandfather create an atmosphere which is more sinister because of this very contrast.

As Trystan Priory was five miles from the sea, one of the attractions of the castle was its closeness to it, for even within those thick walls one was aware of its murmur, especially when it was rough. In comparison our house seemed very peaceful and, to a girl of seventeen who was longing for adventure, peace could appear dull.

Ours was a fine house really though I never realized this until I left it. The old priory had been destroyed when the monasteries were dissolved, and the house had been built on the site with many of the original stones. As it had been constructed in the days of Elizabeth, it was built in the shape of an E out of compliment to the Queen, as so many houses were at that time. It was full of exciting nooks and crannies, and it had its butteries, pantries, and fine old kitchen. The grounds were beautiful. There were rose, pond, kitchen, and herb gardens and some in the Italian style, but mostly English; our mother took a great interest in them as she did about anything in the house because it was the home which sheltered her precious family. This impressed itself on me after visiting Castle Paling, where in spite of Melanie—who was not dissimilar to my mother—one had the impression of something forbidding and menacing.

Bersaba felt it as I did, but it was indicative of our characters that it affected us differently.

The day after our seventeenth birthday I asked Bersaba whether she was pleased we were going to Castle Paling the following week. We were in the schoolroom where we had been left by our governess for what was called "private study."

She shrugged her shoulders. and lowered her eyes and I

9

saw her teeth come out over her lower lip. I knew her habits so well that I understood she was faintly disturbed. But her feelings could be mixed. There was a good deal she hated about Castle Paling but there was one thing she loved. That was our cousin Bastian.

"I wonder how long we shall stay?" I went on.

"Not more than a week I expect," she answered. "You know Mother hates to be away too long for fear Father should return in her absence and she will not be there to welcome him."

Our father was often away from home for months at a stretch because he was deeply involved with the East India Company, which had been founded by his father—amongst others—and which for a time had prospered. In this year of sixteen hundred and thirty-nine it was less successful than it had been, but to a man like my father that was a challenge. Many people connected with the Company visited us at Trystan Priory, and there always seemed something exhilarating to discuss about it. For instance at this time there was a great deal of talk about the new factory they were planning to build on the banks of the Hooghly River in India.

"Fennimore will be primed to send a message if the ship is sighted," I reminded her.

"Oh, yes, but she likes to be here."

"I shall take my new muff," I announced.

"A muff in summer! You are crazy," said Bersaba.

I was crestfallen. My muff had been a birthday present. I had wanted it because I had heard they were now worn a great deal by the ladies of King Charles' court, which meant that they were the height of fashion.

"Besides," went on Bersaba, "where would you wear a muff at Castle Paling? I shall take my sketchbook," she added.

Bersaba had drawn a piece of paper toward her and was sketching on it. She was very good and could, in a few lines, create an impression. I could almost feel that I was at Castle Paling looking out from one of the turret windows.

She started to sketch Grandfather Casvellyn. What a terrifying man he must have been when he could walk about! Now there was something pathetic about him because he looked so frighteningly fierce while at the same time he was so crippled that he could not walk and had to spend most of his time lying on a couch or being wheeled about in a chair. He had been thus for many years—for more than twelve years before we were born. It seemed to us that he had been there for always and always would be there. He was like the Flying Dutchman, but instead of sailing the seas he had been doomed to sit in his chair in expiation of some terrible sin.

"Well," I said slyly, "it will be good to see our cousins."

Bersaba went on sketching and I knew she was thinking of Bastian. He was twenty-three years old and resembled Aunt Melanie; kind and gentle, he had never taken up the patronizing attitude which older people give to the young. Nor did our brother Fennimore for that matter. Our mother would not have allowed it in our house, but Castle Paling was different. I think that at some time Bastian must have shown some preference for Bersaba which won her immediate devotion, for she reacted quickly to any form of appreciation.

There were three girl cousins. Melder, the eldest, was twenty-six and disinclined to marry; she loved housekeeping and coped with Grandfather Casvellyn better than anyone else partly because she remained impassive when he swore and cursed her and everything round him, and quietly went on with what she had come to do. Then there was Rozen, aged nineteen, and Gwenifer seventeen.

As Aunt Melanie, my father's sister, had married my mother's brother Connell, there was a double relationship between us all. It seemed to bind us very closely together but perhaps that had come about because Aunt Melanie was the homemaking family-conscious type of woman—just as my mother was—and they believed in welding families together.

Bersaba had started to sketch Bastian.

"He's not as handsome as that," I protested.

She flushed and tore the paper in halves.

I thought to myself: She really loves Bastian. But the next moment I had forgotten it.

A week later we set out for Castle Paling, Bersaba and I, our mother, three grooms, and two maidservants. We really did not need servants, for there were plenty at Paling, but the roads were not altogether safe and the servants were a protection. My father had made my mother promise never to ride out without making sure that she was adequately guarded against attack, and although the roads between Trystan Priory and Castle Paling were well known to us she would never go against his wishes.

Bersaba looked pretty on that morning. June is such a lovely month when the hedges are gay with wild roses and

11

lacey chevril while great clumps of yellow gorse brighten the
downs and the red sorrel shows itself in the fields. She was
wearing her dark red outer petticoats which we called safeguards and which we always wore for riding. I had put on my
blue ones. Although we sometimes dressed alike we did not
always wear identical clothes. There were occasions when we
liked to because we took a mischievous delight in puzzling
people. I could put on a good impersonation of Bersaba and
she could of me. We used to practice sometimes and one of
the great jokes of our childhood had been to deceive people
in this way. We would laugh until we were hysterical when
someone said to her: "Now, Miss Angelet, it's no use your
pretending to be Miss Bersaba. I'd know you anywhere." It
gave us a kind of power, as I pointed out to Bersaba. We
could put it to good use on certain occasions. Well, on this
day she wore her red so I wore my blue; our cloaks matched
our safeguards and we each had brown, soft boots. So there
would be no danger in our being mistaken for each other on
that journey. But when we were at Paling I knew we would
wear similar clothes at times and enjoy deceiving them.

We rode one on either side of our mother. She was a little
pensive. No doubt she would be thinking of our father and
wondering where he was at that moment. There was always
anxiety in her mind because so many dangers lurked on the
high seas and she could never be sure whether he would
come back.

Once I mentioned this to her and she said that if she did
not suffer these anxieties she could not be so happy when he
did come home. We must always remember that life was
made up of light and shadow and the light was the brighter
because of the contrasting shadow. She was a philosopher,
my mother; and she was always trying to teach us to understand and accept life as it was, because she felt such an attitude would be a cushion if ever misfortunes came to us.

If my father and brother had been riding to Castle Paling
with us she would have been completely happy. I loved her
intensely as we rode along and I started to sing in sheer
thankfulness to God who gave her to me:

> And therefore take the present time
> With a hey and a ho and a hey nonino
> For love is crowned with the prime
> In springtime . . .

My mother smiled at me as though she shared my

thoughts and she joined in the song and told the servants to do the same. Then we all took turns to sing the first line of a song of our choice and the rest of us would come in, but when it was Bersaba's turn she sang alone because no one joined in with her. It was Ophelia's song:

> How should I your true love know
> From another one?
> By his cockle hat and staff
> And his sandal shoon
>
> He is dead and gone, lady
> He is dead and gone;
> At his head a grass green turf,
> At his heels a stone.

Bersaba had a strange haunting voice and when she sang those words I imagined her lying in the stream with her long dark hair floating round her and her face white and dead. There was something strange about Bersaba, something I didn't understand, for all that she was said to be part of me. She had that quiet personality which seems not to intrude and yet can change the mood of all those around her.

She had made us forget the May morning, the sun, the flowers, and the joys of living because she had reminded us of death. We stopped singing then and silently we rode on until the towers of the castle came into view.

The sun picked out the sharp points in the granite and made them glisten like little diamonds. It was indeed an impressive sight which never failed to thrill me. Defiant, bold, arrogant, the castle always seemed like a living thing to me, and I never failed to feel proud to be connected with it. Our house was mellow in a way, although its stones might well be as old as as those of the castle—or almost; but Trystan seemed gentle, homely when compared with Castle Paling. Its four battlemented towers proclaimed it for what it was, a fortress which had remained impregnable for six hundred years, for it had been built in the days of the Conqueror although it had been added to over the passing centuries. My imagination went into action everytime I beheld it and I could picture the defenders of the castle pouring boiling oil and arrows down on those who would assail it. There were marks on a heavy oaken door with its iron bands—the one which was

13

below the gatehouse—which I was sure had been made by battering rams.

Approaching from the west, two of the towers were hidden from us—Ysella's which used to be said to be haunted, and Seaward, which was now haunted by Grandfather Casvellyn. I glanced at my mother. She had grown serious and I wondered what pictures the sight of that castle conjured up in her mind. One day I would read of her life there, which must have been very adventurous and unhappy too, for this must be the reason why she was so contented with the present.

Bersaba's expression had changed too. Her profile was clearcut; she had high cheekbones and long eyes with golden lashes tipped with dark brown at the edges. I often looked at her and thought: in describing her I am describing myself, for I look the same—or almost. It was only our expressions which could change our faces, for the bone structure and the shape of our features were identical. Our mother had once said: "As you grow older you will look less alike. Experience changes faces and it is hardly likely that you will share the same."

Now I thought we may be looking different because she changes when we are at Castle Paling. She is more remote, and I almost feel she has succeeded in doing what she is always trying to—move away from me. There used to be times when I had known what she was thinking but now she could shut me out and when we went to Castle Paling it was almost as though she let down some sort of shutter. I often wondered what it was at Castle Paling that made her do that.

As we were riding under the portcullis and into the courtyard I heard Rozen's voice shouting: "They're here!"

And then there was Aunt Melanie with Melder and Gwenifer coming out of a side door of the castle. There followed the usual bustle while our horses were taken by the grooms and the maids took our baggage and we were embraced by everybody.

Then we went through the guard room to the great hall on the stone walls of which were crossed halberds and pikes and several suits of armor which had been worn by our ancestors.

"Come first into my parlor," said Melanie, "and then when you are refreshed you can go to your rooms. It is good to see you all. The twins look well." She smiled at us and I could see she did not know which of us was which.

Wine and cakes were already there in that chamber which she had made like the one at Trystan. I was always intrigued when I saw her and my mother together to contemplate that

Aunt Melanie's present home was my mother's old one and vice versa.

We all seemed to talk at once and it was just like any other reunion.

We went to our rooms, Bersaba and I sharing as we always did, and Rozen and Gwenifer coming to help us unpack. Gwenifer talked a great deal about the balls that she had attended last season, for although she had not yet reached eighteen, as her elder sister was "out" it was decided that she should join her. Rozen believed that George Kroll was going to speak for her and although it was not a grand match it was one well worth considering.

"There are so few people here," pouted Rozen. "How I wish we could go to Court!"

Court! The very word set us all dreaming of balls and banquets of glittering state occasions and elaborate costumes trimmed with exquisite lace.

Rozen had dressed her hair with a curled fringe which we all admired and she told us that she had heard it was a fashion set by Queen Henrietta Maria. Rozen was very gay and she quite liked George Kroll although he was not the gallant she had hoped for.

"There's a lot of trouble brewing in Court circles," said Bersaba.

Everyone looked at her. How like Bersaba to say something serious when we all wanted to be frivolous.

She went on: "Father is disturbed about the Ship Money."

"Ship Money!" cried Rozen in dismay. "We are talking about fashions!"

"My dear cousin," said Bersaba in one of her superior moods, "if there is trouble between the King and his Parliament there could be no more fashions."

"Which one are you?" said Rozen quite angrily. "Bersaba, I'm sure."

"Of course," I answered for her.

"Oh, Angel, do make her shut up," said Rozen.

I folded my arms and smiled at my twin. "*I* have no control over her," I reminded them.

"It's silly not to face up to what's happening," said Bersaba crossly. "You know very well, Angel, that the people who come to see Father are very anxious."

"They're always anxious," said Gwenifer. "The East India men have always complained about something."

"They're doing wonderful work for the country," I supported my twin.

"Oh, you two and your saintly parents," said Gwenifer. "Let's talk about something interesting."

"So George Kroll is going to speak for Rozen?" I asked.

"It's almost certain," replied Rozen. "And Father will say yes because she thinks George will be a good husband."

"That's one ticked off the list," said Bersaba.

"What a way to look at it," I cried.

"Well, that's what it is," insisted Bersaba. "Our turns will come."

"I shall choose my husband," I said firmly.

"And so shall I," answered Bersaba equally so.

So we talked of balls, and our cousins examined our clothes, and the conversation was on a frivolous level, which pleased me, but I was aware that Bersaba thought it rather foolish. She retired into one of her silences which were so maddening because it seemed as though she were despising us all.

We dined in the great hall because we were quite a large party—nine in all, for Bastian and Uncle Connell, who had been out on the estate, came home in the late afternoon.

While we were dressing I said to Bersaba, "Let's wear our blues tonight."

She hesitated and a slight smile touched her lips. "All right," she said.

"We could have some fun," I said, "pretending I'm you and you're me."

"There are some who'll know the difference."

"Who?"

"Well, Mother for instance."

"Mother always knows."

So we wore our blue silk gowns with their boned bodices caught at the waist with sashes of a toning shade of blue, and skirts open to our feet showing satin petticoats; they had lovely long hanging sleeves. We had had them last year, and although they had not been in the height of fashion even then they were becoming.

"We'll wear our hair piled high," said Bersaba.

"They say it is no longer worn like that."

"It suits our high foreheads," she answered, and she was right.

So we stood side by side laughing at our reflections. Even though we were so accustomed to the likeness it sometimes amused us.

In the hall Uncle Connell kissed us heartily. He was the sort of man who liked women—all kinds, all ages, all sizes. He was

16

big and blustering, not unlike Grandfather Casvellyn—at least seeing him gave one an idea of what Grandfather Casvellyn must have been like in his youth. Even he, though, sometimes seemed afraid of Grandfather Casvellyn, and that made a difference because our grandfather would never have been afraid of anyone. He held us tightly against him and kissed us heartily and he put his hands under my chin and said: "Which one are you?"

I said, "I'm Angelet."

He answered: "Not such an angel if I know anything about it."

And everyone laughed.

"And Bersaba, eh? Well, come here my girl and give your uncle a kiss."

Bersaba went reluctantly, which made Uncle Connell give her two kisses as though repetition could make her like it better.

I had heard it said that Connell was a true Casvellyn and that he had several mistresses scattered around the countryside and more than one of the bastards in the servants' hall had been sired by him.

I often wondered what Aunt Melanie thought about that, but she never gave any sign that she minded. I had discussed it with Bersaba, who had said that she took it as a way of life and that as long as it didn't interfere with her household and family she turned a blind eye to it.

"I should have something to say," I declared, "if I were in her place, wouldn't you?"

"I should find something to *do* about it," answered Bersaba.

Bastian came too. I thought he was as handsome as Bersaba drew him—or nearly: He was as tall as his father, and the fact that he had inherited his father's looks and his mother's nature made him interesting.

He looked from Bersaba to me and back again.

Bersaba laughed then and he said: "Ah, Bersaba." And he kissed her first and then me.

Uncle Connell bade us be seated and we obeyed him. He sat at the head of the long refectory table with my mother on one side of him and Melder on the other. Bersaba and I were on either side of Aunt Melanie and Bastian had seated himself next to Bersaba.

They talked mostly about the affairs of the countryside— all that had to be done on the estate; my mother mentioned the growing difficulties the East India Company were having to face and which she hoped would be a little eased if they could build their new Indian factory.

Bastian said: "There's trouble everywhere. People don't seem to realize it. They shut their eyes to it but one day it will creep up on us."

"Bastian's a proper Jeremiah," commented Rozen.

"There's nothing so stupid as shutting your eyes to facts simply because they're unpleasant," put in Bersaba, placing herself firmly on Bastian's side. He smiled at her—a very special smile—and she glowed with pleasure.

"The King is in disagreement with his ministers," began Bastian.

"My dear boy," put in his father, "kings have been in disagreement with their ministers ever since there have been kings and ministers."

"What other king ever dismissed his parliament and governed—or made some semblance of it—without one for how many years is it? Ten?"

"We haven't noticed the change," said Uncle Connell, laughing.

"It's coming," replied Bastian. "The King believes he governs by God's right and there will be people in the country to disagree with that."

"Kings . . . parliaments," said Uncle Connell, "they seem to have one motive and that is to pile tax upon tax so that the people can pay for their fancies."

"I thought that when Buckingham was murdered that would have changed the situation," said my mother.

"No," said Bastian. "It is the King himself who must change."

"And will he?" asked Bersaba.

"He will . . . or be deposed," Bastian replied. "No king can continue to reign for long without the goodwill of his people."

"Poor man," said my mother. "How sad his life must be."

Uncle Connell laughed. "My dear Tamsyn," he said, "the King cares little for the approval of the people. He cares little for the approval of his ministers. He is so sure that he is right, guided by God. Who knows, perhaps he is."

"At least his home life is happier now," said Aunt Melanie. "I believe it was far from that in the beginning. He is a good man and a good father, whatever kind of king he is."

"It might be more important for him to be a good king," murmured Bastian.

Rozen said: "They say the Queen is very lively. She loves dancing and fashions."

"And meddling," added Bastian.

"She is, after all, the Queen," I said.

"Poor child," put in my mother. "It must be a terrible ordeal to be sent away from home at sixteen—younger than you twins." She smiled at us. "Imagine it . . . sent to a foreign land to a strange husband . . . and she a Catholic and he King of a Protestant country. No wonder there was discord and misunderstanding between them. If they have at last come to understand each other let us be thankful and wish them happiness."

"I do with all my heart," Melanie supported her.

"They won't find it until the King listens to his ministers and we have a parliament to make our laws," said Bastian.

"We are so far from the Court," said Melanie, "that what happens there hardly touches us. Why, we don't even hear of it until months after it has happened!"

"Like the ripples on a pool, in due course they reach its edge," Bastian reminded us.

"How is Grandfather Casvellyn?" asked my mother, changing the subject.

"As usual," answered Melanie. "He knows you are coming, so I suggest when we have finished at the table you go to see him. Otherwise he will complain that you have slighted him."

My mother nodded and smiled.

"Melder will go up with you and she will see that you don't stay too long."

"He has been rather fractious today," said Melder.

"Isn't he always?" asked Connell.

"More so than usual," answered Melder. "But he will be pleased to see you."

I smiled faintly and saw that Bersaba was doing the same. Neither of us could recall any occasion when our grandfather had shown his pleasure in our presence.

Bersaba and my mother and I went out with Melder, and as we passed through the narrow corridor to the door which led from Nonna's Tower to Seaward my hand was gripped in a firm grasp and my fingers pressed warmly. I turned. Bastian was beside me. There was some meaning in the pressure of his fingers.

Grandfather Casvellyn glowered at us as we entered. Although I was prepared for him and knew what he looked like, I always experienced a slight shock when I came face to face with him. His legs were always covered with a rug and I imagined that they would be terrible to behold, mangled as they had been. His shoulders were so broad and from his waist up he looked so powerful, which made it more of a tragedy. I often thought that if he had been a little man it wouldn't have seemed so bad. He had the fiercest eyes I had ever seen. They seemed to start out of his head and the whites all round the pupil were visible. When he turned them upon me I felt as though I were facing Medusa and should not have been surprised to feel my limbs turning to stone. I would always think of the night he had gone out in a boat—strong and well, and been caught in those cruel Devil's Teeth which had made of him the man he was.

He turned his chair and wheeled it toward us.

"So you're here," he said, looking at my mother.

"Yes, Father," she answered. She did not seem in the least afraid of him, which always surprised me in someone so mild and peace-loving. The thought occurred to me that she knew something . . . something he would rather she did not know, and that gave her power over him. Being our mother, she would only use that power not to be afraid.

"And these are your girls. Where's the boy?"

"He has work at home. His father may be arriving home and someone must be there to greet him."

A sneer curved Grandfather's lips. "On East India business is it?"

"But of course," said my mother placidly.

"And these are the girls . . . two of them . . . like as two peas in a pod. It was like you to get two girls. We need boys. There's your brother with all those girls and only one boy to show for years of marriage."

"It's a custom in the family. You had but one, Father, so you can't complain of Connell."

"We're let down by our wives. We can get boys but not on them."

"You have little to complain of. Melanie has been a good daughter to you and Melder looks after you well."

"Oh, yes, I must count my blessings in my own home. I must be grateful because I am allowed to live under my own roof. What do those girls think they're doing standing there like dummies. Come here and let me look at you."

Our mother drew us forward.

"Do they need you to hold their hands while they beard the old lion in his den?" shouted Grandfather. "Don't get too near, my children. I might eat you."

He was terrifying close. His brows grew thick and bushy and under them his eyes were piercing. He stretched out a hand and gripped my arm.

"Which one are you?"

"Angelet," I answered.

"And this one?"

"Bersaba."

"Outlandish names," he said.

"Good Cornish names," answered my mother.

"One named for the Angels and one after a woman who was not such an angel. Bathsheba—that's the origin." He was very interested in origins of words and old customs of the countryside. Linnet, his wife, had been from Devon, but he was proud of his Cornish blood. He peered at Bersaba and his eyes traveled all over her as though he were assessing her capabilities. She returned his gaze fearlessly. Then he gave my sister a little push. "Growing up," he said. "Marry well and get sons."

"I shall do my best," said Bersaba.

I could see that he liked her and that she interested him more than I did, which was strange because he seemed to sense some difference in us which others couldn't see.

"And don't take long about it. Let me see my great-grandchildren before I die."

"The twins are only seventeen, Father," said my mother.

He gave a long throaty chuckle and, stretching out a hand, gave Bersaba a push.

"They're ready," he said. "Ripe and ready."

Bersaba blushed bright red.

My mother said: "We're staying here for a few days, Father. We'll come and see you again."

"One of the penalties of calling here," said our grandfather. "You're expected to take in the old ogre while you enjoy yourselves with the rest of the family."

"Why, you know one of our reasons for coming is to see you," protested our mother.

"Your mother was always one for observing the conventions," said my grandfather, "but I doubt you'll follow in her footsteps." He was looking at Bersaba.

Melder said, "Well, we'll go down now."

"Oh, yes," cried Grandfather. "The watchdog thinks it time you left before I show my fangs. She'd draw them if she could. She's the worst sort of female, your cousin Melder. Don't grow up like her. A shrew, she is. She's a woman who takes

21

sides against a man. She's got a grudge against us because no man wants her as a wife."

"Now, Father," protested my mother, "I am sure—"

"You are sure. . . . There's one thing I can be sure of where you're concerned. You're going to say what you think is the right thing no matter if it means turning your back on the truth. That creature there is scarce a woman, for woman was brought into the world to please man and be fruitful."

Melder showed no sign that she was hurt by this tirade, and indeed he was not looking at her; his eyes were on us and, particularly I fancied, Bersaba.

He started to laugh suddenly and his laughter was as frightening as his anger.

Melder had opened the door.

"Well, we'll be along to see you tomorrow," my mother said as though it had been the most pleasant of visits.

He was still laughing when the door shut on him.

"In one of his bad moods today," commented my mother.

"He's in them every day," answered Melder in a matter-of-fact voice. "The sight of some young girls sets him off on those lines. He seems to find some consolation for his immobility in abusing me. It's of no account . . . if it eases him."

"There's no need for you to take us in tomorrow," said my mother.

I smiled inwardly; I knew she did not like us to hear that talk about women's function in life which the sight of Melder seemed to arouse in him.

She wanted to protect us from the world for as long as she could, but as for us, like most children, we were far more knowledgeable of such things than our mother realized. How could we help it? We had heard the servants talk; we had seen them go off into the woods together; we knew that Bessie Camus had become pregnant and our mother had arranged for her to marry one of the grooms. We knew that babies were not born under gooseberry bushes.

Our own home, where life ran smoothly and there was complete accord between our parents, was different even from life at Castle Paling. Our cousins should be more knowledgeable in this matter of the relationship between men and women than we were. Rozen had said, "Father has been unfaithful all his married life. Whenever a new servant comes he assesses her. He thinks he has a right to her as he is lord of the castle. Grandfather was like that. Of course if he is first he finds a husband for the girl after and he'll give them a cottage so she gets a sort of dowry. That's why so many of the children around are our half-brothers and sisters."

It was hard for us to reconcile this way of life with that lived by our own parents; but we were aware that it happened, which brings me back to the fact that we were not as innocent as our mother believed us to be.

Lying in bed that night, I tried to talk to Bersaba about all this.

"He said we were ripe and ready," I announced with a giggle.

"Grandfather is the sort of man who sees all women as possible bedfellows for some man or other."

"You'd think he would have lost interest in all that now."

"I don't suppose people like that ever do."

"He was looking at you all the time," I reminded her.

"What nonsense."

"Oh, yes he was. It was almost as though he knew something."

"I'm going to sleep," said Bersaba.

"I wonder why he looked at you like that?"

"What?" she said sleepily.

"I said I wondered why he looked at *you* like that."

"He didn't. Good night."

And although I wanted to go on talking, she pretended to be asleep.

Two days passed. We went for rides with our cousins and sometimes we explored the castle. I went down to the sea and looked for seashells and pieces of semiprecious stones on the beaches. We had quite a collection of raw amethyst topaz and interesting quartzes which we had found from time to time.

I used to love to stand on the beach while the waves thundered round me and sent their spray over me, and I would shriek with delight as I stepped back just in time to avoid getting drenched.

I liked to lean against the castle walls and marvel at their strength. They and the sea were like two mighty opponents —the work of man and the work of nature. Of course the sea was the more powerful; it could encroach on the land and sweep over that mighty edifice; but even then it would not completely destroy it. Grandfather Casvellyn had defied the sea and the sea had won that battle—but not completely, for he still lived in the Seaward tower to shake his fist at the mighty monster.

Bersaba had once loved to collect stones on the beach but

now she had lost interest in that and said it was childish. She liked to ride—so did I. On our first day we went off with the cousins and it was not long before we noticed that Bersaba was not with us. She had a passion for getting lost. Rozen and Gwenifer had come with us and there were two grooms.

I said: "She will join us or go back to the castle. She likes to be alone sometimes."

We didn't worry about her as my mother would have done.

I was right. She did come back to the castle. She said she had lost us but had no intention of curtailing her ride just because of that. She knew the countryside well and was not afraid of meeting brigands, for she reckoned she could gallop faster than they could.

"You know Mother doesn't like us to ride alone."

"My dear Angel," she answered, "we are growing up. There may be lots of things we do of which Mother would not approve."

I knew that she was slipping away from me then, and the invisible cord which bound us together was stretching. She had become a stranger with secrets. One day, I thought, it will break, and then we shall be as ordinary sisters.

The next day when I was going to ride again I picked up her safeguards in mistake for my own and I saw that there was bracken clinging to them and mud on the edge of the skirt.

"She must have fallen," I thought.

She came upon me staring at her skirts.

"Look!" I cried. "What happened? Did you take a toss?"

"What nonsense!" she said, snatching the garments from me. "Of course I didn't."

"These skirts have been in contact with earth, sister. That's clear enough."

She was thoughtful for less than a second then she said "Oh, I know. It was when I was out yesterday. There was a lovely pool and it was so peaceful I had the urge to sit by it for a while, so I dismounted and sat there."

"You ought not to have done that . . . and alone. Suppose someone . . . some man . . . ?"

She laughed at me and turned away.

"We've got to grow up one day, Angelet," she said, brushing the skirt. "That's what it was," she went on, and hung the skirts in a cupboard. "And what are you doing examining *my* things?"

"I wasn't examining them. I thought they were mine."

"Well, now you know they're not."

She turned away and I was puzzled.

The following day a strange thing happened. It was midday and we were at dinner in the great hall, for Aunt Melanie said that as there were so many of us it was better to take our meals there rather than in the dining parlor, which was used for a smaller company.

There had always been a big table at Castle Paling. Grandfather Casvellyn had set the custom for hearty eating and Connell had followed it. In our house my father's family had been more abstemious and although there had been plenty of food in our larders should visitors call unexpectedly, we did not consume the large meals which they did at Castle Paling. Aunt Melanie took great pride in her still room and she had Melder to help her and was constantly urging us to try some delicacy or other which she or Melder had concocted from old recipes with little additions of their own.

My mother and Aunt Melanie were discussing the rival properties of the herbs they both grew with such assiduous care, and Aunt Melanie was saying how she had discovered that a solution acquired from the juice of buttercups gave Rozen such a fit of sneezing that it had cleared her head of a very unpleasant cold from which she was suffering, when we heard sound of arrival from without.

"Visitors," said Uncle Connell, looking along the table from his end to where Aunt Melanie was seated.

"I wonder who?" she answered.

One of the servants came running in. "Travelers from afar, my lady," said the man.

Aunt Melanie rose and hurried out of the hall, Uncle Connell following her.

We at the table heard cries of amazement and in a short time my uncle and aunt reappeared and with them were two women—and in that first moment I was aware of their unusual appearance. I often think looking back, that life should prepare us in some way, that when events occur which are the forerunner of great changes which will affect our lives we should be given a little nudge, some warning, some premonition.

But it rarely happens so, and as I sat at the table and looked at the newcomers—one a woman of my mother's age and with her another of my own, or a little older—I was quite unaware that their coming was going to prove one of the most momentous events of our lives.

Aunt Melanie was crying out: "Tamsyn. You know who this is. Senara!"

25

My mother stood up; she turned first pale and then rosy red. She stared for a few minutes before she and the elder of the two women rushed toward each other and embraced.

They were laughing and I could see that my mother was near to tears. She gripped the stranger's shoulders and they looked searchingly at each other.

"Senara!" cried my mother. "What happened?"

"Too much to tell yet," answered the woman. "Oh, it is good to see you . . . good to be here. . . ." She threw back her hood and shook out magnificent black hair. "It's not changed . . . not one little bit. And you . . . you're still the old Tamsyn."

"And this—"

"This is my daughter. Carlotta, come and meet Tamsyn—the dearest sister of my childhood."

Then the girl called Carlotta came to my mother, who was about to embrace her when the girl held back and swept a low curtsy. Even then I was struck by her infinite grace. She was very foreign-looking—with hair as dark as her mother's and long oval eyes so heavily fringed with black lashes that even in that moment I couldn't help noticing them. Her face was very pale except for vividly red lips and the blackness of her eyes.

"Your daughter. . . . My dear Senara. Oh, this is wonderful. You must have so much to tell." She looked round at us. "My girls are here, too."

"So you married Fennimore."

"Yes, I married Fennimore."

"And lived happy ever after."

"I am very happy. Angelet, Bersaba . . ."

We rose from the table and went to our mother.

"Twins!" said Senara. There was a lilt of laughter in her voice which I had noticed from the first. "Or, Tamsyn—you with twins!"

"I have a son, too. He is five years older than the twins."

Senara took my left hand and Bersaba's right and studied us intently.

"Your mother and I were as sisters . . . all our childhood until we were parted. Carlotta, come and meet these two children who are already dear to me because of their mother."

Carlotta's gaze was appraising, I thought. She bowed gracefully to us.

"You have ridden far," said Melanie.

"Yes, we have come from Plymouth. Last night we rested at a most indifferent inn. The beds were hard and the pork too salt, but I scarcely noticed so eager was I to come to Castle Paling."

"What great good fortune that you found us here. We are on a visit."

"Of course. Your home would be at Trystan Priory. How is the good Fennimore?"

"At sea at the moment. We expect him home before long."

"How I shall enjoy seeing you all again!"

"Tell us what has happened."

Melanie was smiling. "I know how you are feeling, seeing each other after all these years. But, Senara, you must be weary. I will have a room made ready for you and your daughter—and you are hungry, I'll dareswear."

"Oh, Melanie, you were always so good, so practical. And, Connell—I am forgetting you and the dear children. But I *am* hungry and so I know is my daughter. If we could wash the stains of travel from our hands and faces and if we could eat some of this delicious-smelling food . . . and then perhaps talk and talk of old times and the future."

Connell came to stand beside his wife. He said, "Call the servants. Let them make ready for our guests."

Melder, good housewife that she was, was already leaving us to issue orders.

"We'll hold back the meal," said Melanie. "In the meantime come to my room and you can wash there. Your rooms will not be ready yet."

She and my mother went out with the newcomers and silence fell on the table.

"Who are these people?" asked Rozen. "Mother and Aunt Tamsyn seem to know them well."

"The elder one was born here at Castle Paling," said Uncle Connell. "Her mother was the victim of a shipwreck and was washed up on the coast. Senara was born about three months after. She lived here all her childhood and when our mother died our father married Senara's mother."

"So this was her home."

"Yes, it was her home."

"And she went away and hasn't been heard of until now?"

"It's a long story," said Connell. "She went away to marry one of the Puritans. I think she went to Holland. No doubt we'll hear."

"And she's come back after all these years! How long is it since she went away?"

Connell was thoughtful. "Why," he said calculating, "it must be nearly thirty years."

"She must be old . . . this Senara."

"She would have been no more than seventeen when she went."

"That would make her forty-seven. It cannot be so."

"She would doubtless have means of keeping herself young."

"How, Father?" asked Rozen.

"Senara was always a sly one. The servants used to think that she was a witch."

"How exciting!" cried Gwenifer.

"There was a lot of talk at the time about witches," said Connell. "You know how now and then there seems to be a fashion for it. The late King was a bit of a fanatic about them. People round here were certain that Senara's mother was a witch and that can be dangerous. She went away."

"What became of her?"

"It was never known. But after she'd gone they came to the castle to take Senara. You see, her mother had been washed up by the sea on Halloween; then she disappeared on Halloween. Everything seemed to point to the fact that she was a witch and the people came to take her. When they found she wasn't there, they said Senara would do, so Senara fled for her life and that was the last we saw of her until now."

"And you and our mother helped her?"

"Naturally we all helped her. She had been as a sister to us."

"And now she has come back," murmured Bersaba.

And we were silent. I was picturing it all so clearly. Senara's mother being washed up by the sea, being a witch, and after Grandmother Linnet died, marrying that fearful old man in the Seaward Tower and then running away from him—which didn't surprise me. And the mob's coming for Senara, who had been young then, with eyes like those of her daughter Carlotta. And who had been Carlotta's father? We should hear, I was sure.

They came back into the hall, accompanied by my mother and Aunt Melanie. My mother was flushed and excited and quite clearly very happy because of the arrivals.

I could not take my eyes from the girl Carlotta. Nor could any of us. She was the most arresting creature I had ever seen. It was something more than beauty although, of course, she was beautiful. In the candlelight her black hair had a bluish tinge, and there was a mysterious look in her enormous almond-shaped eyes. Her skin was very delicately tinged, which prevented its being dead white; it was petal-smooth and her nose was long, patrician, and beautifully molded.

There was something exotic about her which added to her attraction. My cousins could not take their eyes from her any more than Bersaba and I could. Her mother was a beautiful woman still, but even though she must have shown considerable defiance to the years she could not completely elude their ravages, and I guessed that when she had been Carlotta's age she would have been almost as attractive.

They had brought mystery and excitement into the castle. I kept thinking of the mob's marching up the slight incline to the portcullis and storming their way into the castle. They would be carrying torches and shouting what they would do to the witch when they found her.

"Sit beside me, Senara!" cried my mother. "How wonderful it is to have you here. I could almost believe we are young again. You must tell us all that has happened."

"But first allow them to eat," begged Melanie with a smile.

Hot soup was brought; Senara declared it was delicious and it was of the kind she remembered Melanie's preparing before she left the castle.

"We add different herbs from time to time," said Melanie. "We try to improve on it."

"It was always too good to be improved," said Senara. "And see how impatient Tamsyn is. She is really chiding us for talking of soup when there is so much to tell."

My mother said, "Eat, Senara. You must be famished. There is plenty of time to talk afterward."

They ate heartily of the soup, which was followed by lamby pie, and then there were strawberries with clouted cream.

"I have indeed come home," said Senara. "Is it not exactly as I told you it would be, Carlotta?"

Carlotta replied, "Madre, you have talked of nothing else but Castle Paling and your sister Tamsyn ever since you made up your mind to come here."

We were all waiting eagerly for the last of the strawberries to be consumed and when the servants had removed the platters Senara said, "Now you are impatient to hear what happened. I shall give you a rough outline, for I cannot explain all the little happenings that made up a lifetime over a dinner table. But you will learn in due time. You young people may have heard of me. There was a great talk hereabouts when I was here . . . but that was long ago and when faces are no longer here they are forgotten. Yet my mother was different. She came mysteriously, thrown up from the sea. She was a noble lady, the wife of a count and bearing his

29

child . . . which was myself. I was born here . . . in the Red Room. Is the Red Room still here?"

"Why, it's the haunted room," cried Rozen.

"That's right," went on Senara. "The haunted room. But it was haunted before my mother came to it. Colum Casvellyn's first wife died there bearing a stillborn child. That was before he married Tamsyn's mother. Yes, it was haunted then and my mother added another ghost to the Red Room."

"The servants won't go there after dark," said Gwenifer excitedly.

"It's nonsense," retorted Melanie. "The room is not haunted. One of these days I intend to change all the furnishings."

"Several had that idea," said Senara. "Wasn't it odd that no one ever did?"

"Please go on," pleaded Bersaba.

"My mother came and I was born and then she went away, but I grew up with Tamsyn and when her mother died, my mother came back and she married Colum Casvellyn. We were always together, weren't we Tamsyn? I used to shock you, but you thought of me as your sister."

"Always," said my mother.

"Then came the day when my mother went away again and Colum Casvellyn had had his accident and was in his chair. The witch-hunters came for my mother and they were ready to take me in her place so Tamsyn and Connell here got me out of the castle. I was very friendly with my old music master who had become a Puritan and was living in Leydon Hall. You know it of course."

"The Lamptons live there now," said Rozen. "We know them well."

"They bought it after the Deemsters left," added Aunt Melanie.

"I fled there," went on Senara, "and the Deemsters took me in. I was married in the simple Puritan fashion to Richard Gravel—Dickon, my old music master—and we went to Holland together. Amsterdam was the refuge then for those who wished to worship as they pleased, so it was believed; but we began to discover that that freedom was to worship only in a manner approved by the Puritans. I was never really a Puritan at heart. I just changed when I met Dickon. I had brought with me some pieces of jewelry, and to wear jewelry in our sect was considered sinful. At first I wore it in secret and Dickon was so besotted with me that he daren't offend me by forbidding me to wear it."

"I never thought you could be a Puritan, Senara," said my mother with an affectionate smile.

"You knew me well," answered Senara. "We left Amsterdam for Leyden, after which city the Deemsters had named their home. And here we spent eleven years while we made our plans to leave for America. Eleven years! How did I endure them?"

"You had your love for Dickon."

Senara laughed. "My dear Tamsyn," she replied, "you think we are all like you . . . good faithful docile wives. Far from it. I was soon out of love with Dickon and out of love with religion. There was little that was holy about me. All through those eleven years I longed to be back at Paling. I wanted to be young again. I knew that I had wanted Dickon mainly because he was forbidden to me. I knew that I had been wrong to marry a Puritan . . . not that he was always a Puritan. He could forget his religion on occasions."

"They provided an escape for you when you were in danger," my mother reminded her.

"That's true," agreed Senara. "But for them I might have had nowhere to go when I was in danger and that could have been an end to me." She grimaced. "All those years ago I might have been a corpse on that tree in Hangmans Lane where they used to hang witches. Remember, Tamsyn?"

My mother looked uncomfortable.

"They still hang witches there," said Rozen.

"Are they searching them out as madly as they were when I left?"

"Every now and then there is a revival," said my mother. "Thank God we have heard nothing for these last few years. I won't have the servants speaking of witches. It revives interest and that is bad. Why a poor old woman has only to stoop or develop a mole on her cheek or have some spot which can be said to have been made by the Devil and they will take her to Hangmans Lane. Many an innocent woman has been treated thus and I want to see it stopped."

"There will always be witches," said Uncle Connell, "and 'tis well that they should be dispatched to their masters."

"I shall always do all I can to save the innocent," said my mother, fierce when there was someone who needed her protection. "And," she added, "I would like to know more of witches and what made them give their souls to the Devil in the first place."

"Don't attempt to dabble in witchcraft, sister," warned Uncle Connell.

31

"Dabble!" cried my mother. "I only want to know."

"That's what many would say. They only wanted to know."

"Tamsyn, you are just the same," cried Senara. "You always wanted to look after anyone if you thought they needed your care."

"Do tell us what happened when you reached Holland," begged Bersaba.

"Well, for those eleven years I lived as a Puritan I would attend their meetings and listen to their plans. They were going to return to England and sail to America from there. I knew they had bought a ship called the *Speedwell* which they sent to Delftshaven. It was to go to America by way of Southampton. I did not relish the long sea voyage. Months on the ocean . . . prayers . . . endless prayers. My knees grew rough with kneeling. I hated the plain gray gowns I was expected to wear. I learned very quickly that I was not meant to be a Puritan."

"Did you and Dickon have no children?"

"Yes, I had a boy. I called him Richard after his father. He grew up to be a little Puritan. From the age of five he was watching me to curb my vanities. I was stifled. I couldn't endure it. Sometimes I thought that Dickon wouldn't either. I used to think it was a sham, but he was deeper in his Puritanism than I knew. It might have been that he could have escaped at first but it was like an octopus which twined its tentacles about him. When they left for England I did not go with them."

"You let your son go?" cried my mother.

"He was more Dickon's son than mine. He had been brought up in the Puritan manner; he was burning with enthusiasm for the new life in America."

"So you were alone."

"I heard later that Dickon died before they sailed. He was in a tavern in Southampton and there he fell into an argument with sailors about religion. He defended the Puritans and was stabbed. He died of his wounds."

"What a terrible thing to have happened!" cried Melanie.

"Yes, I wished I'd stayed with him. Had I known it would be but a few weeks more. I was fond of Dickon. It was just his fanatical beliefs which came between us. They had alienated the boy, who stayed with them after his father died. And then I was alone."

"Alone in Holland!" cried my mother. "You should have come home then."

"I had friends. One of these was a Spaniard. He took me with him to Madrid and I lived there for some years in fine style. When I lost him I set out to look for my mother because I knew that she was there. I found her. She was married to a gentleman of high nobility, a friend of King Philip. . . . You remember him, Tamsyn. He was here as Lord Cartonel. You thought he came courting me."

"I remember him well," said my mother soberly.

"My mother had never been what you would call maternal. She never wanted me. I was an embarrassment—no, not even an embarrassment—an encumbrance shall we say right from the first. I should never have been born. It was a miracle that I was and that was due to your mother, Tamsyn, who found mine on the shore half dead and to her own detriment brought us both into this castle."

"It was long ago," said my mother, "and you were brought up here as my sister, Senara. There are unbreakable ties between us and I am glad that you have come back to us."

"Do tell us what happened," begged Rozen.

"I went to Court. I married a gentleman of rank. We had a child, Carlotta. I had always wanted to see you but of late the urge became irresistible. I must see you and Castle Paling before I was too old to travel. My husband agreed that I should pay a visit. He could not accompany us. He has a post at Court. So we set out. We arrived in London . . . and we traveled here by stages. That is all and now we are here and right glad to see you."

"You will stay with us for a long while, I hope," said my mother.

"I have a feeling that I shall not be eager to leave this place. I must go back to Spain in due course, but to me Castle Paling is what I think of when I say home."

My mother was deeply moved; so was Aunt Melanie.

Uncle Connell said that we must all drink to the return of Senara with her daughter and she must regard Castle Paling as her home for as long as she wished to, to which my mother replied with some firmness: "Senara was my sister. There is a home for her at Trystan Priory if she so wishes it."

Senara held out one hand to my mother and one to Aunt Melanie.

"God's blessings on you both!" she cried, "and right glad I am to be here. I long to be once more in the Castle, but when I lived here, Tamsyn was my sister. We shared a bedroom at one time, do you remember, Tamsyn?"

"Until you went to the Red Room."

Senara closed her eyes and laughed and I knew that she and Mother exchanged some memory.

"You were my sister and it was to be with you that I came here. Yet the castle was my home . . . all the time I lived here. I will go with you, Tamsyn, for a while and then I will come back and stay at Castle Paling. How's that? Of course it may well be that you will not want me here."

"Not want you!" cried Melanie. "Why, it was your home."

"We change in . . . how many years is it, Tamsyn? Nearly thirty. What time has done to us! You do not look the age I know you must be. You live again in these delightful twins."

"As you do in your Carlotta. Women stay young when they think young and feel young and look young," said my mother.

Senara touched her plentiful black hair, in which there did not appear to be one gray strand. "I have always cared what I look like. As did my mother. She had many secrets."

"She lives still?" asked my mother.

"In Madrid in grand style. It is how she always wanted to live. She resented it here."

"And she has remained young and beautiful?"

"Not young—even she could not manage that. But she still is beautiful. She rules her household like a queen and it is said that she is more royal than royalty."

"Yes, I can believe it. What did she think of your coming to England?"

"She scarcely gave the matter a thought. Perhaps she considered me a little mad. But she knew that I had been brought up by your mother and your influence was strong with me. You had made me sentimental, affectionate . . . a little like yourselves. Therefore I had these odd notions."

Uncle Connell said, "I have a very special black cherry brandy. I shall send to the wine cellars for it. We will all drink to celebrate your return."

"You are good to me, Connell," said Senara. "Never shall I forget how you helped me escape from this house."

"Do you think I would have allowed the mob to lay hands on you?"

"You became master of the castle on that night. Everyone knew then that though the old master lay crippled in his chair, there was a new one as strong to take his place."

I was fascinated. As they talked I was trying to piece the story together. One day I should read it all in the diaries of my mother and her mother, Linnet, who had been the one who had rescued the witch from the sea, that witch who was this Senara's mother.

We sat at the table. No one wished to move. They went on talking and we of the younger generation listened avidly, and as they talked a storm began to rise. The sky grew dark and we could hear the wind rousing the sea.

Melanie called for more candles to be lighted and the servants tiptoed around lighting them while the storm outside seemed to be increasing.

Still we sat on. It was as though no one wanted to leave that table; and Aunt Melanie, my mother, Senara, and Uncle Connell talked of the old days and the picture of their lives began to take shape.

Then suddenly the door was slung open. We heard the roar of a voice which there was no mistaking. It belonged to Grandfather Casvellyn.

He propelled himself into the hall, his eyes looking wilder than ever as they raked the table and came to rest on Senara.

Melanie had risen to her feet.

"Father . . . how did you come here? How did you leave the Seaward Tower?"

He glared at her. "No matter," he shouted. "I did. They brought me down. They carried me and brought me here. I insisted. If I want to come into any part of my castle I'll do so. She's here, they tell me. She's come again . . . as they did all those years ago . . . the witch's girl."

"Father," said Connell, "it's Senara. Your own wife's daughter."

"I know who it is. I was told and I knew they dared not lie to me. What do you want here?" he demanded, glaring at Senara.

She rose and went to him. She was smiling in a way I didn't understand. She knelt before him and lifted her face. In the candlelight it looked young and very beautiful.

"I came back to my old home," she said. "I came to see you all."

"Go back where you came from. You and your kind bring no good to this house."

"Father—how can you?" Melanie cried.

"Don't call me father. You've no right . . . just because my son married you. She'll bring no good here. She's her mother all over again."

"I'm not!" cried Senara. "I'm different."

"Send her away. I won't have her here. She's . . . disaster. I'll not have her here reminding me of her mother."

Tamsyn said, "Father, you are cruel. Senara has traveled

35

far to see us and if you'll not have her here she knows she will always find a home with us."

"Fool!" cried my grandfather. "You were always a fool."

"Was I?" said my mother with spirit. "If I am a fool then I do not know the meaning of wisdom. For I have found happiness in my home and my husband and my children which wise men like yourself—or so you think—ever failed to do."

He glared at her but I could see the admiration for her in his face. He was proud of her and I think it was not the first time he had been.

"Then," he said, "you should have more sense than place them in jeopardy." He pointed to Senara. "That one . . . comes of evil stock. Her mother came here and bewitched us all. She'll do the same. She should never have been born. I warn you, daughter. Be wise. Listen to me. I know. I lived it all." His voice broke suddenly. "By God," he cried, "don't you think I live it all again up in that tower when I look out at the waves and the Devil's Teeth out there? And I say to myself, everything would have been different if the sea had not thrown up Maria the witch on my coast. Your mother was a fool like you. She brought in the witch, who spoiled her life. It's like a pattern, you fool, girl. Don't you see it? The Devil has sent her to take your happiness from you."

"Father," said my mother, "you have suffered so much, you are sick."

"Yes, an old fool of a man, that's what you say. By God, I'd lay a whip about your shoulders, old as you are, if I were not confined to this chair. I've lost the power of my legs but I've a mind that I command still. I'll tell you this, if you take that woman into your house you'll rue the day, and you'll remember this moment and what I've said to you." He began to laugh and it was unpleasant laughter. "All right. I'll not forbid it. I'll watch. I'll see my words come true. I'll look out on you from my tower and I'll prove my words come true. Bring the witch's daughter here . . . into my castle. Let me show you that I'm right."

Then he turned and wheeled his chair away. He called, "Binder—Binder!" And the terrified manservant came to take the chair and push it out of the hall.

There was silence.

It was Carlotta who spoke first. "What a terrible old man," she said.

"He married your grandmother," said Senara. "It was your grandmother of whom he spoke with such venom."

"He must have hated her."

36

"He was bewitched by her."

"He's mad, isn't he?"

"Who would not be mad?" asked Senara. "Such a man as he was to be kept a prisoner in a chair!"

My mother said, "You will come with us, Senara, to Trystan Priory when we leave. You would not want to stay here now."

Senara laughed. "I'll not allow him to decide my plans," she said. "Connell is the master now. If he wanted me to stay—and Melanie wanted it—I would not care for that madman's words. I shall come to Trystan to be with you—depend upon it, Tamsyn, but I want to be in the castle for a while first."

Melanie rose. She was clearly shaken by the scene my grandfather had made.

"It seems as though the storm will not abate for a while," she said. "But there is no reason why we should sit over the table waiting for it. I will take you to the room which will now be ready. You may want to rest."

"I could talk and talk," said Senara. "Tamsyn, come with me to my room. Let us pretend it is years ago and we are young again."

My mother went to Senara and they embraced warmly. Everyone began to talk as though nothing had happened. After all, we were accustomed to Grandfather's outbursts. But I could not forget the wildness of his eyes and the words he had spoken kept ringing in my ears.

News from the Castle

THE change was apparent in the first day. This visit was like no other. Before we had rarely made plans for the days. We would come down to breakfast, which was a tankard of ale and bread with cold bacon, and we helped ourselves to this.

Then we would go our separate ways. There had been a free and easy atmosphere about the castle. Sometimes I would ride with my sister and any of the girls who like to accompany us or I would go to the seashore and add to my collection of shells and semiprecious stones, or I would simply explore the castle. There was so much to do. When we had been young we had been allowed to play all sorts of games in the various towers as long as we did not penetrate Grandfather Casvellyn's Seaward; and the castle had seemed to us an enchanted place.

It was still that in a way, but it was different.

Senara, my mother, and Aunt Melanie seemed to want to talk all the time about the old days; Senara must go round the castle exclaiming, "I remember this well." Or, "Oh, look at that. Fancy its still being here." That left Carlotta to us.

We were wary of each other—particularly was Bersaba wary. Carlotta talked in that half-foreign way which was attractive; her clothes were different; they, with her voice, her manners, and her incomparable beauty, set her apart. It would have been different if she had not been aware of this, but she was.

Bersaba and I with Rozen and Gwenifer took her on a tour of the castle.

"Is it very different from what your mother told you?" asked Rozen.

"Very different."

"And we are different, too?" I asked.

She laughed, shaking her head. "I did not know of you, therefore I could not picture you. You are different from the people I know."

"What? Girls like us?"

"Oh, it is different in Spain. Young girls do not run wild, as here. They practice decorum and have a duenna."

"Who is yours?"

"I have none now. I am here and here I shall live as girls live here."

"Do you prefer it?" asked Bersaba.

She shrugged her shoulders. "I cannot say. It is not a gracious way to live. Yet one has freedom, and that is good."

"We could do with more freedom" said Gwenifer. "We are not allowed to ride out without grooms, are we?"

"Sometimes we get lost," said Bersaba.

Carlotta turned her full-lidded eyes on my sister.

"For a purpose?" asked Carlotta.

My sister shrugged her shoulders, and Gwenifer said, "You came back with Bastian the other day, Bersaba."

"Yes," said Bersaba, "I lost you, and so did Bastian and then . . . we found each other."

It seemed a long and unnecessary explanation. I knew Bersaba had deliberately lost herself. I wondered whether Bastian had too.

"Ah, Bastian, the brother," said Carlotta. "He is a very pleasant young gentleman. I shall miss Spain, where life is so much more gracious, but I think I shall like being here . . . for a while."

"Shall you go back to Spain?"

"Of course."

"Are you betrothed?" asked Rozen.

Carlotta shook her head. "No I could have been but he was not to my liking. He was old, a great nobleman with large estates and a great title, but I said no, I am too young yet for such a union. I will wait a little while. There might be someone to my liking."

We all regarded her with awe.

When we came to the Seaward Tower, she said, "Why do we not enter here?"

"We rarely go in there," said Rozen. "That's where our grandfather lives with his servants. There has to be a special reason for going . . . for instance, when my aunt arrives with the twins. She is expected to call on the first day of her arrival and after that wait for an invitation."

"That mad old man!" said Carlotta. "What a scene he made! He did not like my mother nor me. He does not want us here."

"He gets very angry. For so many years he has been crippled. At first they thought he would kill himself, but he didn't and now he goes on making everyone's life unbearable. But somehow the servants who look after him admire him. I can't think why.

"It is time he is dead," said Carlotta, blowing her lips in an odd gesture as though he were so much dust and she were blowing him away.

We were all a little shocked. Perhaps it had occurred to us that Grandfather Casvellyn's life must be a burden to him and others, but while he had life in his body that life was sacred. Our parents had taught us that.

Carlotta sensed our thoughts. There was something uncanny about her. Perhaps she was indeed a witch or had such experience of life that she understood how the minds of simple country girls worked. She cried out, "Oh, you don't talk of such matters, do you? You all pretend you're fond of him because he's your grandfather. How could anyone be fond of such a horrible old man? He wanted us turned away. Did my grandmother really marry him? She is so beautiful . . . the most beautiful woman I ever saw . . . and she married *him*!"

"He was no doubt very handsome in those days."

She was thoughtful. "Tall and strong and powerful . . . the lord of the castle . . . perhaps. Well, now, I say it is time he was dead and I shall say what I think."

"Don't let anyone hear you," I said.

"I shall not care who does, little twin. Which one are you? How can people tell you from your sister? What fun you must have."

"Yes," said Bersaba, "we do."

"I do not think I should care to have someone so like myself," said Carlotta. "I like to be different . . . no one like me . . . all by myself . . . unique."

"We have our differences," I said. "It is in our natures."

"One is the saint and one the sinner, I believe," said Carlotta.

"And which is which?"

"Our mother says that no person is all bad; none all good. So we shouldn't be so neatly divided," I said.

"How you quote your mother!" said Carlotta contemptuously. "You will have to learn your own lessons from life, won't you? Is the old man watching us now, do you think?"

"It may be," said Bersaba. "I have sometimes seen him at a window watching."

Carlotta turned and looked up at the Seaward Tower. She clenched her fist and shook it.

Again we were horrified and seeing this she laughed at us.

"Let us ride," she said. "I have a fancy to see the countryside."

"We are not allowed to ride alone," said Rozen.

"We shall not be alone. There are five of us."

"We are girls, so we have to take some grooms with us."

"What could happen to us?"

"We could be set upon by robbers."

"Who would take our purses," said Gwenifer.

"Or worse," added Rozen.

"Rape?" said Carlotta with that strange laughter in her voice.

"I think that is what they fear."

"We could elude them," said Carlotta. "Come, we are taking no grooms with us."

"And if we are robbed—" began Rozen.

"Then we shall have gained in experience," answered Carlotta. "Let us change into our riding habits."

"You have yours with you?" asked Rozen.

"My dear cousin—for I suppose we are related in a way since your grandfather was my grandmother's husband, and 'cousin' covers these complicated relationships. So, dear cousin, let me tell you that the pack horses brought our clothes and there are plenty of them, for my mother said the fashions here at Castle Paling will not be of the latest and your English ones of course could not compare with those of Spain."

"I believe the fashions at Court are quite splendid," said Rozen warmly.

"Gaudy, no doubt," said Carlotta, "and I suppose that could be called splendid here. But let us change and then you can show me the countryside."

As we went to our rooms to change, Bersaba said to me, "I don't like her, Angelet. I wish they hadn't come."

"You don't know her," I insisted.

"I know enough."

"How can you in such a short time? You're thinking of Grandfather and what he said."

"He's right. She's going to bring trouble . . . they both are."

When we met in the stable Carlotta looked at us somewhat scornfully. I supposed our riding habits with their safeguards were not very attractive. Her outfit was beautifully cut to enchance her tall willowy figure, and the black riding hat became her well.

She mounted the horse she had arrived on and she stood out among us all. As we were preparing to ride out, Bastian rode in.

He smiled and his eyes came to rest on Carlotta.

"Are you going riding?" he asked. "Take two of the grooms with you."

"We are not taking grooms," retorted Carlotta.

"Oh, but—"

"There are five of us," said Carlotta.

"But you should—"

She shook her head, still smiling at him, and he could not take his eyes from her face.

"I'll come with you," he said.

"It is as you wish," she answered.

And we all rode out together.

41

Bersaba brought her horse up and rode beside Bastian. Then Carlotta was there and Bastian was between them.

Carlotta talked about the countryside and Bastian told her of the quaint customs of the people and the crops that were grown.

I did not think she was very interested in that, but she was in Bastian. So, it seemed, was he in her, for he never left her side during the whole of the morning.

He had said that we must keep together and we did. I was surprised that Carlotta obeyed this because I thought that the very fact that she was asked not to wander off would make her do so. But she seemed content to ride with Bastian and she kept beside him.

Bersaba contrived to keep her place on his other side, but I noticed that he gave his attention to Carlotta, which seemed natural as she was the newcomer.

When we returned to the castle there was great excitement. Our mother came running down to the hall as we came in.

"Your father's ship has been sighted. Fennimore has sent a servant to tell us. He has ridden with all haste from Trystan. We must prepare to go back at once."

"When shall we start?" I asked.

"Within an hour. Your Aunt Melanie knows and is helping me make ready. We shall come again as soon as your father goes away again. But now . . . make ready."

It was a short visit, I thought, but a significant one.

As we came along the coast we saw the ship riding the water and we knew it for our father's. My mother's eyes glistened with joy as she beheld the sight. It was named after her, the *Tamsyn*, and my father had had it built five years before. I had heard my father extol her and say that since she was named after the best woman in the world she must indeed be the best ship that ever sailed the seas. From her poop lantern to her figurehead she was some two hundred and twenty feet in length and forty feet across the beam. She carried cannon of course—a necessity when on her journeys she might meet pirates or rivals masquerading as such. It was a source of great anxiety to my mother that on their return voyage the ships were laden with precious cargoes of silks, ivories, and spices. The figurehead of the *Tamsyn* was an exquisite carving of my mother. My father had said that in some ways that made him feel as though she were with him. He was a very sentimental man and theirs was indeed a rare marriage of minds.

We turned away from the coast to take the road to Trystan Priory and our horses could not carry us fast enough. My father was in the courtyard when we arrived, for he had seen our approach from one of the turret windows, knowing that it would be that day, for he was well aware that as soon as my mother received news of his arrival she would lose no time in setting out.

His eyes went first to her. He lifted her down from her horse and they embraced there. The servants looked on with a kind of wonder. There was something about this love between our parents which was sacred to us all. Bersaba felt it; we had discussed it; we had once both declared that we would never marry because we couldn't marry our father and where in the world would we find another husband like him? There flashed into my mind then a vision of Carlotta's long secretive eyes and I wondered what she would have said had she been here. I was glad she was not. I could not have endured her cynical comments or her looks, which would betray her thoughts about my parents, so I was glad that she had stayed behind at Castle Paling. But I knew that she would come here some day. Then something would change to make it different and I did not want it to change.

My father had turned to us. "My girls," he said, and caught us both up in his arms. "You've grown," he accused us. "You're not my *little* girls anymore."

Our brother Fennimore was smiling rather sheepishly. He was just as happy as the rest.

"And you came while I was away," my mother was saying. "Oh, Fenn, I wish I'd known. We'd only been there a day or so . . . if only I'd been home."

"Well, you're here now, my love."

"I must see the servants. I must go to the kitchen. . . . Oh, Fenn, when did you come?"

He said, "Leave the kitchen. Stay with me. Let us talk and talk."

So we went into the house and for a short time we forgot Carlotta and her mother.

We dined in the intimate parlor—just the famiy—and Father talked of his adventures.

Trade was becoming more prosperous. The great rivals were the Dutch because they were very commercially minded and were seeking maritime expansion. They were good sailors—as much to be feared as the Spaniards had been a few years back. They were as deadly in a way, for while the Spaniards had never lost sight of the desire to bring Catholicism

43

to the entire world, the Dutch had one objective—maritime supremacy, which would make them the biggest and richest traders in the world; and as the very same ambition was possessed by the English in general and in particular those of the East India Company, the rivalry was intense.

"They want to drive us off the seas," Father told us. "And we are determined not to be driven. Why people cannot trade in peace has always been a mystery to me. There are riches enough in the world for us all and let the man who finds them first keep them."

Our mother was in full agreement with my father, and I thought that if everyone in the world were like them it would be a happier place.

My father told us stories of his adventures in strange lands. He made us see palm-fringed islands where the people lived in primitive fashion and rarely saw a white man, how they had been overawed by the sight of the big trading ships and were sometimes hostile. But he always implied that there was no real danger and that he would emerge safe from all his adventures and I fancied that he sometimes colored the stories to give this effect, for the last thing he wanted was to add to our mother's anxieties. We basked in this atmosphere of contentment and neither Bersaba nor I thought beyond the present; we shut our eyes to the truth that one day he would sail away again. While he was home there must be perfect contentment.

We none of us asked on that first day of reunion when he would be leaving us again and it was the next day before we mentioned Senara's return.

Then a faint frown appeared on his face and I thought uneasily, "He doesn't like Senara."

"You knew her well, Father?" I asked.

"Not well," he replied. "I knew her. She left before your mother and I married. I had met her when I visited the Castle."

My mother said, "She will come here. She wants to be with me awhile but I think the Castle has some attraction and she will go back there after visits with us. It was her home. Like myself she was born there."

"So she will be here," said my father slowly.

"You would not have me not receive her?" asked my mother, little lights of horror appearing in her eyes. Was it going to be their first disagreement?

"My love, if you want her here . . . of course you must have her."

"Dearest Fenn," said my mother, "she is as my sister."

"She was not always good to you . . . to us."

"Oh, but she is good at heart. She was wild in those days. She acted without thought. But she was as my sister and I could not turn her away."

My father nodded but I could see that he was uneasy and I wondered what had happened to make him say that Senara had not been good to them.

Bersaba asked her when she was alone with her and she told me that my mother replied, "Oh, she tried to stop your father and me marrying. She was jealous, that was all. She did not want me to go away from her. She was very fond of me. She confessed and then everything was all right. That was all, but your father has not forgotten."

My brother Fennimore wanted to go to sea with my father, but my father thought he should stay at home and look after the estates, but most of all my mother.

My parents used to talk about it at length. I would see them in the garden, arm in arm, in earnest conversation, and I guessed what it was about. My brother Fennimore was like them in that he wanted to do the best for the family, but it is not easy to be denied what you really want to do in life.

My mother knew this and she tried to persuade my father to let him go. She was perfectly safe, she declared; she had good servants and Fennimore's heart was with the Company just as his was.

While my father was home many people came to visit us. There were men in the Company who never went to sea but took part in its management from their offices in England. Some came from London to see us and those would be days of great excitement. The servants would be busy in the kitchen baking pies of all descriptions—all our old Cornish ones would appear to the delight and amazement of the visitors, who had never heard of taddage pies, which contained prematurely born sucking pig and muggety—the entrails of sheep and calves. My mother wondered whether such food would appeal to the fine folk from London but they seemed to eat it with relish and were not told until afterward what the pies contained. Then, besides our old Cornish dishes, there would be beef, mutton, boar's head, duck and snipe, partridge, pigeon, and fish like lampreys, sturgeon and pike, with fruits—mulberries, apricots, medlars, and green figs—to follow. My mother was a devoted housewife and herself supervised the making of many of the dishes, so eager was she to welcome all our father's business colleagues.

There came the day when we heard that our father had relented over our brother Fennimore and he was to go to sea with him when he next sailed. Fennimore was going round in a state of quiet pleasure because of this. He was so like our father and he did not shout with joy or say very much but we were all aware of his contentment.

A week had passed since our return—a week of meals eaten in the great hall, for there were these constant visitors and we never knew when more would arrive. Most of the rooms in the Priory were now occupied and Bersaba and I recalled that this was how it always had been when our father was home.

"I wonder what Carlotta is doing at Castle Paling?" I said one day.

Bersaba answered, "They will not come here until Father has gone. I heard Mother say she would ask them not to, making the excuse that every room was occupied by Father's business associates."

Bersaba always seemed to get such information. Once I accused her of eavesdropping and she did not deny it. But I have to admit that I was always glad to receive the information she was able to give.

There was a good deal of talk at the table and we learned that these men from London were disturbed by the influences at work in the country. The King's popularity was fast waning. He had, it seemed, not the gifts to make him a darling of the public. He was a good and faithful husband—rare in kings—but he did not know how to govern, and his wife, Henrietta Maria, frivolous and strictly Catholic, did nothing to endear herself to the people.

That he had dismissed Parliament and governed without one was an indication of the King's determination to be accepted as the ruler selected by God. He was implying that he did not need a parliament; that he was quite capable of making laws. The people had accepted so much from him, but it was the general verdict, that they were getting restive and they would not go on in this way.

He was alienating the people not only through religion, but through irresponsible taxation which was a direct threat to property.

One of the main topics was of course Ship Money, of which we had heard so much. Fearful of war with the Spaniards or Dutch or both, Charles had commanded that the main ports supply ships for the defense of England. To build these ships money was needed and Ship Money was invented.

A rumbling protest broke out throughout the land. The Puritans, the Protestants, and the Catholics all felt themselves persecuted and stood against the King; Charles had alienated Scotland when he allowed himself to be crowned in Edinburgh by five bishops in white rochets and copes of gold, a ceremony which was attended by much pomp, for this offended the plain Scots and diverted their sympathy from him.

I remembered vividly the conversation at dinner one evening when they talked about the frivolity of the Queen and the King's growing love for her.

My mother thought that it showed goodness in the King and she said that a monarch's happy family life would be an inspiration to the families of the country.

My father smiled at her tenderly and replied, "There have been happy families before this King came to the throne, my love. To have found the ideal companion, to have learned the true secret of living, which is to give happiness to others when happiness will come to the giver unasked, is something which we all may have if we are determined to get it."

"But it is so easy to lose the opportunity to gain that happiness. What if I had lost you?"

There was a sudden shadow between them and I knew instinctively that it was the return of Senara which had reminded them that their happiness might not be secure.

One of the gentlemen from London said, "It would be well for the country if the King were less under the influence of his wife. It was the greatest mistake to deal with William Prynne as they did."

"What happened to William Prynne?" asked Bersaba.

"I forget that remote in the country as you are you miss these things," replied the gentleman. "Prynne wrote a book against stage plays."

"Why should he be against such plays?" demanded my mother. "What harm do they do?"

"It was Prynne's opinion that plays are unlawful because they engender immorality and have been condemned by the Scriptures."

"But is this so?" asked my mother.

"Prynne produced evidence to prove his case."

"He is a killjoy," said my mother. "Miserable himself and wanting everyone else to be the same!"

"That may be," put in my father, "but every man should have the privilege of stating his views."

"That is what many think," put in our guest. "A man may

47

be wrong or right but he must be given leave to air his opinions. Those who don't agree snap their fingers at him; those who do, applaud. There are certain to be those who are ready to take sides."

"On what grounds was he sent to the Star Chamber?" asked my mother.

"This is where the King is foolish in his fondness for the Queen," was the answer. "Prynne attacked the women who appeared on the stage for in his opinion although stage plays in themselves are wicked, the greatest sin of all is for a woman to appear on the stage. Now the Queen loves the play—to witness it and to take part in it—and she and her ladies have recently performed William Montague's *Shepherd's Paradise,* so the attack appears to be on her personally, and on the King too for that matter, for he took great pleasure in watching and applauding the play. And for this Prynne is sent to prison but first set in the pillory and deprived of his ears."

"His ears!" cried my mother, deeply shocked.

"Ah, madam," said our guest, "you live in this peaceful spot. Pray God it may always remain so. But there are changes creeping over our country and they are such that the people will not endure."

I was trying to imagine what a man looked like without his ears and I felt a sudden pain and fear such as I had never known before.

When I rode out I noticed that the people of the countryside seemed thoughtful. It was as though a cold wind had started to blow across the country from Whitehall, so steadily, so relentlessly, that we were even feeling it at Trystan Priory.

We had been home for two weeks when my father was called to Plymouth to discuss the next voyage. My mother begged to go with him, leaving our brother Fennimore in charge of the household.

"We shall not be away long," my mother assured us and when they rode off together I thought she looked like a bride setting out on her first journey with her new husband. The house seemed different without her. We were accustomed to my father's absences, so that did not affect us so much, but the house without her seemed somehow bereft.

After we had bade them farewell in the courtyard, Bersaba and I climbed to the turrets and watched them from there until they had disappeared from sight.

"When I am married I shall be just like our mother," I told Bersaba.

"You will not," answered my sister, "because you are not like our mother."

"I mean I shall have a husband who thinks I am as young and beautiful after thirty years of marriage as I was on the day he first saw me."

"You are not going to marry a blind man?"

"You know what I mean. Father thinks that of our mother."

"There are not many like them."

Sadly I agreed with her.

"Mind you, it would be dull if they were. I want my marriage to be different from that. Theirs is hardly exciting."

"I don't think anyone could ever have a more exciting moment than our mother when she hears his ship is sighted."

"It would greatly depend on what excitement meant to you," Bersaba pointed out.

"Oh, you can never accept things as they are. You always have to probe and dig about and spoil them."

"I like to know the truth," observed my sister. "I wonder what's happening at Castle Paling?"

"It's odd that we haven't heard."

"Do you think they will be asked here?"

"Not until Father goes. He clearly didn't like Senara. She tried to stop his marrying our mother. She was jealous. She didn't want anything to come between her and our mother. She loved her so."

"I'll suggest that she wanted to be the one to marry first."

"It must have been exciting then. I wish we could read our mother's journal. It will be all about Senara and her mother and grandfather when he was young. Have you started writing, Bersaba?"

"No," said Bersaba shortly.

"Are you going to?"

"When I've something that's exciting enough to put down."

"Well, don't you reckon Senara's return with Carlotta is?"

"It remains to be seen." She hesitated. Then she said, "I'll tell you something. I swear someone from Paling will be over soon."

"Who's coming over from Paling Castle then?"

She smiled secretly. "Bastian perhaps," she said.

It was not Bastian who came. It was Senara and her daughter. I wondered if they knew that my father was absent.

Senara cried, "So your mother is not here—"

We told her she had gone with our father to Plymouth.

"Who is in charge?" asked Senara.

"My brother Fennimore," I answered. "And Bersaba and I are the hostesses."

"It's nice of you to welcome us," said Carlotta with a sly smile, reminding us that we had done nothing of the sort.

Bersaba told them that Fennimore was out on the estate and we hastily ordered the grooms to take the horses while we brought them into the hall.

"It's a lovely old place," said Senara. "I always thought so. The Castle is so much grimmer."

"But grander," added Carlotta.

"Our mother will be so sorry not to be here," said Bersaba.

I could not imagine my mother's being in the least sorry while she was with my father. In fact I thought she would be rather pleased not to be here since he would not want these visitors.

"We'll have a room made ready," I said and went away to give orders.

When I came back Bersaba was taking the visitors into the intimate parlor and one of the maids had brought the wine and cakes with which we always refreshed travelers on their arrival.

"I was surprised," Senara was saying, "that your mother did not insist on our coming before."

"It was because our father was home," Bersada was explaining. "When he comes they have so much to talk of because he has been away so long. They just have to be together. It has always been like that."

"Your mother fell in love with him when she was nothing but a girl . . . younger than you are," said Senara.

"And she stayed in love with him ever since," I said defiantly as though there was need to defend her.

"We were not all destined to find such happiness in married life, alas," commented Senara. She smiled at Carlotta and went on: "Let us tell the twins your news. I suppose I should be right to wait until your mother returns. She should be the first to know. But I can see you are all agog with curiosity."

"What news is it?" asked Bersaba.

"Carlotta has already had a proposal of marriage."

"Already . . . but from whom?" My mind went over the people we knew. The Krolls, the Trents, the Lamptons. Surely one of those young men would not be considered good enough by Carlotta, who had gone to great pain to make us aware of her almost royal lineage.

"She has to consider it, have you not, Carlotta? It is not the match she would have expected had she stayed in Spain, but it will bind the families closer and I have never forgotten all through my life the days I spent there in my childhood."

"Who is it?" asked Bersaba almost sharply.

"It is your cousin Bastian. He has asked Carlotta's hand in marriage."

Because I am close to Bersaba I felt the shock which ran through her. It numbed me as it numbed her.

I began to talk rapidly to save her the necessity of doing so. I said, "So soon? How can you be sure? How can Bastian? What do Uncle Connell and Aunt Melanie say?"

"They say it is a matter for Bastian to decide. He is of age. He is his own master and there is no doubt how strongly he is involved. Is that not so, Carlotta?"

"He is determined to marry me."

"And you to marry him?" I asked faintly.

A smile flicked across her lips. "I am not sure. He must wait for his answer."

"We left Paling so that Carlotta could have time to think of this in peaceful surroundings," Senara explained.

"I wanted to know what you felt about it here," said Carlotta. "Would you be happy to have me in your family? I wanted the twins to tell me." She was looking at Bersaba, who stood still, her eyes downcast, saying nothing. "Of course," Carlotta went on, "I shall not listen to what you tell me. *I* shall make up my mind whether or not I shall marry Bastian." Again that look at Bersaba. "And something seems to tell me that I shall."

The atmosphere had grown tense with secret feelings. It affected me strongly because it came from Bersaba. I could see Grandfather Casvellyn's wild eyes, hear his accusing voice. *They'll bring trouble here if they stay.*

Was that prophecy already coming true?

BERSABA

❖ ❖ ❖

The Toad in the Bed

I AM desolate so I am taking up my pen. I had said I would only do so when there was something interesting to write about. I did not think it would be heartbreak. I am so hurt, so humiliated and, I think, above all angry. My anger is none the less fierce because I hide it from the world; it is like a fire inside me, a banked-up fire which is waiting for the moment to burst forth, and when it does I believe I should be capable of killing the one who has brought me to this state.

I put down my pen then and wrung my hands together, wishing that it were her neck I had in my hands. They are very strong, my hands. I could always do things with them that Angelet could not attempt.

At this time I am only half believing it. I say to myself, "It can't be true." But in my heart I know it is. Grandfather was a prophet when he said she would bring disaster to us. He was thinking of me, I know, because Grandfather has a special feeling for me. There is a bond between us. I think I know what it is, for it is a need, a desire which he himself possessed and which came down through him to me. I appear outwardly quiet . . . quieter than Angelet, but internally I am not.

If I had not been as I am this would not have happened to me. I should not have lain with Bastian in the forest and have reveled in that wild exultation which I could no more resist than he could. I used to think that if we were discovered they would blame him; they would say he had seduced me; he was older than I and I was little more than a child. But it would not be true. I was the one who had tempted him—artlessly, subtly, it was true. He used to kiss me and be frightened by the kisses I gave him in return; I would caress him in such a manner as to arouse his desires. He thought it was innocence which made me do these things. He didn't understand that virgin though I was at that time I was possessed by a raging desire to be possessed.

When I was fourteen years old I knew that I wanted Bastian to be my lover. He had singled me out as his favorite and this endeared him to me for although we were so much alike people were more comfortable in Angelet's company. She was not prettier than I . . . how could she be when most people did not know which of us was which? It was something in her manner. When I pretended to be her—it was our favorite game to delude people into thinking one of us was the other—I could assume her nature, open, thoughtless, chattering without thinking very much what she was saying, lighthearted, believing the best of everyone, and being easy to deceive because of that. I just had to think of Angelet's ways to be her. But she never really succeeded in being me because if she lived to a hundred she would never know this deep sensuality which was the strongest force in my nature and which was why Bastian and I had become lovers when I was but fifteen years old and he was twenty-two.

The first time it happened we were riding in the woods near Castle Paling where I was staying with my mother and sister. A party of us had gone out riding and Bastian and I slipped away from the others. We came to a thicket and I said the horses were tired and we should give them a rest.

Bastian said, "Nonsense." We had not long left the castle. But I dismounted and tied my horse to a tree and he did the same. I lay down on the grass and looked at him standing above me. Then suddenly he was lying beside me and I took his hand and held it against my breast. I remember how his body shook with his heartbeats and how excited I was. And then he was beside me saying, "We must go, Bersaba. Dear little Bersaba, we must go back."

54

But I had no intention of going back and I put my arms about him and told him I loved him because he loved me more than he loved Angelet. And all he could say was, "No, Bersaba, we must go. You don't understand."

I understood perfectly but he would not know that. He was the one who did not understand. I knew then that there are people who are born with knowledge and I was one of them. There was one of the servants—we called her Ginny— who was the same. I had heard the servants say that she had lovers since she was eleven years old. But perhaps I was not the same, for I did not want lovers: I wanted my cousin Bastian.

Afterward Bastian was frightened. When we stood up beside our horses he took my face in his hands and kissed me.

He said, "We must never do that again, Bersaba. It was wrong, and when you are old enough I'm going to marry you, and if necessary before."

I was happy then but Bastian wasn't. I thought he would betray what had happened by his mournful looks. For some time he would take great pains not to be with me. I would look at him with hurt and yearning eyes and then one day it happened again, and again he said, "It must never happen like that until we are married."

But it did. It became a ritual and afterward he would always say that we were going to be married.

I thought of Bastian all day. My sketchbook was full of sketches of him. I could not wait until the day I would be old enough to marry him.

He said, "We shall be married on your birthday and announce our intentions six months before."

I used to think, "I shall be married before Angelet is." Another of my characteristics which is almost as strong as my sensuality is the need to better Angelet. She is my sister, my twin, so like me that many cannot tell one from the other, and she is important to me. Sometimes I feel that she is part of me. I love her I suppose, for she is necessary to me. I should hate it if she went away and yet there is an insane desire within me always to better her. I must do everything better than she can or I suffer. People must prefer me or I am consumed with jealousy—and as she has this open sunny frank manner and mine is dark and devious it is often that they turn to her.

Once, when we were very young, my mother bought us sashes for our dresses—mine was red and Angelet's blue. "We shall now be able to tell you apart," she had said jokingly.

And when I saw Angelet in the blue and how people turned to her first and talked to her more than they did to me I became obsessed by the blue sash and it seemed to me that there was some magic in it. I took her blue sash and told her she could have my red one. She refused this, saying that the blue was hers. And one day I went to the drawer in which the sashes were kept and I cut the blue one into shreds.

Our mother was bewildered. She talked to me a great deal, asking me why I had done this, but I did not know how to put my thoughts into words.

Then she said to me, "You thought the blue one was better because it was Angelet's. You were envious of her blue sash, and you see what you have done. There is now no blue sash for either of you. There are seven deadly sins, Bersaba." She told me what they were. "And the greatest of these is envy. Curb it, my dear child, for envy hurts those who bear it far more than those against whom it is directed. You see, you are more unhappy about the blue sash than your sister is."

I pondered that. It was true, because Angelet had forgotten the sash in a day, though it lived on in my memory. But the incident did nothing to curb my envy. It grew from that to what it is today. It's like a parasite growing round an oak tree and the oak tree is my love and need of my sister—for I do love her; she is a part of me. Nature, I think, divided certain qualities and gave her some and me the others. In so many ways we are so distinctly different and it is only my secretive nature that prevents this being obvious, for I am certain that no one has any idea of the dark thoughts which go on in my mind.

After Carlotta and her mother had arrived, Angelet came up to our room. She was very uneasy because although she had no idea of the nature of my relationship with Bastian, she knew that I admired him and sought his company and he mine.

She looked at me anxiously. How relieved I am that I am not one of those girls who shed tears at the slightest provocation. I cry with rage sometimes; never the soft sentimental tears which Angelet gives way to. A sad story will bring the tears to her eyes, but they are easy tears for she will have forgotten what made her cry a very short time afterward.

"What do you think of it?" she cried. "Carlotta and Bastian!"

I shrugged my shoulders, but that couldn't deceive even Angelet.

"Of course," she went on, making an effort not to look at

me, "he is getting old and I suppose it's time he married. He was bound to marry sooner or later. But Carlotta! Why, she has only been there a week or so. What do you think of her, Bersaba?"

"I suppose she is very attractive," I said calmly.

"It's a strange sort of attraction," said Angelet.

"There's something odd about her . . . and about her mother. I wonder if it's true that her grandmother was a witch?"

Horrible pictures came into my mind but I did nothing to suppress them because they soothed me.

Once when I was about twelve years old, we had been riding with our mother and some of the grooms and we had come upon a shouting mob. There had been a woman in their midst and she was not such an old woman either. Her clothes were torn from her body and she was half naked, but it was the look of abject terror in her face which I had never forgotten. The crowd was chanting "Hang the witch. Hang the witch." I don't think I ever saw such fear in any face, before or after.

My mother had said, "We will go now." She turned her horse and we rode off at speed in the opposite direction from that in which we had been going. "These things happen," she told us, "but it will not always be so. People will become more enlightened."

I wanted to ask questions but my mother said, "We won't speak of it anymore, Bersaba. We'll forget it. It's unpleasant; it exists; but in time people will be wiser. We can do no good by talking of it, thinking of it."

That was the attitude in our home. If there was anything unpleasant one did not think of it. If my mother had a fault it was pretending that things were so much better than they were. She told herself everytime my father went away that he would come safely back. She was wise in a way; but it had never been mine to pretend, even to myself. I looked straight into my heart, soul, and mind and asked myself why I did such a thing. I think I know myself better than my mother or Angelet will ever know themselves because of this side of my nature, which demanded the truth however unpleasant or detrimental to myself.

Afterward I went back to that lane and I saw the woman hanging there. It was a gruesome sight, for the crows were attacking her. Her hair was long and I could see even then that she had been a beautiful woman. It was beastly; it was vile; it haunted me for a long time; but at least it was reality.

And now I was thinking of Carlotta in the hands of that mob, Carlotta being dragged to that tree. Her grandmother was a witch. Perhaps she was. Perhaps that accounted for the manner in which she had taken Bastian from me. She had cast some spell upon him. An odd excitement possessed me and I felt better than I had since I had heard.

I said, "Is witchcraft something that is handed down from grandmother to mother and then on and on, I wonder?"

Angelet looked happy because she had come to the conclusion in her light, let's-see-the-best-of-everything manner that my childish fondness for Bastian had not gone as deep as she feared. One of the lovable things about Angelet had always been that my trouble had been hers. I looked at her now with a kind of contempt—which might have been another form of envy, for I admitted it must be pleasant to sail through life without these intense feelings which beset people like myself—as she answered, "Perhaps it is. Oh, I do wonder if Carlotta *is* a witch?"

"It would be interesting to find out," I said.

"How?" she asked.

"We could think about that," I suggested.

"There are good witches as well as bad ones," Angelet said, in keeping with her nature, immediately bestowing benign qualities on the woman who had stolen my lover. "They cure you of warts and sties and give you love potions to enslave a lover. I believe that if you have bad luck some witches can help you find ill-wishers who could be causing that bad luck. I was talking to Ginny the other day. She knows a lot about witches. She's always fancying herself ill-wished."

"We'll talk to Ginny," I said, and all sorts of thoughts were whirling round in my head; they soothed me.

"I wonder if Bastian knows," giggled Angelet. "You'd better ask him."

"Why don't you?"

"Oh, you know he always liked you best."

"Did he show it then?"

"You know he did. Wasn't he always losing himself with you in the woods?"

Now she must see. Her words stabbed me as though they were knife blades. Riding in the woods with him, his pursuing me, intending to be caught, lying on the grass among the bracken. . . . His voice: "This is madness. What if we were seen?" And not caring, because it was so important, so necessary to us both.

And now . . . Carlotta.

I said fiercely, "I'm going to find out if she's a witch."

"We will," replied Angelet blithely. She would be less blithe when they took Carlotta down the lane, when they stripped her clothes from her, when they hung her up by the neck and the crows came.

It was difficult hiding the fact that I was so stunned. Carlotta knew that I had been fond of Bastian, but did she know how far that fondness had carried us? The more I thought of that the more angry I became. I thought of the insult, the humiliation—I, Bersaba Landor, to be cast aside. And his own cousin, too. He must have been completely bewitched.

Carlotta was watching me as a cat watches a mouse, teasing me in the same way, patting me with her paw, letting me run a little way, then clawing me back. I comforted myself with the thought that she didn't know how wounded I was. I was sure she thought I had had a little-girl fondness for Bastian and that I, childish like Angelet, was just a little hurt because he no longer paid me the same attention.

At supper that night Fennimore sat at the head of the table and Carlotta turned her languorous eyes on him. Fennimore was made in the image of his father, and as Carlotta was engaged to marry his cousin Bastian, it would not occur to Fennimore to be aware of her fascination. Like my parents my brother created a sense of security and made even me think that whatever happened, this would always be my home and my parents would shelter and protect me.

Carlotta talked of her coming marriage and what it would mean to her.

"I hesitate," she said. "I am not sure that I would wish to be buried in the country."

"You'll get used to it," said Fennimore easily. "Bastian will be involved with the estates and that can be a full-time job I assure you."

"When we were in Madrid we went to Court often. I am already beginning to find it somewhat dull here."

"Then," said Angelet logically, "you should not marry Bastian unless you have other interests."

Angelet looked slyly at me and I thought, "Oh, no, sister, not now!"

"What interests are there in the country?"

"There's riding for one thing. You can ride far more in the country than in the town. There are exciting things . . . like the May revels and Christmas when we bring in the holly and the ivy. We do have the occasional ball."

"They are nothing like the Court balls, I do assure you," said Carlotta coldly.

"There are exciting things though," insisted Angelet, "like going to see the witch of the woods."

"Who's that?"

"They hanged her some time ago," said Angelet soberly, "but there'll be another. There are always witches."

"What do you know of them?" Carlotta was animated.

"That they do all sorts of interesting things, don't they, Bersaba?"

"They sell their souls to Satan in return for special powers on earth which enable them to get what they want."

"It's strange," said Fennimore, "that witches so often seem to be ugly old women. If they could have what they want you'd think they'd be beautiful."

"Perhaps there are some beautiful ones," said Carlotta.

I thought exultantly, "She is—I am sure she is."

"My grandmother was said to be a witch and I never saw a more beautiful woman," she went on.

"I wonder," I said slowly, "if witchcraft powers are passed down through families?"

Carlotta looked steadily at me. "I think that could be very likely," she replied, and I knew that she wanted me to think that she had special powers, powers to get what she wanted, attract people to her for instance, take them away from those whom they loved by making herself irresistible.

Fennimore—how typical of him—evidently considered the subject unsuitable for his young sisters and determinedly and deliberately changed it.

I didn't listen to what was said. I was excited and felt better than I had since I had heard the news.

Two days after Carlotta and Senara had come to Trystan Priory Bastian rode over. I saw him from one of the Castle windows and I did not know what to do. Part of me wanted to run to our room and shut myself in, but it was Angelet's room too and how could I shut her out? Another part of me wanted to go down to him to rage at him, to abuse him, to tell him that I hated him.

Neither of these actions could I take and there is another trait in my character which I don't quite know whether I should be grateful for or deplore. When something good or bad happens I seem to stand outside the event, to look in and watch myself and others, so that whatever my feelings I can always curb them and ask myself what action will bring most advantage to me. Angelet never stops to think; she does what comes naturally. If she is angry her anger bursts forth; so does her joy. I sometimes think it would be easier for me if I were like that. As at this time. If I did what was natural, either go to my room and burst into floods of tears or go down and abuse Bastian, people would know what I was feeling. But being myself, even in my most abject misery and hatred, and feeling everything so much more intensely than Angelet ever could, I must be outwardly calm and say, "What is the best thing for me to do?" And by best I always meant advantageous to myself.

So now I pondered and I decided that I would go away from the house, so that if he looked for me he would be unable to find me. That would give me time to ponder.

I quickly changed into my riding habit, went down to the stables, saddled my mare, and rode out. As the wind brushed my face and caught at the hair under my riding hat I could smell the dampness of the earth, for it had been raining in the night. I felt the tears coming to my eyes and I knew that if I could have cried I should have felt relieved to some extent. But I would not cry. Instead I nursed my anger. I thought of the insult to my pride and I knew that I had loved Bastian because he had noticed me more and liked me better than my sister and that it was my pride which had made me love him; now he had wounded that pride he had taken away my reason for loving him and I hated him. I wanted to hurt him as he had hurt me.

I heard a small voice within me saying, "You never loved Bastian. You loved only yourself."

And I knew it was true and I wished that I were like Angelet, who never probed her own secret mind as I did.

I went down the old pack horse track where the flowers on the blackberry bushes were out in abundance, and where we came with our dishes at the end of summer and gathered them so that they could make preserves in the stillroom. I started to gallop past the fields of deep green wheat and I came to the woods—the woods where I had lain with Bastian when he visited us at Trystan Priory. The foxgloves were flowering there. Angelet and I once gathered them and took them into the house and old Sarah who worked in the kitchens said they were poison flowers and witches knew how to brew a potion from them to make you sleep forever.

I would like to make Carlotta sleep forever.

I was wrong to have come to the woods where there were too many memories. I thought of the last time we had been here together. It was six months ago—in January and the trees were bare—lacy branches seen against a gray sky. How beautiful they had been; more beautiful, I had said to Bastian, than they were in summer.

"I'd rather have the leaves to shelter us," he had said. "It's dangerous here."

"Nonsense," I had replied. "Who'd come to the woods in winter?"

"We did."

It was cold, I remember—the wind was chill—but I said to him, "While our love is warm what matters it?"

And we laughed and were happy and he said, "This time next winter we shall announce our betrothal." And it was an enchanted afternoon.

When we rode back I pointed out the points of yellow in the jasmine which climbed over one of the cottages we passed.

"Promise of spring," said Bastian. It seemed significant. The future was full of promise for us.

Why did I want to come here to revive memories? Better to have stayed in the house.

Then I saw a man riding toward me and I felt a sudden quiver of alarm because I was doing what was forbidden—riding out alone. I spurred up my horse and, turning off the road, broke into a canter across the meadow. My alarm intensified, for the man who had been on the road was coming across the meadow in my direction.

"There is nothing to fear," I admonished myself. "Why should he not come this way?"

I seemed to hear my mother's voice. "I never want you girls to go out alone. It is all right if Fennimore or Bastian is with you. But always make sure that there are two grooms at least."

He had ridden past me and was pulling up his horse. Strangely enough my fear had left me; excitement took its place, for the rider was no ruffian. Far from it. He was elegant in the extreme and a stranger, for we did not often see such gentlemen in the country.

I noticed his hat first because he swept it off and turned to me, waved it in his hand as he bowed his head; it was of black felt, broad-brimmed and adorned with a beautiful white feather which trailed over the brim. His hair—light brown, almost golden, curled at the tips—fell to his shoulders. We did not wear our hair like that in the country, yet I had heard that it was the latest fashion. Fennimore had laughed at the time and said he would never wear his hair like a girl. But I had to admit that if the face it framed was manly enough the effect was not effeminate. His doublet was black, with wide sleeves caught in at a cuff with lace edges; his breeches were of black material that had a look of satin; and he wore square-toed boots fitting up his leg to just below his knees. I suppose I noticed his appearance so minutely because I had never seen anyone like him before.

"Your pardon, mistress," he said. "I would ask your help. Do you live hereabouts and know the country?"

"I do," I answered.

"I am looking for Trystan Priory, which I believe is in this neighborhood."

"Then you are fortunate to have met me, for I live there and am returning there now."

"Is that truly so, then this is indeed a happy meeting."

"If you ride beside me I will take you there," I said.

"That is kind of you."

Our horses walked side by side as we crossed the meadow to the road.

"I think you may wish to see my father," I said.

"I have business with Captain Fennimore Landor," he answered.

"He is away at this time."

"But I had heard his voyage was ended."

"Yes, it has. He is only gone to Plymouth and will be home within a few days."

"Ah, that is better news. I shall not be too long delayed."

"I daresay it is business concerning the East India Company."

"Your assumption is correct."

"People often come to see him. But you have come far."

"I have come from London. My servants are at an inn. I left them with my baggage and rode out to see if I could find the Priory. You have made my quest easy."

"I am pleased. My brother will talk to you. He knows a great deal about the Company."

"That's interesting. May I introduce myself? I am Gervaise Pondersby."

"I am Bersaba Landor. I have a twin sister, Angelet. She and my brother will be very pleased to see you."

I pictured their astonishment when I rode in with this elegant stranger. I was grateful to him, for he had made me forget temporarily the hurt Bastian had inflicted on me.

The Priory came into sight.

"A charming place," said Gervaise Pondersby. "So this is the Landor home, is it? And how far from the sea?"

"Five miles."

"I had expected it would be nearer."

"Five miles is nothing much," I answered. I told him that the house had been built with stones from the ruined priory as we rode up the slight incline and into the courtyard.

We had been seen and I imagined the consternation that had caused: Bersaba arriving home with a gentleman from London!

I shouted to a groom to take our horses and when we stepped into the hall Fennimore was already there with Bastian. I would not look at Bastian but spoke to Fennimore.

"I met this gentleman on the road. He was looking for Trystan Priory. He has business with Father."

The bow was elegant as he said, "Gervaise Pondersby at your service."

"Why, Sir Gervaise," cried Fennimore, "my father has often spoken of you. Welcome to Trystan. Alas, my father is not here at this time."

"Your sister told me so. But I believe he is not far from home."

"He will be back in a few days. May I present my cousin, Bastian Casvellyn?"

Bastian bowed. I thought, "He seems awkward beside this man," and I exulted in the fact.

"I pray you come into my father's private parlor. I will send for refreshment."

"I will take a little wine and perhaps you can give me more exact information as to when your father will return."

"I can send a messenger to Plymouth to tell him you are here," said Fennimore. I was rather proud of my brother because he did not seem in the least overawed by the stranger.

As Fennimore led him away I ran upstairs. Bastian ran after me but I was fleeter than he.

"Bersaba," he whispered.

"I have nothing to say to you," I hissed over my shoulder.

"I must explain."

I sped on, but he came after me and caught up with me in the gallery.

"There is nothing you can say to me," I told him. "It is I who must say to you, Congratulations."

"You must understand, Bersaba."

"I do understand. You have asked Carlotta to marry you. That's clear enough, is it not?"

"I can't think how it happened. Bersaba, I love you."

"You love me so much that you are going to marry Carlotta. Oh, that is perfectly clear."

"It was a moment of madness. I don't know what came over me. I was sort of bewitched. That's how it is, Bersaba. You must understand. When she is there——"

Every word was like a knife in my heart. I wondered how such a simple man as Bastian could inflict such pain.

I pushed him from me. "Go to her then. Go to your witch. I promise you this. You'll be sorry . . . sick and sorry."

Then I turned and ran and I reached our bedroom. I was thankful that Angelet was not there. I locked the door. He was outside tapping on it, whispering my name.

"I must explain, Bersaba."

Explain. What was there to explain? Only that she was irresistible. He wanted her. He was ready to thrust me aside for her.

"Go back to her," I whispered venomously. "Go back to your . . . witch."

Fennimore immediately sent a messenger to Plymouth to tell my father of Sir Gervaise's arrival, and while he was taking wine my brother persuaded him that he would be more comfortable at Trystan Priory than at the inn and he begged him to come with his personal servants and baggage and rooms would be made ready for him.

Sir Gervaise graciously accepted the invitation, but would not come until my father returned.

At supper everyone was talking about Sir Gervaise, and I explained how I had discovered him when out riding and was immediately reprimanded for riding alone. "You know our mother says you are always to have the grooms with you," said Fennimore. "It was willful of you to do that while she was away."

"I'm not a child any longer, Fennimore," I said sharply.

I knew Bastian was looking at me, and that he blushed a little remembering our unchildlike behavior I was sure. He sat next to Carlotta and I was aware of the spell she had laid on him. He was hurt and bewildered by what had happened to him, which was just the way he would be if he were bewitched. But he could not keep his eyes from her; I saw his hands reach out to touch her. How I hated them both; and I must sit there and pretend that nothing was wrong.

Carlotta said, "He seemed a very courtly gentleman. I saw him when he left—but from a window."

"He will return when my parents are here," said Fennimore, "and then I expect he will stay for a few days."

How I lived through that meal I did not know. Bastian must go home or I would break down. I could not bear to see him and Carlotta together. It was asking too much of me.

After supper the minstrels played soothing music from the gallery and Thomas Jenson, who taught us music and had a beautiful voice, sang madrigals with us. Of course there was the inevitable one about the faithless lover, which did not help me.

As soon as I could I said I was tired and I would go to my room, but my sister had to come up with me to tell me that I looked pale and strained and that I had been very wrong to ride out alone. Chiding me with this tender scolding was more than I could endure and I begged her to leave me alone that I might close my eyes and try to sleep.

Sleep! As if I could sleep.

I had lain there for half an hour when there was a knock on the door. I closed my eyes, thinking it was Angelet returning, but it was not. It was the maid Ginny with some posset Angelet had sent up for me.

I looked at Ginny. She was twenty-one, very wise. She had had a child when she was fourteen and kept him with her in one of the attics because my mother said that it was not right that a mother should be parted from her child. There had been many lovers since for Ginny but no more children. "Foolish girl," said my mother. "She will find herself in trouble again one day." But I understood her. She wasn't so much foolish as helpless.

"Mistress Angelet said you was to take this, mistress," she said now. "Her said it 'ud make you sleep."

"Thank you, Ginny," I said.

She gave it to me. It was hot and soothing.

"Wait a bit while I drink it."

"Yes, mistress."

"Have you ever talked to a witch, Ginny?"

"Oh, yes. I went to one when I had my trouble. It was too late though . . . she could do nothing for me."

"That was Jenny Keys, wasn't it? They hanged her in the lane."

"Yes, mistress, it were. There was naught wrong with Jenny Keys. She'd helped many a girl from her trouble and it was beautiful to see the way she could charm off your warts. She did good, she did. My granny used to say, 'There be

66

white and black witches, Ginny, and Jenny Keys be a white one.' "

"Some didn't think so."

"No, there be some terrible people about. Jenny Keys could turn off a bad spell. Why, when my young brother had the whooping cough Jenny Keys cured him by tying a bag of spiders round his neck. I don't reckon Jenny Keys ever laid a spell. Some of them do though, and there's always them as will tell against a woman who's a witch. Tain't safe . . . being a witch . . . black or white."

"What happened to Jenny Keys?"

"There was people who hated her. They started to talk about her, build up against her like. A cow died in calf . . . so did the calf, and the cowherd he were so mad he said he'd caught Jenny Keys ill-wishing it. Someone else said she'd gone along for a remedy and had seen Jenny Keys in her cottage with her black cat there at her feet and she was roasting a bullock's heart stuffed with pins. She was saying:

> 'Tis not this heart I wish to burn
> But Jack Perran's heart I wish to turn
> Wishing him neither rest nor peace
> Till he be dead and gone.

And when Jack Perran died . . . all sudden in his sleep, people started whispering. They started remembering other witches and how in the times of King James there'd been regular witch baiting. They reckoned a lot of them had been driven underground at that time but now they was coming out again. They reckoned they ought to make an example of one. They talked . . . they remembered . . . they spied on Jenny Keys. Then came the day when they took her and hung her on a tree in Hangmans Lane."

"If she was indeed a witch perhaps it was right."

"Perhaps it were, mistress, but they do say she were a white witch."

"There was a witch once at Castle Paling. Have you ever heard of her?"

Ginny was startled. She looked furtively over her shoulder.

"Why, yes, mistress, everyone have heard of how she come by the sea. My Granny told me. It were always remembered. She came and she went back to the Devil and came back again and then she went back to him and was never heard of no more."

I shivered.

"You be cold, mistress?"

"Someone walking over my grave, Ginny, as they say. You know the ladies here?"

Ginny was very disturbed. "Yes, mistress."

"Well, the young beautiful one is the granddaughter of that witch."

"Yes, mistress."

"I'm going too far too fast," I thought. But nevertheless I went on.

"Do you think the powers are passed down . . . these dark powers, I mean?"

Ginny was a conspirator. Her voice sounded hoarse.

"I've heard it's so. Yes, indeed I've heard it said."

"I wonder. . . . Here, take the dish. The posset was good and warming. I feel I could sleep now."

She took the dish and tiptoed out. I felt like a gardener who has prepared the ground and sown the first seeds.

Now I could wait and see what crop came forth.

I felt better because I had a plan. I became obsessed by it and would awake in the night when a wild excitement possessed me and this soothed my hatred and bitterness. I could understand Homer's saying, "Revenge is sweeter far than flowing honey."

I used to dream of Carlotta's being dragged by the mob to the tree in Hangmans Lane and all the humiliations which would be thrust upon her. I pictured her half-naked body and lewd men watching her and afterward Bastian coming to the lane and seeing her hanging there.

"How wicked I am!" I thought; but the hurt was so deep that I had to soothe it some way and at the back of my mind I believed it to be only a fantasy—like a daydream when one receives comfort for indulging in a fancy that one possesses something which is unattainable.

Carlotta created a good deal of attention in a household like ours. She was so different with her airs and graces; she was exotic, and anything foreign aroused suspicions in the simple. With interest I watched the servants' behavior toward her. They were fascinated and a little afraid, and I did all I could to foster this fear in them. I think Ginny had talked and reminded them of that old story of the witch who had come from the sea.

Once, when we were riding, I saw a woman hurry away as we went by, averting her eyes from Carlotta, and I exulted because it seemed to me that the seeds I had sown were sprouting.

Bastian had left the next day. I don't think he could bear to be in the same house with Carlotta and me together. When he left I did not say good-bye to him but kept out of the way, though I watched him ride off from one of the turret windows and saw how he kept looking backward, for a last glimpse of Carlotta, I thought angrily.

Sometimes when I was in my room I would be frightened at what I was doing. I wanted to kill Carlotta, but not in a straightforward way since I planned that others should do it for me. It was cowardly because I was planning it so that when it happened I could pretend it had nothing to do with me.

Then, when I was with her, I would say to myself, "She deserves it. There is something wicked about her . . . something evil. I believe she *is* a witch, for only a witch could have taken Bastian from me, and if she is, it is better that she be removed."

Nobody could deny her beauty. It was not beauty which is a joy to behold and is the outward manifestation of inner goodness. I always thought my mother was beautiful in that way. Carlotta's was a beauty which came from the Devil— meant for the destruction of those about her. At least that was what I told myself.

Her mother, Senara, was proud of her, but I didn't think she loved her; and I was certain that Carlotta loved no one but herself. Indeed, sometimes I used to think that if Bastian married her that would be sufficient punishment for his treatment of me.

The servants did not like Carlotta. She was too arrogant with them, reminding them always that she was the great lady and they beneath her notice except for what they could do for her. She and her mother shared a Spanish maid whom they had brought with them. Ana was a woman in her mid-thirties, dark-haired with a faint line of black hairs on her upper lip and deepset eyes. She was very quiet and I had never heard her speak, but I imagined she was efficient and an excellent lady's maid, for the manner in which she dressed Carlotta's hair was a wonder in itself. Silent-footed, almost mouselike, one was hardly aware of her. She slept in a small anteroom adjoining Carlotta's bedroom.

When my parents returned and Sir Gervaise with his manservant and two grooms moved into Trystan Priory, life changed. We were now living in greater style, for to have a man such as Sir Gervaise in the house made that a necessity. His business, he told my father, would take up a whole week, he believed, and if he could intrude on Landor hospitality all that time he would be gratified.

Of course we welcomed him. My father was delighted, for Sir Gervaise was as deeply involved with the Company as he was himself.

They rode out together and were closeted together and talking a great deal. They went down to the sea and inspected my father's ship; they discussed the cargoes he had brought back and were constantly in each other's company.

Meals had become ceremonial occasions. Not only was Sir Gervaise our guest, but also Senara and Carlotta, and there was no doubt that our society had become much more grand and sophisticated by these arrivals.

There was a great deal of talk about the Court and in this Sir Gervaise, Senara, and Carlotta had a good deal in common since they had all moved in Court circles, and though Sir Gervaise was connected with Whitehall and Senara and her daughter with Spain there had been a connection between the two Courts when the King—Prince as he was then—had visited Spain in order to arrange a marriage between himself and the King of Spain's sister.

Sir Gervaise told us that as a boy of eighteen he had had a small role in the King's entourage, and it seemed very likely that he and Senara had actually been at the same functions. Senara had met King Charles on one occasion. She said this was before his father's death, when he was but a Prince though heir to the throne, and she had thought him a handsome man, though smaller than was becoming in a king. He had great charm of manner however, and being young and handsome created quite a good impression.

"Of course," she said, "he was more interested in getting help for his sister Elizabeth and her husband Frederick, who had lost his country, than he was in marriage with the Infanta."

"The King saw the present Queen at the French Court when he passed through Paris," Sir Gervaise told us, "but of course she was but a child then, and he did not give her a second glance."

"It's strange," said my mother, "that fate doesn't give us a little nudge when we are face to face with a situation or a person who is going to change our lives."

"You ask too much, my love," said my father.

"There are some people who say they have premonitions," suggested Senara and admitted, "I do now and then."

"Is it because your mother was a witch?" I asked.

There was a silence at the table. My mother was frowning.

"Oh, that's all nonsense, Bersaba," she said. "I can't think where you hear these things."

"But it's true, isn't it?"

"It was said that she was," Senara told us. "That was when she was here. It was never mentioned when I joined her later."

"People build up these fantasies," said my mother. "I am glad they are not talking of such things nowadays. They're . . . unhealthy."

I noticed that the servants who hovered about the table were listening. They would repeat in the kitchen what they had heard in the dining hall. They would remember the witch who had come to Castle Paling and disappeared. That she now lived in Spain would not make her any less of a witch in their eyes.

I watched Carlotta. How beautiful she was! Angelet looked insignificant beside her—and that meant I did too. I had noticed that Sir Gervaise was aware of her—so was she of him, and it was as though she was sending out her tentacles to draw him into her net just as she had Bastian. I noticed how often he addressed his remarks to her.

After supper my father and Sir Gervaise went off together. They had so much business and my mother told me that it had something to do with the Hooghly factory that was going to be built. "They are worried of course," she said, "because there is so much conflict between the King and the people. The fact that he rules without a government is amazing to me. Sir Gervaise says it can't go on like this. There'll be some sort of climax and heaven knows what will happen when that comes."

I said, "Do you think we shall feel it here, Mother?"

"My dear child, we could not escape. This Ship Money is really worrying the people at Plymouth and this certainty that he rules by divine right and is therefore justified in everything he does, is making the King enormously unpopular."

"What does Father think will happen?" I asked.

"That there will have to be an understanding sooner or later. The King will have to change his ways. He is being harsh to the Puritans and it is said that he is influenced by his Catholic wife. I don't like the way things are going, but let us hope they will be put right in time. By the way, I want to talk to you, Bersaba. There was something that was said at supper . . . about witches."

"Oh, yes, Mother."

"I don't want the subject encouraged. I believe it was you who brought it up."

"Was it?" I asked, my voice mildly interested.

"I'm sure of it, dear. I've never liked to talk of it. I can't ever forget the day they came for my stepmother."

"What happened, Mother? Was it very terrible?"

"Yes, it was. I hate to recall it. I dreamed about it for a long time afterward . . . until I was married to your father in fact. I would see that procession in my dreams—lighted torches, chanting voices, and the callous, cruel, gloating, lewd faces of the people marching on that Castle. I never want to see the like again."

"Do you think interest in witches has come back?"

"Never say such things. Has Senara been talking to you?"

"No, Mother."

"I remember when she was young she was constantly talking of witches and reminding people that her mother was suspected of being one. She didn't realize how dangerous it was then. It could still be."

"We haven't heard much talk of it, Mother."

"It's there though . . . sleeping . . . ready to be awakened. People still believe in it, but we have never encouraged it. I don't want people talking about witches just because Senara has come back. So Bersaba, please . . . if anyone speaks of it, brush it aside. I don't want a return of what happened before."

"Of course, Mother," I said.

"You see, my dear, hysteria can so easily be whipped up. Then ignorant people get together and fan the flames . . . you see what I mean."

"Yes, I do, they could march to Trystan Priory just as they marched that night to Castle Paling. They still hang and burn witches; they still tie their arms and legs together and throw them into the sea or the river or any pools deep enough to drown them."

"We'll not think of it. We'll not mention it. If you hear any of the servants talking, stop them. They may well talk, because they remember Carlotta's grandmother. I don't want them to, Bersaba."

"I will remember that, Mother," I said ambiguously, and I wondered whether she would notice my excitement.

As I went up to my room I saw one of the maids on the stairway. She was holding a kerchief in her hand.

"This was dropped by the lady Carlotta," she told me.

"Oh—why do you not take it to her then?" I asked.

The maid looked furtive. "I be feared to, Mistress Bersaba."

"Why?"

The girl cast down her eyes.

"Why? Why?" I demanded.

She couldn't say. I took the kerchief from her. "Are you afraid she's a witch and might ill-wish you?" I asked.

"Oh I dursen't say that, Mistress Bersaba."

The suspicions were spreading fast, I thought exultantly and said, "Give it to me. I'll take it to her room. I'll say a prayer as I cross the threshold. That's what you have to do, isn't it?"

"I do believe so, mistress, but it would be hard to bring myself to."

"All right, don't worry. I'll take it."

I seized the kerchief and went to the room which I knew to be Carlotta's. I knocked, and as there was no response I opened the door cautiously and went in. On the bed lay her nightgown, silk with a thousand frills. How beautiful she would look in it with her dark hair hanging about her shoulders. A soft perfume hung about the room. The fact that it was temporarily Carlotta's had changed it subtly.

I went quietly to the bed and picked up the nightgown. I held it against me and imagined that Bastian was coming in and I was his bride. Then the picture changed from me to Carlotta and the wild misery seized me.

I was suddenly aware of being watched. I turned sharply. The door of the anteroom was open and Ana was standing there.

"Is there anything you want?" she asked in her halting English.

"I brought your mistress' kerchief, which she had dropped. There it is on the table."

Ana bowed her head. I felt foolish standing there holding the nightdress about me so I said, "It's beautiful, this nightdress."

"I make it," said Ana.

"Congratulations. You must be a magician with your needle."

The dark eyes seemed to be probing my mind. I felt exposed, as though this woman read my thoughts—all my hatred of Carlotta; all my desire for revenge.

She came forward silently and, taking the nightdress from me, laid it on the bed.

"She's uncanny," I thought. "It's almost as though she knows what's in my mind. And she will be a watchdog."

The next day I disobeyed orders and again rode out alone. I didn't want anyone with me because I wanted to think. Revenge! It filled my mind, and I thought how clever I was to have formulated a plan which would exonerate me while it utterly defeated my enemy. All my love and longing for Bastian was lost in this new emotion.

I had not gone very far when I noticed that my mare seemed to be going lame, so I dismounted and discovered that she had cast a shoe. By good fortune I was less than a mile from the smithy so I decided to take her along without delay.

I talked soothingly to her as we went along, and in a short time we arrived. Neither Angelet nor I enjoyed our visits there, for the smith was not the most pleasant of men. He was a man of considerable height and girth and we always said that the Devil must look something like him when he stood over his furnace looking as though he would like to cast into it all the sinners of the neighborhood to their eternal torment.

Thomas Gast was a fierce man; he preached every Sunday in one of the barns not far from the smithy and a number of the villagers went to hear him—not so much to agree with his doctrines as to shiver at his fierce language. For Thomas Gast was a Puritan. He believed that pleasure was sinful. I used to misquote to Angelet, "There is more joy in Thomas Gast over one sinner who earns eternal damnation than a thousand who repent in time."

My parents were uneasy because of his fiery preaching, which they feared might bring trouble to the neighborhood. They believed that every man had a right to his opinions on the manner in which God should be worshiped, but it seemed to them the wise way was to keep one's thoughts to oneself. Thomas Gast was not like that. He was a man who believed firmly that Thomas Gast was right and everyone who disagreed with him in the slightest detail was wrong. Moreover, he was not content to leave them in their ignorance. He would chastise them with words and if he got the opportunity, as he did with his own family—with a leather strap.

74

He had ten children—and they and their poor little mother lived in fear lest they incur his wrath by an ill-chosen word or some action which could be construed as sinful.

He was a most uncomfortable man, but as my father said, the best smith he had ever known.

When I took in my mare he looked at me with disapproval, I presumed because I was wearing my riding hat at too jaunty an angle or perhaps my contemplation of revenge had made me appear to cherish a zest for life. However, my appearance displeased him.

I told him what had happened, and gently he examined the horse. He nodded grimly.

"If you could please shoe him right away I'd be glad," I said.

He nodded again, looking at me with his bright black eyes. I could see the whites round his pupils, which made him look as though he were staring like Grandfather Casvellyn, and a little mad. He was a fanatic and when people carry their fanaticism as far as he did perhaps that could be construed as madness.

I said; "It's a beautiful morning, Thomas. It makes you feel good to be alive on such a day."

I really wasn't good at all with Bastian's deceit so recent, but there was in me a grain of mischief and I knew that anyone's finding pleasure even in God-given nature would fill Thomas Gast with the desire to rant.

"You should be thinking of all the sin in the world," he growled.

"What sin? The sun is shining. The flowers are blooming. You should see the hollyhocks and sunflowers in the cottage gardens. And the bees are mad with joy over the lavender."

"You're a feckless young woman," said Thomas Gast. "If you don't see the blackness of sin all around you you'll be heading for hellfire."

"Well, Mr. Gast," I said mischievously, "so many of us are. You seem to be the only one who is without sin. You'll be very lonely when you get to Heaven."

"Don't 'ee joke about matters as is sacred, Mistress Bersaba," he said sternly. "You be watched and all your sins be noted. Never forget that. All your jesting mockery will be recorded and one day you'll answer for it."

I thought then of lying in the woods with Bastian and I knew that Thomas Gast would consider this a cardinal sin which could only earn eternal damnation and for a moment I trembled for there was something about Thomas Gast which made one believe, while one was in his company, that there might be something in his doctrines.

I watched him, his strong face flushed by the furnace, his gentleness with the horse—the only time he was ever gentle was with horses—and he began to declaim as though he were addressing an audience in the barn. The day of judgment was coming. Then those who now strutted in their finery would be cast into utter despair. The torments of Hell were beyond human imagination. He licked his lips.

I think he saw himself as one of God's executioners—a role, I decided, which would suit him very well.

I grew weary of his diatribe and, interrupting it, I said I would stroll off and return when the horse was shod.

So I left the smithy and looked at the gardens in the little row of cottages. There were six of them—all built of the gray Cornish stone which was a feature of the countryside; they had long gardens in front and a patch behind in which most of them grew vegetables or kept a goat or a pig. But the front gardens were full of flowers with the exception of the blacksmith's. He grew vegetables in his, and at the back, pigs were kept. I had been inside the cottage once when the latest Gast was born and my mother had sent Angelet and me over with a basket of good things. Everything in the house was plain and for use, not for ornament. The girls of the household—there were four of them—always wore black garments with collars tight at the neck; so did their mother. Their hair was hidden by caps so that it was not easy to tell which was which. Angelet and I were always sorry for the Gast children.

As I came round by the cottages I saw one of the girls in the garden; she was weeding. I had heard that they all had their tasks and if these were not done to their father's satisfaction they were severely beaten.

As I approached I called good morning and the Gast girl straightened up and spoke to me. I looked at her steadily and guessed her to be the eldest girl. She was about seventeen—my age. I noticed how she took in my riding habit, wich must have seemed as elegant to her as Carlotta's did to me.

"Good day, mistress," said the girl.

I was very curious to know what life was like lived in the blacksmith's house. I could of course imagine to a certain extent and I pictured myself in such a position. If I had been his daughter I would have defied him, I was sure.

"You work very hard," I said. "Which one are you?"

"I'm Phoebe, mistress, the eldest."

Her eyes filled with tears and I said suddenly, "You're unhappy aren't you?"

She nodded and I went on: "What's wrong?"

"Oh don't 'ee ask me, mistress," she said. "Please don't 'ee ask me!"

"Perhaps there's something we could do."

"Ain't nothing you could do, mistress. 'Tis done, more's the pity."

"What is it, Phoebe?"

"I dursen't say."

Strangely enough, as I stood there looking at her I was aware of some understanding between us. And I thought, "It's a man."

Then I thought of Bastian and all my bitterness came back to me and a bond between this girl and myself was forged in that moment.

"Of course," I said, "your father sees sin where others see ordinary pleasure."

"This be true sin."

"What is sin?" I said. "I suppose if it's hurting other people . . . that's sin." I thought of myself leading Carlotta to her death. That was the blackest sin of all. "But if no one is hurt . . . that isn't sin."

She wasn't listening to me; she was caught up in her own drama.

I said gently, "Phoebe, are you . . . in trouble?"

She lifted woebegone eyes to my face, but she did not answer and the fear in her face reminded me of Jenny Keys.

"I would help you if I could," I said rashly.

"Thank you, mistress." She bent down over the earth and went on weeding.

There was nothing I could say to her. If what I guessed might be true then Phoebe was indeed in trouble. I had seen that in her face which I believe Grandfather Casvellyn had seen in me. Did girls change when they took a lover? Was the loss of virginity apparent in their faces? I wondered. For I was absolutely certain that Phoebe had had a lover, and that now she was faced with the consequences.

The consequences. A child! Then I was overwhelmed by the thought that it might have happened to me. "I will marry you when you are old enough or before if necessary," Bastian had said.

There had been a certain recklessness in our loving, for we had not to consider the consequences too seriously. I knew that my parents, shocked as they might have been, would have given me love and understanding. So would Aunt Melanie, and Uncle Connell being the man he was would laugh and say Bastian was a chip off the old block.

How different for poor Phoebe Gast. To wear a ribbon, to undo a button at the neck on a hot day, to wear a belt which might hold in the waist of those shapeless black smocks they wore—that would be sinful. But to have lain in the fields or the woods with a man. . . .

I went back to the smithy. The mare was waiting for me. Thomas Gast looked more like one of Satan's henchmen than ever and I could not stop thinking of poor Phoebe Gast.

Yesterday I overheard two servants talking. I had come in from the stables and they were dusting in one of the rooms which led out of the hall. They could not see me so I sat down and listened because what they were saying interested me. One of them was Ginny and the other Mab, a girl in her middle teens who had a reputation among the servants as one who was ready for adventure, and had an eye for the men.

As soon as I caught the name Jenny Keys I had to listen.

"She truly were," Ginny was saying. "White she was but white can turn to black . . . and it could have been that was what happened to her."

"What did she do, Ginny?"

"Her did lots of good. Why if I could have gone earlier to her I'd have been spared my shame."

"But you wouldn't have been without young Jeff for the world."

"Not now. But then I would."

"How was Jenny Keys brought out, Ginny?"

"You mean, how was it known what she were? I'll tell you something. One day two of the servants from the Priory went down to see her. 'Twas just a love draught they wanted. There was this stableman who wouldn't look at one of them and all she wanted was to turn his eyes to her. And what did they see . . . right there in Jenny Key's laps was a toad . . . a horrible slimy toad . . . but 'twas no ordinary toad, they did say. There looked out of his eyes something as told them he were the Devil in toad form. They shook with trembling both of them and then they turned on their heels and ran for their lives. 'Twasn't long after that one of them took sick and she swore 'twas something that toad had sent out to her—for he weren't no ordinary toad. He were what they do call her familiar, and that showed Jenny Keys was a witch."

"How would you know when a toad was a familiar? There's

lots of them round the ponds. I've heard 'em croaking at night in the spring when they come out looking for a mate and then they go down to the ponds to lay their eggs."

"They're just ordinary toads . . . they ain't familiars."

"But toads is nasty things. I suppose it's because they come out at night."

" 'Tis so, but don't do to mistake them all. There's some as just goes about their business . . . same as any other creature might. 'Tis only when a witch do take one up and to her bed maybe and in him comes the spawn of the Devil, who lives and shelters in the toad.

"Like in the toad they saw with Jenny Keys?"

"Maybe so, and when it was known that Jenny Keys harbored a toad and took him to her close like, the trouble started. They said she carried him in her bosom and that he crawled over her body and was familiar like."

Mab burst into giggles and Ginny reproved her. "You laugh now but you wouldn't be laughing if witches heard you."

"Jenny Keys be dead though."

"Jenny Keys ain't the only witch, remember."

"Who else is?"

"You don't have to look far."

There was an awed silence.

"You mean . . . *her* . . ."

"Why not? Her grandmother were. Powers be passed down, I reckon."

"I reckon we ought to keep our eyes open."

I rose and went swiftly and silently up the staircase to my room.

Angelet—with that special feeling that was between us—began to sense that I wanted to be alone. She had guessed of course that this was concerned with Bastian and I had seen her look at Carlotta with something like distaste, for she was very loyal to me.

When we lay in bed at night it was our custom to talk over the events of the day, and although since I heard of Bastian's perfidy I had had no wish to talk to her, I could not suddenly break the habit.

She said to me one night after the conversation at the dinner table had been particularly sparkling and Carlotta with Senara and Gervaise had discussed the Courts of Spain and England at great length—thus making it very difficult for the rest of us to participate: "Has it occurred to you, Bersaba, that Sir Gervaise and Carlotta are getting very friendly?"

"I think Carlotta is of a nature to pay attention always to the male members of the company."

"You are right. Of course she is beautiful. One has to grant her that, and having been at Court I suppose does something to one. I wonder if we shall ever go to Court?"

"Do you want to?" I asked.

"It would be amusing. Besides, we shall have to marry sometime, shan't we? Mother obviously meant something like that when she said our next birthday party would be different."

I yawned. "It's a long way away."

"There are the Trent men and the Krolls and the Lamptons. One of them I suppose. Oh, isn't it dull living in the country! I would like never to have known my husband and then the next day he is there. Do you feel like that?"

I felt the anger surge up in me. No, I had expected Bastian to be my husband and I've known him all my life . . . and yet I never really knew him. I used to think he was quiet and steady and that I could tease him about this. Then I found that that wasn't true at all. He had only to see Carlotta and he forgot all his vows to me. How little we knew people whom we thought we understood so well.

"Do you?" urged Angelet. "You're not asleep, are you?"

"What's that?" I cried, pretending to be starting out of a doze.

Oh, go to sleep," she said. "You never want to talk these days."

It was better to be alone for if I talked to Angelet I might betray something of my feelings. I was afraid that I might let fall some little comment which would betray me when the time came.

So I rode out alone doing the forbidden thing. Down the blackberry track, past the smithy. I glanced in the direction of the cottages and thought of poor Phoebe, wondering how she was faring. I could visualize clearly the misery she must be enduring with a heavy burden of guilt upon her. I wondered what Thomas Gast would do if my surmise was correct.

It was a misty evening and darker than usual when I took my mare to the stables. I wandered down by the garden to the pond on which the water lilies were growing and as I did so I heard the croaking of a toad and as I came nearer I saw him.

He was seated there by the pool—drowsy, I imagine, after a good feed of insects—and I suddenly felt my heart begin to beat wildly as memories of the conversation I had heard between the servants came back to me.

On impulse I took a large kerchief from my pocket and, stooping, wrapped it round the toad and carried him into the Priory. I went straight up to our room and was thankful that Angelet was not there.

I was excited. I knew what I was going to do with the toad. It was part of my plan and seeing him there, waiting for me, as it were, had forced me to act before I had meant to.

But why not? There was no point in delay.

In the evening the servants went into the bedrooms to prepare the beds for the night, to turn back the quilt and if it were cold put in hot bricks wrapped up in flannel.

Ana did not turn down the beds for Carlotta and Senara any more than she cleaned their rooms. That was a housemaid's task and Ana, as lady's maid, would consider it beneath her. It was Mab who did the beds and I was particularly amused because she was the one whom I had heard talking to Ginny. When I considered that it seemed as though I were being guided by fate, for I knew what Mab would find when she turned down Carlotta's bed. There was a tall livery chest in the corridor outside the bedroom door and when I heard Mab going up to the rooms I followed at a discreet distance and hid myself behind the chest.

It happened just as I knew it would. It was not long before I heard Mab's piercing scream and she came running out of the bedroom, her face white as a lily petal. She didn't see me because her one thought was to get away from that room as fast as she could.

I slipped out and went into Carlotta's room. There on the pillow was the toad. He seemed to glare at me with baleful eyes, so I smothered him in the kerchief and hurried from the room. As I did so I felt my blood run cold and my heart began to beat so wildly that it was like a drum beating against my bodice. I was standing there by the bed when I had a strange feeling that I was not alone. I looked around the room. No one was there. The door of the communicating room where Senara slept was open a little but I could see no one.

What was it—this sudden fear? It had seemed so easy. All I had to do was put the toad in her bed, leave it there for Mab to find when she came to do the beds, then when she ran out as I was sure she would, I was to go in and remove the toad so that when she brought the others to see it, it would have disappeared, which I felt was just the sort of thing a familiar would do.

As I stood there in that room and I could feel the toad moving in the kerchief I had an impulse to drop it and run. I thought to myself: "Suppose she is truly a witch? She bewitched Bastian. Suppose the toad *is* her familiar! Suppose it is a devil in toad form!" But I had found him— a perfectly harmless toad by the pond in the garden and it was I who had placed him in her bed.

It was just a feeling that eyes were watching me. Why? I went swiftly to the door between the two rooms. I looked inside. No one was there. Then I ran from the room, out into the corridor. I could hear Mab's voice explaining what she had seen.

Ginny was saying: " 'Tis nothing. You dreamed it. 'Twas because we was talking of toads."

And Mab: "I can't go in there. I'd die rather."

I waited in one of the rooms while they went up to Carlotta's room, then I came swiftly along the gallery and down the stairs praying I should meet no one. I went out through a side door and across a courtyard to the gardens.

I sped across to the pool and laid down the kerchief. The toad remained still for several seconds. I watched him fearfully, half expecting him to turn into some horrible shape, but seeming to realize that he was free and on his home ground, he made his cautious way to the edge of the pool and hid himself under a large stone.

I picked up the kerchief and went into the house.

On the way I met several of the maids, who were chattering wildly together.

"What's happened?" I said.

"Oh, 'twas Mab, Miss Bersaba. Her be well nigh in hysterics."

"Why?"

" 'Tis what her have seen in the lady Carlotta's bed."

"In her bed?"

Ginny said, "Mab could have fancied it. There were no toad there when I went up."

The maids were silent, their eyes on my face.

"Whatever made Mab imagine such a thing?" I asked.

" 'Tis talk, Miss Bersaba," said Ginny.

"I did see it," Mab insisted. "It were there . . . on her pillow. The way it looked at me . . . 'twere terrible. It was like no other toad I seen."

"Well, where is it now?" I asked with a hint of impatience.

"It have clean disappeared," said Ginny.

"Well, that's a blessing," I answered infusing skepticism into my voice.

And I passed on.

I knew that that night the great topic of conversation among the servants would be the toad Mab had seen in Carlotta's bed. I knew too that the story of the toad would not be confined to the Priory. It would spread to the village. I wondered what Thomas Gast would say when he heard it. The habits of witches would be great sin in his eyes.

I dreamed of him that night standing by his furnace with his wild eyes gloating on the flames.

Journey Through the Rain

IT WAS late afternoon and I was in our orchard lying beneath my favorite apple tree and thinking of Bastian and wondering what he was doing at that time. He had looked so unhappy when he had left and although I had pretended to be unaware of him I was far from that. I hoped he was unhappy. He should be. He had deceived me and now he was parted from Carlotta, for she was undecided whether or not she would marry him, and when one considered her growing friendship with Sir Gervaise, the wealthy courtier, it seemed unlikely that she would take Bastian, the country squire.

So I hated her on two counts—one for taking my lover and the other for finding him not good enough for her. When I considered that, I could gloat over the toad incident. I knew the servants talked of little else because I eavesdropped continuously. Often I would come upon them in a room, on the stairs, or in the gardens whispering together. They would stop when I approached, but not before I had discovered the subject of their conversation.

Sometimes I would grow impatient. What if Carlotta decided to go back to Castle Paling? She would then go away . . . back to Bastian . . . and when she was out of sight people here would forget their suspicions.

While I was brooding in this way Ginny came out to the orchard.

She said, "I saw 'ee come out here, Miss Bersaba, so I knew where you were to. There's someone as wants a word with you . . . and in secret."

Ginny spoke in a quiet voice with a tremor of excitement in it which made her seem conspiratorial. My feelings of guilt were growing very strong. I would start when anyone spoke to me because I suppose I felt that someone had watched me put the toad in the bed and remove it and understood what I was doing, so that when the time came they would know what part I had played in the drama.

Ginny's next words quashed my fears in that direction but startled me nevertheless. "It's Phoebe Gast," she said.

"What does she want?"

"She wants to see you, Miss Bersaba. She be in the barn. She have asked me to come for you and ask you if you'd talk to her like."

The barn was a stone-walled building in which corn was stored. It was apart from the other outbuildings and one had to cross a small field after leaving the garden to reach it.

"Does anyone know she's there?"

"Oh, no, mistress. She be scared out of her wits I do tell 'ee. She waited in the lane for me for she knows I came along that way and she darted out and said to me, 'Tell Mistress Bersaba. Tell her I must see her.' Then she told me she was going to the barn."

"I'll go and see what's wrong," I said, but I knew and I felt exultant in a way because she had come to me.

When we reached the barn, I pushed open the door and looked in. The creak of the door brought Phoebe to her feet and as soon as she saw who it was relief flooded over her poor sad face.

I felt adult, in charge of the situation, as Angelet, who lacked my experience, could never have been.

I said, "Ginny, go back to the house. Don't tell anyone that Phoebe is here. I will see you when I get back."

Ginny ran off and I shut the barn door.

"Oh, mistress," cried Phoebe, "I had nowhere to go. And I thought of you. You was terrible kind to me the other day."

"I did nothing, Phoebe."

" 'Twas the way you looked at me. As though you understood like."

"Now, Phoebe," I said. "You have been with a man and you are going to have a child. That's it, isn't it?"

"You be terrible sharp, mistress. How did 'ee know?"

"I did know," I said. "I am . . . perceptive." I think she thought I meant I had special powers and she was so desperate, poor girl, that she seemed to look upon me as some goddess who could drag her out of her trouble. A great pleasure swept over me to be so regarded. It was strange to have been thinking of bringing disaster, possibly death, to one woman so recently and then to feel gratified because I was going to save another. It was a sort of expiation, placating the angels. Moreover, I felt a sense of power which was very gratifying—and like a balm laid on the wounds which Bastian had inflicted.

I sat down beside her. "How did it happen?" I asked.

"He said I were pretty and he did like the look of me. He said he couldn't keep his eyes off me. I hadn't thought I could be pretty to anyone before that. It just made me soft like, I reckon."

"Poor Phoebe," I said, "it must have been hard living in that cottage with a father like yours."

At the mention of her father Phoebe began to tremble.

"I fear him, Mistress Bersaba." She unbuttoned the shapeless black gown and showed me the marks of a lash on her shoulder. "He gave me that for singing a song about spring on the sabbath day," she said. "What he'd give me for this I don't dare think. He'd kill me I reckon. I deserve it, I don't doubt. I've been so wicked."

"Why did you do it, Phoebe?"

"The need came over me, mistress."

I nodded. Who could understand better than I?

"Let us be practical," I said. "Does he know?"

"Oh, God help us, no. My mother does and he might beat it out of her. He'll blame her for my sins. He'll say she knew of my wanton ways and let them go unpunished. What can I do, Mistress Bersaba?"

"I'll think," I said.

"You be terrible good to me. No one ain't ever been so good before."

I felt somehow ashamed. I would never have believed I would. I was learning something about myself. I could put myself so easily into Phoebe's place. I could feel the need coming over me and I could see myself if I had been Thomas

85

Gast's daughter finding myself in the same position as she was. It was for this reason that I could give out this comfort, this understanding, and even in that moment I thought: "Angelet could never be the same. Innocent Angelet could not understand."

I said, "Could the man marry you?"

She shook her head. "He be married. I did know at the time. I can't think what came over me."

"How old is the baby?"

"Well 'twould be six months nearly. There comes the time when it can't be hid no more . . . and that time's come now."

"So you ran away."

"Yes. My mother knew. Her's known for a day or two. Her's beside herself. She keeps saying, 'Gast'll kill you. He's a hard man . . . but a good man. He can't abide sin and I reckon this is about one of the biggest sins there is.' She was frightened for me. So I ran away. I thought it best."

She was looking at me with pleading eyes, and I said, "Don't worry, Phoebe, I'll see to it. You mustn't get too upset. It's bad for the baby."

"Oh, the baby. I wish it dead, mistress. I wish I was dead. I did think of doing away with myself but . . . I couldn't somehow."

"You mustn't talk like that. Now, that *is* wicked. Listen. You will stay here for tonight. Nobody knows you're here except Ginny and she won't dare tell anyone because she knows I'll be angry if she does. I'll bring you a wool cloak to wrap yourself in and I'll bring you food. There's a bolt on the barn door. When I go pull it across the door and don't open it for anyone but me. In the morning I'll have a plan."

She started to cry. "Oh, Mistress Bersaba. You be terrible good to me. You're like an angel, that's what you are . . . an angel of mercy. I won't ever forget this."

"Don't say any more. Just wait there. I'll be back."

I came out of the barn and heard her pull the bolt as I had bidden. I felt exultant, powerful, godlike as I went into the house.

The next morning I realized that I could not keep Phoebe indefinitely in the barn and there was only one thing I could do and that was tell my mother. I could have done that the previous night, for I knew very well what her reaction would be. She would never turn away a girl in Phoebe's condition. I was beginning to take a sharp look at myself, and I did not disguise the fact that I had behaved as I had because of a love of power. I had wanted to take all the glory of saving Phoebe for myself and no one else was to have a share in it. So it was I who had taken food and covering down to her. It was I who kept her secret for a night.

But now I must tell my mother before Phoebe was discovered. I found her in the stillroom with one of the servants, and she looked up with pleasure when she saw me. She always liked us to come to the stillroom because she thought it was so good for us to learn the secrets of preserving and such culinary arts.

"Mother," I said, "I want to speak to you."

I must have looked very serious for she immediately said to the servant, "You carry on, Annie." And to me: "Come to my bedroom, Bersaba."

So we went there and I told her that Phoebe was going to have a child and had run away from home and that I had hidden her in the barn for the night.

"Oh, poor, poor girl. What will become of her? Thomas Gast is such a cruel man. Why didn't you come to me last night?"

"She was so distressed, Mother, and I didn't quite know what you would say. I had to save her for at least a night. I said I would do what I could. We must help her."

"Of course we must. She can't go back to that father of hers."

"Could she stay here?"

"She will have to. Where else is there? But what of the child?"

"Ginny's child stays here."

"I know. But Ginny was one of our servants. We mustn't let people think that they can have children as they like and that the Priory is a sort of home for them."

I knew that while she was talking she was wondering what she could do for Phoebe. She would never turn her away and she would let the child stay here because she would say that a child cannot be parted from its mother. I could see the horror in her eyes which meant that she was contemplating Thomas Gast's avenging anger if the girl ever fell into his hands.

"Mother," I said, "she is terrified. If you could see her you would have to help."

"My dearest child, of course we shall help her. She will have to come here at least until the child is born and then we will see what can be done."

"Oh, thank you, Mother."

She looked at me, her eyes full of love and approval. "I am so happy, Bersaba, to see how compassionate you can be."

"I have not done wrong to promise her, to give her hope?"

"I wouldn't have you do anything else. Go down to the barn and bring her to the house."

Exultantly I went.

Phoebe drew back the bolt when I said who it was. Her eyes were shadowed and still filled with terror.

"It's all right," I told her. "You are going to stay here. I have spoken to my mother. She says you are not to worry. The baby will be born here and then we'll see."

Phoebe fell to her knees and, taking my hand, kissed it.

I felt wonderfully happy. I had not felt like that since I had heard of Bastian's deception and I had thought I never would again.

It was impossible to keep Phoebe's presence at the Priory a secret. Not that we had attempted to. My parents said that Thomas Gast would have to know sooner or later and the sooner perhaps the better. His daughter's disappearance would have to be explained, and it could only be a matter of hours before one of the servants talked to someone in the village and such news would spread like wildfire.

It was not therefore surprising that the following day Thomas Gast presented himself at the Priory.

Phoebe saw him coming and—much to my gratification—immediately came to me as though I was the one who could best protect her.

She, Angelet, and I went to one of the peeps in the solarium where we could look down on the hall without being seen, and where not only could we see but hear what was going on. Angelet and I had used those peeps in our childhood when we had watched our parents entertaining in the great hall. My sister had thrown herself wholeheartedly into Phoebe's cause as I had known she would, and was as determined as I that Phoebe should not go back to the fiery blacksmith. With characteristic enthusiasm she had been busy finding discarded garments which Phoebe would be able to adjust to her ever-increasing size and materials which could be transformed into baby clothes.

The blacksmith looked less fierce in our hall than he did in the smithy. I missed the glow which the fiery furnace cast over his face and the ring of the anvil which because of him sounded Satanic. I think he was perhaps a little subdued by what would seem to him the grandeur of our home. At the same time he would disapprove of it and I could imagine his thinking of it as treasures upon earth which rot and decay.

Our mother came down to the hall. She looked very fragile confronting that mighty man, but there was that air of dignity about her of which he could not help but be aware.

"My lady," said Thomas Gast, "it's come to my ears that you have my daughter here, and I am come to take her from you."

"For what purpose?" asked my mother.

"That I may treat her according to her deserts, ma'am."

I could feel Phoebe tremble beside me. "Don't be afraid," I whispered. "You're not going. Watch."

"It is for that reason that we have decided she shall stay here at least until the child is born. A girl in her condition must not be subjected to harsh treatment if only for the sake of the unborn child."

Thomas Gast was temporarily taken aback. My mother was speaking as though this was a child about to be respectably born. He spluttered. "I don't follow you, ma'am. It must be you don't know—"

My mother seized her opportunity. "I know what has happened. Poor Phoebe has been seduced by a man who can't marry her. She is young, little more than a child herself. We must be merciful. There is a new life to consider. I am sure she will realize the error of her ways and that it won't occur again."

The blacksmith's fury broke out. "Ma'am, she be my daughter, more's the pity. I would she had been strangled at birth rather than bring this disgrace on me and mine. I want that girl. I'll thrash her till she screams for mercy. 'Tis the only way to cast out the blackness of her sin. Not that it will ever be cast out. She'll know the folly of her ways when she goes to Hell . . . but first she must have a taste of Hell on earth."

"She has had that most of her life," said my mother tartly. "Thomas Gast, your Puritan piety has brought misery to your entire family. We are not going to give Phoebe back to you. She is staying here. We shall employ her in the household and that's an end to it."

The blacksmith was like a lion cheated of his prey. "I'd respectfully remind you, ma'am, that she be my girl."

"That does not give you the right to ill-treat her."

"Begging your pardon, ma'am, I have every right. Give her

over to me that I can help her mend her ways and maybe save her soul from eternal damnation."

"If we gave Phoebe back to you, Thomas Gast, and if any ill befell her or the child through your treatment of her, do you know that would be murder?"

"You seek to bemuse me, ma'am. I only want my girl."

My father had come into the hall. He stood beside my mother and said quietly, "You will go now, Thomas Gast. Your daughter will remain here until her child is born. I forbid you to harm her and you are trespassing on my land. I gave you no permission to come here."

"You've got my girl, master."

"Your daughter is here and stays here. Now go, and remember this: The smithy belongs to me and if you wish to stay there you must obey my wishes. If aught happens to your daughter through your ill-treatment I shall accuse you of murder and that will not be very pleasant for you."

"I'm a godfearing man, master, who only wants to serve the Lord and do his duty by his family."

"Harsh duty, Thomas Gast."

"They be my children and I be responsible to God for 'em."

"You are also responsible to God for yourself," said my father.

"I, master! There's no more religious man in these parts. I'm on my knees four hours a day, and I'll see it's the same with my family. This girl of mine have brought terrible disgrace on us all and God calls for vengeance."

"Mind you do not bring disgrace on us all by your cruelty to your wife and children."

That stung Thomas Gast to retort. In that moment he was ready to fling away his very smithy in his righteous anger.

" 'Tis a sorry matter when such as I am is chided by those as harbor whores and witches among them."

With that he turned and went out.

I could see the horror on my parents' faces as they looked at each other; and I knew what was responsible for it.

It was the reference to witches.

The aura of glory in which I had been living since I went to Phoebe in the barn seemed to evaporate. My father slipped his arm through my mother's and they went out of the hall together. He was clearly reassuring her.

During the next two days Phoebe would not venture out. Angelet and I looked after her. We had reminded our mother that she had once said that when we were eighteen we should

90

have a personal maid between us—one who would look after our clothes, sew for us, do our hair—and take our messages. Well, here was Phoebe and we both wanted her. We weren't eighteen yet but soon would be.

Our mother, delighted by our sympathy for Phoebe, readily agreed and at first I was afraid that Angelet with her more appealing ways might win Phoebe from me. But that was clearly not to be. Phoebe remembered what I had done—and I believed she always would. I was her savior and she told me that was something she would never forget as long as she lived.

"I'll be your slave all the days of my life, Mistress Bersaba," she told me.

"We don't have slaves nowadays, Phoebe," I replied. "If you'll just be my maid that's good enough."

"There's nothing I wouldn't do for 'ee," she answered fervently. "You changed everything for me. You've even made me love the baby."

I was very happy.

Ginny told me that Thomas Gast was preaching hellfire every night on the village green.

"Crowds do go and listen to him, mistress. Once there was just the few . . . them like himself. They want to stop dancing and singing and have nothing but church and prayers all day long."

I watched Carlotta with Sir Gervaise. They often went out riding together. They were becoming very friendly, which seemed to please Senara. I heard her say to my mother, "It would be quite a good match. Carlotta would never settle in the wilds."

My mother replied, "You were happy enough here once, Senara . . . until you went away, and then you didn't want to go."

"I liked adventure, but it's true I often wished I was back. Carlotta is different. I was brought up here. The place where you spend your childhood means something to you."

Once when I was standing at our bedroom window watching the moon, which was nearing its fullness, Phoebe came and stood silently behind me.

I turned and smiled at her. I took great pleasure in her devotion to me and I was constantly amazed that it did more to soothe me than my plans for revenge had done.

"Look at the moon, Phoebe," I said. "Is it not beautiful?"

" 'Twill soon be full, Mistress Bersaba."

Her brows were puckered and she looked anxious. I said, "What's wrong Phoebe? Everything is going well, isn't it?"

"There's something I think I should tell 'ee, mistress. 'Tis about the moon."

"The moon! What on earth do you mean?"

"I know you don't like her, mistress, and that is what have held me back. But 'tis for you to say what should be done."

"What are you trying to tell me, Phoebe?"

"There be a lot of grumbling in the village, mistress. My father have always spoke against witches. And now I be here it have made a hate in him against this house. He's a man with a mountain of hate in him for all his goodness and that he never laughs or sings seeing it as sinful. He hates sin, and he hates that you have sheltered me and robbed me of my punishment and he hates witches. He says he wants to see every tree with a witch hanging on it. Then perhaps we'll be free of them."

"There has been a lot of talk of witches lately."

"Oh, yes, mistress, 'twas since the ladies came and it was remembered. There's the one they came to get long time ago at Castle Paling and her fled. But now 'tis the daughter they'm after. She have a look of the Devil in her and she have bewitched the fine gentleman from London. He be always seen with her. There was not many as would listen at first, on account of her being at the Priory. Witches by rights lives in little huts and they're easy to take. There was some who wouldn't believe the lady was a witch . . . not until the toad was found on her pillow."

"Oh!" I gasped. "And now. . . ."

"They've had their proof, mistress. They're going to take her the first opportunity they get and they're going to hang her on a tree on the night of the full moon. If they can take her easy, they'd like that better, not wanting trouble with the Priory . . . but if they can't . . . well, they'll take her some way."

My first thought was: "It's worked. I've done this. I've roused them up against her, and no one will know that I did it. I shall have my revenge. They will kill her . . . in most horrible fashion and I shall be avenged."

Then I saw her in my mind's eye being dragged to the pond. Would they tie her right arm to her left leg and her left arm to her right leg and throw her into the water? If she sank she would be innocent but dead and if she floated she would be guilty and put to death.

This was the perfect revenge. Ugly death, humiliation. Carlotta, the dignified lady, to be submitted to such.

Why not? She had taken Bastian from me, and then she had rejected him in his turn for Sir Gervaise—or so it seemed she would. She deserved the worst that could happen to her. I should not be sorry for her.

Since the toad had been found in her bed. . . .

Phoebe was looking at me. "You're so good, Mistress Bersaba. You won't let it happen."

I pressed Phoebe's hand and went to my mother.

"I must speak to you at once," I said. "Please, quickly . . . there's no time to lose."

Once more she took me into her bedroom.

"They are going to take Carlotta," I said. "If they can't capture her before they'll take her on the night of the full moon. They are going to kill her . . . hang her on a tree or drown her. . . . Perhaps . . ."

"My child," cried my mother and held me against her. "I feared it," she went on. "That man is wicked. He seeks revenge. And he calls himself godly. He yearns to inflict torture on everyone. It is not the concept of Heaven that he loves, but that of Hell."

"What shall we do, Mother?"

"Thank God you discovered this in time. It is two days before the full moon. They must leave tonight. Your father and I will arrange it."

That night Senara and Carlotta left and Sir Gervaise, his business with my father completed, accompanied them.

I lay in bed bewildered. I could not sleep. What had I done? I had planned so carefully and when my plans were nearing fruition I had deliberately ruined them.

I could not understand myself. What had come over me? I hated Carlotta and yet I had saved her.

My mother came into the room and stood by my bed.

"They are safe," she said. "They will soon be in Castle Paling."

I did not answer and she stooped over the bed and kissed me.

"You have saved them," she said. "I'm proud of you, my darling."

When she had gone Angelet said to me, "You've become a sort of saint. Mother's proud of you and Phoebe thinks you're a god or something."

"And you know different," I answered, and added: "So do I."

Angelet went on talking about witches and I pretended to be sleepy.

"I think she *was* one," was Angelet's verdict. "After all, there was that toad in her bed. How could a toad have got there . . . and then it disappeared, didn't it?"

I remained silent, asking myself what had possessed me to do what I had and the answer was: I did not know.

The night of the full moon passed without incident, for it was soon common knowledge that Carlotta had left with her mother and the fine gentleman from London. This seemed further proof of her special powers. But it was an anticlimax. The fevered excitement had died down. There was to be no witch baiting on the night of the full moon and Thomas Gast's pregnant daughter had become a maid at the Priory where her child would be born. It was not the first time that the Big House had sheltered wayward girls and it seemed in the natural course of events that the affair would soon be forgotten.

Life went on normally at the Priory. We no longer ate in some state in the main hall but took our meals in the small dining parlor. Estate affairs were discussed between my father and Fennimore and they were planning together how the estate should be run when they had both gone to sea. There was already a very good manager and he would take over much of Fennimore's work and everything would be satisfactory while Fennimore would be doing what he wanted to.

My mother was uneasy at having two men at sea but as usual she curbed her misgivings and believed in the best.

It was about a week after Carlotta, Senara, and Sir Gervaise had left that we had news from Castle Paling. Carlotta was betrothed to Sir Gervaise and they were leaving for London as he must be close to that city that he might hold his place at Court. He and Carlotta would be married when they reached London, and Senara was to accompany them and stay awhile with them before returning to Spain.

I thought about Bastian then and I must admit I felt a certain pleasure in his misery, for I was sure he was miserable after being so shamefully treated by Carlotta.

Within two days Bastian rode over to the Priory.

I heard his voice so I had warning, and I shut myself in our room trying to compose myself. It was not long before Angelet came running in.

"Who do you think is here? Bastian! Come down and see him."

I hesitated. Not to go and see him might be construed as an indication that I was emotionally moved. I didn't want that to happen. My pride was fierce and strong and all I was afraid of was that when I saw him it would melt and I should be ready to go back to the old relationship. That was what I did not want. If I forgave him, I should never know when he was going to turn from me because someone more attractive had appeared.

No, his conduct was something I could not forgive.

I went down to the hall and there he was . . . Bastian, who used to arouse such joy in me. When he looked at me his eyes shone with the old pleasure and I was delighted that it scarcely moved me. I kept the vision of himself and Carlotta before my eyes.

"Good day to you, Bastian."

He seized my hands and held them firmly. I made sure that they gave no response. "Oh, Bersaba, I'm glad to see you."

Angelet stood there smiling benignly at me. I knew she was thinking: "It's all right now, Carlotta is out of the way and he is free for Bersaba."

Nothing could infuriate me more. Did he think he could pick me up and drop me at will? My feelings had changed toward Bastian. I realized then—in this revealing self-knowledge which had come to me recently—that it was not so much Bastian I had loved, but his admiration, the fact that he singled me out, that he preferred me to Angelet. All my emotions were concerned in some way with Angelet—for they grew from an intense desire to prove that I was as good in every way—no, better—than my sister.

She, dear simple Angelet, felt nothing of this. She was uncomplicated, predictable, and perhaps that was what made her so much more lovable than I.

"It is pleasant to see you, Bastian," I said.

"I have so much to say to you."

"You'll be wanting to tell us all about your broken engagement."

"Oh. . . . it never seemed real to me somehow."

"It was real enough to be broken." I turned to Angelet. "I'll go and tell Mother that Bastian is here."

"I'll go," said Angelet.

"No, you stay and talk to Bastian." I was halfway up the stairs before she could protest.

I went and told my mother and she went down to the hall,

but I did not accompany her. Afterward I wondered whether it looked too pointed. What I really wanted to convey was the fact that Bastian was no longer of any special interest to me.

By suppertime I had still not seen him alone. Whenever I was in his company I always contrived that others should be there and he would look at me with anguished appeal. But I was enjoying the situation. This was revenge . . . far better than that I had planned on Carlotta. After all, it was Bastian who was the guilty party.

It was inevitable that he should catch up with me at some time. It happened the next morning when I had gone into the gardens to gather some flowers. I had in fact arranged it should be so and I wanted it to happen in daylight in view of the house. I was a little uncertain, not so much of my love for Bastian—which I think I understood and which was based on his preference for me, so that it was not real love—but of what Phoebe called "the need." That was there. I thought of lying on the cool grass with him bending over me and I had to confess that I thought that would be pleasant—well, more than pleasant.

But my pride was urging me and that *must* remain stronger than my senses.

So I contrived this meeting in the garden where anything other than a change of words would be impossible.

"Bersaba," he cried, "I have to speak to you."

I pretended to be interested in the rose I was cutting.

"Listen to me. I've come to ask you to marry me."

I raised my eyebrows. How I should have longed to hear him say that just a short time ago. I was not yet eighteen and we were to have been married then, but now everything was changed. I had seen Sir Gervaise from London and I had to admit that although he did not appeal to me in the way Bastian had done, I liked well his elegant mode of speech and the easy manner with which he wore his clothes. He had shown me that there was a life outside this narrow country one in which we had spent our lives. I had been fascinated by the talk of Courts in which he, Carlotta, and Senara had been engaged so often. I thought: I am young for marriage. If I marry Bastian I should be here for the whole of my life. Is it what I want? Don't I want to see the world? I should like to go to London, to see the King and the Queen and the people whose names have been bandied about at our table. Carlotta's coming has indeed changed everything and changed me too.

Marriage was more than lying in feather beds—more comfortable than the hard earth but more binding—it was growing up, changing, seeing life from a hundred different angles. Yes, the events of the last weeks had made me realize that I was very young and inexperienced of life.

Realizing this so clearly showed me how to deal with Bastian.

I replied, "Thank you, Bastian. I am indeed honored. It is good of you to think of me now that Carlotta has rejected you, but I am too young for marriage and have no intention of entering into that state yet."

"Bersaba, don't be a little idiot. You're talking like Gervaise Pondersby."

"That must be interesting. She preferred it, didn't she, to your rough country speech?"

"You're jealous, Bersaba. There's no need to be. I don't know what came over me. It was like a spell. I just couldn't help it."

"So you forgot that you had talked of marriage to me?"

"I always meant it to be you, Bersaba . . . after what used to happen."

"We can forget that," I said sharply.

"*You* can forget it?"

"Yes," I said boldly, "and if I can you should . . . and it is obvious that you did."

"Bersaba, my dearest little Bersaba. . . ."

"I am not your dearest. There was one who was dearer. It is only because she preferred someone else that you are here now."

"I am asking you to marry me. Have you forgotten what you gave me? That is what you should only give your husband. Don't you know that? I have seduced you, Bersaba. What would your parents say?"

"Nothing, because they won't know. You didn't seduce me, Bastian. I seduced you. I wanted experience. Well, I've had it and as far as I'm concerned there's an end to the matter."

"You're talking like a . . . like a . . ."

"Yes, like a what?"

"Like a courtesan."

"Perhaps that's what I am. You thought me such, didn't you? You were my lover and as soon as Carlotta came along you forgot me."

"I never forgot you, not once. And now I want to make amends."

"Amends." I knew my eyes were blazing. "There is no

97

need, Bastian. Fortunately there are no . . . consequences. It is all over. I no longer want you. I no longer need you. Can you understand that?"

"You're so different, Bersaba. I can't believe you're the same."

"You find it hard to believe that I am not eager for you. That's it, isn't it? I've grown up, Bastian. You have helped me to grow up. That's all you mean to me. I'm grateful in a way. I'm not a child anymore. I know something of what life is about. I shan't go to my husband as a shrinking virgin, shall I? Thanks to you."

"You would never have shrunk, Bersaba."

"From some I should . . . as from you now. Bastian, I must ask you not to bother me anymore."

"I shall speak to your parents," he said.

"They would never force me to marry against my will." I looked down at my fingers. "These thorns are sharp." I sucked my finger without looking at him. Then I went on cutting the roses and he stood there watching me, helplessly.

My mother asked me to come to her sitting room as she had something to say to me.

"Bersaba," she said when we were alone, "Bastian has asked for your hand in marriage."

"I have already refused him, Mother."

"I know how you feel, my child. He was betrothed to Carlotta and she rejected him. He is impetuous. He should have waited. But it can be a long engagement. Indeed, it would have to be as both your father and I consider you too young for marriage."

"There is no need to consider it at all, Mother. I will not marry Bastian."

"You two used to seem so fond of each other."

"He is my cousin."

"That need provide no real obstacle."

"But it is better for cousins not to marry unless they both feel determined to because there is a great love between them."

"I always hoped that Bastian would marry one of you."

"Perhaps Angelet will oblige."

"My dear Bersaba, you sound a little bitter. Don't take the affair of Carlotta too seriously. She is a very fascinating creature. You see how a noble gentleman like Sir Gervaise became so quickly attracted to her that he is going to marry her. Bastian was temporarily bemused but he tells me he always loved you and intended to marry you."

"Except when he became betrothed to Carlotta."

"Ah, you were deeply hurt. I knew it. But it's over."

"Mother, please understand. It taught me something and that is that when I marry it will not be Bastian. Never! I was fond of Bastian but I don't love him. Please do not ask me to take him because I won't . . . I won't. . . ."

"You know very well that neither your father nor I would force you into a marriage which was not of your liking."

"Then the matter is settled."

"Let us leave it for a while, Bersaba. Think about it. Bastian would be a good, kind, and gentle husband. He would help you slowly to realize all that marriage means."

I smiled inwardly at the innocence of my mother and I wondered what she would say if she knew of those passionate encounters in lonely places in the woods. She had accepted Phoebe's dilemma. What would she have said if she now found her own daughter in such a position?

"I will never marry Bastian," I said. "I am determined."

She sighed and kissed me. I was sure that she believed that one day I would change my mind.

But Bastian knew I never would. He had sensed the change in me. He thought it had come about because of his entanglement with Carlotta. It had to some extent, but there was more than that. I learned something about myself and that was that I did not know all I had thought I had. Life was bewilderingly complicated. I had much to learn and I was eager to begin. I felt I had had all I needed from Bastian.

A few days passed. I was coolly aloof and now did not care if I was alone with him and because I could compare him with Sir Gervaise he no longer seemed the handsome young god he had. I no longer felt the urge to embrace him.

I was free from my ardent desires for a while.

He understood more than my parents could because they had no idea of how far our relationship had progressed.

Before he left, Bastian asked my father if he could join in his enterprise and go to sea with him and Fennimore when he left.

It was a hasty decision, said my father. He must not think that because I had refused his offer of marriage that was the end of the old way of life.

Bastian implored him to consider him and my father eventually said he would.

So he left us and in due course we heard that Carlotta had

become Lady Pondersby and was living in some state in a mansion not far from London and Senara was with her.

My father decided that he could find a place for Bastian, and in September of that year when my father and brother sailed away, Bastian was with them.

Just before they left a messenger arrived from London, with letters from Sir Gervaise to my father and among these was one for our mother from Senara and one for Angelet and myself from Carlotta.

Angelet and I seized it and with great excitement took it up to our bedroom to read it. She had written:

> MY DEAR TWINS
>
> I wished that you could have come to my wedding. You would have been so interested to see how these matters are conducted here. I have been thinking of you there in the country and what fun it would be if you came to visit me. You said you always wanted to see London. Well, now is your chance.
>
> I am writing to your mother to tell her that this is an invitation.
>
> I hope she will spare you.
>
> We had an exhausting journey to London, but it was worthwhile to be here and my mother and I did so much enjoy our little sojourn in the country.
>
> I shall hope to see you both, or if both cannot be spared at the same time, then one of you.
>
> I look forward to hearing your news.
>
> CARLOTTA

Angelet and I looked at each other with sparkling eyes.

"To London!" we cried.

Angelet threw herself into my arms and said, "We'll both go. One of us couldn't stay behind. I wouldn't let you go without me."

"Nor you without me."

"We should need clothes."

"We'll take Phoebe. We shall need a maid."

"It will be wonderful to see London. Do you think we shall see the King and Queen?"

"She said to London, not to Court."

"Yes, but Carlotta goes to Court, doesn't she? So perhaps she'll take us."

Angelet turned out all her clothes from the cupboard. She tried them on, smiling, frowning. She was very excited.

When we saw our mother we realized that she was not so happy at the suggestion.

"You can't go," she told us. "Not yet. Your father is going and Fennimore with him." She looked so woebegone that Angelet cried, "Of course we won't go, Mother. I'd forgotten. You'd be all on your own." Then she was smiling. "But why shouldn't you come with us?"

"I'd have to be here for when your father comes back."

"But he's only just gone. He'll be away for months."

"We'll see," said our mother; but I knew that she did not want us to go.

When our father had left we paid another visit to Castle Paling. My mother and Aunt Melanie talked a great deal about Senara's suggestion and my mother said she feared the difficulties of the journey and she would be very anxious for her girls traveling without her. If she could have gone it would have been different but she was never sure when my father would be home. He had just left, it was true, but sometimes there were reasons for returning almost at once. She had never felt she could leave the Priory when Fenn was away and when he was there she must be there with him.

We paid our visit to Grandfather Casvellyn, who glared at us in the way to which we had become accustomed and shouted at us because we did not speak and roared to us to say something sensible when we did.

I noticed that his eyes were on me. He singled me out and I was sure he knew which one I was.

"Come here," he said and he drew me to him so that I was touching the rug which covered his mangled legs. Then he gripped my chin in those bony fingers and made me look at him. "What have you been doing?" he asked.

I said, "I have been helping Aunt Melanie to gather the flowers."

He laughed. "I didn't mean that. You know I didn't. You're a sly one, I fancy."

He gave me a little push.

My mother was watching and smiling as though she were delighted that one of her children pleased her father. She was a very innocent woman, my mother; it came of believing the best of everybody. Grandfather Casvellyn had been a great rake in his day; there were dark stories about him and his activities; they concerned women too. He was telling me that he believed there was something of him in me.

Perhaps there was.

He made me feel a little uneasy though, because I wondered if sometimes he had seen me coming in with Bastian and knew what had happened between us.

Gwenifer and Rozen discussed the invitation at length and were envious because they had not received one.

"I expect," said Angelet, "she wants to thank Bersaba for saving her. There was a plot to take her, you know. Bersaba heard of it and stopped it."

They were very interested. It was amazing how excited people became whenever witches and witchcraft were mentioned.

We stayed at the Castle for a week. During the journey back it rained all through the day and we arrived home soaked to the skin. Mother insisted on our putting our feet in bowls of hot water into which was added some herb which was supposed to ward off chills.

However, I caught one and it seemed to hang about for quite a time.

Phoebe by now was getting near her time. She was large and the baby was supposed to be due in mid-September. The time came and passed and still it was not born.

I was very interested in Phoebe's baby. So was Angelet, but to me there was something special about it. I wanted her to have a healthy child to whom in due course she would tell the story of my bringing her to the Priory and the child would realize that it owed its existence to me.

September was almost over. Each morning I would look anxiously at Phoebe, who seemed to be getting larger and larger, but the baby gave no sign of wanting to be born.

Ginny said, "Oh, that Phoebe—she's misjudged the time, I reckon. That father of hers scared her out of her wits."

The last day of September came and still the baby was not born. It was a dark morning with a heavy mist in the air when I said to Angelet, "I reckon the baby will be born today."

"It must be," she answered. "It's already three weeks late."

Phoebe was beginning to look frightened.

"I feel something awful be happening to me, Mistress Bersaba," she said. "Do 'ee think the Lord be punishing me for being wanton like?"

"No," I said sharply. "If He's going to punish people for being like that He shouldn't have made them that way."

Phoebe looked frightened. I think she expected the wrath of Heaven to descend upon me to punish me for my blasphemy. It was to be expected. Hadn't she been brought up in the smithy?

In the afternoon it started to rain, great heavy drops that fell steadily down. At four o'clock I thought Phoebe looked ill and she said she was in pain so I went down to the stables and told one of the grooms to ride over to the midwife and tell her to come without delay. She lived some two miles away in a little group of cottages just outside our estate.

He went off and I went back to Phoebe. I made her go to bed and I stood at the window, watching for the midwife.

Phoebe looked very ill and I wasn't sure whether it was the pain she was suffering or the fear which had returned now her time had come. For seventeen years she had listened to her father's ranting about the vengeance of God so it was small wonder that she was reminded of it now.

I kept telling her that there was nothing to fear. A great many girls had been in her position and come happily through. I was almost on the point of telling her my own experiences just to comfort her, but I stopped short of that in time.

I was at the window when I heard the sound of horse's hooves in the stables, so thinking it was the groom returned with the midwife, I ran down.

It was the groom but the midwife was not with him.

"Where is Mother Gantry?" I demanded.

"Her couldn't come, Mistress Bersaba."

"What do you mean she couldn't come? I sent you for her."

"I hammered on her door but she wouldn't answer. I said, 'You'm wanted at the Priory. One of the maids is giving birth.' "

"What did she say to that?"

"She just come to the window and shook her head at me. Then she pulled down the blind and said, 'Go away, or you'll be sorry.' So I rode back to tell 'ee, mistress."

"You fool," I cried. "We need a midwife. Why do you think I sent you if it don't matter whether she came or not. Saddle my horse."

"Mistress Bersaba—"

"Saddle my horse!" I shouted and, trembling, he obeyed.

"Mistress Bersaba," he repeated, "I'll go back—"

I jumped on my horse and rode out. The rain was teeming down. I was not dressed for the saddle. There was nothing on my head, and my hair was soon streaming down behind my back.

I took a certain glory in what I was doing. I had saved Phoebe from her father; I had saved Carlotta from the mob—

although I had done my best to throw her to them; and now I was continuing in my heroic role. I was going to arrive just in time with the midwife whom that fool of a groom had not brought back with him simply because the woman was too tired or too lazy to answer a summons for a mere maid.

I came to her cottage. I banged on the door. I heard a feeble voice and I lifted a latch and went in. "Mistress Gantry—" I began.

She was lying back in a chair and I went to her and shook her before I noticed that her face was fiery red, her eyes glassy.

"Begone," she cried. "Don't 'ee come near me. Stay away, I tell 'ee."

"Mistress Gantry, a baby is about to be born."

"Get you gone, mistress," cried Mother Gantry. "I be sick of a pox."

I understood why she had not opened the door to the groom, and that by coming in I had placed myself in acute danger.

I went out of the cottage and mounted my horse.

It seemed a long time before I got back to the Priory. I went into the stables where the grooms stared at me. Then, wet and bedraggled as I was, I went up to Phoebe's room.

My mother was at the door.

"Bersaba, wherever have you been?"

"I've been to Mother Gantry. She can't come. She's sick . . . she says of a pox."

"You saw her."

"Yes," I said. "I went into her cottage to get her to come to Phoebe."

"Oh, my child," said my mother. "You must get those things off."

"Phoebe's baby?"

"It is born . . . dead."

I stared at her. I could see her concern was all for me.

"Phoebe?" I began.

"She is very ill but she has a chance of recovery. I want you to get those wet clothes off. Come with me."

She led me away.

I was feeling limp, deflated, and exhausted.

ANGELET

❖ ❖ ❖

In Paul's Walk

I WAS sad as I rode along, for this would be the first time in my life that I had been parted from Bersaba. There was a terrible anxiety in my heart, too, for this was a turning point in our lives and I instinctively knew that nothing would be the same again.

I had longed to go to London; so often I had visualized the trip and I had an uncanny feeling that my very longing had made it come about. Once a wise woman—I think she was certainly a white witch—had come to Castle Paling with her husband, who was a kind of traveling peddler. Aunt Melanie had given them shelter for the night and the woman had earned her lodging by telling fortunes, which amused us young ones. I always remember what she said to me. It was something like this: "If you want something badly, believe you will get it, think of it, see yourself getting it. It is almost certain that if you do this your hopes will come true. But you may have to pay for it in a way you hadn't expected—and that way may not be pleasant. In fact, it could be that you might wish you had never asked for it."

That was how I felt now on the road to London. I was here because Bersaba was so ill. I had seen the fear in my mother's eyes and that she wanted to make sure of my safety, for when Phoebe's baby was born dead Bersaba had caught the small-pox from the midwife. We did not know this immediately of course. Bersaba rode out to bring the midwife in the teeming rain and actually went in and shook the old woman before she noticed the terrible signs of illness on her face and thus she had come into physical contact with her.

When she came back and told us what had happened my mother herself put her to bed and made her stay there. The next day, however, we heard that the midwife had died and that several people in the village were suffering from the smallpox.

My mother—usually so meek—became like a general gathering her forces about her, going into the attack determined to defeat the enemy—in this case a disease which could kill.

She sent for me and I was immediately aware of her purpose. "You will no longer sleep in Bersaba's room," she told me. "Your things are being moved to a little room on the east side."

This room was about the farthest from the one I shared with Bersaba.

"I don't want you to see your sister until I say you may."

I was horrified. Not see Bersaba! I who had been with her almost every hour of my life! I felt as though part of myself was being taken away.

"We must be sensible," said my mother the next day, very calm in spite of the anxiety she was suffering. "The fact is that Bersaba has been in contact with a woman who has the smallpox. She had a chill at the time so may well be in a receptive state. We shall know in a week or two at most whether she has contracted the disease. If she has then I want you to go away."

"To go away . . . from Bersaba when she is ill!"

"My dear child, this is a dangerous sickness which can result in death. We must be brave and we shall not be that if we shut our eyes to the truth. I am going to send you to London . . . if this develops."

"To London . . . without Bersaba?"

"I want you to be far away. This is going to be distressing and if Bersaba really has contracted the disease we are going to need all our skills in nursing her."

"I should be here to help, then."

"No. I would not let you run the risk."

106

"But what of you, Mother?"

"I am her mother. You don't think I would allow anyone else to nurse her?"

"What if you caught it?" My eyes were round with horror.

"I shall not," she said confidently. "I *must* not, for I intend to nurse Bersaba. But as yet we are unsure. I want you to stay away from her. That is why I have changed your room. Promise me that you will not see her."

"But what will she think?"

"Bersaba is sensible. She knows what has happened. She understands the danger. Therefore she will agree that we are right."

"Mother, how could I go to London when she may be ill?"

"You can because I say you must. You are so close . . . so accustomed to being together, that I fear it might not be possible to keep you apart."

"But to go to London . . . without Bersaba!"

"I have been awake all night thinking of the best course to take and I have come to the conclusion that this is it. If you were at Castle Paling you would be too near . . . and I think it would be good for you to have a change of scene. In London everything will be fresh for you. You won't fret so much."

"Mother, you think she may die. . . ."

"She is going to live. But we have to face the facts, Angel. She is already weak. She has seemed in a highly strung state these last weeks . . . and then the chill. But I shall nurse her through it. I have sent a message to London telling Senara that in all probability you will be leaving in two weeks unless she hears to the contrary. Make your preparations. I'm afraid you will only be able to take what you have and there will be no time for making new garments. Be of good cheer, Angelet. It may not come to this."

I was bewildered. I had so longed to go to London but I had never for a moment thought of doing so without Bersaba. I just could not visualize a life she did not share.

Those two weeks passed somehow. Every morning I would look into my mother's face to read what I dared not ask. The whole household seemed to be plunged into melancholy. Bersaba stayed in her room and only my mother went to her. She told me that Bersaba understood and realized that it must be so.

Then came the morning when I read the terrible truth in my mother's eyes. The first dread symptoms had shown themselves.

That was why on that October morning I was traveling to London. I had Mab with me to act as my maid and six grooms to protect me and to look after the baggage. And as I rode along I was thinking of my sister and wondering whether I should ever see her again.

I remember very little of the journey because all the time my thoughts were occupied with Bersaba. We stayed the first night at Castle Paling, and that was a somber occasion because everyone was so shocked by the thought of what might be happening at the Priory.

I could see that they didn't have much hope of Bersaba's recovery and their assurances that it would certainly be a mild attack and that she would have the best attention and that so much had been learned about the disease now that many people were cured, lacked conviction.

The journey took two weeks. To me it seemed like going from inn to inn, then starting off almost as soon as it was light and going on till the horses needed a rest at midday and then another inn and food before we started off again.

We kept to the byways as much as possible, for the groom in charge believed that there was less likelihood of meeting road robbers that way. He said that highwaymen haunted the main roads because more travelers used them and although there might be rich people on the byways robbers might have to hang about in wait for a whole day and meet no one, so they preferred the more regular traffic on the highways.

This seemed to me logical and I suppose we had our share of thrills, but nothing seemed to touch me because I wasn't so much on the road as in that bedroom at Trystan Priory with my sister. When the rain teemed down I scarcely noticed it; when the roads were impassable and we had to retrace our way I accepted it stoically.

Mab said to me, "You'm not here, Miss Angelet. That's what 'tis."

And I answered, "I can't be anywhere, Mab, but back at Trystan Priory with my sister."

And I kept blaming myself in a way because I had so wanted this and it had come about in this strange uncanny way, for I knew my mother would never have consented to our going to London together; she would have thought of all the dangers on the road her darlings would have to face, and perhaps too of other dangers in London society. But there was no danger as great as that which now threatened my sister Bersaba and my mother would agree to anything that took me out of its path.

So the journey progressed. We crossed the Tamar at Gunislake and traveled across Devon to Tavistock and thence to Somerset and to Wiltshire, where carved on the hillside I saw the strange white horse which was said to have been done in the era before Christianity came to England. As we came to Stonehenge, that impressive and most weird stone circle, I thought vaguely of the rites which were doubtless performed there long before the Romans came to Britain and was reminded of the strange murmurs there had been about Carlotta and wondered whether she really had been a witch.

And so Stonehenge and on through Basingstoke to Reading, when I found myself a little excited and being ashamed of it, hastily sending my thoughts back to that sickroom in Trystan Priory. I caught a glimpse of Windsor Castle through the trees. It looked magnificent with its gray towers and battlements and the Great Park which surrounded it; and I thought of history lessons in the Priory schoolroom where I had sat beside Bersaba and we had learned of how Edward the Third had picked up the lady's garter there and created the motto: "Evil be to him who evil thinks"—a story which we both loved to hear repeated; and how King John stayed there before signing the Magna Carta at Runnymede, and Henry VIII hunted in the forest. Seeing the very castle of which we had heard so much aroused my interest and excitement, but it was overshadowed by memories of my sister.

I thought then, "She will always be there. I shall never escape from Bersaba." It seemed strange to use the word "escape," for that sounded as though I were in some sort of captivity from which I wanted to get away.

We were drawing nearer and nearer to London and my thoughts were not: What is awaiting me in London, but any day there might be news of Bersaba.

And so we came to Pondersby Hall, the residence of Sir Gervaise, which lay not far from the village of Richmond close to the river—the river on which craft of all sizes and shapes sailed in and out of the city of London.

It was a magnificent house but I was accustomed to great mansions, having been brought up between my father's Priory and my grandfather's Castle, and there is nothing quite so inspiring as a castle with its gray battlemented towers and fortresslike exterior, dating back to the Norman era. But Pondersby Hall had a different personality from either the

Priory or the Castle. It was haughty—if one can apply such a term to a house—but it was the word which occurred to me. It had a well-cared-for look which the houses of Cornwall lacked. I supposed that, situated in the more cosy southeast corner of England, it escaped the gales to which we were subject, and the colder drier climate had not played such havoc with its walls. It was not old as houses go. It must have been built round about 1560, so it was less than a hundred years old and it had an air of modernity which the Castle certainly lacked.

Perhaps this impression was strengthened by the fact that everything was in such good condition. The grass in the forecourt was neat and looked as though it had been freshly cut that morning. The gray walls looked clean, as if they had just been washed—a silvery gray rather than the darker shade of Castle Paling. I was immediately aware of the ornamental scrolled gables with carved masked corbels at their bases. There was a projecting porch and on the right of this an enormous window, mullioned and transomed, contained panes too numerous to count. The glass of those panes was of blue and red and green and very effective.

I thought, as I was to think so often during the next weeks, "I wonder what Bersaba would think of that?"

As we came into the forecourt a manservant appeared. He was in green and blue livery, which I was soon to learn were the Pondersby colors.

He presented himself to me and, bowing, said, "Good afternoon, ma'am. We have been expecting you since yesterday. Orders are that you are to be welcomed and taken to your apartment. I will call the grooms and your servants shall be told where to go."

I thanked him and asked his name.

"James, ma'am. I am the majordomo. In any difficulty if you will acquaint me of it I will endeavor to remedy the fault."

I wanted to laugh and thought how amused Bersaba would have been by his dignity.

I dismounted, stiff from so long in the saddle, and I immediately felt at a disadvantage. I had an idea that the impeccable James was inwardly raising his eyebrows and asking himself what this was which had arrived to sully his beautiful Hall.

Mab dismounted and took her place behind me. The men followed the groom, I presumed to the quarters assigned to them.

James led us up the two steps to the projecting porch with all the dignity of a man performing a most important ceremony; I was soon to realize that he brought that attitude to everything he did, for whatever it was it had to be shown to be worthy of the attention of James.

We followed him into the hall where the colored glass threw a flattering light onto our faces and I looked up at it admiringly at the same time taking in the fine plaster ceiling decorated with scrolls, and the minstrels' gallery at one end of the hall.

A woman in a blue gown over which she wore a green apron of the same shades as James' livery was waiting for us and I recognized her at once as Ana, who had accompanied Carlotta to Cornwall.

"Our guest has come," said James. "Take her and her maid to their rooms and make sure that everything Mistress Landor needs is available."

Ana nodded, less overawed I fancied than we were by the dignity of James.

"If you will come with me I will take you to your rooms," she said, "and when her ladyship returns I will inform her of your arrival."

We followed Ana up a staircase which led from the hall to a gallery. Along this we went and mounted another staircase. On this landing were our rooms. A large one for me and a small one leading from it for Mab. I had a window not unlike that of the hall—only much smaller with a window seat and my panes of glass were uncolored. My bed was a four-poster and several mats, of the same tones as the blue of the drapes at the window and the curtains of my bed, covered the wooden floor.

I said, "It's luxurious, isn't it Mab?"

" 'Tis certain surely so," replied Mab.

"I will bring you hot water," said Ana and did so.

I washed and in a short while two menservants—in the usual livery—brought up my baggage.

I asked Mab what she thought of it.

"It be very grand, Mistress Angelet," she said.

"Yet it's not much different from home," I pointed out.

"Oh, there be grandness in the air, mistress."

That was it. Grandness in the air. I looked down at my dusty boots. They looked out of place in this room and I daresay I looked the same.

Mab unpacked my clothes and as I watched her their glory

seemed to diminish before my eyes. I knew instinctively that they would look most unfashionable here.

It was late afternoon when Carlotta came in. She had been riding and I heard her voice as she walked across the forecourt.

I looked down at her. How elegant she was! Her habit was of pale gray and she wore a hat with a curling feather.

"They are here then?" She laughed as though there was something amusing about my being there.

She came up to my room and stood on the threshold, looking at me.

"Angelet!" she cried as she came forward and, taking my hands, drew me to her. It was scarcely a kiss she gave me. Rather did she knock her cheek against mine—first on one side and then on the other.

"A pity your sister couldn't come with you." Her mouth twisted slightly and I knew then that she really would have liked to have Bersaba here. I remembered how she had taken Bastian and upset Bersaba quite a bit—although she had pretended not to be—and I thought that perhaps because of that she had a special interest in my sister.

"Has there been news of Trystan?" I asked.

She shook her head. "How was she when you left?"

"Very sick."

"Some recover," she said. "You mustn't brood. Where are your clothes?"

"Mab has hung them in the cupboard."

She went there and, looking at them, groaned.

"Don't you like them?"

"They are a little old-fashioned. You will need new things here."

"They're all I have."

"We'll remedy that. I foresaw this so I'm prepared. Ana has already started a gown. She'll fit you and it will be ready tomorrow. I shall take you into London and buy some fripperies for you . . . a fan, some patches, and some rouge and powder."

"Patches and powder!"

"Yes, we must subdue that blooming country complexion somehow. It will make you look such a bumpkin."

"But . . . isn't that what I am?"

"Assuredly you are. That is why we shall have to work hard to make you otherwise."

She sat down on a chair and laughed at me.

"You look startled. You are in London—where society is

smart. I can assure you it is a little different from Cornwall."

"I am sure it is. Perhaps. . . ."

"Perhaps what?"

"As I am so unsuitable I should go back."

"We'll make you suitable. It's just a matter of time. And you can't go back. Your sister is ill. That's why you're here. I doubt your mother would ever have submitted you to the wicked ways of the world but for that."

She laughed again and I said coldly, "I seem to amuse you."

"Oh, you do. And you'll amuse yourself. In a month's time I'll remind you of what you are like now and you'll laugh like mad."

"I'm sorry I'm so unsatisfactory," I said.

"Never mind. It's a challenge. You'll soon grow up here. That's the difference really. You are young for your age."

"I shall not be eighteen until next birthday."

"But eighteen in your dear old Priory is not quite the same as being eighteen in the outside world. You'll see."

I said, "Where is your mother?"

"She is on a visit at the moment. She'll be delighted that you're here. She always wanted to do something for Tamsyn's girls and said it was a pity you were condemned to life in the country."

"And your husband?"

"Gervaise is at Court. We have a residence close to White-hall and I am there often. We are not so far from Whitehall here, so it is not really like being in the country."

"Are you happy in your marriage?"

"Life has been amusing," she answered.

"Is that the same as being happy?"

"I assure you, my little country mouse, it is the essence of contentment."

I was uneasy. I disliked being talked down to. Bersaba would have known how to deal with the situation much better than I did. Oh, how I missed her! I was realizing more and more how much I had always turned to her when I was not sure how to act.

Carlotta was aware of my discomfiture and seemed to enjoy it.

"You will soon fall into our ways," she said, "and how glad you will be that you have escaped the dull life. Now let us be practical."

Later she showed me the house, introduced me to some of

113

the servants, examined my wardrobe in detail, and discarded most of it.

She said I would be tired after my journey, that I should retire early and tomorrow I could start my new life.

We ate together in a small room off the main hall as we did at home when we were just the family, and she talked all the time about her life, how exciting it was and how different I was going to find it, behaving all the time as though she were my benefactress.

As soon as supper was over she said I should go to my room and sleep, for she was sure I was tired out. I was certainly glad to escape.

Mab came in and helped me get to bed, but when I lay there I could not sleep. I kept thinking of how Carlotta and Senara had arrived at the Castle and how Grandfather Casvellyn had looked like an angry prophet when he had said no good would come of their return into our lives.

Now Bersaba was ill and perhaps I should never see her again. I felt bereft. We were as one. How could I go on living without her?

I could not stop thinking of her lying in that room we had shared for so many years while the dread disease afflicted her. Bersaba tossing in fever, delirious . . . no longer my calm self-possessed sister—the clever part of us, the one whom I had thought I should never have to do without.

A few days passed during which I did not go far afield. Carlotta was anxious that I should not until I was adequately dressed and as she said had cast off some of my country manners, which she made me feel would be despised in London. I must learn to walk with more dignity, hold my head high, to move with grace, to bow, to curtsy, and to overcome a certain accent which would not be acceptable in London society.

I allowed myself to be primed and took an interest in it largely because it turned my mind from brooding on what was happening at home. I had to shut out the thought of Bersaba's face on the pillow—fevered, her eyes wild, and the horrible signs of her illness upon her. I kept telling myself that I could do no good by dwelling on it, so I meekly allowed myself to be turned into a copy of a town-bred girl.

Carlotta was certainly enjoying the operation. I wondered whether she enjoyed scoring over us for some reason. Although I was parted from Bersaba I still thought of us together, and I asked myself now whether Carlotta had taken up Bastian as she did because she knew of Bersaba's fondness for him. It seemed that that might be characteristic of her.

On the third day after my arrival Senara returned. She embraced me warmly and seemed really pleased to see me, and asked a good many questions about Bersaba. I had the impression that she really cared about my mother.

"Poor Tamsyn," she said. "I can picture her distress. She was always more like a mother to me than a sister though she was but a year older. She mothered everyone . . . even her own mother. I know she will be in great distress. I am glad to have you here with us and I shall write to your mother and tell her so."

She was more sympathetic and understanding than her daughter and I was able to talk to her and tell her how homesick I was and how I was wondering whether I ought to go home as Carlotta did not seem to think I fitted into the London scene.

She shook her head. "You have a certain charm, Angelet, which is appealing, and I am sure many people here will appreciate it. Your fresh country innocence will seem charming to people who are weary of the society ways, which are often false."

"Carlotta wants to change me."

"We must see that she doesn't succeed too well."

Senara certainly comforted me, particularly when she talked about her childhood and how she and my mother had been as close as sisters. "I know how you feel about Bersaba," she said. "Of course your mother and I were not twins, but the manner in which I came to the castle made her feel she had to protect me and I always enjoyed that motherly security she threw around me. She does it to many. It's her way."

So I felt better when Senara returned, and when I went riding with her and we passed along by the river I was temporarily forgetful of everything but the wonder of it, for as we approached the city the boats on the river were so numerous that they almost touched one another.

Senara was pleased at my wonder. She told me that I was in the greatest port in the world and that ships came here from every place I could imagine. I was excited and comforted to see some of the ships from my father's East India Company because that made me feel that I was not so very far away. How wonderful they looked! How powerfully built! They were equipped to face the storms they would meet at sea as well as armed against pirates. Then I began to wonder what my father was doing now—and Fennimore and Bastian

—and fear touched me that some ill might befall them and if Bersaba were to die. . . .

Senara, glancing at me, saw the misery in my face and she said kindly, "Everything will come out well, I promise you."

"How can you know?" I asked.

"I know these things," she told me. I thought, "She *is* a witch," and I wanted to believe she was so that I could assure myself that she was right.

She showed me the wharves where goods were being unloaded—some by the Company's ships and others from Amsterdam, Germany, Italy, and France. I could not help being enthralled, and after that a little of the burden of fear lightened. Senara had said that all would be well and that meant that my family would be safe. I believed Senara. As a witch she could have special knowledge of these matters.

The days, which had seemed endless by the end of the first week, began to fly past. I had a new wardrobe now and I was pleased that my clothes were looser than those we had worn in the country. Ana, who was a good seamstress, told me that the stiff fashions which had once come from Spain were quite outmoded now. Farthingales were never worn and one did not put stiffening under skirts to make them stand out. Ruffs were completely of the past, so were high collars, and it was smart and becoming to wear low-cut dresses. The wrists and arms were often shown and some of my new gowns had sleeves which came only to the elbow. When I wore these I had long gloves and a great deal of attention was paid to getting the right ones.

Ana dressed my hair too. She gave me a fringe of curls on my forehead which had to be crimped each day.

Mab, like myself, had to go through a certain tuition. I think she enjoyed it, for she started to give herself airs and talk disparagingly of the poor maids of Trystan who had no idea what fashion meant.

I was beginning to feel that but for the anxieties about what was happening at home, and if Bersaba would have been with me, my trip to London would have been a great adventure.

Sir Gervaise appeared a few days after my arrival. He was kind and asked solicitously after my family. He was quite clearly concerned and I thought he was much more kindly than his wife and I wondered if he was happy in his marriage. I believed that Carlotta would be a demanding and not very affectionate wife. Of course he admired her beauty, which was something one could not help but be aware of. When I looked at myself in the mirror with my fashionable fringe and my rather bony wrists I often thought what a contrast I made to the elegant magnificence of Carlotta. She seemed to be aware of it, too, for she viewed me with great complacency.

So I began to feel a little happier for Senara's certainty that all would be well, and Sir Gervaise's gentleness was also of great help to me.

Every day I would hope for a message from home, but Senara said, "It is as yet too early. Your mother would wait to tell you until she was certain that the crisis was over. I promise you it will be, but remember it will take a little time for the messenger to get here."

Sir Gervaise told me that he knew several people who had suffered from the smallpox and survived. Careful nursing, the sickness taken in time . . . these things worked wonders!

They did all they could to sustain me, and I began to accept their conviction. "All will be well," I told myself. It must be. There could not be a world without Bersaba.

I dreamed of her; it was as though she were with me, laughing at my fringe and my shyness with Carlotta. It was almost as though she injected some of her qualities into me. Sometimes I used to think, "We are really one person," and I believed she was thinking of me at that moment as she lay on her sickbed just as I was thinking of her, so that part of me seemed in that bed of fever and part of her was here in this elegant house learning something of fashions and ways of London society.

I liked to listen to Sir Gervaise talking. He knew that I was interested and seemed to enjoy it when I listened so intently.

He told me that he was rather concerned about the way in which the country was moving. The King could not be aware of his growing unpopularity and the Queen did nothing to help.

"The people here are suspicious of her," he said, "because she is a Catholic and she will do all she can to bring Catholisism into England. Not that she could ever succeed. The people here will never have it. Ever since Bloody Mary's reign they have set their hearts against it."

I asked about the King and he told me, "A man of great charm, of good looks—for all he is of small stature—and perfect manners. But he will never win the popularity of the people. He is too aloof. They do not understand him nor he them. He is proud with a firm belief that God set the King on the throne and that his right to be there is unquestioned. I fear it will bring trouble . . . to him and the country." He looked at me and smiled. "I am wearying you. Forgive me."

"Indeed you are not," I assured him. "I long to learn something of what is happening at Court."

"I fear," he said ominously, "that before long the whole country will be aware of what is happening at Court."

I gradually began to understand what he meant and my education began the next day when Carlotta took me into London to buy lace and other materials such as ribbons, gloves, and a fan or two. We went in style, for Sir Gervaise, being a rich and important gentleman, was the owner of a coach. And because Carlotta had the ability to wheedle anything out of him, she persuaded him to allow her to use it. It was grand, like a padded box, with seats for two at the back and front and a window with velvet drapes which could be pulled if one wished to shut out the street scene. Sir Gervaise's family crest was emblazoned on the side and it was drawn by two magnificent white horses. The driver was resplendent in the Pondersby livery and so was the footman mounted at the back.

Thus in state we set off and as we approached the city I became aware of an atmosphere of bustle and excitement; there were people on horseback and people on foot, all behaving as though their business was of the utmost urgency, matters of life and death. For the first time I saw one of the new hackney coaches which could be hired for short distances; a carrier's wagon trundled past us and, with a great deal of noise, turned into an inn yard. There were so many barges and other craft on the river that the water was almost invisible; and everywhere people seemed to be shouting, calling to each other, sharing jokes, quarreling, cajoling, threatening. I saw men and women in the most exaggerated of costumes. The low-cut dresses of the women seemed distinctly immodest to me, but at home we were still in the fashions of twenty years before, I supposed, when even ruffs and certainly the high collars which followed them were still being worn. The men were more surprising than the women, for they wore wide sashes and their garters, just above the knee, were made of ribbon with big bows at the side; and there were rosettes on their shoes.

But this elaborate costume was not general, for there were of course the beggars—ragged, sharp-eyed, darting hither and thither, pleading and threatening, and there was another kind of citizen who by the very somber nature of their dress called attention to the splendor of others. These were men in cloth doublets and dark-colored breeches, their collars were plain white and their tall crowned hats were unadorned by feathers; the women who were with them were dressed in plain gowns, usually gray in color, with white aprons protecting their skirts and white caps or plain tall hats similar to those worn by the men. They were like a different race of people; they walked quietly, eyes downcast except when they cast looks of contempt at those who swaggered by in their flamboyant garments.

I asked Carlotta who these people were.

"Oh, they are the Puritans," she said. "They believe it is wicked to enjoy life. See how they cut their hair."

"I do," I said. "It's a great contrast to those who wear theirs long like women."

"Long hair is so much more becoming."

"The contrast is so great," I said. "In the country no one looks as grand and no one as somber."

"They will. Fashions arrive in time . . . even in remote places like Cornwall."

I disliked the denigration in her voice when she talked of my home so I said no more and gave my full attention to the scene before me.

I had never seen women such as those I occasionally glimpsed. Their faces were highly colored in a manner which could never be natural, and many of them had black spots and patches on their faces. I saw two of them in an argument and one started to pull at the other's hair but the coach passed on so I did not see the outcome of that affair.

When we stopped, beggars looked in at the window and called a blessing on us if we would give them just a little to buy a crust of bread. Carlotta threw out coins, which clattered onto the cobbles, and a ragged boy who could not have been more than five years old darted forward and seized them. The beggars set up a wail but the coach passed on.

We left the coach at St. Paul's and Carlotta told the coachman to wait for us there and guard well the coach while we explored Paul's Walk for the articles we had come to buy.

My experience grew more astonishing with every passing minute. There, in Paul's Walk, which was the middle aisle of St. Paul's Cathedral, was a market and a promenade and a meeting place for all kinds of people.

Carlotta bade me keep close and I could see why. We were watched as we passed along and now and then a lady or a gentleman as grandly dressed as Carlotta would stop and exchange a word with her when she would present me as "a visitor from the country" at which I could be graciously smiled on and then ignored.

People pressed close against us; cunning faces studied us; it would have been frightening to have been alone; but the promenades were filled mainly with people like ourselves and as there were stalls containing materials of the finest quality and ribbons, laces, fans, patches, books, and ornaments, the vendors were eager for our patronage and frowned on the beggars who lurked around and I was sure were intent on picking the pockets of the unwary.

I saw a man with his tailor, who was telling him how much material he should buy; there were notices on the pillars offering services of all nature. There was a woman with a young girl and boy who looked downcast and indeed terrified. I guessed she was offering them as servants for some rich household. I saw a woman with an evil face talking earnestly to a young dandy in a cloak of crimson velvet with gold lace on his breeches; a very young girl was with her—and as she was clearly being shown off to the young man even my country innocence could guess the nature of that transaction. It was all rather terrifying and yet exciting. The place seemed to have a life of its own such as no other I had ever known had had.

Carlotta suddenly announced that she could not find what she wanted in the Walk so we would go to the New Exchange in the Strand. So we got into the coach, and it was not easy to move along, for people crowded round it, laughing at our vehicle, touching it, peering in the window at us, offering us all sorts of merchandise—from silver chains to silk kerchiefs —many of which had been I had no doubt but a short time before been snatched from some unwary passerby.

So we came to the New Exchange and ascended to an upper gallery which was lined with shops offering for sale ribbons, laces, cloth of all description, powder, rouge, patches, cuffs, and collars, some very fine, embroidered in gold and sivler.

Carlotta made a few purchases and we returned to the coach.

I was fascinated by the Strand and the grand houses there whose gardens ran down to the river; I loved the narrow streets at the end of which I could see the water lapping; in fact I was ready to admit that I had never dreamed there could be such a place and the very fact that underlying its grandeur was something so certainly sinister but added to its attraction.

We had left the Strand well behind and were coming toward Whitehall when I saw the most fearful sight I had, to that time, ever seen.

I had seen men in the pillory before, for there was one in our village and offenders were often put in it and made to endure the ridicule of passersby in order to impress on them the error of their ways; but I had never seen anything like this.

These two men were in the somber garments which proclaimed them as Puritans. They did not look like men, because I could not see their faces for blood; it had splashed onto their hands, which protruded through the holes.

I stared in horror and Carlotta followed my gaze.

"Puritans," she said. "They have been making trouble."

"What trouble?"

"Perhaps talking against the Court. They are always trying to stop all sport and pleasure. They criticized the Queen no doubt and accused her of trying to foist Catholicism on the nation."

"And for that?"

"They have lost their ears," she said.

We had passed on. The coach carried us on through green fields and the pleasant villages of Kensington and Barnes until in due course we arrived at Pondersby Hall. For me every impression of that colorful scene had been overlaid by the sight of those two Puritans in the pillory.

I began to understand what Gervaise meant when he talked about the uneasiness in the country.

Carlotta was pleased because there was to be a ball at one of the fine houses near Whitehall and she and Sir Gervaise had received an invitation which included Senara and the visitor from the country—myself.

"You have been noticed," said Carlotta. "This is at the house of Lord Mallard, who is a confidant of the King, so it is almost certain that their Majesties will be present."

There was a great deal of excitement as to what must be worn and even Carlotta was less languid than usual. Ana was pressed into service and as the time drew near it was discovered that we were short of the lace with which Carlotta's gown was to be trimmed and that ribbons were needed for my dress.

We would therefore take the coach and there would be another trip into the city. My feelings were a little mixed. I was uneasy about the ball for Carlotta had so impressed on me my lack of social grace, and although I felt a great excitement at the prospect of visiting the city again I had not forgotten the sight of the two men in the pillory.

We set out early in the Pondersby coach. It was misty down by the river, which gave an aura of enchantment to the scene. There was a blue haze on the trees which I found entrancing and I felt my spirits rising as high as they could, oppressed as they always were by anxieties about what was happening at home.

We came to St. Paul's Walk and I was again fascinated by the people there. I was listening to a moneylender with whom a languid gallant, most extravagantly clad, was trying to arrange a loan; then my attention was caught by a horse dealer who was explaining to a prospective buyer the points of the animal he was leading; there was a man writing a letter at the dictation of an anxious-eyed woman and I found myself wondering what tragedy had brought her there. Carlotta was busy with the lace seller and had moved around to the side of the stall, and as I stood there a woman approached me, her eyes full of anguish.

"Lady," she said in a hoarse whisper, "spare me something. My husband is dead . . . drowned in the river when his boat overturned. I have six starving children and not a bite has passed their lips these last two days. You have a kind face. You'll give, I know."

And I knew that if I turned away as Carlotta would have bidden me I should never be able to forget her face, so I took out my purse and opened it but at that moment a boy who could not have been more than eleven years old darted up and snatched the purse from me.

I cried out, but he was already disappearing, and without thinking I ran after him. I could see him darting in and out of the crowd and I followed, calling, "Come back! Give me back my purse!"

The crowd impeded the thief's progress as well as mine and I kept him in sight until he broke free and ran down an alley.

Without thinking I followed. He ran round a corner and I went after him, but he had already turned another corner and when I followed I could no longer see him. I stopped short. Two men were coming toward me and I felt myself go cold with fear, for they had such evil looks. Their unkempt hair fell over their faces, their ragged garments hung loosely, and through the rents in them I caught a glimpse of dirty skin. They were smiling in a way which was horrifying.

I turned to run but I was too late and I realized in that moment that I did not know where I was.

There was one of them on either side of me, their leering faces close to mine. One pulled at the chain about my neck, which my mother had given me, and I cried out in protest.

My arms were pinioned and I started to scream loudly.

"You're caught, my pretty," said one of the men, his face so near mine that I smelled his foul breath and saw his ugly broken teeth.

"Let me go! Let me go!" I shouted wildly.

"Not yet," said the other and they began to drag me toward the door of a dwelling which I had not noticed before.

I began to pray to myself because I had never been so frightened in my life and I knew that these men meant to inflict on me the worst of all evils and possibly death; and it had all happened so suddenly, for one moment I had been thinking of laces and ribbons, letter writers and moneylenders, and now here I was captured. And even in such a moment I thought of my mother when she would learn what had happened to me.

Then I heard a shout from behind: "Hold. Hold, you villains, hold!"

A man was running down the alley. I had a fleeting glimpse of him and I cried out in thankfulness, for there was something about his appearance which told me that I could trust him to help.

He was elegantly clad, but not foppishly so, and there was a sword in his hand which he was brandishing menacingly. The change in my captors was immediate. They did not wait to face him. They simply released me and ran.

I was trembling and could not keep my voice steady as I stammered, "Oh, thank you . . . thank you."

"I saw it all," he said. "The boy snatching your purse and your attempt to catch him."

"I am so grateful."

"You are new to London, I am sure. Let me escort you from this warren. It is not good for you to be here."

He returned his sword to its scabbard and, taking my arm, led me through the alley the way I had come.

"It was unwise," he said, "to follow the boy."

"But he had my purse."

"It was equally unwise to take out your purse as you did."

"The woman had six starving children."

"I doubt that. She's a professional beggar. Tomorrow she

will have a dying husband or a dying mother. They vary their stories, you know."

"I see that now, but I believed her."

"Next time you will be more skeptical. Tell me your name."

I told him and that I was staying at Pondersby Hall.

"I have made the acquaintance of Sir Gervaise," he told me. "I am Richard Tolworthy, a soldier of the King's army."

"I can only say again thank you, sir. I have never been so terrified in my life."

"It is a lesson learned. Look on it that way."

"But if you had not seen . . . if you had not been there to save me—"

"I was and it was my pleasure. Where do you wish to go?"

"I left Lady Pondersby buying laces in Paul's Walk. We came in from Pondersby Hall in the coach."

"Then I will take you back to Paul's Walk and we will find Lady Pondersby."

We were very quickly there. Carlotta had been engrossed in the lace buying, which she had just completed, and she was looking around wondering what had become of me when she saw me with my rescuer.

She cried out, "Whatever has happened?"

"Something terrible," I answered. "I've lost my purse. A boy snatched it. I ran after him and there were two men. . . . This gentleman saved me."

Carlotta was gravely surveying Richard Tolworthy, and I thought with a little stab of jealousy: "I suppose he is thinking how beautiful she is."

He bowed and said, "Richard Tolworthy at your service, ma'am."

"Why, sir"—she laughed—"it seems you have indeed been at *our* service. Mistress Landor is newly arrived from the country."

"I gathered so," he said.

I felt deflated and sad suddenly, as Carlotta went on: "And as she does not seem inclined to present me, I will tell you that I am Lady Pondersby, wife of Sir Gervaise."

"Of whose acquaintance I have the pleasure," said Richard Tolworthy. "May I escort you to your coach?"

"Thank you. I would be glad if you did. I see Mistress Landor has been considerably shocked by the adventure."

"I fear so," he said, glancing briefly at me. "But at least she will know how to avoid such an experience if—may God forbid—it should occur again."

"It would have been terrible if you had not been there. I

should never have forgiven myself!" said Carlotta. "Oh, here is the coach. Could I take you to your destination?"

"Thank you. I have business in the Walk."

He handed us both into the coach and stood back bowing.

As we moved away, Carlotta said, "Well, you have had a little adventure, have you not?"

"I was terrified . . . until he came."

"I should think so. Two men you say . . . with evil intent. Robbery with rape, doubtless. You have learned something of the streets of London this morning. Let it stand you in good stead."

It was characteristic of Carlotta that she should see the incident as an example of my folly rather than her neglect and should seek to make me feel the more foolishly inexperienced because of it.

But she did not dwell on that. She was clearly interested in my rescuer.

"I have heard his name," she said. "I believe him to be one of the King's generals."

"He said he was a soldier."

"Yes, a high-ranking one. It was obvious in his bearing. It was civil of him and gallant of him, was it not?"

"It was indeed."

She leaned back against the upholstery of the coach.

"What is it I have heard of him? Something I fancy. I believe there is some mystery about him. I must ask Gervaise."

She half closed her eyes, smiling. I realized that she was indeed intrigued by Richard Tolworthy.

As for myself I could not shut out of my mind the terrible moment when those two men had loomed up beside me and somehow conveyed their purpose. I could not imagine what would have happened to me if Richard Tolworthy had not appeared. It was quite beyond my ability to do so. But I knew that I would rather they had killed me.

And then he had come. I remembered certain things about him. It was a stern face, as became a high-ranking soldier. It was a strong face—cold, though. I suppose he had despised me for walking so foolishly into such a trap. I had lost my purse but fortunately I had had very little money in it, and I would make sure that such a thing never happened to me again, so perhaps the experience was well worth the price I had paid for it.

He was tall and his skin slightly bronzed, so I supposed he had fought the King's battles in other countries. I wondered whether I would ever see him again and I felt a flutter of excitement because it did not seem unlikely. He would move in Court circles—those of which Sir Gervaise was a member. I wondered whether he would notice me if we met again. When Carlotta had appeared I had the impression that she had shown him that I was to be despised for my folly, although before he had been kind, understanding of my inexperience.

When we arrived at Pondersby Hall all thought of the man and the adventure receded, for there was a letter from my mother. I seized it and ran to my room with it because I could not bear to read it under the scrutiny of Carlotta's eyes.

My fingers were trembling as I opened it. My fears of what I would read made it impossible for a second or so to see the words which danced before my eyes: "My dearest Angelet, I hasten to tell you the good news. Bersaba is going to recover. She is very very weak but. . . ." The letter slipped from my hands. I just buried my face in them and I started to weep as I had not since the terrible anxiety had begun—tears of relief, tears of joy. Life would go on again.

Senara came and sat with me. She too wept a little and we sat side by side holding hands. I loved her in that moment because of her true affection for my mother.

She kept saying, "Thank God. Thank God. It would have killed Tamsyn. This is due to her nursing, you can depend upon it. Her mother's care has defied the laws of nature. Tamsyn is one of the truly good women in this world."

She put her arms round me and held me fast.

"Did I not tell you so?" she demanded.

And I answered, "You did!" And I thought: "You are truly a witch."

Mab was happy.

"I couldn't believe Mistress Bersaba could die," she said. "She's too sharp for it."

I laughed at that observation. It was with the laughter that is born of relief and happiness because that great black cloud had been dispersed and the skies were blue again.

Carlotta said, "Now you can stop fretting and begin to take a real interest in everything. It's been exasperating to have you so lukewarm when I take so much trouble to launch you."

I laughed at her too—the same sort of laughter.

At dinner Carlotta told Sir Gervaise of my adventure.

He was most concerned.

"My dear Angelet," he said, "that was a most unwise thing to do!"

"I know it now. But you see, it was my purse."

"You could have lost so much more."

"It was great good fortune that Richard Tolworthy was at hand. Gervaise, you've met him. What do you know of him?"

"He's a good soldier. He's had great success in several campaigns."

"I mean . . . personally," said Carlotta with a trace of impatience.

Sir Gervaise looked thoughtful. "There was something about him. It slips my memory."

"Oh, do try to think."

"I don't know. A somewhat unsociable fellow if I remember rightly. He doesn't mix in society a great deal. Devoted to his profession, of course, which occupies him. Lost his wife. . . ."

"So he was married."

"I believe so."

"How could he have lost his wife if he wasn't?" said Carlotta with some show of exasperation.

"I'm not sure," said Sir Gervaise. "Perhaps it was something else. However, there was some story."

I lay awake a long time that night. I was thinking of the rejoicing at home. Bersaba no longer in danger, but very weak still and she would be for a long time. We could bear that. My mother would nurse her back to health and when I went home she would be there.

I slept at last and dreamed that I was at home. Bersaba and I were in the hall and as we sat there a man came in. He bowed and I said, "This is Bersaba, whose life has been saved and, Bersaba, this is Richard Tolworthy, who saved mine."

And he sat down between us and we were very happy together. I awoke reluctantly from that dream.

The Betrothal

I FORGOT that unpleasant adventure and thought about the exciting new experiences which were crowding in on me. I could now say to myself I will tell Bersaba that, without the terrible foreboding coming over me that I might never be able to. I could, in other words, be happy and carefree, so I let myself think about the Mallard ball. I was to have a very special ball gown which Sir Gervaise wished to give me—a thanksgiving offering for two happy events, he told me: my escape from the London villains and the recovery of my sister, and he wanted me to be very happy wearing it.

"Gervaise doesn't want you to look like a little country mouse at the Mallard ball," said Carlotta, attempting to douse my pleasure as usual; I replied spiritedly that I thought the reason was that Gervaise wanted to be kind.

She shrugged her shoulders. The important thing was the dress. It was to have a rose-pink silk bodice and flowing skirt over a most elaborate cream satin petticoat embroidered in gold thread, and it would be cut very low to enhance my long neck, which Carlotta rather grudgingly admitted had a certain grace. But the immaturity of my bosom would have to be disguised.

Ana, who was making the dresses, whispered to me that that which Carlotta disparaged was in fact my youthfulness, which to many would be very attractive, so I must not be depressed by my immaturity.

"There are many aging ladies who would give a great deal to possess it," she told me.

I discovered during the making of that dress that Ana was interested in me. She would kneel beside me and encourage me to talk. She liked to hear about Bersaba.

"You look so alike," she said, "yet there is a difference."

"Most people can't tell it," I replied.

"Do you know," said Ana, "I think I could."

I told her how Bersaba had gone to the midwife because she was so concerned about one of the servants whose baby was overdue.

"I remember," said Ana, "she warned us that there was murmuring in the village against my mistress . . . and yet . . ." She hesitated and I looked at her expectantly and Ana said, "I did not think she was so fond of my mistress."

"I do not think she was either," I answered, thinking of Bastian.

"Yet she warned her."

"Of course she would warn her. The mob can be terrible when they are on the march. I once saw them taking a witch. It was horrible. There is something frightening about a mob. Ordinary people become like savages when they get together, and what is supposed to be a righteous cause rouses them to madness and cruelty."

"Your sister is a strange lady," said Ana.

"Oh, I know her well. I understand her. Sometimes I think we are one person because there are times when it seems that nature divided the human qualities between us and gave all to one of us and none to the other. She is so much cleverer than I. It didn't occur to me to go for the midwife although I knew that the baby was overdue. I'm thoughtless I suppose, thinking less of other people."

"*I* think you inherited your share of good points, my lady," said Ana. "Indeed, I should not think your sister has them all. It would be a mistake to think so if some occasion were to arise. . . ."

I looked at her sharply and she went on: "But I talk too much. Look at the set of this bodice."

I was mystified as much by her manner as by her words. It was almost as though she were trying to warn me. Warn me against Bersaba! What nonsense!

But she did seem fond of me, almost protective, and I was beginning to feel that I had kind friends about me. Senara was anxious to make me happy for my mother's sake but very soon she would be leaving for Spain. She told me how delighted she was to hear of my sister's recovery and that if Bersaba had died she would have gone back to be with my mother. Now all was going to be well, it was only a matter of Bersaba's getting strong again, and it occurred to me that now there was no longer any fear of infection I should soon be returning home.

The night of the ball arrived. I was thrilled to see myself in the most elaborate and exquisite ball dress I had ever possessed. Ana came in to make sure that Mab had helped me dress in the right manner. She whispered to me that she would have liked to do my hair herself but her ladyship was demanding her full attention. She glanced with approval at the dress and said I did it credit but she was not quite happy about my hair and was going to find some time to come to me and do it as it should be. She came in due course and combed my curled fringe in the right manner and my long thick hair was coiled up at the back of my head.

The Mallard residence was a large mansion with gardens which ran down to the river. Our hosts received us and looks of interest were bestowed on me before we passed on. People gathered around Sir Gervaise and Carlotta, who appeared to be very well known, and I was introduced to a young man gloriously attired in breeches of satin the shape of the bellows we used at home for getting the fire to burn and I laughed to myself to wonder what he would think of such a homely description, for they were of pale blue satin tied at the knee with a bunch of multicolored ribbons.

He was a little languid and I was afraid that I was out of step in the dance, which seemed to surprise him. I was relieved when the dancing stopped abruptly and there was a sudden silence over the ballroom. This heralded the arrival of the King and Queen. The company immediately formed itself into two lines through which the royal party passed, and I had the privilege of getting a close view of their Majesties. The King was undoubtedly handsome, with clear-cut features, a well-trimmed beard, and hair which curled on his shoulders. He looked kindly but stern, and although his stature was not great there was about him such an air of dignity that I would have known him in any gathering as the King. As for the Queen, she had a fascination of her own, largely due to a vitality which was apparent even in her smile. She was far from good-looking, for her nose was long and her prominent teeth not good, but she had large dark eyes, which shone with interest in all about her, and her pale skin was smooth and delicate.

I felt deeply moved as I swept the curtsy I had been instructed in while they passed on. And I thought, "How I shall enjoy telling Bersaba this!"

I had lost my languid gallant, who had doubtless taken the opportunity to find a more sophisticated partner. While I was feeling rather lost, and looking for Senara or Sir Gervaise, a voice close to me said, "So we meet again." And standing before me was the man who had rescued me from the alley.

I felt myself flushing with pleasure and a certain tingling excitement which he inspired. He went on: "It occurred to me that we should meet again before long."

"I hope," I answered, "that I thanked you adequately."

"You did indeed. Your appreciation was apparent. Do you care to dance?"

"I enjoy it but I am not so practiced in the Court dances as I should like to be."

"To tell the truth no more am I. I'll warrant you excel at those which are performed in the country. I think they capture the spirit of dancing more surely than these ballroom dances. I'll warrant you excel at Leap Candle and Sellengers Round as well as Barley Break and John Come Kiss Me."

I laughed aloud. "I love them all. We dance them at Christmastime, and when we've brought the harvest in we make our corn dollies to ensure a good harvest next year."

"Ah, you make me envious of the joys of the country. I'll tell you what we'll do—we'll go into the garden. We can find a seat there and we'll talk. Would you like that?"

"I should greatly enjoy it."

"Come then. We'll slip away."

He made a way through the press of people, and I was delighted to be in the fresh air, for fortunately it was a mild evening. The gardens were very beautiful. The sound of the river washing the stone steps at the water's edge gave a soothing charm to the scene.

He found the seat. It was in a kind of arbor facing the river, its trellis sheltering us from the breeze, and there we sat.

"Tell me about the country," he said. So I told him about my home and how because of Bersaba's illness I had come to London.

He expressed his relief that she had recovered and asked if now I should be returning to the country, to which I replied that I should in due course.

He suggested that my sister would need a long convalescence after her illness. He was sure of this because he had a friend who had the great good fortune to recover from the disease. He went on: "And believe me it is the greatest good fortune and rarely happens. My friend believed he had had one foot in the grave and regarded it as a miracle that he had been able to draw it out in time."

I shivered and he asked if I were cold.

"No," I said, "I was just wondering what life would be like without my sister."

"You are twins. Tell me—is she like you?"

"So like that our mother is the only one who can tell us apart on every occasion."

"She looks like you; she speaks as you do. Tell me, does she *think* as you do?"

"Ah, there is the difference, and that is great. She is much cleverer than I. She used to do my sums for me and write my essays. I did her needlework. That was about the only thing I could do better than she could. There, that tells you all you want to know about us."

"Not all, for I confess to a great curiosity."

I don't think I had been so happy since I had left home. I suddenly felt that the world was a new and exciting place. A miracle had happened. Bersaba had been snatched from the grave and she would in time be well and strong again; and here was I in London in this enchanting garden, talking to a man who was one of the King's generals—an important man who seemed interested in me and admitted he wanted to know me better.

I should never have known him but for my frightening adventure. I should never have felt this elation because of Bersaba's recovery if she had never been ill. So with every experience, it seemed however alarming at the time, came compensations.

I said, "We talk so much about me and my affairs. You do not talk of yours."

"Tell me what you wish to know."

"You are a soldier. You must have seen a great many adventures, perhaps abroad."

"Oh, yes, I have seen service overseas. As soon as I had matriculated at Cambridge I knew I wanted to be a soldier. It is in fact a tradition in my family. My father sent me to the Low Countries to learn the art of war. Later I was fighting in Spain and then France."

"And at the moment you are at peace."

"A soldier is always prepared for war."

"And you are going abroad for a while?"

"Not until the need arises."

"So now you train your men and you keep yourself in readiness. Do you have a home in the country?"

"It is outside the town. We have estates in the north which are managed by my younger brother. He did not go into the Army. My home is Far Flamstead. It lies west of Hampton. But I have quarters in the town naturally."

"As Gervaise has."

"He is connected with the Court so it is necessary."

"And is yours an ancient manor?"

"No, built last century, when so many such places were."

"And you go there whenever possible to enjoy the peace of the country?"

There was a sudden silence, and I looked at him sharply. His features seemed to have set themselves into a mask as he said, "I do not get much opportunity. My duties keep me in the town."

I remembered then that Sir Gervaise had said there was some story about him which he couldn't remember and that the General had lost his wife.

I could not of course ask him questions on such a subject, but a great deal of the pleasure seemed to have evaporated.

His easy manner had dropped from him; he had become secretive.

I talked about home and Castle Paling although I was longing to hear about him, but he encouraged me to do this and expressed great interest in my background, which I believed was due to the fact that he did not want to talk about himself.

While we were talking we heard footsteps and a man and woman came by. They knew him evidently because the man addressed him by his name.

Luke Longridge and his sister Ella were presented to me, and I thought they regarded me with some disapproval. I wondered for the first time whether I had committed some breach of etiquette by being discovered here in the gardens alone with a man.

They were much less elaborately dressed than most of the company and there seemed to be a rather disapproving attitude about the pair of them.

Luke Longridge said that he would like to share the seat with us and he and his sister sat down.

They talked of the flowers and the mildness of the night for a few moments, and then Luke Longridge said that the King had seemed serene and quite unaware of the storm which was blowing up around him.

"One would not expect His Majesty to be aught else on such an occasion," commented the General.

"The Queen is frivolous as ever," went on Luke Longridge. "I declare, she does not appear to have a thought above dancing and light conversation except it is to introduce her hated religion to the country. That she will never do."

"Indeed she will not," said the General.

Ella Longridge replied vehemently, "There will be plenty to see that she does not."

"His Majesty would never allow it to happen. He knows the will of the people," replied the General.

"Since Buckingham's death—and thank God for it—the Queen has become his chief adviser," said Luke Longridge.

"That is an exaggeration," retorted the General.

"He has a doting fondness for her—after ignoring her for years and disliking his marriage he has now become an uxorious husband led by the nose; and who leads him . . . the frivolous Catholic Frenchwoman!"

"The King is happy in his marriage, which is fruitful," said the General. "And you will admit, my friend, that that is good for the country. It is not true to say that the King listens only to his wife. His Majesty has a great sense of duty."

"Is that why there is so much unrest in the country?" demanded Luke Longridge. "It will not be endured, I promise you, General. There is murmuring throughout the land. The country is divided against itself, and by God, I know on which side I shall be . . . and it won't be the King's."

"You speak treason, Longridge. Have a care," said the General.

"I speak what's in my mind," answered Luke Longridge.

"Be careful, Luke," said his sister.

I wanted to beg of the General to be careful too. I looked at him pleadingly, but he seemed unaware of me.

A passion burned in Luke Longridge. He cried suddenly, "I'd see an end to all this. It'll come to it in time. A King to rule without a parliament. . . ."

"Luke, Luke!" cried his sister.

I suddenly had a vision of the men I had seen in the pillory. A short while ago I had thought this was an enchanted night, and now it had suddenly changed. I had been dreaming and I was awakening rudely to reality. Nothing was quite what it seemed. In that ballroom the debonair King and his fascinating wife were receiving the homage of subjects; they did not know some of their subjects such as the Longridges were murmuring against them. Or did they? What of the men in the pillory?

"You have insulted the King," I heard General Tolworthy cry, "and the King's Army. I shall need satisfaction for this."

"You know full well I speak sound sense."

"I know full well you have insulted the King and his Army. You may name the meeting place."

"You will hear from me in due course." Luke Longridge bowed and walked toward the house, his sister clinging to his arm.

"It is chill," said the General to me. "Allow me to escort you back to your friends."

I stood my ground firmly.

"What did it mean? You are surely not going to fight?"

"He left me no alternative."

"But he merely expressed a point of view."

"Which was an insult to the Crown."

"But not a personal one."

"My dear Mistress Landor, I am one of the King's generals. Any insult to His Majesty is indeed my affair."

"Does this mean there is to be a duel?"

"Pray do not concern yourself. It is a fairly commonplace affair."

"Which could end in death for one of you!"

"It may be, but perhaps not."

"But—"

"Come, it grows chill."

He would say no more, and I could do nothing but allow him to lead me in.

He took me to Senara, who was in conversation with a group of people, then he bowed and departed.

I was glad when the evening was over and we were going home in the coach, and so relieved that no one was inclined for talk. I could not stop thinking of what seemed to me that most stupid quarrel which could well end in the death of one of those men.

I knew that if Richard Tolworthy were killed I should remember him for the rest of my life.

I passed a miserable two days. Richard Tolworthy would either be killed himself or kill the other man, and I could see no satisfaction in that. How could he have challenged the other in such a senseless manner? Luke Longridge had insulted the King. Well, I thought angrily, let the King fight his own battles.

But Richard was a soldier . . . a man of ideals. Of course he was right, I assured myself. I thought of Luke Longridge, whom I was beginning to hate because he had provoked this duel.

I asked Carlotta what happened if a man was injured in a duel.

"Sometimes he dies. It depends how deeply he is wounded."

"And the other?"

"He would probably flee the country. After all, it is murder."

"I see."

"Why do you ask?"

"I just wanted to know. I am supposed to learn the manners and customs of the nobility, am I not?"

"That's a morbid one."

"I have noticed that many customs end in morbidity."

"Ah," she mocked, "you are becoming quite observant."

I tried to put the matter from my mind and to tell myself how foolish I was to be involved with a man whom I had met only twice, though they had been two unusual occasions— one when he had saved me from a horrible fate and the other when he had challenged a man to a duel.

How I wished that Bersaba was with me so that I could tell

135

her of my feelings. I wondered when my mother would suggest that I return. She would need me to nurse Bersaba, to be with her perhaps. She had said in her letter that it would be a long time before she was herself again and had hinted that the disease was still in the village and that she did not want me to return until the neighborhood was, as she called it, clean again.

I thought that if General Richard Tolworthy were killed or fled abroad I would like to go home without delay. Then I could put the whole London adventure behind me and look back on it as something rather unreal.

However, a week after the ball Richard Tolworthy called at the house.

By great good fortune Senara had gone to say good-bye to neighbors, for she was leaving the following week. Carlotta had accompanied her, and Sir Gervaise was at Whitehall. The General was apparently making a conventional call on Sir Gervaise, and when he was told that he was not at home he asked if I were.

As a result I was receiving him in the parlor which led from the hall, and floods of joy swept over me when I saw that he was neither maimed nor had the look of a fugitive.

"I was hoping that I might have a word with you," he said, "because you were so concerned on the night of the ball."

"Indeed I was. I could not understand what had happened so suddenly and why it should be a matter of life and death."

"I had no alternative in the circumstances but to deliver the challenge. However, it was not taken up. I received an apology. The offending words were retracted and so we did not meet."

"I am so pleased. It was wise of him."

"He is a Puritan at heart and doesn't believe in shedding blood."

"Then I think there is a great deal to be said for Puritanism."

He smiled at me. "You were really anxious, I know."

"Oh, I was. I thought you would be killed or perhaps kill him and have to go into exile."

"I am grateful for your concern."

"But of course I'm concerned. Didn't you save me?"

"That was nothing."

I just could not help showing my relief and I think he was very pleased.

He talked for some time asking me more questions about my home. He wanted to know how long I was staying in Lon-

136

don, and when I told him that I might be leaving at any time and that it would depend on my sister's health and when the plague vanished from the neighborhood, he listened very intently.

Then he said, "I hope you will stay a long while. Or do you get a little homesick?"

"I was at first. Now I am not sure. There is so much of interest here."

"Encounters with beggars, duels?" he suggested.

"And meeting interesting people," I told him.

"There must be interesting people whom you meet in your home."

"Yes," I admitted, "but . . . different."

And I thought then, "I have never met anyone like you." I knew then that as long as I lived I never would.

When he left he took my hand in his and kissed it.

He said, "I shall call again."

I watched rim ride away and then I went up to my room because I wanted to be alone to think about him. If I had to return to Cornwall now, how should I feel? I should be wretched. Wretched to go to my beloved home, to see my dearest mother and the sister who was part of myself! What had happened to me?

I half suspected that, in my impulsive thoughtless way, I was in love with Richard Tolworthy.

The weeks slipped quickly by. Senara left and I was sad to say good-bye to her, for I felt I had lost a friend. True to his promise, General Tolworthy called on us. Sir Gervaise could not understand at first. "General Tolworthy seems to have become very friendly toward me suddenly," was his comment. We were invited to functions where we met him and we had many conversations together.

Carlotta thought he had conceived a passion for her which, being the man he was, he would keep secret. She made much of him and consequently she frequently invited him to the house. I was rather amused because deep in my heart I knew that it was not Carlotta who interested him. There was something inherently serious about him—almost secretive; but there was a rapport between us; we did not have to speak much; he did not even have to single me out particularly, but I knew in my heart that I was the one he came to see.

Now I was afraid that my mother would say I must return, and I had visions of slipping out of his life and I wondered whether he would let me go. Much as I longed to see my family, I could not endure the thought of leaving him.

My mother wrote but she did not suggest that I return. She wrote:

My Dearest Angelet,

First let me tell you that your sister is improving though she has a long way to go. I can tell you now that she has come very near to death. She is so weak still that she must keep to her bed. She sends her dearest love to you, my darling, but is too weak to take up her pen to write to you herself. You may be sure that when she is strong enough she will do so.

My aim is to nurse her back to her former strength. The physicians tell me that will take months and that it is little short of a miracle that we have her with us. I want you, my daughter, to endure this long separation as best you can. I would not have you here just yet and if you can assure me that you are well and happy I will content myself and look forward to your return as we all do. . . .

I read that letter over and over again. It filled me with joy. I was pleasing my mother by staying and I knew now that more than seeing my sister, more than being with my mother, I wanted to be here where each day I awoke with the thought: "It could happen today."

I meant that General Tolworthy might that day ask me to be his wife.

Winter had come. I had never before spent a Christmas away from home. My mother had written to me, sending me silk to make a gown and telling me not to be too unhappy because I should not be with them this year. The festivities at Trystan would be less merry than usual, for Bersaba was so easily tired and must spend several hours each day on her bed.

The mummers would come, she doubted not, and there would be the carol singers; Aunt Melanie and Uncle Connell had insisted on coming to be with them but my father, Fennimore, and Bastian would not be there, so a great deal of usual activities would not take place.

"Next Christmas," wrote my mother, "I trust we shall all be together."

So Christmas was celebrated at Pondersby Hall, and although we did have a lord of misrule it was far less simple than our Christmases at home. For instance there was a masque where we did a Spanish play, which Carlotta managed for us and in which we all had to play a part. We rehearsed for two weeks before Christmas and we performed it both on Christmas Day and Twelfth Night. Carlotta of course was the central character, and she acted with great skill and charm and it was true that numbers of the young men regarded Sir Gervaise enviously and gazed at Carlotta with longing eyes. So it was not surprising that she counted Richard Tolworthy among her admirers.

He went away immediately after Christmas and weeks elapsed before I saw him again. I began to fret, thinking that he had forgotten all about me.

January came and with it the snow. We had it so rarely in Cornwall that I could only remember seeing it three times. Then, how excited we had been! We had pelted each other with snowballs, and I remember that Bastian was there and had made Bersaba his special target.

Now it was different. We did not play at snowballs but we skated on the ponds and that was good fun, but all the time I was thinking of Richard and wondering if I should ever see him again.

It was a dark early February day when he rode over. The roads, which had been impassable, were clear again and all that was left of the recent snow was mounds of it in the fields and against the hedgerows.

There was a great fire in the hall when he came in. I heard him asking the footman if Sir Gervaise were at home and I went into the hall trying to look as though I had come down by chance.

I held out my hand to him and said as calmly as I could, "It is a long time since we have seen you, General."

He replied that he had been in the north on business. Then Sir Gervaise appeared and I hung back while he was conducted to the parlor. Sir Gervaise ordered that Carlotta be told that we had a visitor.

I went to my room. I did not want to see Carlotta paying him that very special attention she reserved for men. I had come to the conclusion that I had allowed myself to imagine what I wanted to believe and that Richard Tolworthy had no more interest in me than he would in any young girl whom he had rescued from a pair of ruffians, and who had shown some concern because she had heard him challenge someone to a duel.

I combed my hair, patting it into shape, hoping that he would ask to see me, but he didn't.

A few days later he called again. This time I was alone, and he asked if I would see him and I received him in the parlor.

"I have to confess a little duplicity," he told me. "I learned that Sir Gervaise and his lady would not be at home today. So I called in the hope that you would be."

"You . . . wanted to see *me*, then?"

I felt as though the sun had suddenly burst forth and was shining more brilliantly than it did in the summer and that the entire universe was singing with joy.

"I wanted to talk to you rather specially."

"Yes?" I asked breathlessly.

"Pray sit down," he said. I sat on the window seat and folded my hands in my lap. I dared not look at him in case I should betray my feelings and that I had misconstrued his words and would betray myself.

"I think," he said, "that we have become good friends. Do you agree?"

"Oh, I do. Indeed I do."

"You exaggerated what I did on my first meeting. It was no more than any man would have done."

"I shall never forget that you risked your life for me."

"Oh, you must look at life rationally. Villains like that are always cowards. They attack women and children. Moreover, I was armed and I assure you I ran no risk. But what I was saying was that we have become friends. I have hesitated over this, and perhaps I should have been wise to hesitate still further. You are very young, Angelet. I may use your Christian name?"

"Please do. I like you to."

"It is a charming name and may I say it suits you."

"Oh, please, you must not have too good an opinion of me. I shall never live up to it—"

I stopped short. I had made it sound as though we would be together. I was blushing hotly.

He ignored my outburst and said, "How old are you, Angelet?"

"I shall be eighteen in June."

He sighed. "That is very young. Do you know how old I am?"

"I hadn't thought of age in connection with you."

"What a charming thing to say! It is good, too, because I am considerably older than you are. I shall be thirty-four years of age in September. You see there is a great difference in our ages."

"Does that matter with . . . friends?"

140

"It is a question I have been asking myself these last weeks. Perhaps I should not have spoken to you yet."

"I am sure it is always better to say what is in one's mind."

"I have made up mine to ask you to marry me."

"Oh!" I could say no more. I felt my whole body tingling with delight. It had really happened then. I had not been wrong. I said to myself, "Oh, Bersaba, I am going to be married. Think of it! I am going to be married to a General in the King's Army, the most wonderful, most gallant man in the world."

Bersaba had once said, "I wonder which of us will marry first?" and Bersaba had wanted to be the first. She always wanted to be the first in everything and somehow I had wanted her to, for it had seemed her right.

But this was different. More than anything I wanted to marry Richard Tolworthy.

"Yes," he said, "you are startled. You are wondering how I, who am so old, can dare suggest such a thing to you who are not yet eighteen. That's what you mean, is it not?"

I laughed—strange, rather hysterical laughter it sounded. I could never be clever as Bersaba was and I tried fleetingly to imagine what she would say in these circumstances. But what was the use? I was myself, not Bersaba, and I had never been able to say anything but that which first came into my head.

"I mean nothing of the sort," I cried. "I mean only that I am so happy that you asked me. I have been so immodest. I thought perhaps you were interested in me and I let myself dream that you wanted to marry me and . . . I just could not have borne it if you hadn't."

He came toward me then and I stood up. I expected him to take me into his arms and hold me tightly. But he did not. He took my hand and kissed it as he might have done if we had just been introduced at a ball.

"You are a dear child," he said, "but impetuous. Can you really mean this?"

"With all my heart," I said.

He pushed me back gently onto the window seat and sat in a chair some distance from me.

"You must not make a hasty decision, my dear."

"I don't understand you. Were you hoping I would say no?"

He smiled at me. "I asked you because I hoped you would say yes. But you are young."

"That," I said rather tritely, "will in due course be remedied."

141

"But as you grow older so shall I. You must listen to what I have to say very carefully. When you are twenty-four years of age I shall be forty. Think of that."

"It seems good arithmetic to me." I was growing frivolous in my happiness.

"Now let me talk to you very seriously. Have you thought very much about marrying?"

"Only vaguely. My sister and I used to talk about it sometimes. We used to wonder whom we would marry and who would marry first. You see, being twins we have always done everything together. There were so few eligible people surrounding us, and we guessed we would marry two of the young men of the neighborhood."

"And you came to London and met me."

"And how glad I am! I was never more glad of anything in my life."

"You are at the beginning of your life, my dear. Let us remember that. I must make you see what life would be like if you married me. You have been here in this house and you have been to one or two balls and masques and there is no doubt that you have found life here a little more exciting than that in your country house. That's true, I believe."

"Yes," I admitted, "but not because of the balls and masques."

"I am glad of that," he said. "I lead a quieter life."

"I shall be happy to share it."

"You have a good sweet nature and I believe you will make me very happy . . . if this marriage should take place."

"But it *is* going to take place. You have asked me and I have accepted. If we both want it, it must take place, must it not?"

"Yes," he answered, "if we both want it and there is no objection from your family."

"My parents would want me to be happy. They always have."

"Then I shall ask their consent. I shall speak to Sir Gervaise, who is your temporary guardian, and ask him to recommend me to your parents."

I clasped my hands blissfully.

"But first," he went on, "I want you to be absolutely sure what this means."

"I know that I want to be with you more than anything." I spoke fervently and the truth of what I said astonished me. Truly I loved this man.

"I have pointed out to you the disparity in our ages."

"Which I accept and rejoice in. Do you think I want a young man with breeches like bellows tied up with fancy ribbons?"

He smiled. I noticed then that he rarely laughed and sometimes it was as though he smiled in spite of himself. He was a very serious man, this one I loved. I thought: "I shall change that. I'll make him so happy that he will laugh all the time."

"There are certain things you must know about me. I have been already married."

"Did she die?" I asked.

"She died," he answered.

"And it was very sad, I suppose."

"Yes, it was very sad."

"Then please don't talk about it if it distresses you."

"I think you should know of it."

"Was it long ago?"

"Ten years," he said.

"But that is a very long time."

"Yes," he said, "it has seemed a very long time."

"And did you never want to marry anyone until now?"

He hesitated. Then he said, "I thought of it once . . . but decided against it."

"So you weren't really in love."

"I thought it might be unwise."

I got up and, going to him, stood behind him and placed my hands on his shoulders and laid my face against his head.

"And you do not think it unwise now?"

"I think this could perhaps be the right thing for me. I have to consider whether it would be right for you."

"No!" I cried vehemently, "that is for me to say."

He took my hand from his shoulder and pressed his lips to it.

"As you see, Angelet, I am not a very merry man."

"No, you are serious. I like that. You are the King's General. You have a high position in his army."

"Which takes me away from home frequently. Would you like that?"

"I should not like you to be away from me but I would accept it."

"Then life is rather quiet in Far Flamstead. It is different from here. I do not entertain there very much. I never have. In fact I am not the most sociable of men."

"I am not very good at balls and banquets."

"We should have to attend them occasionally. Sometimes we should have to be at Whitehall."

"Then I should enjoy that because it was not often."

"You are determined to find everything to your liking."

"I believe that is how it is when one is in love."

"Oh, Angelet," he said, "I can't do this. You are too young. You have had no experience of living."

"You will give me my experience. Is that not what a husband should do?"

"I am afraid," he said.

"Please do not be afraid that I will not be suitable."

"I am afraid that I am the one who will fail you."

"This must be the strangest proposal ever made," I said. "You ask me to marry you and then you proceed to tell me why I shouldn't."

"All I want is for you to be sure and not to discover that you have made a terrible mistake."

"I am sure," I cried. "I am. I am."

Then he stood up and he held me in his arms. I had never been embraced by a man before, so I had no way of judging it. I thought he was very tender, and I knew that I was going to be very happy.

He called next day and asked to see Gervaise. They were together for some time, during which I waited in a fever of impatience. I knew that all would be well because the decision would rest with my parents, and I was sure that if I told my mother I loved this man and could never be happy without him, she would surely give her consent. Then I supposed I would have to wait for my father's, but that need not be so, for he would sanction anything of which she approved and she knew it.

Gervaise sent for me and when I went in Richard was with him.

I could see that Gervaise was a little disturbed, for I had come to know that he was a man who felt he had a duty toward me and would regard that duty with the utmost seriousness.

"You know, my dear," he said, "that General Tolworthy is asking for your hand in marriage. I believe you have accepted his proposal."

"Yes," I said warmly and happily, "I have."

"Then," said Sir Gervaise, "I will write at once to your mother, and you perhaps should do the same as the General will, and the letters can be dispatched today."

"I understand Angelet's father is on the high seas," said Richard.

"He often is," I cried, "and we never know when he will be home. My mother will speak for them both."

Richard looked askance at Gervaise, who said, "I believe that could be so. Let us all write our letters and they can then be dispatched without delay."

I went to my room, my head whirling with delight. I wrote to both my mother and my sister, and I knew that they would read the happiness in my letters. When I tried to describe him it was difficult. I could not say he was like this or that one, for there was simply no one like him. He was different from all other men. He was important. He was a general in the King's Army. He was a friend of the King's and the Queen's, and he would defend them with his life. He was serious. They need not think he was a frivolous man of the town. No, he was a steady clever soldier and his great concern was that he should make me happy.

I knew my mother would never be able to withhold her consent when she read my letter.

Carlotta was piqued when she heard the news.

"I simply do not believe it," was her first comment. And afterward: "I always thought there was something strange about Richard Tolworthy."

"There was a time when you thought him rather attractive," I pointed out and added maliciously, "That was when you thought he preferred you."

"That's nonsense," she said. "In any case you're far too young for marriage."

"I shall be eighteen."

"You are immature for your age," she told me and walked out of the room.

Yes, she was very angry.

Ana whispered to me, "She is angry because she does not like any but herself to be preferred."

Mab said the same, and I knew that they were right.

Richard left on duty and said that he would be away for a week or so and as soon as he was free to do so he would call on us.

Meanwhile we waited and I lived in a dream. I did not look into the future. I could not because I found it very hard to imagine what it would be like. There was a house, Far Flamstead, which I had not seen and which Richard had not described very clearly. He was not good at descriptions, I thought fondly. I knew its whereabouts roughly but he had never suggested taking me there, which was perhaps rather

145

strange, but I had a notion that he wanted to wait for my family's consent before he regarded us as betrothed.

It seemed along time before the letters came. My mother wrote:

> My Dearest Angelet,
>
> I was surprised to hear the news and your happiness came through to me. I wish it were possible for us to come to London but that is quite out of the question. Bersaba is not yet strong enough to travel. My dear child, I understand how you are feeling. This is a wonderful thing that has happened to you. Sir Gervaise has written to me and so has General Tolworthy. He sounds a very serious man and eager to care for you. And you are truly in love with him. You could not disguise your true feelings from me if you tried.
>
> I wish your father were here, but you know we can never be sure when he will return, and Fennimore is not even here either. I know that you do not want to wait. I have experienced this myself when I was your age so I am writing to General Tolworthy and to Sir Gervaise and telling them that they have your family's consent to your marriage.
>
> Oh, my dearest, how different it is from what I imagined! I had planned that you should be married in this house and naturally I thought it would be someone hereabouts and that you would live near to me and Trystan Priory. But this is clearly what you want and I know how unhappy you would be if I withheld my consent.
>
> So, my dear, be happy. You may become betrothed. Perhaps you could come down here to be married. I wonder if that is possible?
>
> Bersaba is writing to you. It will be but a short note. There is a great change in your sister but she is gradually though slowly regaining her strength.
>
> I hope to hear from you soon, my darling.
>
> My deepest love as ever,
>
> MOTHER

I kissed the letter. How like her. So calm, so reasonable. It was not what she had planned. Of course it wasn't. Who would have believed Bersaba would have fallen ill and I should come to London and find my husband there? But she accepted it. It was life, and she remembered the time when she and my father were young and how dearly she had loved him!

And from Bersaba:

DEAR ANGELET,

So you are to be married. Fancy! I always thought we'd be married together. I hope you will be happy.

You will see a great change in me when we meet. I have been so ill, as you know, but you can't know what a change there is in me. I have to rest a great deal, and there are you going to balls and meeting interesting people and now you are going to be married. I want to see you, Angelet, so much. There is such a lot I want to say. I can't write more now because I am so tired and they are waiting to take the letters.

Do come home and bring your future husband. I long to see you both.

Your loving twin,
BERSABA

It was the first letter she had written to me in her life because we had always been together and she had been too weak to write before.

Try as I might I could not imagine her languid in her bed, she who had always been so vital in her somewhat secret way.

But I confess I was too excited to think very much about my home. My future was here.

Richard rode over and was closeted with Sir Gervaise and after a while he came to the parlor where I was waiting for him.

"This is good news," he said. "We have your mother's consent and she assures us that she speaks for your father. There is nothing now to prevent our betrothal."

He took my left hand and put a ring on the third finger. It was a strange ring—a twist of gold very elaborately engraved with a square-cut emerald set in it.

It seemed to fit me perfectly.

"A good omen," he said. "It's the family ring, always worn by the brides of the eldest son."

I admired it. It was certainly unusual.

Then he kissed me very solemnly.

He supped with us and he and Sir Gervaise talked at length about the insurrection in Scotland and the covenant the Scots had entered into which was against the government.

"There could be trouble there," said Richard, "and we have to be ready to meet it."

"There is a great deal of unease everywhere," admitted Sir Gervaise. "What do you think will be the outcome?"

"I can't say of course, but if this trouble goes on I should be prepared for . . . just anything."

Sir Gervaise nodded gravely.

Carlotta clearly found this conversation boring and changed it to matters more agreeable to herself, which was the affairs of people she knew and what entertainments were planned in the future, which Richard—I was gleefully aware—found as trivial as she found his interests dull. I wondered how she could ever have thought that he was interested in her. I wanted him to know that I would be happy to learn the serious side of the country's affairs and would listen enraptured while he talked to me of the hazards of government.

After Richard had left I retired to my room and I had not been there very long when there was a knock on my door and Carlotta entered.

She threw herself onto my bed and looked at me quizzically.

"What a bore!" she cried. "I fancy you are not going to have a very lively life with the brave General."

"It is the life I have chosen."

"My dear girl, you can hardly call it a choice. There was no one else to choose from, was there?"

"I didn't need anyone else."

"Your first proposal and you accepted. I can't tell you how many I had before I took Gervaise."

"I knew of my cousin Bastian, of course."

"Oh, that was never serious."

"It was to him."

"A country boy! He just did not understand. That could hardly be called my fault."

"I should call it that."

"Oh, dear, you are giving yourself airs. It doesn't become you, Angelet. You got your General by that little-girl manner . . . someone whom he can mold. I can see his thinking that he'll train you like a recruit in his army to go weak at the knees every time the General appears. Don't you think you should consider a little and not rush into this?"

"I have considered."

"Now that my mother has left I feel responsible for you."

"You surprise me."

"You are after all a guest in my house."

"I feel that Sir Gervaise is my host."

"You have a hostess too, my dear, and you only knew Gervaise when he came briefly to Cornwall, but you and I are a kind of cousin, aren't we? Not blood relations but . . . my mother and your mother brought up as sisters. So I feel I can talk to you as poor Gervaise couldn't."

"I feel complete confidence in *poor* Gervaise."

"And you say 'poor' in that way implying that he is so because he is married to me. Let me tell you, my dear Angelet, Gervaise is very content with his marriage. There is more to the condition you should know than being polite in company. In some respects—and I fancy you know little about this—I am very satisfactory indeed."

I had a notion of what she was referring to. There was another side to marriage, and it was true I had never experienced it though I knew of its existence. I had seen lovers at home, secret meetings in secret places. Fumbling embraces . . . and such like.

I had to admit she had made me apprehensive, for she was right that I had no conception of what that would mean, and she was implying that Sir Gervaise and she were in tune in this rather special way.

She was fully aware that she had aroused my uneasiness and this gave her some pleasure.

"Let me see the ring," she said.

I held out my hand and she slipped it from my finger.

"It has an engraved *T* inside, I see."

"It has been worn by the brides of the eldest son through the ages."

"Do you care to wear a ring that has been worn by so many before you?"

"It's a tradition," I said.

She stared down at the ring in the palm of her hand.

"So it was worn by your predecessor," she said slowly. "It must have been taken from her finger when she was dead."

She handed me back the ring with a smile.

"Good night," she said. And she added: "And good luck." The implication was that I might need it.

After she had gone I sat in my chair staring at the ring in the palm of my hand. I was picturing a woman in her coffin and Richard leaning over her to take off the ring.

It was an unpleasant image and I couldn't get it out of my mind. So much so that it haunted my dreams in a vague intangible way and I woke up in the darkness trembling. I think I had thought that I was lying in my coffin and Richard was saying, "All right. We mustn't forget the ring. I shall need that for the next one."

I found it difficult to sleep after that.

The betrothal had taken place at the beginning of April

and then the preparations began, for the wedding was to be in May.

"A month or so before your eighteenth birthday," said Richard.

I couldn't help remembering my last birthday when we had been out in the fields near Trystan Priory. I mustn't forget it was Bersaba's birthday too. It was then that our mother had said, "Next birthday will be different. There will be parties and suchlike." And she had given us our journals to write and I had started immediately. Bersaba had said she would only write in hers when she had something important to write about. Poor dear Bersaba! She would have something to write about now. What a lot had happened in a short year! There could not be a better example of the truism that life was made up of light and shadow. The tragedy of Bersaba's sickness; the joy of my marriage. I embroidered a bag for her which I would send for her birthday. It was exquisite and I had put a good deal of work in it. She would love it for that reason because she would know that with my approaching wedding I should have so much to do and yet I still set time aside for her.

The sudden April showers and brief sunshine were giving way to more settled weather. May was a beautiful month that year—more so than usual, I was sure. The scent of the hawthorn hung heavy in the air and I thought it intoxicating. But perhaps it was my happiness after all. Ana was working hard for me. Carlotta had graciously allowed her to do so. Poor Mab was not very good. She was in a twitter of excitement about the coming marriage and thought herself to be so lucky to have been chosen to come to London with me, where so many exciting things could happen.

We went frequently into the city to buy what was needed. I began to enjoy these jaunts and forgot the unpleasantness I had experienced there. I was never foolish enough to leave whoever I was with and I did avert my eyes when I saw a pillory, but I never saw that grim spectacle again.

There seemed always to be something going on. I saw people dance round the maypole on May Day and crown the May Queen; I saw lovers embracing in the fields on sunny afternoons; I heard their laughing as they shouted to each other—apprentices and serving girls. I saw them on the river and arm in arm in the streets. I watched the traveling peddlers—and they often came to Pondersby Hall and spread their packs for us to see—calling their wares as they went through the streets. I listened to the chat between them and their customers. I would watch the corn-cutter, who in addition to dealing with painful feet could pull out a troublesome tooth, and this usually attracted a crowd to watch the anguish of the poor victim. There were jugglers and fiddlers and often there would be cockfighting in a corner of the street, a practice which filled me with disgust, but I never had to see the actual contest because so many crowded around to witness the so-called sport that I could not have looked in had I wanted to.

Then of course there were the shops—the object of our visits—and so much beautiful cloth to examine, so many ribbons to choose. Ana and I would spend hours in this fascinating occupation. She said it was all part of the preparations for marriage. Perhaps there should have been other preparations. If my mother had been with me, or Bersaba, I could have talked to them. Perhaps I could have learned . . . But I should learn gradually, and Richard would be kind, respecting my ignorance.

But how I longed to talk to Bersaba.

The time was passing. It would soon be my wedding day.

I saw little of Richard. He was with his company, he told us. The Scottish unrest was occupying much of his time. There could be trouble with these Covenanters.

It seemed plausible enough when he explained to me. "You see, the Covenant has always been important to Scotland. It was started nearly a hundred years ago when the Scots feared a revival of Popery. This year the King wished to introduce the English liturgy into Scotland and they have revived the Covenant."

"It seems to me," I said, "that there has to be perpetual trouble over religion."

"It has always been so," he answered. "And this means of course that we have to be watchful of events on the border. If there should be trouble I shall have to be ready."

I understood that, though I was sorry that it meant he could not enjoy these exciting preparations with me.

Carlotta came to my room one evening. I wondered why she always chose the evenings just before I was about to retire for this sort of thing. I fancied her object was to disturb me because she resented my happiness. I was becoming more and more convinced that she had taken up with Bastian because she had known that Bersaba and he were friendly. Of course that was just a childish friendship but nonetheless important to them because of it.

There was a strain of evil in Carlotta, something that loved mischief. I began to wonder whether she was not after all a witch.

She sprawled in the chair and surveyed me.

"We don't see very much of our bridegroom," she said.

"Mine do you mean?"

"*The* bridegroom, shall we say. I was wondering whether we can be so sure that he will be yours."

"I don't know what you mean."

"I have been thinking about this since I heard and I wondered whether I should warn you."

"Warn me? What about?"

"I heard the story. It created quite a stir at the time. It was five years ago."

"What story?"

"He was going to marry, you know, and changed his mind."

I felt myself go cold with fear. "What are you trying to tell me?"

"Our Richard was married when he was quite young, and she died."

"You're not suggesting—"

"Suggesting what?"

"That she . . . that he . . ."

"That he dispatched her? I never heard that. It's an interesting idea. There is something odd about him. He's a cold fish. I never could abide cold men."

"I thought you were rather interested in him at one time . . . when you thought he preferred you."

"I did think he was normal then—just a little quiet. But what I want to tell you is that he changed his mind before. He was betrothed, the arrangements were going ahead, just as now, and then a few weeks before the wedding . . . it was all off."

"Why?"

"That's the mystery. There was no wedding. Whether she discovered some dark secret or whether he decided to jilt her, we don't know. It was all a great mystery. But I think you ought to be *prepared*."

"Thank you. It's kind of you to be so considerate."

"Well, it would be most awkward if it happened again, wouldn't it?"

"We want a quiet wedding."

"Of course. I think you're wise . . . in the circumstances." She stood up and regarded me almost superciliously. "I just thought I ought to warn you."

"That's so kind," I murmured.

And she was gone. Was it true? I wondered. No, it couldn't be. He wanted this marriage. Why should he have suggested it otherwise? Carlotta was just piqued because he had preferred marriage with me to a flirtation with her. To be ignored was something she could not tolerate and she persisted in denigrating anyone who did that.

But I was uneasy, for I had to admit that the nearer I came to marriage the more did I realize that Richard was by no means the conventional bridegroom.

Mab was a little envious of Ana. She found fault with her needlework and grumbled that she could have done it so much better herself. She was disappointed because I did not make a confidante of her. Mab, I was coming to the conclusion, was really rather a silly girl. She was constantly trying to turn the conversation to babies.

"Oh, Mistress Angelet," she would murmur, "I can't wait for the first little baby. I do hope you won't have to wait so long as your poor mother did."

Then she talked about her sister Emily, who had had a child out of wedlock.

"Emily was like that," she said. "She couldn't leave the men alone and nor could they leave her. She got caught she did . . . caught good and proper. And me mother says that if she don't take care she'll have another to feed before long. I said to her once, 'Em, you are silly. You'll get caught again.' And she said that she couldn't help it if she did. It was just her way. She couldn't say no."

Mab would look at me speculatively and I became angry with her, one of the main reasons being that I was so ignorant of that side of marriage and indeed a little fearful of it.

Richard returned and came at once to Pondersby Hall to see me.

I went down to the parlor. He took my hands and kissed them, and as soon as I saw him I was happy, for my doubts vanished and I realized how uneasy Carlotta had made me with her hints that I might be treated as someone else had been and the marriage canceled at the last moment.

I said, "You still want to marry me, Richard, don't you?"

He looked at me in astonishment. "Why on earth do you say that?"

I laid my face against his coat. "I don't know. I'm just so happy I'm afraid it's too good to be true."

He lifted my face and looked at me intently.

"You are a dear good child," he said. "It is small wonder that I love you."

"And we'll be happy, won't we?"

"We must make sure that we are."

"I will make sure."

"Do you doubt that I will?"

"No, no. Not when you are here."

"You must never doubt me . . . particularly when I am not there. You do understand, don't you, that I shall be away from home for long periods?"

"I do understand it. It was something my mother had to endure."

"So you are prepared for it?"

"Yes, and . . . perhaps we shall have some children so that I shan't be lonely."

There was a silence and, looking up into his face, I saw a strange expression there which I could not understand. But then he took my hand and gripped it hard.

"It is what I want," he said. "Yes, I do want that very much."

"I hope . . . I shall please you," I said.

He put me from him suddenly and, going to the door, opened it abruptly.

Mab fell into the room.

I felt very angry with her, for she had clearly been listening at the keyhole.

"What are you doing, Mab?" I demanded.

She rose awkwardly to her feet and stood there not knowing what to do and I saw that her eyes, which had been alight with curiosity a moment before, were now apprehensive.

I said, "Go away. I will speak to you later."

She ran out, shutting the door after her. I looked at Richard in dismay, for I saw that he was very angry.

"That girl will have to go," he said. "We will not have her at Far Flamstead."

"Go?" I stammered.

"Yes. Send her back to your home. I'll not have her prying . . . listening at keyholes."

"She's a silly girl. I'll give her a good scolding and warn her."

"No, Angelet," he said sternly. "That is not enough. I will not have her in Far Flamstead. She is to be dismissed."

"She will be heartbroken. I know her well. She has been with my family since she was about eleven. My mother thought she was the most suitable one to send with me."

"She is most unsuitable and I will not have her in my house."

"It was just a moment's folly, I know. She is a silly frivolous girl and so interested in us. . . ."

He said, "Angelet, you will dismiss that girl. Let her go back when the next messengers come with letters."

He was adamant. It was in the nature of a command, and although I knew it was rather harsh treatment for poor silly Mab, I knew I must do as he wished for I greatly feared to displease him.

I said, "All right. She shall go, but it will be hard for her . . . and I have grown used to her. She was just beginning to know how to do my hair."

He stroked my hair gently. "We will find you a maid who is better at it. Tell her that she must prepare to go at once."

I said I would and tried to dismiss the matter. But it had me uneasy. I wondered why he should have been so insistent about a rather trivial matter.

Then the thought flashed into my head. Listening at doors! Prying! It almost seemed as though he were afraid Mab might discover something.

Could it be that there was something to hide at Far Flamstead?

Poor Mab was indeed heartbroken. She sobbed bitterly when I told her she was to go back. At first she stared at me in astonishment.

"But Mistress Angelet, I've always been with you. You couldn't send me away now."

I said, "You'll have to go back to what you were doing before I left. My mother will allow you to do that."

"But what have I *done*, mistress?"

I tried to whip myself to an anger which matched that of Richard.

"You were caught listening at the keyhole. It was a foolish, wicked thing to do."

"I didn't mean no harm. I just wanted to know that it was all right for you. He seems so . . . so . . ."

I shook her a little. "So, so what?" I demanded.

"He seemed so cold like . . . not like a husband. I was just worried about you and wanted to be sure. . . ."

"Don't make excuses, Mab," I told her. "You were caught and now you must pay for your folly."

I wanted so much to forgive her. To tell her not to be silly and not listen at doors again. That was what my mother would have done.

I even tried to speak to Richard again about it, but I saw his face harden when I mentioned her name, and I dared go no farther.

When the next batch of letters arrived I read them avidly and poor Mab left for Cornwall when the messengers returned there.

The Folly

SO, on the tenth of May of the year sixteen hundred and forty, I was married to Richard Tolworthy. As he had wished—and so had I—it was a quiet wedding. Sir Gervaise gave me away, Carlotta attended, and it took place in the small church at Pondersby. Several of the servants sat at the back of the church and after the ceremony we went back to the Hall for a meal.

It was not elaborate, for Richard had insisted on this, and when it was over in the early afternoon he wanted us to set out for Far Flamstead.

It did occur to me that it was rather unusual that I should never have seen my new home, which was not after all so very far distant from Pondersby Hall. I had suggested that I should visit it and Richard had been in agreement, but looking back I now realized that something always had happened to prevent the visit.

At first he had said he was having a certain amount of renovation done for me and he did not wish me to see it in an unfinished state; and on the other occasion when I had been going, he had been called away and there was a postponement.

"Never mind," he had said, "if there is something you don't like you can alter it afterward."

I was beginning to see that my husband had a gift for making the unusual seem normal. It was something to do with the manner in which he dealt with it. I had learned through Mab that he did not like emotional scenes, and I was doing my best to be the sort of wife he wished me to be, which I suppose was a very good resolution to have made at the beginning of one's married life.

It was early afternoon when we left Pondersby. We took with us two grooms with saddle horses containing certain things I should need. The rest of my baggage, the wardrobe I had been gathering together and which formed my trousseau, would arrive within the next few days.

Richard did not speak very much as we rode along, but I sensed in him a certain contentment as though something which had caused him apprehension was now settled satisfactorily. I felt very tender toward him and I was happy because I knew that whatever awaited me in my new home, of one thing I was certain and that was that I loved my husband.

As the afternoon wore on and we had left the familiar countryside behind us the scenery seemed to change—but perhaps that was my mood. I noticed wild roses in the hedgerows, and the purple loosestrife growing by a stream reminded me of the days when Bersaba and I used to go out and pick armfuls of it.

We walked our horses, for the road was rough and stony and my husband said to me, "How quiet you are, Angelet. It is not like you."

"It is a solemn occasion," I reminded him.

"A happy one, I trust, for you."

"I have never been happier."

"Is there nothing more you would ask for?"

"Oh, yes. I should have liked to see my mother and my sister and for you to know them."

"As I shall in time, I trust."

We had come to the village of Hampton and we stopped there at an inn where Richard said we would refresh ourselves. We were immediately offered a private room and served with ale and partridge pie, which looked delicious, but I was not hungry and I don't think Richard was either.

"We are not far off now," he told me and I wondered why if that were so we had stopped and it suddenly occurred to me that he was in no hurry for us to reach our home.

It was evening when Far Flamstead came into sight.

"There," said Richard. "Your home, my dear."

I could only stare at it. It was large—larger than Pondersby

Hall—red brick and E-shaped with its central part and east and west wings. I saw several outbuildings and the green sward all around it.

"It's beautiful," I said.

He was pleased.

"I hope you will grow to love it. My brother lives in Flamstead Castle in Cumberland where my family have lived for generations. This was built later and we called it Far Flamstead because so many miles separated it from the old home."

"That's interesting," I said. "So your younger brother took the castle and you Far Flamstead."

"As a soldier I needed to be in the south. It works very well."

As we came nearer the house I noticed that it was surrounded by a shallow moat which was crossed by a bridge. Looking up, I saw how impressive was the central block; above the gateway was a window with eight-light windows—a sort of lookout because from those windows one would be able to see a party approaching for some distance. I wondered if we had been watched. On either side of the central tower were the projecting octagonal towers of the east and west wings.

We passed through the gateway and were in a courtyard bounded on three sides by brick walls with two corner turrets.

As we entered the courtyard a man appeared. He bowed to us and Richard said, "This is Jesson. Jesson, your mistress."

"Welcome to Far Flamstead, my lady," said the man; he had a sharp clipped voice and there was something in his bearing which told me that he was an old soldier.

"Are they prepared?" asked Richard, dismounting and helping me to do the same.

"Yes, sir," answered Jesson. "We have been awaiting your arrival since late afternoon."

Richard took me by the arm and we went through a door into a hall. The first thing I noticed were the people there, standing in a line waiting to receive us and give the traditional greeting of the household to the new mistress.

There were eight of them—not so many for such a large house, I supposed—three women, I noticed, and five men.

"We have ridden far and are tired," said Richard, "but I must first present you to my wife." He turned to me. "Jesson you have already met. Mrs. Cherry."

A plump woman came forward and curtsied. I thought her name suited her, for she was somewhat rotund and her cheeks had the reddish tinge of a ripe cherry.

"Mrs. Cherry is the housekeeper, and Cherry her husband." A man came forward.

"Cherry served with me at one time before he received a wound in his leg. He now serves me here at Far Flamstead."

There were two women—one in her mid-thirties, I imagined, and one slightly younger. They were Meg and Grace Jesson, daughters of the man who had been in the courtyard.

The others were brought forward and presented to me but I forgot their names. I could not help feeling that I was inspecting an army parade. It was faintly amusing.

"Now," said Richard, "you have met them all. We will go to our rooms and then we will eat, for you must be hungry."

I was very much aware of eight pairs of eyes studying me intently, which was natural. They must all have been agog with curiosity to see whom their master had married. They seemed relieved, I fancied, and that would no doubt be because of my youth.

The hall was lofty, some fifty feet in length with the hammerbeam kind of roof that was at Pondersby; the floor consisted of marble slabs; the walls were whitewashed and an array of banners and trophies hung there with a suit of armor at either end. A large refectory table stood in the center, and of the same oak were the companion benches on either side. Pewter implements had been placed on the table and I was immediately aware of the high polish on tables and benches and how the armory shone.

The servants had fallen back, their eyes following me as Richard led me along the hall to a staircase. We mounted this and came to a gallery along which we passed and, mounting yet another staircase, we came to what was to be our bedchamber.

I confess to a shiver of apprehension as I was led into this room and my eyes fell on the big four-poster bed; this was draped in crimson velvet and the counterpane was of the same colored satin.

Richard shut the door and I was alone with him.

He took off my cape and threw it on the bed.

"That which you will need tonight will have been brought by the pack horses," he said. "Tomorrow the rest of your baggage will come."

"Yes," I said, "I shall have adequate."

He took me by the shoulders and turned my face up to his.

"You tremble," he said. "Are you afraid?"

"No . . . not really. I'm just hoping that I shall not disappoint you."

"You are such a very dear child," he said.

"But I must stop being a child, must I not, now that I am your wife?"

"You will always be yourself," he said, "and that is what I ask."

I said, "The house is a little—"

"Yes?" he prompted.

"Well, overpowering. So many menservants."

"That is because I am a soldier. They have all served with me at one time. The country is not very good to soldiers who can no longer be of use to it."

"So you brought them here?"

"They are all men whom I can trust."

"There will only be four women in this house, then?"

"Do you want more? You can choose either Meg or Grace Jesson for your personal maid. Give yourself a day or two to decide which."

"What are their duties now?"

"I don't know. Mrs. Cherry and Cherry work that out. But you only have to ask for what you want, you know."

"Everything seems very well looked after."

He smiled. "That is army training, I'll swear. Now you would like to wash and we will eat. It has been a strange day for you."

"The only wedding day I ever had," I said lightly, and then wished I hadn't, for my words might have reminded him that he had had two—and almost a third if Carlotta was right.

He left me for a while, and alone in the bedchamber I peered about me. It was a large room and contained a carved chest, a court cupboard, several chairs, a table on which stood a mirror, and two heavy pewter candlesticks.

I tried to avert my eyes from the great four-poster bed, for I had to admit to myself that I was very uneasy about what would be expected of me. I felt so stupidly ignorant, but I supposed all I should have to do was submit. It seemed to me then that I heard Bersaba's mocking laughter. How strange! But a room like this would make one imaginative. I couldn't help thinking of all the husbands and wives who had slept here and he of course would have shared that bed with his first wife.

I went to the deep bay window set in an embrasure. There was a window seat with padded velvet cushions and heavy embroidered curtains which matched the bed hangings. I knelt for a moment on the window seat and looked out. Before me lay a green lawn and, not more than a hundred yards away, though largely hidden by a high wall, the crenellated towers of what looked like a miniature castle.

There was a knock on the door. It was one of the Jesson girls with hot water.

"Master said to bring it, my lady," she said.

"Thank you," I said. "Are you Grace?"

"No, I'm Meg, my lady."

"Thank you, Meg."

I washed my hands and as I did so Grace came in with the light baggage I had brought with me, so I was able to change my riding clothes for a gown, and when I had done this Richard appeared to conduct me to the meal which he said was waiting for us.

Together we went to the dining room.

"I shall lose myself here," I commented.

"At first perhaps," he said. "But there will be plenty to show you the way."

The dining room was lofty, with a beautiful carved ceiling. By now the candles had been lighted although it was not yet quite dark. The walls were covered in tapestry with predominating blues and reds depicting the War of the Roses on one side and what Richard told me was the battle of Bosworth Field on the other. He said I might wish to do some tapestry myself as I was fond of needlework.

"It will be something for you to do while I'm away," he added.

"You will not go yet," I said fearfully and tried to imagine myself alone in this big house with strangers.

"I think not, but a soldier always has to be ready when the call comes."

I felt it was a warning. "Tomorrow when daylight comes it will all look different," I thought; and I suddenly thought of Trystan Priory, where everything seemed suddenly homely.

Supper was served by Jesson and two menservants, which seemed strange because we always had girls to serve at home and so did they at Pondersby Hall. But I had to admit that everything was done with the greatest precision and efficiency.

There was cold duck and beef and mutton and venison together with pies, which I was not hungry enough to tackle. Richard urged me to take a little of the malmsey wine which was served in fine Venetian glasses, and as I drank I felt less apprehensive. As the darkness fell and I smiled across the table at my husband, his face mellowed by the candlelight, I told myself I was going to be happy. I thought, "It is all so strange

161

and I am young and so inexperienced and Trystan Priory, my mother, and Bersaba seem so very far away. . . ."

The meal was over and I went back to our bedchamber. My nightgown had been laid out on the bed and I undressed and looked out the window.

There was a half-moon and it was a clear night as I stood there and saw again the towers of the miniature castle. It looked ghostly in moonlight and if I hadn't seen it by the light of day I should have thought it wasn't quite real.

As I stood there I felt a pair of hands on my shoulders.

I swung round, alarmed. Richard was standing behind me.

"I startled you," he said.

"A little. What is the castle out there? Is it a castle? It looks like a toy one."

"That," he said, "is Flamstead Folly."

"What does that mean?"

He took my hand and stood beside me. "It means that an ancestor of mine, my great grandfather, had it built."

"A little castle?"

"He thought it would be amusing. It was going to be much bigger, but he found the building too costly so he contented himself with a small one because he had vowed he would have a castle. It was called a Folly because it was rather a foolish thing to do."

"I must explore it!" I cried.

"No, don't. You see, a fairly high wall has been built around it. That's because it's not safe. It was not very securely built. One of these days I shall have to pull it down. But don't go near it. You mustn't. Promise me you won't."

"Of course I'll promise. You sound so . . . earnest."

"Well, I don't want a ton of bricks to descend upon this defenseless head."

"I'm sorry. It looks . . . exciting."

"You must not go there. I insist. Promise me."

"I already have."

"Remember it, please."

His face was stern as it had been when he had insisted on my getting rid of Mab.

"Come," he said, "it's cold here."

He drew me toward the bed.

I awoke to sunshine and remembered where I was. I put out my hand and felt that I was alone.

I sat up in bed. The curtains about the bed were half-drawn. I shivered with a sort of thankfulness because I had survived the night. I did not want to think about it. There was no one with whom I could discuss it. Perhaps I might have done so with Bersaba. I wondered whether I were pregnant. I should love to have a child. That was the side of marriage which I should enjoy, and the very fact that I expressed my feelings in that way was in itself an admission that there was another side which I did not enjoy.

I pulled the bell rope, which was the signal for Grace to bring my hot water. I washed and put on my riding habit and went downstairs.

Richard was in the dining room having breakfast. I found it difficult to look at him, I felt so embarrassed. But he rose and, putting his arms about me, kissed me.

"Good morning, my dearest," he said warmly, and a little glow of happiness came to me.

"Perhaps I was all right after all," I thought, and my spirits rose.

"I see you are dressed for riding," he said.

"I have only my riding habit and the gown I wore last night."

"Your things will be here today. Grace or Meg will unpack them for you. Today I am going to show you over the house. Then you won't lose yourself. And perhaps we will ride around the neighborhood a little. Would you like that?"

"I should love it." I was happy now, assuring myself that everything was going to be all right after all.

During the day I began to think I had worried unnecessarily and I told myself that the night was a long way off and that Richard gave no sign that his affection for me had diminished.

He was very anxious to show me the house and this he did. There was no doubt that he loved the place. I followed him up the staircase lighted by small quatrefoil oeilets, which he pointed out to me and showed me how the soffits formed a continuous spiral vault which he said was quite unusual. Lovingly he stroked the molded brick handrail and told me that a great deal of assiduous care had gone into the construction of this house. The castle in Cumberland had been originally built as a fortress and then added to over five centuries, but Far Flamstead had been built as a place for people to live in in comfort.

In the gallery were portraits of his ancestors. "I had some of them brought here from the castle," he told me. "You see from these that there has always been a strong military tradition in our family."

He took me to the chapel with its linenfold-ended pews and barrel-vaulted ceiling. The wooden ribs of the ceiling were engraved with Tudor roses. It struck a chill into me and as our footsteps echoed on the glazed tiles a feeling of foreboding came over me and I felt a quick rush of nostalgia for the Priory and my family.

It was so insistent that for a few panic-stricken moments I would have been ready to run out of the house, leap onto a horse, and gallop off in the direction of the southwest.

"What's the matter?" asked Richard.

"I don't know. It's so cold in here."

"Yes, and too dark."

"I have the feeling that a lot has happened here."

"A priest was murdered at the altar there. One of my ancestresses was a Catholic during Elizabeth's reign. She had a priest here in secret. Her son discovered him at mass and murdered him while he stood there with the chalice in his hands."

"How . . . terrible. You think he haunts the chapel . . . that priest—"

"He died instantly. That was the end of him."

"Do you believe people come back to haunt a place where they have died violently?"

"I believe that is nonsense. Just think of all the people who have died violently. The world would be full of ghosts."

"Perhaps it is."

"Oh, come, my dear, you are fanciful. And you don't like the chapel. We don't have a resident priest now and I don't think the King could bring in laws against the Catholics since his wife is such an ardent one."

"But he is not so kind toward Puritans."

"Ah, that is another matter."

"It's intolerance just the same."

"Of course it is. Do you give a lot of thought to these matters?"

"Not really. Only when we were in Cornwall there was periodical outcries against witches."

"That persists not only in Cornwall but all over the country and through the ages."

"But if there is such a thing as witchcraft and people want to practice it, why should they not?"

"It's worship of the Devil, and witches are said to ill-wish and often bring about the deaths of those who offend them."

"There are good ones, I believe . . . white witches. They

understand the properties of herbs and cure people with them. But they suffer often just the same."

"There will always be unfairness."

"And," I went on, "those who follow the Catholic faith or are Puritans harm no one."

"That's true enough, but it seems to me these different sects all wish to impose their will on others and that's where the conflict comes in."

"One day perhaps there will be a world where people allow each other to think as they wish."

"I see you are an idealist. Also that you have had enough of the chapel. Come, I shall take you now to the solarium . . . the warm room of the house. I imagine your sitting there on sunny afternoons with your needlework, for you are going to make a tapestry, I know, to hang on the walls and which will last for hundreds of years."

"I should like that."

"You will choose your subject. What will it be?"

"No war," I said. "There is too much war. I don't like it."

"And you married a soldier!"

"I think you are the kind of soldier who fights for the right."

"And I can see that you are going to be a loyal and loving wife."

"I shall do my best, but you will have to be patient with me. I know I have a great deal to learn of . . . er . . . marriage."

"My dearest," he said, "we both may have a good deal to learn."

My spirits lifted in the solarium. It faced south and the sun streamed in through the great semicircular bay window. The hangings were of deep blue with gold fringe and the window seats had cushions of the same rich color. The ceiling was most beautiful, delicately decorated and adorned with pictures of two cherubs floating on a cloud carrying between them the family crest. It was full of light and color and a complete contrast to the cold dank chapel.

Tapestry hung on one side of the wall . . . and here again the subject was battle—that of Hastings this time. Richard told me that it was the family's proud boast that they had come to England with the Conqueror.

From the solarium we went to the King's Chamber, so called because the King himself had spent a night there. The brick fireplace had been put in specially for him. With loving care Richard pointed out the four-centered chamfered arch and jambs and the beautiful carving round the sides. The King had given his permission for the royal arms to be placed over the door.

"Do you think he will come again?" I asked.

"It's not unlikely."

I tried to picture myself as hostess to the King and Queen and failed.

"The King's manners are impeccable," said Richard. "He would always be charming so you would need to have no fear if he did. But he is too concerned now with state matters to come visiting." Then he turned to me and, drawing me to him, kissed my forehead tenderly. "You disturb yourself unnecessarily, Angelet," he told me. "You believe you will be inadequate. Let me tell you this . . . in a short while you will be asking yourself what there was to fear."

I knew that he was telling me that everything would be well between us and I was suddenly as happy as I had been when he had first asked me to marry him and marriage seemed to me to be the most romantic adventure in the world.

I was almost blithe as I was conducted through the house. I was shown bedrooms so numerous that I lost count of them. Many of them were named after the colors predominating in them—the Scarlet Room, the Blue Room, the Gold Room, the Silver Room, the Gray Room, and so on. Then there were the Paneled Room and the Tapestry Room and the Pages' Room where china of all kinds was kept.

There was one door which Richard passed by and I asked what it was.

"Oh, just like all the others," he said. "There is really nothing special about it."

He opened the door. It seemed to me that he did so almost reluctantly, and because of that I felt a great urge to see what the room contained.

He was right, there was nothing special about it. It contained a table and a few chairs and a very large court cupboard with linenfold sides.

"What do you call this room?" I asked.

"I think it has been known as the Castle Room."

"Oh, I see why. You get a good view of the Folly here."

I went to the window and stood there. He was beside me and I sensed his apprehension. I knew then that he had not been going to show me this room. The same sort of uneasiness which had enveloped me in the chapel returned to me. From the window there was a better view of the castle than I had seen anywhere else. The walls looked almost white in the sunshine. It was indeed a high wall which surrounded it, and of course this room would be called the Castle Room because it was high up and gave a good view of the miniature battlements.

"It was a pity that high wall was built," I said. "It looks not so old as the castle."

"How observant you are. How can you tell?"

"It just looks newer. When was it built?"

He hesitated. "Oh . . . er, about ten years ago."

"Then you built it!"

"Yes, I ordered it to be built."

"Whatever for?"

"Perhaps I wanted to shut out the Folly."

"Wouldn't it have been easier to pull it down . . . particularly as it's crumbling and you don't like it?"

"Did I say I didn't like it?"

"You implied it . . . calling it a Folly and all that."

"It was not I who called it a Folly. It was called that before I was born."

"I suppose you didn't like to pull down what your ancestor had taken such pains to build, so you had the wall made to shut it out to a certain extent and prevent people's going there as it might be dangerous."

"Yes," he said, "that's so." Then, deliberately, he turned me away from the window.

He had a rather curt way of conveying that he wished a subject closed and I was learning to take his hints. My husband was a man who expected unquestioning obedience. As a commanding soldier I supposed that was natural.

I began to examine the room. I said, "It has a lived-in look."

"A lived-in look! What do you mean by that? It's rarely used."

"Then I'm wrong. What is kept in the court cupboard?"

"I don't know."

"Shall we see?"

"Oh, come, there are more interesting things to look at. I want to take you up to the roof."

"The roof. That sounds exciting."

He shut the door of the Castle Room firmly and led me to the newel stairs. The air was warm yet fresh. I stood up there breathing it in with relish. I could see over the gardens to the wooded hills and beyond a house in the distance. I examined the detailed ornamentation of the turrets and looked for the Folly, but I could not see it from this side of the house.

On the way down we passed through the long gallery and I paused to examine the portraits. There was a fine one of Richard himself and next to him the portrait of a young woman. I knew without asking that she was his first wife, and I could not help a great curiosity. She was pretty and very young, even younger than I was. Her pretty fair hair was dressed high above her head, which made her face look small; she had large appealing blue eyes. There was an expression in her face which fascinated me. It was almost as though she were pleading to be helped, as though she were afraid of something.

Richard said, "Yes, that's Magdalen."

"Magdalen," I repeated.

"My first wife."

"Was she very young when she died?"

"Nineteen."

I had the same uneasy feeling that had assailed me before. I suppose I couldn't help imagining that girl with him and I knew I should go on doing so.

"Was she very ill?"

"She died in childbirth."

"So there was a child."

"It was a double tragedy."

Again that secret command: *We shall not talk of this.*

"Well," I thought. "I understand that." He then led me down to the outhouses, and I saw what a fine stable he kept. He showed me the bolting house, the washing house, and the winery. I was aware that I had become mistress of a fine establishment.

"I said I shall write and tell my sister and my mother all about my new home."

"You must do that," he said.

"And when my sister is well they must come and visit me."

"Indeed they must," he answered warmly and I was happy contemplating their arrival.

"How proud I shall be to show them everything," I said.

He pressed my arm, well pleased.

That afternoon we went riding, for he wished to show me the countryside. He did not have a large estate, as the family land was in Cumberland and Far Flamstead was merely a soldier's country house. The grounds were extensive enough, consisting of the gardens, the paddocks, and the copse of fir trees.

We supped together as we had on the previous night and as before we shared the velvet curtained bed.

For two weeks we lived to a sort of pattern. Each morning he worked in the library and I was left to myself, when I would wander through the gardens, which consisted of ten acres, so there was plenty for me to see. There was a walled rose garden and a pond garden, a kitchen garden and a herb garden. I wrote letters to my mother and to Bersaba—telling the former the details of the flowers we grew here and how the colder drier climate seemed to affect certain things. It was easy writing to her. It was less so writing to Bersaba. I used to think often of her lying in bed, where she still had to spend a certain amount of time, regaining her strength, my mother called it, so I was afraid to write too glowingly of my happiness, which was certainly there, but it is the nature of happiness to be elusive. I had discovered that it stayed usually for a few fleeting moments and, if it remained for a day, that was rare. The nights hung over me not exactly frightening but bewildering. I had never thought about this side to marriage, and it always seemed to me that the man I met behind the red curtains of the four-poster bed was a stranger—not the one who was so noble, dignified, and commanding by day.

I loved him dearly. I never had any doubt of that, and the fact that at times he seemed rather remote in his daytime personality made him more than ever attractive to me. I used to fancy I could hear my mother's explaining, "You were very young to marry. Had you been at home I should have talked to you and warned you of what you must expect. You would have been prepared. But as it happened so suddenly, so unexpectedly, you are groping in the dark a little. Have no fear. You love him and he loves you. You are a little in awe of him because he holds a high position in the country. Well, it is a good thing to respect your husband."

I used to wonder if she had felt thus with my father.

I thought if Bersaba were here I could talk to her. But I could not bring myself to write my innermost thoughts even to her.

In the afternoons, when Richard's work was done, we would ride together. He delighted in showing me the countryside. He had a great feeling for nature and he loved trees. He would point them out to me and tell me about them; and there were a great variety round Flamstead. It was like a lesson in botany to ride with Richard. He would pause by a stream where the willow trees grew. "See how they love the moist damp earth," he pointed out. "Look, their roots are almost in the water. This is a male tree, for the flowers of the male and female are on separate trees. You should see the furry silvery tufts breaking out in the spring and the males have golden-tipped stamens and the females green. When they're in full seed they look as though they are covered in tufts of white wool."

He would point out the Scots pines and the yews.

"Look at that yew. It has been there for over a hundred years. Doesn't that give you pause to think? Imagine what changes it has seen. It was there when Queen Elizabeth first came to the throne and before that when her father was dissolving the monasteries and cutting us off from Rome."

"There is something rather sinister about yews," I said.

"Well, they are poisonous to cattle."

"There's something witchlike about them. One could imagine their having secret knowledge. But the berries are not poisonous, are they? The birds eat them."

"My dear little Angelet, you see good everywhere. I hope you always will."

He talked at length about the yews; how they grew very slowly and could live for over a thousand years, and the flowers were of distinct sexes and grew on different trees—the male flowers small, round, and yellow, their stamens producing a considerable amount of pollen, the female flowers small green ovoids which grew on the under part of the twigs.

I felt that he was explaining that there was a similarity between nature's laws with flowers and with people. He knew that I was uneasy and he was telling me that I would grow accustomed to what seemed a little strange and alarming to me at first. Hadn't it been happening throughout the world since the Creation, because it was nature's way of replenishing the earth?

I listened avidly and tried to convey to him that I understood and would in time accept life as it was.

He had interesting stories to tell of the trees and said that they were the most beautiful of all nature's creations. There was no time of the year when a tree was not beautiful. In the spring it was a joy with its buds and promise; in the summer it was rich and full; in the autumn the turning color of its leaves was an inspiration to the artist. Best of all was the winter, when its denuded branches could be seen against a winter sky.

"I had not thought you could be so lyrical," I told him.

"I am usually afraid of mockery," he said.

"Not with me."

"Never with you."

I felt happy then.

Then he showed me an aspen—the trembling poplar—and it was fascinating to watch how it quivered in the light breeze.

"It is said that the cross of Christ was made from the wood of an aspen and that ever after it has been unable to rest."

"Do you believe that?" I asked

He shook his head. "The leaves tremble so much because their stems are so long and slender."

"Do you have a logical explanation for everything?"

"I hope so."

I was learning a great deal about him. In the evenings he liked to talk to me about his battles and I tried to learn about them. Oddly enough he had sets of soldiers—tin ones, infantry and cavalry such as children play with. I was astonished when I first saw them. To imagine Richard playing with soldiers was the last thing I would have thought possible. But it was scarcely playing with them. He showed how certain battles had been won or lost, and he would take a large sheet of paper and draw out the battle field and place his soldiers on them.

He would show a rare excitement as he moved the soldiers about. "You see, Angelet, the foot soldiers came along here, but what they didn't know was that the cavalry was lying in wait behind this hill. You see? They were so strategically placed that they were hidden from sight. It was a mistake on the part of the foot commander. He should have sent out spies to assess the enemy's position."

I tried to follow because I was so anxious to please him. It moved me deeply to see him there with his miniature soldiers. It made him seem young and vulnerable in a way.

I wished that I could have been interested in the battles, but I could only pretend to be. I had always hated talk of fighting. My mother used to say that wars were made by the folly of ambitious men and although they brought temporary gain to one side it was rarely worth having. Of course they had still talked now and then of the defeat of the Armada, but that was a sea battle and we had been fighting for our lives and our freedom then.

So I would sit there in the evenings while he played out his battles and engaged me in a game of chess—a game at which I had never excelled. Bersaba and I used to play together and I so rarely defeated her that it was a red letter day when I did.

171

After the game was over Richard would sit back and survey the board and tell me where I had gone wrong and often he would put the pieces back and want us to start again at that point.

He was born to command and to teach I suppose, and he seemed to take a special delight in instructing me. Sometimes I thought he looked upon me as a pupil—a beloved and cherished pupil, but one nonetheless who needed a good deal of instruction.

I did not mind. I was happy, desperately wanting to please him. I had to remember that I would seem such a child to him. I was going to try to grow up, to enjoy the things that he enjoyed, to be able to plan my chess moves as far ahead as he could and to understand why the infantry should have gone forward instead of remaining where they were—or vice versa.

So this life went on for those two weeks. It was a sort of routine—a tender teacher with his pupil.

Then one day a messenger came. He was in the uniform of the King's Guard, and he had a letter for Richard.

This captain and Richard were closeted in the library for a long time and then Richard sent one of the servants for me.

I went down to the library and Richard smiled at me—rather sternly, I thought.

He presented the captain to me and said, "I shall be leaving tomorrow, Angelet. It is necessary for me to go north for a brief spell. Trouble is expected on the border."

I knew I must not show my disappointment. He had told me that a soldier's wife must be prepared for sudden calls such as this, so I tried to be the wife he would have wished me to and said, 'What would you like me to tell the servants to prepare?" My voice was a little tremulous but I was rewarded with a look of approval.

The next day he left Far Flamstead.

The house seemed different without him. I had the sudden odd feeling that it was secretly amused because I was now at its mercy. I had always been fanciful; I lacked that logical mind which Richard had cultivated. He had left in the afternoon and I went right up to the roof and watched him until I could see him no more. Then I descended the newel staircase and as I came down I paused at the door of the Castle Room. My hand was on the latch but I hesitated. He had not wanted me to go into that room for some reason. What would he think of me if I went in within half an hour of his departure? Resolutely I went back to our bedroom.

I stood at the window and looked out. I could just see the pseudobattlements of the castle, and I wondered why he had looked so stern when he had told me I was not to go there. I turned my back on the view and, sitting on the window seat, looked at the four-poster bed. I should sleep there alone tonight, and it was no use telling myself I was not relieved because my feelings were too strong to be denied.

"I shall get used to that," I told myself. And I thought of the lessons of the trees and the laws of nature and I fell to wondering if soon I would know that I was to have a child. There was no doubt of my feelings about that. I imagined the letters I would write home.

It was strange eating alone but I felt that the attitude of the servants had changed and that I was not served with the same military precision. Another facet of Richard's character was that he could not endure unpunctuality. He would arrive exactly at the appointed time and on one or two occasions when I had been a few minutes late his expression had shown his disapproval although he had said nothing.

After supper the evening seemed long. I went to the library. Most of the volumes dealt with military matters. I smiled wryly. "Well," I told myself, "you did marry a soldier."

Then to bed.

How big the bed seemed—how luxurious and comforting. I slept soundly and when I awoke in the morning I felt a sense of desolation because he was not there.

Life, I assured myself, was full of contrasts, light and shadow, pleasure and endurance. During the day I would miss him so much, but I had to admit I was relieved at night.

I spent the morning in the garden as I always did. I ate a solitary dinner, and the afternoon stretched out long before me. Should I ride? If I wanted to go far I would have to take a groom with me just as we always had to at home, so I had no great desire to go.

I found myself climbing the newel staircase to look at the view from the roof, but as I came to the Castle Room the urge came to me to go in and it was so strong that I couldn't resist it. Even as I stood on the threshold I felt uneasy. I suppose because I was doing something of which my husband would not approve.

It was an ordinary room. There were table chairs, a little writing table, and a court cupboard. What was unusual about it? Only the fact that from it there was a good view of the castle.

The castle! This room! Forbidden territory. I wondered

why. As the castle was unsafe, the stone was crumbling, why not remove it? It seemed to be of no use, but it had been put there by an ancestor. But why should this most logical man care about that? I could hear his voice as he bent over his toy soldiers. "The infantry here were useless . . . quite useless. If they had been here now . . . they could have done very good work and that might have been another story."

The site of the castle could be used for another building. Something useful. Or gardens perhaps.

I went to the window seat and, kneeling there, looked out. It really was rather absurd. Just a modest little house really, with grinning gargoyles on its turrets and tiny machicolations from which no boiling oil or hot tar had ever been thrown down on intruders.

I turned back to the room. "Homely," I murmured. Yes, it did look as though it had been lived in. I wondered by whom. I tried to open the doors of the court cupboard. They were locked, but one drawer opened and in it was a key. It was that to the cupboard, so I was able to open the doors. It was full of canvases.

I was interested. Richard had said that he wanted me to start a tapestry and I thought it is just what I needed to fill the hours while he was away, and here were the canvases. I took them out and examined them. They were of varying sizes. I opened another drawer and found a quantity of beautiful colored embroidering silks.

I took out the canvases, spread them out on the table, and as I did so a small worked piece fell out. I picked it up. It was one of those samplers which most children were expected to make at some time as a lesson in patience and diligence. This one was neatly worked and the cross-stitches were minute. I had worked one myself, but Bersaba had cobbled hers and had asked my mother what useful purpose it served to have to sit there making neat little stitches—though Bersaba's were never neat—in the form of the alphabet, numbers one to nine, and a verse from the Bible, "Blessed are the meek: for they shall inherit the Earth" or something like that, followed by one's name and the date. My mother had seen Bersaba's point and she did not have to pursue hers. I finished mine and my mother showed it to my father with great pride.

This was similar.

The letters of the alphabet, the numbers, and:

My lips shall not speak wickedness neither shall my tongue utter deceit.

The price of wisdom is above rubies.

And underneath that, *M. Herriot in the year of our Lord 1619*.

"Magdalen," I thought. She lived here. This was her room. It was for that reason that Richard had not wished me to come here.

Now that Richard was not here, the servants' attitude definitely changed towards me. Mrs. Cherry liked to talk to me, and when I went to the kitchen my stays were longer than they had been.

Richard had wanted me to learn the duties of the mistress of the house and this was something in which I did not need a great deal of tuition, for my mother had always been a woman deeply concerned with domestic matters, and she had brought us up to feel the same. It was one of the areas in which I did better than Bersaba and I was often in our kitchen at Trystan when my mother gave the orders for the day.

So I had no difficulty with Mrs. Cherry, who sensed this and respected me for it.

I made a point of going down to the kitchen each morning to tell her what I would have for dinner and supper. She would sit down with me, purring slightly. "She seems a very contented woman," I thought.

She called me "my lady" as all the servants did and she spoke of the General in hushed whispers which implied great respect.

I asked her if she had done a lot of cooking at any time and she answered yes, she had, for there were occasions when the household was full of guests. "Military gentlemen," she said. "They'd come here and stay for a few days. The General would ride out from Whitehall with them. Big appetites they had, and good drinkers most of them. That's why the General keeps a good cellar. Cherry says we've got some of the finest malmseys and muscatels in England."

"You must tell me what happens on these occasions, Mrs. Cherry. I shall want to make sure that they are a success."

"You can rely on me . . . and Cherry as well as Mr. Jesson, and we see that the rest of them behaves if you know what I mean. There's nothing we wouldn't do for the General."

"It must have been difficult for him without a hostess all these years."

"Well, I reckon you'll be a help, my lady, but I can tell you that these military gentlemen like to eat and drink and fight their wars on the table and they're content. I remember one night when we went in to clear away after supper and there they were . . . my best game pie was some fort or other and my boar's head was the enemy's cavalry, if you please. There they were arranged there all over the table . . . you never saw the like . . . and one of them started making pellets of bread and throwing them around. Shot and shell they was."

I laughed. I could well imagine that.

"Their profession is fighting, Mrs. Cherry, and preserving the country from our enemies."

"I don't doubt that, my lady. But as I was saying . . . give them a good sirloin of beef and a leg of mutton and plenty of pies and plover and partridge and hare or peacock and something good to wash it down with and they're content."

"I am sure everything will work splendidly."

"Oh, you can rely on me, my lady . . . and Cherry. And the rest of them too."

"Thank you."

"There's one thing we have to be ready for. At any time the General can arrive. You can be sure that he'll be back here as fast as he can . . . he being such a newly married man."

"Mrs. Cherry," I said, "how long have you been here?"

"It was before the General . . . er . . . before his first marriage. Cherry got a wound in his leg, and the General, thinking highly of him, and Cherry being unfit for service, he says—the General, I mean—'Well, come along and be my general factotum.' That's what he said, and, 'Mrs. Cherry can be the housekeeper and cook for me.' Cherry jumped at it, and so did I. Always a high regard Cherry had for the General —who wasn't a General then—that came after."

"So you were here at the time of his first marriage."

"Oh, yes. I remember the day he brought her here. We talked of it here in the kitchens only the other day. Your coming reminded us—those of us who were here, of course. I said, 'He's not made a mistake this time,' and Cherry agreed with me."

"A mistake?"

"Oh, I'm speaking out of turn again. Cherry's always telling me I talk too much. Well it's good to be sociable. Well, since you ask, my lady, and it's as well to know what's gone before I reckon, she was a delicate little thing. Too young she was."

"How young?"

"Seventeen—going on for eighteen."

"Oh," I said.

"I know you're a young lady yourself, but she seemed younger if you know what I mean. One of the Herriots. Thought a good deal of themselves, the Herriots did, one of the finest families in the north. The families were in favor and I think that had to be the reason for it. So they were married, and the General—only he wasn't a General then— brought her home. She knew nothing about housekeeping. She was frightened of her own shadow."

"She liked needlework."

"Yes, indeed, my lady. She'd sit up there in the Castle Room and she'd have her tapestry set up there and she'd work away and sometimes you'd hear her singing. She had a pretty voice—oh, a very pretty voice—but not strong, and she'd play the spinet and sing as she played. It was very pretty to hear her. There was one song she used to sing . . ."

"Yes, Mrs. Cherry?" I prompted.

"We were trying to remember the other day because Grace was saying it was funny in a way—oh, not to make you laugh. I don't mean that . . . queer if you like. The song was about her being laid in her grave and she hoped her wrongs wouldn't be held against her. The last line used to go, 'Remember me, but forget what brought me to this state,' which was very odd in a way."

"You mean because she died so young . . . and unexpectedly?"

"Oh, it was expected. She'd been ailing all the time. The midwife—Mrs. Jesson, that was—she died a few years later— spoke to me a few days before and said she didn't think her ladyship could survive."

"She was very ill, then?"

"Every woman must be a bit afraid of her first. It's natural and there's many who give their lives for the sake of the child. It's nature's way. But it ain't natural for anyone to be quite so frightened. That's what I reckon."

"And so she and her baby died."

"It was a sad time, I can tell you. The General he just went away and the house was quiet and dead-like for more than a year."

"How very sad."

"Oh, well, things are different now. You're a strong healthy young lady if you'll forgive me the liberty of remarking on it. I reckon when your time comes . . ."

She looked at me intently, and for the first time I noticed an alertness in her eyes which did not quite accord with her placid rotundity. I supposed that she was naturally interested

177

to know if I had already conceived. Women like her would like to have children in the house.

I stood up suddenly. I felt I had talked enough and I had a sudden notion that Richard would not approve of this chattering with the servants.

So I said, "There is no need to cook a great deal, Mrs. Cherry, as I shall be alone."

"Well, of course not, my lady. You just tell me what you want and I promise you it will be just to your liking."

I had always had a strong curiosity about what was going on around me, and I thought a great deal about Richard's life with Magdalen and wondered whether he had fought out old battles with her and admonished her about her lack of concentrated effort over the chessboard.

I smiled indulgently. Well, he wouldn't have wanted a wife who could beat him, would he? I was not sure. There was a great deal about him that I did not understand. I was glad of it, for it made our future life full of interest and discovery.

I feared I was much more easy to read.

I was longing to work on a canvas. I wished Bersaba were there. She used to draw my pictures for me, making the finished work a joint affair. When people complimented me on the finesse of my stitches I would always draw attention to the design. "That is my sister's work," I would say.

As I went through the canvases I found one of them already mapped out. The design was beautifully drawn, and I thought, "Magdalen was quite an artist." It was a garden scene. There was a pond with lilies on it and I realized at once that it was a study of the pond garden, which was enclosed by a hedge and surrounded by a pleached alley. I studied it intently. What beautiful colors one could use! And then I saw that above the alley there was a glimpse of the towers of the Folly without the tall wall which was now there.

I thought, "I must work that canvas, for it will solve the problem of the drawing." When I found exactly the silks I needed I could not wait to begin, so I sat down there in the room, for it was an ideal spot and I could understand why she had used it so much. The light was exactly what one needed for such work.

As I sat there a strange feeling came over me. I felt at home and as though I were not alone.

"I hope, Magdalen," I said aloud, "you don't mind my using your canvas."

The sound of my voice startled me and I laughed at myself

but at the same time it was almost as though I heard a murmur of contentment as I sat there, selecting my silks. How I loved working with bright colors! The room was full of sunshine and I thought, "Could I make this my room? Richard wouldn't like it. Or did I imagine that? Perhaps he had merely been eager to show me the rest of the house and that was why he had not wanted to linger."

I worked on for a while and then suddenly the room darkened. I turned sharply and went to the window. It was only a dark cloud passing across the face of the sun. There was a tetchy wind and quite a number of clouds had sprung up.

I watched them scurrying across the sky. Now the sun was completely hidden and darkness hung over the towers of the Folly. My mood had changed and I fancied there was a menace in the air. I turned away to look round the room. It was different now it was darker. My canvas lay on the table and the room had lost its homely atmosphere.

It seemed full of menacing warning, and I had the feeling that I wanted to get away.

As I went out I could almost hear Bersaba's voice mocking me as she had when I had wakened sometimes from my nightmares.

"You're too easily afraid, Angelet. Why should you always be afraid? You should make other people afraid of you sometimes."

I hurried down to the room I had shared with Richard.

Meg was there putting my clothes away.

"It's getting really dark, my lady," she said. "I reckon we're in for a storm."

The days began to speed past. A messenger arrived after three weeks with a letter from Richard in which he said he was in the Midlands and would be going north shortly. He believed he might be away for as much as six weeks. "You can be sure that as soon as I can I shall return to you."

That was as near as he could get to saying he loved me, but it was enough; and I knew he would be as good as his word.

In the meantime I would learn all I could about the management of his house and would surprise him. It was a lonely life because no one called. I suppose his friends knew that he was away, and when he was home it would be quite different. They had left us alone for the weeks following our marriage because they would reason that would have been what we wanted; and now they would wait for his return.

I had several talks with Mrs. Cherry, and I was getting to

know the girls, Grace and Meg, very well. I chose Meg as my special maid—well, it was not exactly that I chose her as that she seemed to fall naturally into the role. I learned that Jesson had been with the General as long as the Cherrys had and that he had brought his wife and daughters with him to serve the household. I was glad they were there because without them and Mrs. Cherry it would have been a household of men.

Meg was more talkative than Grace; the younger of the two, she was thirty-seven and told me proudly that she had been born in the January of the year the great Queen died. Grace could say she had actually lived during that glorious reign.

She remembered the previous lady of the house. "Very gentle she was and kind," she told me. "She'd sit up in that room with her stitching just like you're doing. Funny you should like sewing, too. I used to dress her hair for her. She didn't have one of them curly fringes though. Beautiful hair it was and she was as pale as a lily. I used to love to hear her play on the spinet, and when she sang with it that was lovely."

"Did she play and sing for the General?"

"Oh, yes, and when there was company she would, too. But there was something sad about her. And then of course she was going to have the baby—" Meg stopped short.

"Yes," I said, "what was she like then?"

"Oh, I wasn't with her so much then," she said evasively.

"But you used to do her hair."

"Yes . . . but it wasn't the same."

"Was . . . the General very upset about what happened?"

"Oh, very. He went away for a long time and then it must have been a year after the poor lady had gone they started building that wall."

"The wall round the castle, you mean?"

"It darkened the place a bit."

"It was put there because the castle is in a dangerous state, I believe."

"That's right, my lady. We're none of us to set foot there. I reckon one of these days one of them turrets will fall off."

"It ought to be removed."

"Well, that sort of thing's best to be left to crumble on its own, don't you think?"

"No, I should have thought it could be demolished quite simply."

"Oh, yes, but the story is this old ancestor built it and he

180

might get nasty and start haunting the place. Not that that would be much worse. I reckon it's haunted already."

"What makes you say that, Meg?"

"Oh, nothing, my lady, only that that sort of place often is."

"But you said it was haunted. Have you seen anything?"

She hesitated, and a little too long at that, and I saw her press her lips together as though she were determined to prevent words escaping which she should not.

It was clear to me that there was some mystery about the castle, and that someone—it must have been Richard—had given instructions that I was not to be frightened by gossip about it.

The days began to pass tranquilly enough. I worked for several hours on my canvas and felt my fingers itching to work on the castle, so I deserted the pond and stitched happily in the gray wool I had found and which was a fair match for its walls. Then I worked a little on the simples in the gardens, and gathered them and made some of them into possets and potions as my mother had taught me, for there was a good stillroom at Far Flamstead. Mrs. Cherry was very interested and told me that she was "a dab hand" with the simples. She had recently cured Jesson of a pain he had which, between ourselves, she was sure was due to overeating, and Meg swore by her cure for headaches. She was eager to add my mother's recipes to her own. "You're always learning something," she said.

I scarcely ever rode out because I found plenty to do in the house and when I did I went round the paddock where I could be by myself.

Letters came from my mother and Bersaba. My mother's were full of advice as to my housekeeping and telling me how she longed to see me. Bersaba's were brief, so I suppose she was still easily tired. The intimate rapport between us seemed to have been lost. I suppose marriage had changed me, for I felt I had left the world of my childhood far behind me and had to start living a new life, but I was constantly thinking how wonderful it would be to see my mother and my sister.

I did not realize how I was thrown inwardly on my own resources and that I was becoming obsessed by the past, yet desperately as I wanted to please my husband, I had to understand him and learn all I could about him. I therefore had to discover all that was possible of his life before he had known me and one of the most important events in that past must naturally have been his marriage.

Working on Magdalen's canvas, sitting in her room, I felt I was getting to know *her*. She was one of the Herriots—a very well known family. "High places at Court they had," Mrs. Cherry told me. "There were a lot of girls—six of them—and husbands had to be found for them. My lady was the youngest. She was always timid."

Poor little Magdalen, who had been so frightened of the trials of childbirth. I shouldn't be like that, I knew, for if only I could have a dear little baby everything would be worthwhile. After all, the best things in life had to be worked for, suffered for.

I found a great pleasure in being out of doors. On warm days I would take my canvas and sit in the pond garden. It was rather amusing to sit there in the very surroundings which I was stitching onto my canvas. I would wander around a good deal. I watched the flowers opening in the enclosed gardens, and it occurred to me that I might bring in some of my own ideas. I thought, "Perhaps I should tell Richard what I would like to do before consulting with the gardeners." However, there was no harm in making plans.

I found my footsteps led me often in the direction of the castle, but the high wall made it impossible to see it at close quarters. I knew, however, from the Castle Room view, that surrounding the building was a thick growth of fir trees forming themselves into a little wood.

I wondered a great deal about it and what it was like inside. I imagined a tiny guardroom, suits of armor, a little keep, spiral staircases—Castle Paling in miniature.

The fir trees grew thick on both sides of the wall. Some of them could have been quite young trees planted perhaps when the wall was built. They were of the cupressus variety, the kind which grows very quickly, and in a few years a little sprig becomes a bushy tree. The thought occurred to me that they might have been chosen for that purpose.

The more I thought of it the more strange it seemed. "Of course," I thought, "Richard is fully occupied with his military career. He doesn't want the nuisance of having workmen pulling down the castle. It would be a major undertaking. That was why he left it, and because it had been neglected for some years it probably was dangerous. But why build a wall around it?"

I could not keep my thoughts from it. It was the first thing I looked at when I went to the Castle Room, and when I explored the gardens again and again it seemed my steps almost involuntarily led me there.

One day when I was walking through the trees close to the wall I felt suddenly alert, for I sensed that someone was near me in the copse. I didn't know why that should startle me so much, for one of the servants might easily be there. But why should they be there? They might ask, why should I? *I* was there because I was naturally curious about anything that concerned my new home and my husband, and I could not quite reconcile myself to the explanation he had given me of this mysterious castle.

I listened. The swish of a branch as someone brushed it aside; the dislodgement of a stone; the startled scurry of a rabbit or some such animal; but most of all the awareness of a presence. Someone was watching me. Perhaps someone who had seen me come here before and was alarmed by my curiosity?

I was going to find out.

I went forward quickly, then paused to listen.

Yes, there was the unmistakable sound of retreating footsteps.

"Who's there?" I called.

There was no answer. And then . . . through the trees I saw a face. It was there and it was gone. Whoever it belonged to must have been hiding behind one of the trees and I had just caught him peering out.

It was a face, though, that once seen would not be easily forgotten. The dark hair grew low on the forehead and the bushy eyebrows were jet black; the face was very pale—unusually so—and there was a vivid birthmark on the left cheek.

It was the sort of face that could be a little startling, especially disembodied, as it were, for the tree hid the rest of him.

"Who are you?" I cried.

But the face disappeared, and for a few moments I could do nothing but stand there, because I was more than a little startled by what I had seen.

Then I went on through the woods, calling to whoever it was to stop. But there was no response. I went through the trees until I came to the wall surrounding the castle. It was the first time I had approached it from this direction, and that was how I discovered the door in the wall. I stood for a moment examining it, looking, furtively I must admit, over my shoulder, expecting at any moment to see that rather unearthly apparition. A door in the wall! There was an arch which betrayed it, for the wall at this point was covered with creepers which festooned over it almost obscuring the door.

I pushed aside the creepers and examined it closely. There was a keyhole which would take a large key. I lay against the door and pushed it. It was locked fast.

It was very strange, and as I stood there a sense of apprehension came over me. I felt alone suddenly and very isolated from the household of Far Flamstead. I kept thinking of that face which had looked at me through the trees. The strange expression of the eyes. They had not been threatening, far from it. They had seemed almost afraid of *me*, which was perhaps why I had somewhat recklessly followed.

But now I felt a great urge to get out of the copse. I started to run and did not stop until I was through the trees and in the clear.

I was quite breathless and the first person I saw was Mrs. Cherry. She was coming out of the herb garden, and in her apron she was carrying some leaves and sprigs, which she must have just gathered.

"Why, you look startled, my lady," she said.

"I . . . I just saw someone in the copse."

"In the copse, my lady?"

"Yes, the one by the castle wall."

"Oh?" Her round eyes seemed to have taken on an alert look. "Trespassers then . . ."

"It was a man with dark hair and brows and there was some birthmark on his cheek."

She hesitated for a few seconds, her brows drawn together while she looked down at the grass. Then she lifted her face and was smiling. "Oh, that would be Strawberry John. So he were there, were he? He'd no right, the rascal."

"Strawberry John. What's that?"

"He have this mark on his cheek like. In strawberry season it comes up just like a strawberry. They say his mother had a terrible fancy for strawberries when she were carrying him and he were born with it—right on his cheek it is—so you can't fail to see it. He makes a bit by poaching where he shouldn't, if you get my meaning. Yes, I know Strawberry John."

"I called out and he didn't answer. He ran."

"He knew he'd no right to be in them woods, that's what. Why, you look really scared. There's nothing to fear from Strawberry John."

I had explored the gardens and I wanted to go farther afield. I knew that I was supposed not to go riding beyond the paddock but I was thinking a great deal about Bersaba, who had often gone out riding alone, so I decided I could come to no harm and one day I set out.

I took a different route from the one I had taken with Richard and rode on through pleasant lanes for about three miles when I came to a farmhouse. It was large and comfortable-looking, with stone walls and a tiled roof. Close by were several small cottages, and they all seemed part of the farm estate.

I approached with interest, for it struck me that the owners of the farm must be our nearest neighbors. As I stood there a woman came out of the house, went to the well to draw water and, seeing me on horseback, she called a greeting.

There was something familiar about her and she certainly noticed the same about me, for she approached looking at me curiously.

Then I recognized her. She was Ella Longridge, the sister of the man whom Richard had challenged to a duel.

"Why," she cried, "we have met before."

"You are Mistress Longridge, I believe."

"And you are the new mistress of Far Flamstead. We met at a ball."

"I remember it well. You and your brother were together there, and there was an unfortunate incident."

"It was satisfactorily settled," she said. "You are riding alone?"

"Yes. My husband is away on military matters and I have grown tired of keeping within bounds and had no wish to bring a groom with me."

"Would you care to come in a while? My brother is out, but he would not wish me to be inhospitable."

"It's kind of you. I should greatly like to do so."

I dismounted and tethered my horse to a post near the mounting block and went with her into the farmhouse.

I noticed the simplicity of her gray gown, and she wore a white collar and white apron. Her shoes were strong and serviceable and her hair taken back from her brow in the plainest of styles.

We were in a large kitchen with an open fireplace at one end and a long refectory table with benches for seats and two chairs with arms at either end. On a dresser were pewter vessels, and hanging from chains over the fireplace was a large black pot in which something savory was cooking; from the wall oven came the appetizing smell of baking.

I said I was surprised to find that we were neighbors.

"Our families were very friendly at one time," said Ella

Longridge, "but differences arose and you saw the climax at the ball. My brother had not so openly expressed his disapproval of certain matters before, and your husband took exception to his view. It may well be that he would not wish you to come here, but shall we say this is a meeting between two women who do not care so ardently for the quarrels of men?"

She looked round the farmhouse and said, "You see we live simply here. My brother manages the farm but that is not his only occupation. He was a Member of Parliament and writes papers on political matters. I fear sometimes he is too outspoken; he was never one to consider the effect of his words."

I could not help liking Ella Longridge, and the thought of having her as a near neighbor lifted my spirits considerably, for I was realizing how lonely I had been.

She went to the oven and brought out a batch of little pies, golden brown and looking appetizing.

"We will sample them while they are hot from the oven, and if you would care for it I will give you some of our home-brewed ale."

She put the ale from a cask into two pewter mugs and set them on the table. Then she took two of the hot pies and placed them on platters.

"It is not every day that I have a visitor," she said.

"We are very near neighbors."

"By a shortcut we are a mile and a half from each other and our farmland extends almost to the grounds of Far Flamstead."

"Have you lived here long?" I asked, sipping the delicious ale.

"All our lives. We have a residence in London which Luke used when he was a Member of Parliament. He is always hoping that this state of affairs will end, and he with others is working to that purpose. But we are of the land, farming stock, and sometimes I think it would have been better for Luke if he had not dabbled in politics. It can be a dangerous game in such times as these."

"We seem far removed from all that in Cornwall."

"Luke seems to think that the storm that is brewing will envelop the whole country—even the most remote areas."

I shivered. "I hate conflict. My mother used to say that our family had suffered a great deal from it in the past."

"All families have, I imagine. But the country is in a sorry state, Luke says. There are too many people bent on enjoying what they call the good things of life. They should live more simply."

"As you do," I said. "These pies are very good."

"I do most of the baking myself. We have but two maid-servants in the house. Of course there are several people working on the farm. I will show you later if you would like to see. There are the brewhouse where this ale is made, and the dairy, the woodstack barns, the cattle sheds, and we have a separate bakehouse, for there are many to feed."

"You work very hard, Mistress Longridge."

"I am content in my work, for it is that to which I have been called."

She asked me questions then about my family, the reason for my coming to London, and about my marriage. I found it pleasant to have someone to talk to.

And when we had eaten and drunk she showed me the farmhouse; we ascended the wooden staircase and went through a number of rooms, some of which led into each other; they all had the heavy oak beams and small leaded windows, and all were fresh and clean though rather sparsely furnished.

I said I had to go now as they might well be wondering where I had been and would be alarmed if I did not return in time for dinner.

Ella then said that she would not detain me, but if I wished to call again I should be very welcome. She had few friends in the country because Luke had upset so many of them by his views. It seemed that most of the people they had known were in opposition to him.

As I was about to mount my horse, Luke Longridge him-self rode up. He was astonished to see me, and like his sister he recognized me at once.

"So we have a visitor," he said, dismounting and bowing to me.

"It was a surprise call. Mistress Tolworthy was riding by and paused to look at the farm. So, recognizing her, I invited her in."

"You are welcome," said Luke. I immediately noticed his plain dark doublet and breeches and hair which was cut close to his head quite different from the fashion.

"I was just about to leave, as I did not want them to be anxious about me."

"You rode here alone?" he asked.

"Yes. It is not far and I did not want a groom to accompany me."

"And your husband?"

"He is away from home and has been for some weeks."

"You must allow me to take you home," he said.

I could not refuse such an offer. Moreover, I was interested in him and I felt I should be civil to him because I had always thought that Richard had provoked him on that occasion when I had first met the Longridges.

He mounted his horse and we rode off together.

I said I had had no idea that we were such near neighbors.

"We have been so all our lives."

I thought it was no use pretending I did not remember his and Richard's disagreement so I said, "I am glad you did not fight my husband."

"It was a challenge given in the heat of the moment. I should not care to shed blood over such a trivial matter. I think General Tolworthy realized that later, for he accepted the situation."

"People become ardent over matters which seem important to them. My husband is in the King's Army and he is naturally completely loyal to His Majesty."

"And it is right that he should be. But a country can be more important than its king."

"I have always thought of them as one: King and Country."

"That is as it should be. I trust General Tolworthy will not object to your calling at the farmhouse."

"I am sure he would not."

"When he returns you must tell him that my sister invited you in and that I escorted you home."

"Yes, of course I shall."

"It might be that he will object to such neighborliness."

"I am sure he would be pleased for me to have friends so near, since he has so often to be away from home."

"We shall see. And if that is the case my sister will be delighted with your friendship."

"And I with hers. It has been a most interesting morning."

Far Flamstead had now come into sight and he said he would leave me.

He bowed and I knew that he waited and watched until he saw me ride into the stables.

Soon after that I began to suspect that I was pregnant. I wasn't sure of course and it may be that I wished for this so fervently that I imagined it was so. I used to sit in the Castle Room and dream about the child and thought: "This time next year it will be here—that's if it is so."

I was a little absentminded and of course this began to be noticed. I caught Mrs. Cherry looking at me intently, and once when I went into the kitchen she was whispering with Grace and Meg and as the whispering stopped abruptly as I entered I guessed they were discussing me, for while Mrs. Cherry retained her rotund cheerfulness the other two looked a little embarrassed.

When she was doing my hair Meg asked me if I felt well.

"Of course," I answered. "Why do you ask? Don't I look well?"

"Oh, yes, my lady, you look very well . . . but different."

"How different?" I asked sharply.

She was again embarrassed.

"Well, we was wondering, my lady . . . I hope it's not out of place, but you see, being as it was in the family, we got noticing things."

"Really, Meg," I said, "I don't know what you're talking about."

She hung her head and looked very uncomfortable and because I insisted on her telling me what she meant she said, "Well, it would be lovely to have a little baby in the house. It's what we'd all look forward to."

I felt myself flushing scarlet. "But what makes you think—"

"It was Grace, my lady."

"Grace!"

"Well, you see, she learned it from my mother and she was going to be one herself. She does now when she's needed . . . roundabouts, you know. If anyone wants her. She's got a natural way for it."

"Really, Meg," I said, "I haven't the faintest notion of what you are talking about."

"Our mother was a midwife, my lady, and she taught Grace all she knew. Grace would have been the same, only we came here and she has other duties. I reckon she earns her keep as I'm sure you'll agree."

"I do, but what about Grace?"

"Well, Grace has second sight, you might say, my lady, where babies is concerned and she reckons that you're what she might call in the family way if you'll excuse the expression to a lady."

"How could Grace know?"

"Well, she always says that people change when they get that way . . . no matter who they be, and she says she'd take a wager on it, my lady."

I said, "Grace may be right. I shall hope so."

Meg smiled, very well content.

As the days passed I began to feel Grace's insight had not failed her.

August would soon be with us. The wheatfields of the Longridge Farm were already changing color and were now a golden brown, and the barley and oats and his root crops made a patchwork quilt of the land—yellow, white, blue, green, and purple. Mine was not a poetic nature but I told myself that the whole earth was symbolically fruitful.

How I longed for a child! In my mind I talked to my mother and Bersaba, but I was afraid to write to them for fear I should be wrong.

However, I couldn't resist talking to knowledgeable Grace.

"Grace," I said, "I'm almost sure."

"Oh, my lady," she answered, "I *am* sure."

"I feel so excited about it."

"Bringing little lives into the world is the most exciting thing in life, my lady."

"Yes, I believe it is."

"Ain't no doubt about it, my lady." She came close to me and looked into my face. Then she laid her hands on me.

"I'd say 'tis just about two months, my lady. There's some as takes to breeding like the flowers to rain. It'll be an easy birth, I can promise you. You've got that sort of figure for it. Little waist and hips enough—like an hourglass, and that's good for babies."

"You're very comforting, Grace."

"Oh, I know my business. There's not a child of eight and under in Longridge Cottages who wasn't brought into the world by me—and them that's older was brought in by my mother. You can rely on me. I'll be beside you all through."

"Of course it's very early days yet."

"Don't you fret, my lady. The baby's here all right. I don't have a shadow of a doubt. My mother was the finest midwife in the country and she taught me all she knew. She was well thought of. The highest ladies in the land knew they couldn't do better than have her in attendance. She always believed in being there a day or more before she was needed. None of that last minute arrival on the scene if she could help it. A lot of harm could be done before she arrived. She was ready a week before—"

Grace stopped suddenly and I said quickly, "She attended the General's first wife, then?"

" 'Tweren't her fault the poor lady died. She said before that it were no ordinary confinement. She were very weak

190

and my mother knew there wasn't a hope for her, but she did all she could for her. All her skill she used . . . 'Tweren't no good. The best midwife in the world can't go against fate. Oh, she were different from you. You're a fine strong healthy lady. No need to think of her."

"I'd like to know more about her, Grace."

Grace's mouth was tightly shut. "I reckon you don't want to go getting fancies, my lady. You want to think about your own dear little baby. Why, I reckon next April you'll be holding that little 'un in your arms and calling him the masterpiece of creation."

I smiled at her. She was already assuming the role of nurse. It amused me, and it was comforting to know that when my time did come I should be attended by the best midwife in the country.

A messenger came with a letter from Richard. Trouble had not developed in the north as he had feared, and the situation was under control. Before the end of the month he would be with me.

I thought it was safe to write to tell him of my hopes, for I knew that they would delight him. I wrote:

> I am not sure, but it could well be so. Grace, the dedicated midwife whose mother taught her all she knows—and that seems to be everything there is to know on the subject— is absolutely certain and she is treating me as though I were a very priceless piece of china. By the time you come home I shall be quite certain. I am so happy because I feel in my heart that it must be so. I have not written to Trystan Priory yet. My mother will be delighted and of course anxious. I don't think I could ask for anything in the world, only just to see my mother and my sister.

Within a week a letter came back from Richard. He must have read mine and sat down immediately to reply. He wrote:

> MY DEAR WIFE,
> Your letter filled me with the utmost pleasure. I must impress on you to take care of yourself. I shall be with you just as soon as is possible, which must be by the end of the month. Then I shall hope to stay for a longer time—unless of course something unforeseen should happen. At the moment this seems unlikely. It might well be that your mother and sister

could visit us. I should not wish you to undertake the journey to them at this time and as the weeks go on you will need to take more and more care. I assure you that I am thinking of you when I am not occupied with military matters. You know how deep my affection is for you.

Your husband,
RICHARD TOLWORTHY

I smiled over the letter. It was not a passionate love letter by any means; but it was sincere, and every word in it rang true. I would not have had it otherwise.

There was one night when I could not sleep. I lay in the big bed and thought of Richard's coming home and how we would talk and plan for the child. Life had taken on a new dimension. The thought of being a mother must make it so. I felt older, wiser. I had to be. I would have a new life to guide. I wondered whether I should be adequate.

My mother would be delighted and apprehensive. She herself had waited five years for my brother Fennimore and she would be so pleased because no bride could have been quicker to conceive than I had.

I used to talk to Bersaba when I lay in bed, whispering and making up her comments. It seemed so strange that our lives should have suddenly diverged when they had run along side by side for so many years.

And as I lay there musing I was suddenly aware of a strange sound which broke the silence of the night. I wasn't quite sure what it was, but it sounded like laughter . . . strange uncanny laughter though not in the least mirthful. I sat up in bed and looked toward the window. A light flickered and went out. There it was again.

I knew whence it came. The castle!

I was out of bed in a second and, wrapping my robe about me, went to the window and watched. Then I heard the sound again. Laughter followed by a piercing scream. It was very odd.

I thought, "Someone is in the castle."

From the window I could only see the turrets, but there was one room from which I could get a better view.

I lighted a candle, mounted the newel staircase, and went into the Castle Room. It looked eerie by the faint light of a moon. I stood at the window and held up the candle. I could only see my own face mirrored there, so I placed the candle on the table and, going back to the window seat, knelt there watching the turrets.

Then I saw the light again. It flickered and went out. It was as though someone was carrying a lantern, the light of which showed as he passed the machicolations of the turret.

I opened the window and leaned out, trying to get a little nearer to the castle, and then suddenly I was sure I saw a face. It appeared on the battlements—a disembodied face as it were—peering out at me.

I felt my blood run cold, for it scarcely looked human, and for a matter of seconds it seemed to be staring at me. Then it disappeared, and the light with it.

I had seen that face before. I knew it belonged to the man I had seen in the woods. I had recognized the thatch of hair and the heavy brows, though I could not make out the mark of his face.

"Strawberry John," I murmured.

Then I felt my hair stand on end, because as I knelt there at the window I knew that I was not alone in the room. For a few seconds I believed myself to be in the presence of something uncanny, and I was afraid to turn round. Indeed, in those seconds I felt as though I were petrified, for I could not move. I was trembling with terror.

Someone was standing behind me. Someone was coming toward me. Fleetingly I remembered how Richard had not wanted me to come to this room.

I forced myself to turn sharply.

Mrs. Cherry was standing behind me. She looked unlike her daytime self because her hair was in two plaits which hung one over each shoulder and she was wearing a cloak of brown worsted which she clutched around her.

"Mrs. Cherry!" I cried.

"My lady, what are you doing up here? You'll catch your death . . . and the window open."

"I thought it was—" I began.

"I know, you've been having nightmares, I reckon. What possessed you to come up here? I heard footsteps on the stairs. I'm a light sleeper, and I thought it was Meg walking in her sleep. We have to watch her. Then I come in here and find you, my lady . . . and in your condition."

"Mrs. Cherry, something's happening . . ."

"Look, my lady, I'm going to get you back to bed. Why, you're shivering with the cold. This is a nice thing, this is. The General would never forgive us if aught happened to you. Now you come on. It's chilly in this room. I'm going to get you back to bed and quick as a flash of lightning."

"There's somebody in the castle," I said.

"Nonsense. No one could get in. It's all locked up. The General's orders. It's dangerous, he says, and it's downright forbidden for any one of us to go in there."

"I saw a light there. And I saw . . . a face."

"Now, my lady, you've been having nightmares. A nice soothing posset is what you want. I'm going to get that for you right away."

"I tell you I was not dreaming. I was wide awake and I heard the noise, a sort of laughter, and then I saw the light so I came up here to see better and then there was the face."

"It was a trick of the light, I reckon."

"No. It wasn't. I think it was—the man I saw in the woods."

"Strawberry John!"

"I couldn't see the birthmark. It was just the shape of his head and all that hair."

"Oh, no, my lady. That couldn't be. Come along down. I want to get you back to bed. I wouldn't go wandering round in the night if I was you. Some of these stairs are tricky. A fall in your condition wouldn't be the slightest bit of good to you and it might cause great harm. It wouldn't be the first time a nasty fall had put an end to someone's hopes. Now come on. I'll have no peace till I see you back in your warm bed. And I'm going to bring up a hot brick for you . . . wrapped in lovely flannel, and one of my best soothing possets. Then in the morning you'll feel right as rain and see it was only a nightmare."

I could see it was no use talking to her so I allowed her to lead me back to my room. I was at least comforted by her presence. I don't know what I had expected to see when I turned from the window and came face to face with her. It was such an anticlimax, when I had been expecting something supernatural to see that round rosy face looking at me in concern.

I was still shivering as she carefully tucked me in.

"Now you wait and I'll get that hot brick and my posset. We'll be quiet because we don't want to wake the rest of the household."

I lay in bed waiting for her return. It was no use her stating I had had a nightmare. I had seen the flickering light. I had seen the face at the turret. I was not such an imaginative person that I had made that up.

She came first with the brick, which was a comfort.

Wrapped in red flannel, it gave out a gentle warmth and the shivering was soon giving way to a cozy comfort. "I'll be back in a minute," she said, and she was as good as her word. She had a small pewter goblet and in it some concoction which she said was sweet to the taste and soothing to the body.

She handed it to me and said, "Sip it, my lady. That's the way it does most good. I don't reckon there's many as knows more of the secret of herbs and things that grow in the ground than I do and if there are I'd like to meet them, for it's always a good thing to improve your knowledge. Some of the General's important guests—great soldiers like himself —have talked of the flavor of my stews, and all it was was a touch of burdock, lady smock, or old man's pepper. You can do a lot with them. There they are, all in the ground, given us by the good God and all we have to do is make use of them. Now, in this posset, I've got a sprinkling of thyme. That gives pleasant dreams, so my grandmother found out, and she passed it on through the family like, and there's just a spot of poppy to make your sleep easy. Is it pleasant, my lady?"

"Yes, it's sweet . . .but not too sweet and it does have a pleasant tang."

"I knew you'd like it. You'll be asleep in no time."

"But I am sure I saw the light and the face. I won't have it that it was fancy. As for a nightmare, I was fully awake."

She was thoughtful for a moment. Then she said, "Strawberry John, you say. This face—it had a look of him?"

"I can't be sure. There was only the moonlight and his face was against even that. It was therefore in shadow. The shape of his head reminded me."

"I'm just wondering if that crazy Strawberry John got into the castle somehow. That just could be."

"How could he?"

"If he got over the wall."

"Could he climb it? And there are glass flints at the top."

"You know that then, my lady."

"Yes, I noticed them when the sun was shining the other day. The little bits of glass were glistening."

"The General is so determined that everyone should stay out. But there is Strawberry John. He's not quite right in the head, that's why we don't take much notice of him."

"He's a poacher, you say?"

"Yes, he does a bit of poaching. People round about are generous to him. They're sorry for him. He being what you might call two happorth short. Now, since you're so sure you saw the light and the face I just wonder whether he got in somehow? I'll speak to Cherry and Mr. Jesson. I'll get them to run him to earth one day and question him. The General would want to know if it's possible for anyone to get in there . . . and you can be sure he'll put a stop to it if he knows what's going on."

I felt soothed by the thought that Strawberry John might have got into the castle. I would not allow Mrs. Cherry to convince me that I was a stupid hysterical creature who had imagined the whole thing.

I was beginning to grow sleepy. The warmth of the bed and soothing posset were working.

"Thank you, Mrs. Cherry," I said. "It was good of you to look after me."

"Oh, I'm only doing what the General would wish, my lady. We've got to take special care of you . . . now."

She tiptoed out and I was soon asleep and did not wake until the sun was streaming into the bedchamber.

The next day I thought I would like to talk with someone about what had happened, and I immediately thought of Ella Longridge. There was something about the farmhouse kitchen that was in direct contrast to the castle. Everything there was so simple; I imagined there was nothing in that big and homey room that was not of practical use. There was something direct about both the Longridges—matter-of-fact, down-to-earth, honest good people.

Of course Richard did not agree with their views, which I knew were against the King in some way. For Richard, as a soldier, would be intensely loyal. It occurred to me that he would support the King even if he disagreed with his policies. Richard was a man who would have a certain standard of behavior and never diverge from it. Luke Longridge was different. I wondered what he wrote in those articles which his sister had mentioned.

But it was not Luke I felt an urge to see. It was Ella, and the more I thought of that kitchen with the appetizing smell of baking coming from the oven and the sound of ale being poured into a pewter tankard the more I wanted to be there.

I rode out in the early morning. I would call, spend an hour there, and be back in time for dinner. No one would know that I had been there. After all, they had invited me to call when I wished and it might be that when Richard returned he would not wish me to continue the friendship. How friendly could one feel toward a man whom one had challenged to a duel? Perhaps it was not good wifely conduct to seize an opportunity to act against what might well be her husband's wishes, but I did want the Longridges to know that I at least felt nothing but friendship for them no matter how their views differed from those of my own family. My mother used to talk a great deal about tolerance. She believed it was a good thing, and that belief was something I had inherited from her.

So I set out and in a short time the farmhouse came into view. I rode into the yard and was about to dismount when I was seized by cramping pains.

I managed to get off my horse and as I did so I was dizzy and I knew that I could not stand much longer so I let myself slide to the ground. It was there that a serving maid found me.

"You're ill, mistress," she cried and ran into the farmhouse. Ella came out, all concern.

"Why, it's Mistress Tolworthy," she said. "Here, Jane, help me into the house with her."

I was able to stand and they helped me in, and very soon I was lying on a settle with rugs around me.

The dizziness passed but the pain continued.

"I don't know what is happening to me," I stammered. "I meant to call on you. . . ."

"Never mind now," said Ella. "Stay there and rest."

That was all I wanted to do and very soon I did know what was happening to me. I was losing my baby.

Ella Longridge put me to bed and sent over to Far Flamstead for Grace, who came and very soon confirmed my fears.

"You're safe enough, mistress," said Grace. "Why, 'twas nothing to speak of. 'Tis just the sorrow of losing it. But at this stage you soon recover and you'll have more. 'Tis a warning to us, though, that we'll have to take special care of you. Must have had a shock like."

She had brought some of her herb medicines with her and she said that I shouldn't move for the rest of that day but I'd be well enough to go home tomorrow, she was sure, but she'd want to see me first.

Ella said that Grace must stay the night and accompany me back the next. She would feel happier with Grace in the farmhouse.

So there I lay in this plain bedroom with its bare boards and somber colors and I thought of what losing my baby would mean. My dreams had evaporated. I had lost the child just as I was becoming sure of its existence. I was glad I had not told my mother and sister; I was sorry that I had told Richard. I would have to write to him now and tell him that I had lost the child.

Ella came and sat by my bed; she brought her sewing with her, not embroidery, which I supposed she would consider frivolous, but the plain material she was stitching into garments for herself and her brother.

She told me how sorry she was that this had happened. Although she was a spinster who had no intention of marrying, she could well understand my feelings.

"I wonder what went wrong?" she said.

I told her what had happened the previous night.

"That explains it," she said. "The shock must have brought on this miscarriage."

"I felt nothing at the time."

"I believe it happens like that sometimes. I wonder who was there in the Folly?"

"You have heard of Strawberry John, have you, Mistress Longridge?"

"I have. He is a strange-looking man. Very strong, I believe. His father was a very strong man indeed and John inherited that strength. He has this mark on his face and it is easy to identify him because of it. One doesn't hear of him often. I don't know where he lives . . . nobody seems to know."

"Mrs. Cherry, our housekeeper, suggested that he found some way into the castle."

"That seems a very likely explanation. What a pity that you happened to be disturbed by it."

"I don't know what my husband will say when he comes back. He is insistent that no one go near the castle, as it is unsafe."

"I daresay he will demolish it."

"I don't know. He feels it would not be right, as his ancestor set such store by it."

It was comforting talking to Ella, and later in the day her brother came in, but as she insisted on my remaining in bed and the Longridges would not think it fitting for me to receive a gentleman in my bedchamber, I did not see him.

I slept peacefully that night and in the morning felt well enough to get up.

Grace pronounced me fit to travel, but Luke Longridge would not hear of my riding and he took Grace and me back to Far Flamstead in one of the farm carts, which was drawn by two horses. He said he would send a man over with my horse and Grace's later that day.

Mrs. Cherry seized on me and, murmuring something about my night's adventure in the Castle Room, which had brought this on, insisted that I go to bed.

I felt a little weak and very depressed so I allowed her to take me there.

I was indeed sad. I did not realize until now how much I had counted on having my baby. I recalled the nights in the big bed which had filled me with apprehension and which I had been inclined to forget while Richard was away. In my heart I had said it was worthwhile because I was going to have a baby. But now there was no baby.

These thoughts I could not explain to anybody, and when Grace and Meg kept telling me that I should soon have another I could not help dwelling rather morbidly on the necessary preliminaries.

I wondered whether I was unusual, but I didn't think so. I had heard it said by married ladies, whispering together, that it was a woman's duty to submit to her husband's needs, however uncomfortable and distasteful this might be; and I knew now what they meant.

I was certainly depressed and I thought more and more of Trystan Priory. It occurred to me that what I wanted more than anything now was to see my sister.

I told myself I could talk to her. There was a good deal she would not understand, of course. How could she, an unmarried girl and a virgin? But still I should find some comfort in talking.

Then Richard returned home.

He was solicitous and very concerned because of what had happened.

He seemed taller and more remote than I had been imagining him and was a little embarrassed with me, not knowing how to tell me of his affection.

For one thing I was grateful. He said I must be strong again before we thought of having another child, because what had happened, although so early in my pregnancy and therefore not dangerous to me, might well have weakened me. And we must take no risks.

During that first week of his return I slept in the Blue Room, so called because of its furnishings, which was on the same landing as our own bedchamber.

"You will find it more restful to sleep alone," was his comment. "Just at first," he added.

How grateful I was.

I hoped that he did not sense my relief but I feared I could not hide it.

Of course I told him of the night before my miscarriage, how I had seen the lights and thought I had glimpsed Strawberry John on the battlements. I saw his face whiten, and I could not understand the expression in his eyes. His mouth was tight; angry, I thought it.

"Could you have imagined it?" he asked, almost pleadingly, I thought.

"No!" I said vehemently. "I was fully awake and in possession of my senses. I saw the light, heard something, and there was no doubt that it was a face up there."

"And you recognized that face?"

"Yes—well, I'm not absolutely sure. The light wasn't good. But I had seen this Strawberry John in the woods near the castle."

"I wonder if it is possible?" he said. "I shall discover."

I said, "Wouldn't it be better to demolish the castle?"

"No," he said. "I couldn't do that."

"But if it is dangerous and people can get in?"

"People cannot get in. I don't understand this. It was unfortunate, but I shall look into the matter. You should never have left your bed and gone up to investigate. It was foolish."

"It seemed natural. After all, I wanted to know what was going on in my home."

"I will see this Strawberry John at the first opportunity, and if by chance you saw him, I must ask you not to be afraid if by some chance you should do so again. If you do, come to me at once. I shall take the necessary steps. I do not wish you to attempt to investigate without telling me. Please remember that, Angelet."

It was a command, spoken in a stern voice. "So he must talk to his soldiers," I thought.

"It is a painful subject," he went on. "Your wanderings in the night in all probability have lost the child. You must take care in future. Perhaps it would be better if you came to Whitehall and stayed in London for a while."

I was silent. A terrible depression had come over me and I could not shake it off.

Then began the evenings, when he brought out the soldiers and made a battlefield. He did not always involve me in this; and sometimes he would go to the library and become deeply

200

immersed in some of the books there. We had the occasional game of chess, but I was afraid my game had not improved and I knew that there was little excitement for him in our battles over the board.

I knew too that soon he would be back with me in the red-curtained bed.

One day he said to me, "You are not really happy, Angelet. Tell me what would make you so?"

I answered promptly: "Perhaps if I could see my sister. We have been together all our lives until I came to London. I miss her very much."

"Why should she not come to visit us?"

"Do you think I might ask her?"

"By all means do so."

So that day I wrote to Bersaba.

> "Do come, Bersaba. It seems so long since I have seen you. There is so much I want to talk to you about. I miss you and mother terribly, but if you could come it would be a wonderful help to me. Bersaba, I need you here. You are stronger now. Are you strong enough for the journey? I do hope so and I do believe you will want to come when I tell you how much I need you."

I read the letter through when I had written it. It sounded like a cry for help.

BERSABA

❖ ❖ ❖

Escape from the Grave

I AM changed. It is no use their telling me I am not. I have come near to death and only by a miracle—which was brought about through the assiduous care of my mother and Phoebe— have I survived. This terrible disease has set its mark on me. Who ever heard of anyone who escaped unscathed! I know that either my mother or Phoebe remained at my bedside through day and night and not once did they sleep while they were there, but they took it in turns to spend the long nights with me.

It is because of this that I am not completely disfigured. On my brows there are one or two of those horrible scars, more on my neck, one on my left cheek, but my mother and Phoebe saved me from the worst and there are few who have suffered the dreadful disease and come through it who show as few signs as I do. My mother bound my hands to my sides that I might not in my sleep touch the hateful sores; they watched over me; they bathed me in special oils made by my mother and learned from hers; they fed me broth and milk and beef tea; and they would not let me see myself in a mirror until they were sure that the disfiguration was going to be slight.

Although I was grateful that it is, I cannot pretend I am the same. I have grown thin and my eyes seem too big for my face. My mother says it has not impaired my looks, but I often ask myself if that is truth or mother love which makes her see me so.

For months, even after the infection had left me, I was conscious of a lassitude. I did not want to do anything but lie on my bed and read, and sometimes brood and ask fate why this had had to happen to me.

When my mother first told me that she had sent Angelet away I was relieved because I knew that everyone in the household ran the risk of taking the disease which I had brought in from the midwife. Afterward I began to feel a little resentful. It seemed unfair that Angelet should be having gay adventures while I should have this fearful one. But when Phoebe came into my room, her eyes round with adoration, I felt better, for there is no doubt that to Phoebe I am a mixture of saint and Amazon—a goddess of power and virtue. I like that, for my nature is one that revels in admiration. I suppose most people like it, but my love of it is inordinate. That was why I always wanted to score over Angelet. Now she is married to a very important man, it seems—a General in the King's Army—and my mother says that he is well known to people who have called at the house and they think that Angelet has made a very good match indeed.

And it is all because of what happened to me, for if I had not contracted this disease, both Angelet and I would be here in Trystan Priory, and since we had passed our eighteenth birthdays my mother would have been bestirring herself to get us husbands. Who would have believed that Angelet would find her own!

I often think of her and wonder what she is doing. We had been so close, we had always done everything together . . . well, not everything. She had known nothing of my affair with Bastian. And now we were miles apart, separated by distance and all the experiences she must be having in her new life.

I have taken to riding each day. The first time I sat in the saddle since my illness I felt like a novice, terrified that I was going to fall, but that soon passed, and my mother agreed that I should ride a little each day. Sometimes she accompanied me and often I went with the grooms.

I am very conscious of the marks on my face.

"They are nothing," said my mother. "In fact no one would notice them. You must wear a fringe on your forehead, which I hear from Angelet's letters is most fashionable."

Phoebe cut my fringe and curled it, but whenever I looked at myself in a mirror my eyes went to the scars. I used to get angry sometimes and think of Angelet, who had had an exciting adventure ending in marriage while her skin remained as smooth and fresh as mine used to be.

It was as though she were constantly with me. I used to read her letters again and again. She described Far Flamstead with its quaint folly to me so that I could see it clearly, and when she wrote of her husband I sensed that she thought him wonderful. Yet at the same time there was something which she held back. I couldn't help thinking of them together . . . as Bastian and I had been, and I was filled with a bitter envy.

Soon after my eighteenth birthday my father's ship returned. That was a day of great rejoicing in our household. My lassitude dropped from me then, for not only had my father returned, but my brother Fennimore and Bastian with him.

When the news came that the ship had been sighted there was the bustle of excitement and preparation which I remembered so well. My mother shone with an inner radiance and the whole household seemed to come alive. Only at such times would she allow herself to contemplate the hazards of the journey. That must have been a very happy trait to possess.

We rode down to the coast to greet them as they came ashore.

My father embraced my mother first as though he was never going to let her go again, and then he looked around for his daughters. It was difficult explaining so much in a few breathless sentences. My mother had evidently practiced how she would tell him so that he should suffer no unnecessary anxieties even for a few moments.

"We are all well and happy, Fenn. But so much has happened since you have been away. Our darling Angelet has married, most happily, and Bersaba has been ill but is now quite recovered. It is too much to tell now."

My brother Fennimore embraced me, and so did Bastian. I felt myself flushing with bitter anger, wondering how much of the change he noticed.

"Let us get back to the house," said my mother. "I can only think that you are back . . . safe and well."

So we rode back to Trystan Priory—myself between Fenni-more and Bastian.

I told them as briefly as I could. I contracted smallpox; Angelet was sent away to stay with Carlotta and there had met her husband. We had recently had the news that she had married and everyone seemed pleased with the match.

"Bersaba!" cried my brother Fennimore. "You have had smallpox. But it is a miracle!"

"Yes," I agreed. "The miracle of love, I suppose. You can imagine what Mother did for me. And there was Phoebe to help her. The blacksmith's daughter, you know. Her father turned her out and I brought her to the Priory. She seems to think that makes her my slave for life."

Bastian said nothing, but I could sense his emotion and I felt elated. It was at this moment that I started to come alive again.

There was the well-remembered atmosphere of festivity about the Priory. My father was delighted to be back, so concerned about what had happened in his absence. As we came into the house he had me on one side of him, my mother on the other, and kept pressing my arm against him and I knew how thankful he was that I had survived.

Everything had to be told him in detail. Angelet's letters had to be produced. He wanted to hear how I had gone to the midwife and how my mother had nursed me. He sent for Phoebe and thanked her for what she had done, and she said it was nothing to what I had done for her and she'd give her life for me.

There were sentimental tears in their eyes, and I felt like an outside observer looking on at the scene; and all the time I was conscious of Bastian.

We supped in the hall that night and it was like long-ago days, for the servants were at the table too. The only thing that was missing was the massive old salt cellar, which a hundred years ago used to stand in the center of the table, dividing the members of the household and their guests from the menials. It now stood in the kitchen as a sort of ornament and memento of other days. My father sat at the head of the table and Mother beside him, with Fennimore on my mother's left hand and I on my father's right. Bastian sat next to me.

Everyone was happy, for the servants loved my father and regarded him as the best of masters. I once remarked to Angelet that their regard for him was due in part to the fact that they saw him rarely. It is so much easier to love someone who is not always there to irritate and inspire something less than loving. I remember how horrified she was, and how we argued about our father and the servants and our different characters, hers and mine. "You're a sentimentalist, Angelet." I clinched the discussion with that remark, for I invariably had the last word. "And I am a realist." I could always nonplus her with words, but now of course she had escaped from me. She was the one who had had the fine adventure; she was the one who had made the good marriage.

So that was a merry meal except for the fact that my father regretted the absence of my sister. He would have liked to have her living a few miles away and to be here with her new husband on this occasion.

I asked Bastian how he had liked voyaging and he replied that it had been a great adventure but he was not sure that he wished to go again.

He looked at me earnestly and said, "I want to stay here. There is so much to keep me."

I wondered if he noticed those hideous pockmarks. My hair hid them on my brow where they were at their worst, and I kept my left cheek turned away from him.

He said, "To think that you were so ill, Bersaba, and I knew nothing of it! You might have died."

"It is considered a miracle that I did not," I answered.

My mother said that she supposed he would like to go soon to his family and he replied that he would be very happy to stay at the Priory for a few days if she would allow it.

She reproached him warmly for asking, for she hoped he regarded the Priory as his second home.

My father said there were business matters in progress and he would want to discuss them with my mother, Fennimore, and Bastian.

Bastian looked contented, and I knew that he was watching me.

The next morning he asked me to ride with him and we went out together.

It was a beautiful morning, or perhaps it seemed especially so to me, because I was regaining an interest in life. I was beginning to feel well again perhaps, or it might have been because Bastian was here and clearly in love with me. I noticed afresh the beauties of the countryside to which for so long I had been oblivious. I was struck by the bright yellow flowers of the vetch, which we called lady's fingers and which grew on the hillside, and the pale blue of the skullcaps close to the streams. There also grew the woody nightshade—yellow and purple—the flower which always seemed to me to be of special interest because it could look so pretty and yet could be deadly. We were always warned not to touch it, and we called it "bittersweet."

On this day it seemed especially significant. For that was my mood—bittersweet.

Bastian said, "I have thought about you so much, Bersaba. I remember so much of—"

"Of what should be forgotten," I answered.

"It never will be," he answered vehemently.

I shrugged my shoulders. "You did forget for a time."

"No, I never did."

I laughed and spurred up my horse. He was after me, beside me pleading, "Bersaba, I must talk to you."

"Well, pray talk."

"I want to marry you."

"Now that your first choice, Carlotta, is out of reach I make a good second, is that it?"

"You are first, Bersaba. You would always be first."

"My experiences would suggest otherwise."

"I must try to explain."

"Everything is clear. No explanations are needed."

"When I think of everything we used to be to each other—"

"That makes it all the more clear," I retorted sharply. "You knew that and yet you preferred Carlotta. Alas for you, *she* preferred someone else. Poor Bastian! Now you say, 'Very well, since I can't have Carlotta, I'll take Bersaba.' Alas again for you. Bersaba is not one to be picked up and dropped and then to beg for the return of past favors."

"You have a sharp tongue, Bersaba."

"It is one of the reasons why it would be unwise for you to marry me."

"Your parents would be delighted."

"Would they? Have you asked them?"

"I have spoken to your father."

"We are cousins," I said.

"What of it? That didn't bother you at one time."

"I've grown up. There is so much you don't know. I have had a deadly illness, Bastian. I'm changed." I had pulled up my horse and dramatically took off my hat and shook back my hair. "Look!" I showed him the scars on my forehead.

"I love them," he said. "They make me want you more than ever."

"You have strange tastes, Bastian."

"Give me a chance, Bersaba."

"How? Shall we go to the woods and find a secluded spot and lie there together? Shall you come to my bedchamber this night when the household is asleep? It would be safe, you know. Angelet is no longer there."

I saw the lights leap into his eyes and I felt a great surge of desire for him, but I held it in check, for my bitterness was as strong as my desire and my pride was as great as my need.

I turned away from him and put on my hat. "Then," I said, "you could enjoy our adventure until someone more desirable came along, someone to whom you could offer marriage."

I spurred on my horse and galloped away, and as we sped over the soft turf a sudden realization came to me. It was not that I really cared for Bastian, that I needed Bastian, but that I was a sensuous woman who would always need men; I had more than my share of desire than most women and I wondered then about Angelet and her husband and I knew of course that this was one of the assets—could one call it an asset or a liability?—of which I had taken the lion's share.

I knew that I must not be too often alone with Bastian, for old desires would torment me. But I did not love Bastian. I merely wanted that which others could give me, but my need had blinded me to the real reason. As I sped past fields where the rough-headed poppy was peeping out among the corn, as I saw the white flowers of hemlock and the purple bells of foxgloves among the lush grasses, I laughed aloud, because I had reached a new knowledge of myself, and experience had taught me that in knowledge was strength.

My father had decided that the Company would build new offices in Plymouth, and Fennimore had expressed a desire to go there and superintend the management of these.

"Fennimore is not at heart a sailor," said my father. "I am glad he took this voyage, which has been a revelation to him. He is a Company man. He will be invaluable on land, for that part of the venture is as important as the sea voyages."

I believe I understood his pleasure. He did not want Fennimore to face the hazards of the sea; he preferred him to remain at home so that my mother did not lose them both now that Angelet had left home. And, naturally, her place would be with her husband, and that was not in the West Country. They were aware of Bastian's feelings for me and although the fact of our close relationship may have caused them some qualms as to the wisdom of the match, they could see many advantages. I knew that I only had to say I loved

Bastian and their consent to our marriage would be given. Bastian, as he had said, had already spoken to my father.

This amused me very much because I was aware that everyone was waiting for us to announce our betrothal. My mother was in a state of contentment. Her husband was home and it seemed as though his stay would be longer than usual, for he had the matter of the Plymouth office to concern himself with. Fennimore was not to go to sea with him when he next went; Angelet, though sadly missed, was satisfactorily and, it seemed, happily married; and I, Bersaba, had been snatched from what had at one time seemed like the tomb itself and was clearly regaining my health and strength, having been only mildly scathed by the experience.

All my mother needed for her personal happiness was that of her family. Each day she looked for letters from Angelet and when they came she read them aloud and then we all read them separately. I had letters from her too, and I could sense something in mine which the others failed to see.

Angelet was holding something back. My sister had a secret, and I longed to know what it was.

Meanwhile I amused myself with Bastian. It was an interesting game I played, and I had to be careful, too, which added to my zest; for I had to guard my own nature. It would have been so easy to give way, for with my returning health I realized that my desire for a certain kind of pleasure had increased rather than diminished and that, I supposed, was something to do with the matter of growing older.

I would allow Bastian to think I was relenting. I would smile at him beguilingly and suggest we ride out together. Then I would torment him—and myself as well, which was by no means unpleasurable—and I used to feel so proud of myself when I resisted temptation that it was worthwhile having placed myself in a position to feel it. Often, when the household was asleep, he would slip out of the house and stand beneath my window and throw up soft clods of earth to attract my attention. Sometimes I would pretend not to hear; at others I would open my window and look out.

"Go away, Bastian," I said.

"Bersaba, I must see you. I *must.*"

"I am not Carlotta, you must remember," I retorted, shutting my window.

Then I would laugh and feel very excited.

Once he came to my bedroom door, but I had been expecting this and had pulled the bar across.

"Go away!" I hissed. "Do you want to waken the household?"

It occurred to me that it would be most amusing to let him in and pretend I would allow him to stay and then deny him. But I was afraid of my own reactions and the last thing I wanted to do was to give way.

"Bastian seems not in the least anxious to go to Castle Paling." said my mother. "I have sent a message to Melanie to tell her they are back and that Bastian is well. I have told her that there is much to do about this office in Plymouth." She smiled at me. "But somehow I don't think that is the only reason."

How she would have liked to think of her dear daughter only a few miles away at Castle Paling! For if I married Bastian I should one day be the mistress of that castle. She wouldn't think of one that, though. She wanted her brother to live for years and years and she wanted me close to compensate for the loss of Angelet.

So I amused myself during those weeks while Bastian stayed on and I became alive again. My disfigurations had not detracted from that certain allure which people like myself seem to have for the opposite sex. I began to realize that life was becoming exciting again and I thought a good deal of Angelet.

Her General sounded rather stern, and old too. Playing games with soldiers—how odd! And chess. Well, poor Angelet had never been very good at that. One of our governesses had said, "You have a grasshopper mind, Angelet. Try to concentrate as Bersaba does." Dear Angelet! She could never concentrate for very long . . . not long enough to win a game of chess.

I should like to see her and this stern old man; and I wondered very much about their lives together.

Then there came the letter from Angelet. She had miscarried and had been so excited because there was to be a child, but had hesitated to tell us, as she was not entirely sure. It had all happened so quickly and she would very shortly be well, for the miscarriage had taken place only about two months after conception. Still, she had felt unwell and her husband had thought it would be a good idea if her sister could pay her a visit. His profession made it necessary for him to be away from home a good deal and although Far Flamstead was not a great distance from London it was still in the country.

There was a letter from Angelet to me: "Do come, Bersaba. I can't tell you how often I have thought of you and longed for you to be here. There is so much to tell you. Strange things happen sometimes and I want someone to talk to. Someone who understands me. . . ."

I thought then: "So her General doesn't." I wasn't surprised. He was a good deal older than she. He was very solemn and serious. Angelet ought to have married someone young and lighthearted.

"No one ever did as you did, Bersaba. Please, please come."

I was excited. I had resented her going and leaving me behind and if I went I should have a chance to escape from the rather stifling—if comfortable and deeply loving—atmosphere of home. Moreover, I wanted to see something of the world outside Cornwall.

How glad I was that I had not succumbed to Bastian!

My mother said to me, "Have you had a letter from your sister?"

I told her I had and that she was very insistent that I go to see her.

"My dearest Bersaba. You won't want to go because of Bastian perhaps. Angelet wants you; she writes as though she *needs* you. We must remember that you and she have always been together until now. It's not natural for you to be apart. But of course she has her life to live and you have yours. You must do whatever you think best. I know how much you want to be with her, but perhaps even more you prefer not to go."

I said, "I must think about this, Mother." I felt ashamed, as I always did when I deceived her, for of course I had already decided that I was going to London.

Bastian was stricken.

"You can't go," he said. "What about us?"

"I shall doubtless meet Carlotta. I'll tell her how desolate you are."

"Please, Bersaba," he implored, "be serious. That was a momentary madness, an aberration. Please, please understand. It was you I loved . . . I always loved you."

"I would prefer you to tell the truth. Lies would not be a good foundation on which to build a marriage."

That raised his hopes. I really believed he thought that I was going to marry him.

The conceit of men is past understanding. Didn't he know that he had wounded my pride so deeply that I would never forget it? Those scars were as indelible as those of the smallpox. He didn't understand that I was not the sort to forgive. I wanted reparation. I wanted revenge. I was having it now, and it was as exciting as giving way to my carnal desires would have been.

"Revenge," my mother had once said, "brings no happiness to the one who seeks it, while forgiveness brings nothing but joy."

That may have been for her. It was not in my nature to forgive.

"The Bible tells us to forgive," she said.

That might be, but I wanted an eye for an eye, a tooth for a tooth, and nothing less would satisfy me.

So I had my triumph for the day came when I told them I had definitely decided to go to Angelet.

Bastian went to Castle Paling. I was up at the top of our house to see him go. He did not know that I watched him and saw him turn and look at the house in anguish.

I had finished with Bastian. I had made him suffer as I had, and this was indeed true, for I knew that he had loved me. I had learned too the exhilarating fact that there was within me a certain attraction which had not been diminished by my illness. Moreover, I had my journey to plan and although I felt some sadness at leaving my parents I could not help but be excited at the prospect of adventure ahead and, of course, reunion with my sister. I loved my family but not with the same dedication which I think the rest of them shared. I was too self-centered for that and I had always known that my own desires and inclination must be of greater importance to me than those of others. I think many people shared this characteristic, but I had the rare virtue that I could see it and admit it. But my relationship with my sister was outside affection and family bonds; it was a mystic union. After all, we had begun life together even before we had made our appearance in the world. We were in a way necessary to each other. I sensed that in her letters. She had a husband and I was sure she loved him, but that was not enough for her. She needed me too; and in my way I needed her.

I tried to explain this to my parents because I was aware of my good fortune in possessing such: I did not have to because my mother immediately understood and told me that she was happy it should be so. Much as she hated parting from me and my sister, our happiness was of far greater importance to her than her own sorrow, and the fact that there was this bond between us had always been a great comfort to her.

"Your father is staying for some time," she told me, "and

Fennimore will not go to sea again in the foreseeable future. I am content with that, and if you can be happy with Angelet, my darling child, it is all I ask."

I told Phoebe I was going and did not mention that she would come with me. For a few moments I savored desolation which parting with me would bring her.

Then I said, "You foolish girl, you are coming with me. I shall need a maid and can you think I would take anyone else?"

She fell on her knees—she was a little dramatic, poor Phoebe—and clasped my skirts, which was a most awkward and undignified posture, as I told her sharply. She rose then, her eyes shining with admiration.

It was small wonder that life was growing rosy for me.

I wrote and told Angelet that I should soon be setting out and that brought an ecstatic response. She longed to see me. She could not wait for me. She had so much to tell me.

There was a letter which amused me from the General. It was addressed to my parents. It was extremely stilted and precise, written in handwriting which was small and neat, and yet somehow bold.

He would welcome me, he said. I would be a great comfort to Angelet, who had just had an unfortunate experience. He was discreetly referring to the child she had lost. He had mapped out my journey, which he was able to do with some knowledge, for he traveled the country a good deal in the course of his duty. He mentioned the most satisfactory inns with accounts of their virtues and shortcomings.

I was very amused. The Monarch's Head, in Dorchester, was a worthy stopping place; they would care well for the horses. The White Horse, in Taunton, was another good inn and so on. My final resting place should be at the Bald Faced Stag, in the village of Hampton, and I should reach it if I followed his route on the thirtieth of August, providing I left on the date I had suggested.

My mother said, "I think he is the sort of man who would take good care of his wife, as he has gone to such trouble to make your journey easy."

I was amused. "Poor Angelet!" I thought. "No wonder she is in need of comfort."

The Juice of the Poppy

MY SPIRITS were high as I set out. My mother was a little sad, but determined not to show it, and with my father beside her she could not be completely so. They, with my brother Fennimore, were in the courtyard when I mounted and as I turned to take a last look at my mother I wondered when I should see her again.

Phoebe was almost ecstatic. She was with me, which seemed all she needed to make her happy, and I think too she was secretly relieved to be leaving and putting so many miles between her and her self-righteous father. She had lived in terror of the blacksmith's catching her one day and taking her back to the life from which she had escaped.

It was a lovely morning. Whenever I smell the pungent odor of water mint I shall remember it; whenever I see barber's bush growing at random on wasteland I shall experience that feeling of wild exhilaration which was with me then.

Phoebe and I rode together between two grooms in the lead and two behind, and I felt like singing as we went along.

I said to Phoebe, "I am longing to see my brother-in-law. I fear he is a very stern gentleman. I wonder what he will think of us?"

"He will admire you, Mistress Bersaba."

"I doubt that."

"He must do because you're the living image of the lady he married."

"Oh, but she hasn't been ill. There will be a difference."

"Your illness has made you more beautiful, mistress."

"Now, Phoebe, that's too much!"

" 'Tis true in an odd sort of way, mistress. You're thinner and it makes you look taller and graceful like and then too . . . I don't know. It does, I know it's true."

"You are a good girl, Phoebe," I said, "but I like to have the truth, even when I don't like what it tells me."

"I swear it, mistress, and Jem was saying the same. He said, 'My word, Mistress Bersaba's illness have done something for her.' I don't know what, mistress, but 'tis true."

"Jem?"

"Him in the stables, mistress."

"Oh," I thought. "So I appeal to stableboys, do I!"

But I was happy, because although Phoebe was prejudiced, the stableboy had said that, and it was a comfort even from such quarters.

Our journey was uneventful, taking in the usual mishaps which one does not expect to travel without. One of the horses went lame and we sold it and replaced it from a dealer in one of the Wiltshire horse markets; some of the roads were flooded, which meant making a detour; another was forced on us when we heard that a certain notorious highwayman was reputed to be lurking nearby. The road across Salisbury Plain was a distance of forty miles, but there again we delayed our journey that we might not be too far from inns and villages and this added miles.

I was amazed though by the accuracy of the General's instructions, and oddly enough when we reached the Bald Faced Stag on the thirtieth of August I felt a kind of triumph as though I had taken a challenge and proved something.

The host was expecting us.

"General Tolworthy was sure that you would come this day or the next and he has asked me to reserve the best room for you," he told us.

It was indeed a pleasant room, its walls paneled, its windows leaded, and the ceiling beams of heavy oak. In it was a four-poster bed, the usual court cupboard, a chest, a small table, and two chairs, so it was very adequately furnished. Phoebe would sleep in a small adjoining room. It could not have been more comfortable.

An excellent meal awaited us of sturgeon, pigeon pie, and roast beef served with a good malmsey wine. I was hungry after a day in the saddle and as the long and arduous journey was in its last stages the thought of seeing Angelet the next day made me wildly happy.

I had retired to my room where Phoebe had taken out the things I should need for the night and I sat on the window seat which overlooked the yard, looking down at the activity below. I saw a carrier coach for the first time. These, I had heard, could only be hired in London and they did journeys of no more than thirty miles' radius. All travelers had to be prepared to stay at certain selected inns where the horses could be properly looked after. The descending passengers looked tired and I supposed only those who could not afford to travel in any other way would go by carrier coach.

A man rode into the courtyard. Tall and of commanding appearance, he wore his fair hair onto his shoulders and he had a small mustache brushed away from his lips. He was elegantly but not foppishly dressed. There was something which I could only call magnetism about him of which I was immediately aware.

On impulse I opened the window and leaned out and at that moment he looked up and saw me.

I cannot explain what happened because I did not understand it and I had never experienced it before. I felt a response in every part of my body. It seemed absurd that someone whom I did not know and whom I had not met until that moment and had only looked at for a few seconds could have this effect on me. But it was so. We seemed to gaze at each other for a long time, but it could have been only for a few seconds.

Then he took off his hat and bowed.

I inclined my head in acknowledgment and immediately moved backward and shut the window. I went to the table, on which stood a mirror, and I stared at myself. The scar of my cheek seemed to stand out white against the scarlet of my skin.

"What happened?" I asked myself. I only knew that he aroused in me some great emotion which I could not understand.

I went back to the window but he had disappeared. He must have come into the inn.

He was obviously staying here, and I wanted to see him again. I wanted to know what had happened to me. It was extraordinary. One did not feel this odd emotion—why not admit it? desire—for someone to whom one had not spoken a word. Yet somehow I thought I knew him. He had not seemed like a stranger to me.

I wondered what he had thought when he had looked up and had seen me.

I patted down my fringe and smoothed my hair, but it would not cover the scar on my left cheek. When I descended the stairs I saw him at once. He saw me too for he came forward, smiling.

"I knew you at once," he said. "The likeness to your sister is amazing."

"You are—"

"Richard Tolworthy. I thought I would come here to meet you and take you back to Far Flamstead tomorrow."

My emotions were mixed. What did the future hold, then? I knew my nature. I sometimes wished that I did not. I would have to live under the same roof with this man, and he was my sister's husband.

He had ordered that a room be kept clear for us that we might talk. The landlord had lighted a fire because he said it grew chilly in the evenings and insisted on bringing us more of the malmsey wine, of which he was very proud, and we sat at the table.

"How glad I am that you have come," he said. "Angelet has been pining for you. And how like her you are! I could almost believe she is sitting there now, but of course there is a difference—a great difference."

I could not read the thoughts in his eyes; he was not a man to betray much, so I could not ascertain what sort of impact I had made on him; I was still staggering from that which he had made on me.

I watched his fingers curl about the glass—long fingers, almost artistic, strong yet delicate, not, I should have thought, the hands of the soldier. There were fine golden hairs on the backs of them, and I felt a longing to touch them.

"Yes," I said. "There is a great difference. My illness has left its mark on me forever."

He did not deny that he could see the pockmark. I knew that he was straightforward and would never flatter.

All he said was, "You were fortunate to recover."

"I had expert nursing. My mother was determined that I should get well, and so was my maid."

"Angelet has told me."

"She must have told you a good deal about me." I suddenly began to wonder how I appeared to Angelet, how much she knew of me. I believed I understood her through and through. Did she understand me? No, Angelet would never probe into the secret minds of those about her. She saw everything black and white, good and bad. Did she adore her General? I wondered. I thought of them together, making love.

"She told me about your illness and how you contracted it."

I thought, "She would make me appear a heroine." I wondered if he thought me so. He would not for long. I could see that he was a man it would not be easy to deceive.

"I am so pleased that you have come. Angelet is a little depressed at this time."

"Yes, the miscarriage. How ill was she?"

"Not seriously, but of course she was disappointed."

"As you too must have been."

"She will soon be well again. We are living quietly at the moment. My duties have taken me up to the north. The times are somewhat unsettled."

I did know that. I had always been more interested in political matters than Angelet had.

"Yes, I understand that there are elements in the country who are not pleased with the manner in which its affairs are being conducted."

"Scotland is the trouble at the moment."

I was glad I had been reading a great deal during my illness. "Is the King wrong, do you think, to enforce the use of the prayerbook?"

"The King is the King," he said. "He is the ruler, and it is the duty of his subjects to accept him as such."

"It seems strange," I said, "that there should be revolt in the very country which nurtured his father."

"The Stuarts are Scottish and therefore there are some English who do not care for them. And the Scots complain that the King has become too English. There have been riots up there and the fact is we do not have enough money to equip the kind of army we need to subdue Scotland."

"And this of course gives you great concern and I doubt not takes you frequently from home."

"Of course a soldier must always be prepared to leave his home."

"It seems a pity to quarrel over religion."

"Many of the wars in history have been connected with it."

I tried to talk intelligently about the affairs of the country and managed tolerably well by subtly leaving him to do the talking. All the time I was learning about him. He was not a man given to trivial conversation, but he was soon telling me about his campaigns in Spain and France, and I listened, avidly, not so much because I was interested in the manner in which battles were fought, but because I wanted to know more of him.

We talked for an hour—or rather he did and I listened; and I knew that I had made an impression, for he seemed a little surprised by himself.

He said, "How knowledgeable you are of these matters. One rarely meets a woman who is."

"I have become knowledgeable tonight," I answered; and I did not mean only of the wars in France and Spain.

"I came to welcome you," he said, "and to conduct you to Far Flamstead tomorrow. I had no idea that I should pass such an interesting evening. I have enjoyed it."

"It is because you find me so much like your wife."

"No," he said, "I find you very different. The only real likeness is in your looks."

"We can be told apart . . . now," I said, touching the scar on my cheek.

"You have honorable battle scars," he said. "You must wear them boldly."

"How can I do otherwise?"

He leaned forward suddenly and said, "Let me tell you. They add an interest to your face. I am so pleased that you have come to stay with us and I hope your visit will be of long duration."

"You should reserve judgment until you know me better. Sometimes guests in the house can be quite tiresome."

"My wife's sister is not a guest. She is a member of the family and will always be welcome however long she wishes to stay."

"That, General, is a rash statement and I should never have believed you guilty of rashness."

"How can you know? We have only just met."

"But this is no ordinary meeting."

For a moment we looked full at each other. I believed my eyes were glowing warmly. His were cold. To him I was merely his wife's sister and he was pleased that I was not unintelligent. That was as far as his cautious mind would take him. But it was not all. No. Perhaps I was more knowledgeable than he in spite of the difference in our ages. Sometimes I believe that women such as I am are born with knowledge in the matter of this attraction between the sexes. I knew that somewhere, latent perhaps beneath that glacial exterior, there could be passion.

I thought of how I had teased Bastian, how I had withstood temptation with him, and now I knew of course that Bastian had meant nothing to me. I had merely penetrated briefly the edge of discovery.

I said, "I have known you through my sister, for you appeared frequently in her letters, so you see you are not a stranger to me. Moreover, my sister and I are twins . . .

identical twins. There is a bond so strong between us that the experiences of one are felt by the other."

I stood up. He took my hand in his and said earnestly, "I hope that you enjoy your stay with us."

"I know I shall," I assured him.

He conducted me to my room where Phoebe was waiting. She swept a curtsy to the General and I left him at my bedroom door.

I went to the bed and sat down. Phoebe came and unbuttoned my gown.

"You like the gentleman." It was a statement rather than a question.

"Yes," I answered, "I like the gentleman."

"He was down there alone with you."

"And you think that was wrong do you, Phoebe?"

"Mistress, 'tis not for me—"

I laughed at her. "You concern yourself unduly, Phoebe. The gentleman in question is General Tolworthy, my sister's husband, and therefore my brother-in-law."

Phoebe looked at me with wide eyes for a few seconds, then she lowered them quickly, but not before I had seen the apprehension there.

I was sure that Phoebe knew that I had had adventures. As a girl who had had her own, she would have noticed that strange elation in me; moreover she would know what it meant. She may have felt it herself when she lingered in the cornfields with the man who had fathered the child who had been her disgrace and her salvation.

I could not sleep that night. I kept going over our conversation in my mind. His face haunted me: the outline of his features, the fine but well-marked brows, the cold glitter of the blue eyes, the correct manner, the absence of any awareness that I was a woman; and yet . . . there was something . . . some little spark of understanding, some rapport that flashed between us.

I reversed our positions. Suppose I had been the one who had come to Carlotta; suppose Angelet had been the one who had caught the pox? I would have been his wife. Or should I? Why had he chosen her? She told me about her adventure in the streets of London. I could imagine that when he rescued and protected her, her helplessness would have appealed to him. I suppose had my purse been snatched I should have attempted to retrieve it. Suppose then that I had been Angelet and his wife. Angelet would be lying in this bed now coming to stay with me.

I had to know what it was like between them. Was he in love with her and she with him?

I should soon discover when I lived in that house with them. And what would be the result of my living there?

I tried to talk to myself secretly. You know your nature. You need to be married. Phoebe knows it. Perhaps she does also. Should I try to find a husband for her . . . someone who will adore me for giving him the opportunity of marrying Phoebe and coming into my service? Why did I always want people to admire me? Why couldn't I be simple and uncomplicated like Angelet? But perhaps she was no longer so simple. She had married; she had slept in this man's bed; she would have borne his child if something had not gone wrong. She must have changed.

Did I not know myself? I had been ill for so long and I am suddenly awakened to life. I had flirted with Bastian again and although my pride would not let me take him as a lover, I had wanted to. But then it was not necessarily Bastian I had wanted. Now I met this man and he was different from anyone I had known. He was not like the Kroll boys and the Lamptons, with whom I had grown up. There was a remoteness about him which intrigued me; he was worldly; he had lived; he had fought battles and faced death. He fascinated me, therefore. And he was my sister's husband and because of this strange relationship between us which I do not altogether understand I must have this feeling for him.

At last I slept and I was awakened by Phoebe in the early morning because we were to leave the inn precisely at seven of the clock.

We breakfasted together and talked easily as we had before.

He told me of his home in the north, and I told him I could imagine his ancestors defending their homes against the Picts. He had a look of the Dane about him and I said that his ancestors must have come in their long ships and ravaged our coasts.

He said that may have been, but they claimed to have come with William the Conqueror, and we talked about war and how it had always existed in the world. I said how much better it might be if these matters could be settled in other ways.

As a soldier he could not see how else they could be settled because there would always be people who would not

222

keep their word and the only real way of enforcing law and order was by force.

"It's strange," I said, "that to produce peace one must go to war."

"Antidotes are often like that," he told me. "I have learned something of the use of herbs, and I find that the effects of one poison are often nullified by the action of another."

Then he talked about herbs and how he had often used them after battles, and so the breakfast hour passed quickly.

We were to leave at seven and we did—on the stroke. I was amused at his precision. I guessed that unpunctuality was something which would seem almost a crime to him, and I wondered how Angelet fared, because punctuality had never been one of her virtues.

I rode beside him and I thanked him for the courtesy of coming to the Bald Faced Stag to escort me to his home. He waved that aside and said that of course he would come to meet his new sister and it had been a thoroughly enjoyable experience. His face was very earnest as he said, "I hope you will not find it too quiet at Far Flamstead. Later of course we shall go to my residence in Whitehall and there of course you will meet people from the Court. At this time I feel that Angelet needs to regain her strength, and I wish her to live quietly."

"Of course. I live in the country, which I imagine is far quieter than Far Flamstead, so you need have no fears on that score."

"I am sure your coming is going to be of great benefit to us both."

He pointed out the features of the landscape as we passed along and I was struck by the difference in the country from that to which I was accustomed. Our trees bore the marks of their battles with the southwest gales; here in the southeast of England, the trees—lime, plane, horse chestnut—seemed stately; there was a neatness about them as though their branches had been trimmed, and although the grass might seem of less verdant green than ours—but only slightly so— fields often gave the impression that the grass had just been cut. There was almost an elegance about it which our rougher Cornish landscape lacked.

And finally we came to Far Flamstead. I noticed his pride when he pointed it out—a gracious house, clearly built during the early years of the great Queen—red brick, half-timbered with latticed windows surrounded by pleasant gardens.

I caught a glimpse of a gray tower and I cried, "That must be the castle of which Angelet told me."

Because I was so much aware of him and had become most susceptible to his changing moods, I knew he was sorry I had mentioned the castle. There was something about it which disturbed him.

"It's a ruin, isn't it?"

"Hardly that. A folly is a better description."

"Which means something that is useless."

"Oh, er . . . yes, of course."

"Doesn't it take up space which could be used for other purposes?"

"My ancestor built it and there is a legend about it. It is not to be disturbed."

"Because if it were it would bring ill luck to the family or something like that?"

"Yes, I suppose so."

"Are you superstitious?"

"We all are at times. Those who declare they are not are often proven to be more so than the rest of us. It is a natural instinct for mankind to be superstitious. Imagine him when understanding first began to dawn on him. He was afraid . . . afraid of the moon, afraid of the sun, afraid of the wild beasts which roamed the land, and out of fear superstition grew. It's a natural instinct."

"So you believe that while we have something to fear we shall be superstitious about it. I know. There is a legend that while the castle remains all will go well with the house."

He was silent, and I longed to know the real truth about the castle.

But now we were riding into the courtyard, and there was my sister.

"Bersaba," she called. I dismounted, and she flung herself into my arms.

We talked. How we talked! There was so much to say. She must know what had happened at home since she had left, but she was not more anxious than I to hear what had happened to her.

She told me of her rescue by Richard; she spoke of his courtship and their marriage and how she had come to Far Flamstead to be mistress of it.

But although she talked incessantly and described in detail, she told me nothing of her relationship with her husband. In fact I noticed a certain reluctance in her to do so.

She took me into a charming bedchamber which she called the Lavender Room and which was to be mine. The curtains about the bed were embroidered with sprigs of lavender, as were the curtains, and the rugs were of a delicate shade of mauve.

Next to it was the Blue Room, which she often used as a bedroom.

"Not always?"

"No." She was faintly embarrassed. "I have slept in it . . . since. . . . Not always of course. But after my miscarriage I had to rest a good deal, and it was decided that I ought to have a bedroom of my own."

"Apart," I said, "from the connubial chamber."

"Well . . . yes. It's a very restful room."

There was that about my sister which was still virginal. It was hard to believe that she had been married and but for an accident might have been about to become a mother.

The Blue Room was charming, very much like the Lavender Room. I wondered whether it had been Richard Tolworthy's idea that she should have this retreat.

She talked about the events which led up to her miscarriage and how she had heard it said that the castle was haunted and one night, seeing a light there, she had gone up to the castle room to look. She had seen . . . something . . . she was not quite sure what. A face, she had thought, and oddly enough she believed she had seen the face before. The servants were convinced that she had had a nightmare, but she didn't really think that was so. In any case she had had a fright and they said that had brought on her miscarriage.

I remembered the strange look in Richard Tolworthy's face when he had talked of the castle and I longed to know more about it, because I felt that in learning that I would know more about him.

Those first days were full of vivid impressions. I rode out with my sister and she showed me the Longridge Farmhouse.

Richard had ridden over, she told me, to thank them for what they had done for her, although relations were strained between them. She told me how Richard had once challenged Luke Longridge to a duel.

"A duel!" I cried, because this seemed to shed a new light on his character. I could not imagine his being romantically rash "What? Was it over a woman?"

Angelet laughed. "Certainly not. Luke Longridge was disloyal to the King."

"I see your husband is an ardent Royalist," I commented.

She was thoughtful. "He is a soldier, and his duty is to be loyal to the King."

"Yes." I thought, "he is a man who would always act conventionally. He might not admire the King, but he served him and therefore would defend him to the death if need be."

He was the sort of man who would adhere strictly to the conventions.

So I rode and walked and talked with Angelet. Sometimes, when the evenings were drawing in, I would see a certain apprehension in her eyes. Sometimes I would go quietly to the door of her room and peep inside. If she were not there I would know that she was in what I called the connubial bed with him.

Once he spent a night away, and I was struck with her relief. Yet when she talked of him her eyes glowed with such admiration that anyone would have said that she was deeply in love with him.

I tried to sound her about that side of her relationship with him.

"Soon," I said, "we shall be hearing you are with child again."

I saw the shiver pass through her.

"What's the matter, Angelet? You want children, don't you?"

"Of course."

"And he . . . your husband?"

"Yes, naturally he wants children."

"Well then since you both do . . ."

She turned away from me, but I caught her arm. "Are you happy, Angel?"

"Of course."

"Marriage is everything you want . . . *everything.* . . ."

I made her look at me, for she had never been able to lie to me. Now I could see that blankness in her eyes which showed me she was trying to hide something.

"There are things about marriage," she said, "of which you would be ignorant."

I felt laughter bubbling up inside me.

"Such as?" I asked.

"I can't explain. You will have to wait until you have a husband yourself."

From that moment the situation became clear to me. I knew that my sister had endured with stoicism those occasions which her contract had forced her to spend in the marriage bed. I wondered what effect her attitude had on him. He must be aware of it and it would give little comfort to him.

I looked forward to the evenings when he was with us. I played chess with him and now and then beat him. That surprised him a little, but at the same time he was pleased.

Bringing out his miniature soldiers and placing them on a mock battlefield, he would show us how he had fought and won battles.

I watched intently, determined to gain his attention. I would ask questions about the tactics and once expressed doubts as to the wisdom of employing them. Those well-marked eyebrows would shoot up as he talked to me, as though amazed at my temerity in questioning a professional soldier.

Once I took the infantry and placed it in another position. Instead of reproving me or trying to stop me, he said, "Then in that case I should have brought the cavalry over here."

"The infantry is behind this ridge of hills," I pointed out. "Your cavalry would not have been aware that they had changed position."

"They would have seen."

"No, they moved by night."

"My spies would have informed me."

"Ah, but my spies recognized your spies. You have used the same men too often. They misled you and you are under the impression that they are concealed by *this* ridge. They moved silently on to another."

I saw the glint in his eyes as mine met his and held them.

"What do you know of battle?" he demanded.

"Battle is strategy and tactics. A woman, you know, is rather skilled in these arts."

He was amused and, I knew, excited; and we played out our mock battles.

Angelet sat in her chair, watching us.

Afterward she said to me, "You shouldn't have talked like that to Richard. It was rather arrogant, wasn't it? As though you knew as much about fighting battles as he does."

"They are only battles with toy soldiers."

"They are real to him. He is reconstructing battles he has fought and won."

"Then it is well for him to have an opposing general to outwit him."

"You . . . Bersaba!"

227

"Yes," I retorted, "why not?"

"I don't think he was very pleased."

But of course he was, and we went on playing our games on the mock battlefields and the chessboard. I looked forward to those evenings when I would be so aware of him and try to make him aware of me. Then, when I was alone at night, I would think of him. I knew that the terrible fascination which I had felt when we had first met had by no means diminished. In fact it grew every day.

Once Angelet said to me, "Richard was talking of you last night."

"Yes?" I asked eagerly. "What did he say?"

"He said that we must entertain. He would rather we did it in London, though. He said that would be more interesting."

"But you said he was talking of me."

"It was of you. He said we should find a husband for you."

I felt angry with him, and I said, "Does he want me out of the house?"

"Oh, no, Bersaba! You mustn't think that. He likes to have you here because he knows I do. He said you are amusing and attractive and ought to be married. Just for now he wants us to stay here because of my health. He doesn't think I'm well enough yet for anything but the quiet life."

He had said I was amusing and attractive, but he wanted to find a husband for me.

I felt half pleased yet half angry and frustrated.

I was uneasy about this household of servants. Had I been mistress of Far Flamstead I should have wanted to know more about them. The chief ones of course were the Cherrys and the man Jesson. The latter was a silent-footed, self-effacing, yet efficient man of whom one saw so little that one was inclined to forget he existed. He was a sort of gray eminence, I imagined, for the servants spoke of him with awe. His daughters were very much in evidence. Meg was Angelet's personal maid and her sister Grace was a sort of part-time midwife, according to Angelet. Her services would not be in great demand in the house, as most of the servants were men, but she would be useful if Angelet ever needed her. She had a great belief in Grace's wisdom, for it seemed the woman had known she was pregnant before Angelet had been sure of it herself.

I thought how like Richard it was to have a house managed by his own sex. All these men had served under him at some time, I gathered, and had left the Army for some reason. He would be their benefactor and would reason, in his cold analytical way, that they would doubtless give him better service because of this.

Mrs. Cherry and her husband seemed a conventional enough couple. She was in charge of the kitchens and he acted with Jesson as a general factotum. I had to admit the house was run smoothly. Every clock kept exact time and meals were served precisely on the stroke of the intended hour. It was amusing. Angelet scarcely behaved like the mistress of the house, for she had made no changes. I thought I should have done so just to show these people that I was the mistress.

There was no doubt that I was regarded with some interest and. I imagined, mild suspicion. I would often find Mrs. Cherry's eyes watching me with a wary look in them as though she were pondering what I would do next.

I had been fascinated by the castle from the first and became more so when Angelet told me not to approach it as it was a ruin in danger of collapse and Richard had given firm orders that no one was to go near it. She told me she believed he would be very angry if any of us disobeyed his orders.

She took me up to the Castle Room, which had been used by his first wife. A brief marriage that had only lasted a year before she died in childbirth.

What did she know of the wife? I asked. Had she learned anything about her?

Very little, she answered. People didn't talk about her. She had died more than ten years ago.

"And Richard? Don't you ask him?"

"I don't think he would like that."

"You are a very good wife I'm sure, Angelet. Do you always do as he wishes?"

"Of course. Why does that amuse you?"

"I was just thinking that were I in your place I would at times be a little rebellious."

"You would not. You have not been married and know nothing of the relationship between a man and his wife. Naturally I wish to please him in all things. . . ."

Her voice faltered. "Oh, yes, little sister," I thought. "You want to serve him in all things even though it is so distressing for you to submit to his embraces."

The situation amused and intrigued me; and there was the perpetual excitement of his presence. I found that all through the day I was waiting for the evening—those seemingly quiet evenings when Angelet sat at her embroidery and he and I talked or played out our battles on the chessboard or paper battleground.

I read some of the books I found in his library. He discovered me there one day, coming upon me rather silently and looking over my shoulder.

"What are you reading, Bersaba?" he asked.

I showed him.

"And it interests you?"

"Enormously."

"You should have been a soldier."

"They do not recruit women, I believe."

"There is certainly one woman I know who would be as efficient as any man."

"I might not excel on the battleground, but I should like to plan the battles."

"You would be a general without delay."

The faint lift of the lips was gratifying, for he was a man who did not smile very much. I wondered why. Was it because life had been difficult for him? I longed to know. I was not sure whether I was in love with him. I knew that I wanted to be with him, that I wanted him to make love to me so fervently that this obscured all other feelings. It had not been like this with Bastian. There had been no mystery about my cousin. I knew everything of importance that had happened throughout his life. But here was my sister's husband with that immense physical attraction which had overwhelmed me from the moment I had seen him and was growing every day. It was enhanced by that cool exterior, but being the woman I was I knew that was but a covering—a protective one perhaps —a disguise such as he would employ in battle tactics. Every day I learned something of him because I made him the subject of my main interest. He was conventional in the extreme; he had been brought up to believe in certain ideals. He would never swerve from them although he was extremely logical in all other matters. Loyalty to the King and the family would remain. I admired him for this (and yet I felt a perverse desire to break through them). Something had happened to him— something tragic, I knew that. Often I fancied that the secret was in this house. These servants of his—the Cherrys and the Jessons—did they know anything? They had been in his service for a long time. His young wife had died in childbed. Had he loved her tenderly, passionately? What a tragedy to lose both his wife and the child he had longed for . . . for he was the sort of man who would want sons. It would certainly be a tradition of the family to carry on the line. There was a younger brother in the north, at Flamstead Castle, I gathered. I suppose he visited him there when he went on his travels. Why had he waited ten years after his first wife's death before he had married? And why Angelet? Was she pretty? It was hard to say when you are judging a face so like your own. She had an innocence which I lacked. She would always have it. It went with her virginal nature. She was loving, emotional, romantic—and passionless. Once again I pictured nature neatly dividing our characteristics. "That one for you, Angelet, that for Bersaba." Gentleness, mildness, simplicity for Angelet. And for Bersaba an overwhelming sensuality which when at its pitch blindly demanded satisfaction without thought of consequences. That comes first and that force will govern her life. For the rest she is selfish; she is proud; she is arrogant. But she has a lively mind and an ability to learn and perhaps —but she is not yet sure of this—an ability to get what she wants.

But she is not all bad, I defended. I touched the scars of my brow and I thought of how the determination to save Phoebe had seemed more important to me than anything, although I had not known of course when I set out on that journey in the rain to bring the midwife what effect it was going to have on my life. Would I have gone then? Certainly not. I was not all that noble.

So the days passed and I had been in the house a month. Angelet still professed herself to tire easily, but I knew that this was to excuse herself from sharing the big four-poster bed with her husband. He was never insistent, I was sure.

She was always hoping that she would become pregnant, though. She did want a child. She would make a very good mother I was sure, and I fancy too that she believed that if she conceived she could reasonably hope to escape from those nightly embraces.

Then temptation came suddenly and without warning.

During the day a messenger came for Richard and he left for Whitehall immediately, telling us that he thought he might well be back the following afternoon.

I felt depressed because the day would be empty without him, and I wondered how I would get through it. I could not sit as Angelet could for hours over a piece of needlework. I would read as long as the light was good; I rode; I walked a little. I enjoyed exploring the grounds and I often found myself skirting the castle surrounded by its high wall the top of which I discovered was covered in small pieces of broken glass. Richard had certainly gone to great lengths to prevent anyone's gaining access to the castle over that wall.

During the afternoon Angelet and I had arranged to ride out together, but Meg came to my room when I was about to change into my riding habit to say that my sister wanted to speak to me. She was in the Blue Room and I went to her at once. She was lying on her bed looking very sorry for herself, and I saw the reason was a swelling on the left side of her face.

"It's toothache, mistress," said Meg. "My lady has had it all the morning."

I went over to Angelet; her eyes were half closed and she was evidently in some pain.

"You want some of Mother's camomile concoction," I said. "It never fails."

"Mrs. Cherry has a good one," said Meg. "She be clever with herbs."

"I'll go and see her," I said.

Mrs. Cherry was in the kitchen, rosy from baking. She gave me that quick look of suspicion which I had noticed previously before her features settled into the benign mask of friendly bonhomie.

"Mrs. Cherry," I said, "my sister is suffering from a raging toothache. Meg says you have something for it."

"Why bless you, mistress, indeed I have. I've got my own little stillroom here. I can give her something that'll send her to sleep and that's going to soothe the tooth."

"My mother made a mixture of camomile and poppy juice and something else. It was most effective."

"Mine has these. It'll cure it in time but she may need a dose or two."

"Could you please give it to me?"

"With the greatest of pleasure, mistress."

She gave me the bottle with the mixture in it and I took it immediately to my sister. I smelled it. It was slightly different from the one our mother made.

"Take this, Angelet," I said, "and then you'll sleep."

She obeyed and I sat with her for a while until she went to sleep. I stood over her bed, looking at her. She looked so young and innocent lying there in that deep sleep; her hair had fallen away from her smooth white brow. I felt my fingers go involuntarily to my own. If people saw us lying side by side they would tell the difference. The scarred one is Bersaba. I felt a sudden wild envy because she was his wife, and I could think of nothing I wanted more than to be just that. Then I thought of the frightened look which used to come into her eyes when darkness fell, and the excuses she would make to stay in the Blue Room and I was sorry for her.

I went out to the stables and told the groom to saddle my horse. He wanted to come with me because it was understood that neither I nor Angelet would ride out alone; but I had to be alone. I wanted to think what I was doing here and how long I was going to stay.

I thought of his coming back. He might say, "We are going to Whitehall. There we shall entertain. I will bring interesting people to my house; perhaps we shall find a husband for Bersaba."

There was an anger in my heart for a fate which had used me so unkindly—which had scarred me and then brought me after he had become my sister's husband to the man whom I wanted as I believed I never would another. My nature was such that it needed fulfillment; I was beginning to know myself. I cared nothing for Bastian. I never had. I had been mistaken in a certain natural need and called it love.

But Richard Tolworthy obsessed me. I thought of him during the night and day; and a day such as this one, when he was away, was a day without meaning. I suppose this was what people called being in love.

I rode on without taking much notice of where I went. I said to myself, "I must write to my mother. I must go home. I can't stay here. It is unwise and I don't know to what it might lead. I will say Angelet is getting well and I miss my home."

A man was riding toward me. As he drew up he lifted his hat and bowed to me.

"Good day to you," he said. "It's long since you called on us."

I looked at him in amazement and he returned my gaze. Then understanding dawned on me.

"You must be mistaking me for my sister. I am Bersaba Landor."

"Indeed. It is so? Mistress Tolworthy has mentioned that she had a twin sister."

"I am that twin sister."

"Then I am happy to make your acquaintance and so will my sister be. Would you care to call on her? Our farmhouse is but half a mile away."

I was ready for such an adventure on this day of emptiness and I expressed my readiness to meet his sister.

I studied him as we rode while he chatted in a rather reserved manner about the crops and the harvest. I could always be interested in other people's affairs. It was a quality I had which made up for the lack of that sweetness (of which Angelet had taken the major share) and while she would have expressed polite interest it would have been clear that her mind was wandering off somewhere else. But mine was a genuine desire to learn what people were doing and this was one of the reasons why I sometimes seemed to win people's admiration, for there is nothing to delight them more than a show of interest for their concerns.

I gathered at once that this man who introduced himself as Luke Longridge was a Puritan. His dress proclaimed him as that and when I met his sister in her plain gray gown I was convinced of this.

The farmhouse was cozy and I was given some of their homemade brew and hotcakes to go with it, which was pleasant, and the sister, Ella, asked after Angelet. I told them of the toothache and they in their turn wished their condolences to be taken to her. I heard from Ella what I had already heard from Angelet, how my sister had ridden over and been taken ill there at the time of her miscarriage.

I asked a great deal of questions about the farm and learned that that January had been a very bad time, as the inclement weather had made lambing difficult, and how busy they had been planting the runcival or marrow fat peas. The barley sowing had gone well in March and Ella had had her hands full in April as she always did, sowing flax and hemp and of course the herbs in her own garden. Hops were very profitable and since they had been introduced into the country during the reign of Henry VIII a great many farmers were growing them even though they needed very special attention.

Then we went into the difficulties of the hay and the corn harvests, for which of course they required extra labor and had to call in traveling laborers to give a hand.

I sensed though that the real interest of this household was not so much farming as politics and I realized that Luke Longridge had a burning desire to make his opinions known.

He was a reformer. That was obvious. I must compare him with Richard Tolworthy, for I compared all men with him. Richard's mind ran along the lines it knew it should go. He was a strong man, with firm ideals. Luke Longridge was a rebel against those very conventions which Richard upheld so strongly.

I thought suddenly of what Angelet had told me about a man she had seen in a pillory, his face blooded because someone, by order of the law, had just deprived him of his ears.

I said, "I suppose one should be careful of making too much comment lest it come to mischievous ears."

He smiled, and I saw a fanatical light in his eyes. This man would be a martyr if the occasion arose to demand it. I had always thought martyrdom foolish, for what good did it do to die for a cause? Surely it was much better to live and fight for it in secret? I said something of this and I saw an expression in his eyes which I realize I kindled. I was not quite sure what it meant but I was aware of it.

I went on to say that I thought that there was peace with the Scots over the matter of religion, which had been causing a great deal of trouble there, and he answered that the Parliament of Scotland had confirmed the acts of the General Assembly, which was right and fitting, and that they were in communication with some of the leading Puritans in England.

"Of which you are one," I said.

He looked down at his plain garb and said, "I can see that you are aware of my opinions."

"They are clear to see."

"And you come from a Royalist household so you will doubtless not wish to call on us again."

"I would certainly wish to call on you, to hear your arguments. How can one form an opinion unless one hears from both sides?"

"I doubt the General would wish you to come here to talk politics. He has not forbidden his wife to call, no doubt because my sister was of some use to her when she was ill and he is grateful, but I feel sure he does not wish for regular visits between our families."

"The General may command his armies if he wishes but he could not command me."

I saw the faint color in his cheeks and I knew that he found it difficult to take his eyes from me. Women such as myself, who are attracted by men, attract them in turn. Something passes between us. I was aware of it now with Luke Longridge; though my thoughts were obsessed by Richard Tolworthy, strangely enough I could still be interested in Luke Longridge and feel an upsurge of spirits because he, this stern Puritan, was not entirely indifferent to me, although I came from what he called a Royalist background.

So it was an interesting hour I spent in the Longridges' farm kitchen and afterward Luke insisted on riding back with me.

He admonished me mildly as we rode, telling me that it

was unwise for me to take solitary rides. "There are footpads lurking around," he said. "A lady alone would be easy prey."

"I would never be easy prey, I do assure you."

"You do not realize how rough these men can be. I would beg of you to take care."

"It is good of you to concern yourself," I told him and he replied, "I look forward to more interesting discussions. Do you think I could turn you to our way of thinking in time?"

"I doubt it," I answered. "Although I have an open mind."

We soon came to Far Flamstead. He bowed gravely and as I took my leave I was aware of that expression in his eyes which I aroused in others, and I was amused, he being a Puritan.

The encounter had made something of that dull day. I had discovered that scarred or not I was still attractive.

I went into the Blue Room where Angelet was still asleep. Meg was hovering about and I asked if her mistress had not wakened since she had had the posset.

"No, she have been in this deep and peaceful sleep, mistress."

She was still sleeping in the evening and I went down to see Mrs. Cherry.

I said, "The posset is very potent. Mistress Tolworthy has slept all through the day."

" 'Tis the poppy juice," said Mrs. Cherry comfortably. "There is nothing like deep sleep to get us through our ills."

"Should she have another dose when she awakens?"

"The tooth will have recovered, I doubt not. But keep the bottle in case she should need it."

She slept through the night and when I went in to see her she declared her toothache was better.

The next morning we went for a ride and in the afternoon Richard returned. He had a great deal of work to do, we were told, and he went to his library.

We supped together in the small parlor and Richard told us that as he thought that he would have to be in Whitehall often it might be a good idea if he stayed there. It would save the journey back and forth from Flamstead.

I asked if the trouble with the Puritans and the Scots had anything to do with his business there.

"Not any more than other matters," he told me. "The Army is below strength and I am constantly attempting to have that rectified. This entails meetings with the King. There have been too many troubles. The war with Spain was a disaster."

"I believe he went into that to gratify his great friend Buckingham."

"There is no doubt that Buckingham had immense influence with the King."

"His murder, while untimely for him, was timely for England."

"Who can say? But our troubles seem to be rising through the financial embarrassments caused by the wars with France and Spain and this means that everyone not in the Army fails to see the importance of it. This is what I have to drive home."

"Perhaps if the King did not govern like an absolute monarch, there would not be this trouble."

Richard looked earnestly at me. "Who shall say?" he said. "But I regret the murmurings against His Majesty. I cannot see that they will bring aught but ill to the land, and I want us to be ready to meet whatever comes."

"How knowledgeable you are, Bersaba," said Angelet.

"Knowledgeable enough to realize how little I know," I replied. "I read a good deal and listen when I can and thus I pick up certain information."

Richard smiled at me approvingly and, remembering the admiration I had seen in Luke Longridge's eyes, a glow of confidence came to me and I think perhaps it was this which made me act as I did.

As she was eating, Angelet suddenly put her hand to her cheek.

"The tooth?" I asked.

She nodded. Then she said, "I had a rather painful tooth while you were away, Richard. Mrs. Cherry prescribed one of her possets. I must say they are good."

He expressed concern that she had suffered and his pleasure that Mrs. Cherry had produced the cure. And we talked of the effects of the ship tax and other such matters, which excluded Angelet from the conversation, and when the meal was over he went back to his study to work.

After we had left the supper table Angelet complained of her tooth. Eating had brought it on again and she was in pain. I suggested that she have a dose of Mrs. Cherry's concoction, which had done her so much good before, and she eagerly agreed that this had helped her once and would do so again. I could see that she was telling herself that if she had a violent toothache Richard would not expect her to join him and the thought comforted her considerably. I even wondered whether in some ways she welcomed this painful tooth.

"He can be told that my tooth is bothering me—" she began.

"I'll send Meg," I said.

I helped her undress and poured out the liquid myself. "It seems a little more than last time," I said.

"Never mind. It will make me sleep the better."

She drank it eagerly, and it was not long before the poppy juice had its effect. I sat by her bed for a while, watching her. I was struck by the youthful innocence of her face; there was a certain smile about her lips which suggested satisfaction, and I knew this was because she had escaped from a situation which was distasteful to her.

I rang the bell for Meg so that she could take a message to the study where Richard was working. She did not answer it. I remember then that Angelet had said something earlier about her bell's being out of order and that it was going to be repaired.

I went to my room, but my thoughts were so full of what was happening between Richard and Angelet that I forgot Meg. I undressed slowly and sat before my mirror for a while. I did not see myself, but my sister's innocent face with that smile of relief on her lips, and I thought how different we were and what I would have given to have been in her place. I remembered then that Richard had not been told of her toothache and that I had promised that Meg should take the message.

On impulse I decided that I would tell him myself. I went quickly to the library, but he was not there. The house seemed very quiet as, with a wildly beating heart, I made my way to their bedroom.

He must have heard my footsteps, for as I lifted my hand to the handle the door was opened. He took my hand and drew me in.

His touch unnerved me. Fleetingly, my need of him swept over me, subduing everything else. He did not speak. It was as though some spark had ignited the passion in us both. He drew me to him and then it was too late for me to resist.

"Angelet . . ." he began softly.

Now was the moment to explain. I almost did . . . and then it passed. Of course I looked like her. He could not see the scars by candlelight. While I despised myself, I was making a bargain with fate. Let this happen. . . . Just once, and I'll go away. I'll never come back. I'll never see him again.

And then I did this wicked thing. I went on letting him believe I was Angelet. I deceived him and I deceived myself in the belief that it could do no harm to my sister.

The excitement was intense, for when I was in his arms his response was immediate. I don't think either of us could have turned back then. I had to give myself up to this over-powering desire. I could think of nothing else. I would leave remorse for the morrow.

Exploration in the Night

I AWOKE with the dawn. He was sleeping beside me and the enormity of what I had done swept over me. I was horrified. It could not be true. I had dreamed it.

Quietly I slipped out of the bed, terrified that he would awaken and see me. What could I say to him? How could I explain?

Trembling, I sped across the room and quietly opened the door. I reached the Lavender Room unobserved but before entering it I looked in at the Blue Room where Angelet was sleeping peacefully in her poppy-juice sleep.

I went to my bed and lay there.

"You have betrayed your sister's faith in you," I told myself. Then I wondered: Had he known? Was it possible that he could have been deceived?

How young and inexperienced I had been to think that I had reached the heights with Bastian! My intuition in the inn yard had not been false. We were meant for each other.

What would come out of this? I was torn between a certain exultation and desperate shame. How could I ever explain my feelings to anyone? I was in love with him, if love was obsession. I wanted to be with him, to talk to him, to discover his needs and supply them, to learn of everything he did and be beside him throughout his life. How could I go into battle with him? I allowed myself to make the most ridiculous images. I saw myself disguised as a soldier in his army. I would go to his camp secretly in the night as I had gone to his bedchamber last night. Always there would be this adventure of loving and possessing.

The room was growing light and fantasies disappeared in the cold brightness of day. What I had done was unforgivable. Knowing my sister had taken a sleeping draught, I had gone to her husband. It was like something out of the Bible. Retribution would follow. I had committed the sin of fornication and induced him to commit adultery without his knowledge. Or was it? How could I know what he was like with Angelet? What had he thought to find his frigid wife changed into a demanding passionate woman.

He *must* have known. What would he do now? I could not guess, for the truth was that although I knew he was the one man in the world for me, I did not know him.

Phoebe had come into the room. I saw her startled eyes go to the bed and her relief when she saw me there. She knew. She had betrayed that much. She must have come in and found my bed not slept in. Perhaps she looked in through the night. I need not fear Phoebe. She was there to protect me.

"It's a bright morning, Phoebe," I said, trying to make my voice sound natural.

"Yes, mistress, 'tis very bright."

She had her back to me while she set down the hot water and I had a fancy that she did not want to look me in the eyes.

"I trust my sister's tooth is better," I said. "It was very bad last night."

"I saw Meg on my way in, mistress," she said. "Mistress Tolworthy be still sleeping."

"A peaceful night will have done her the world of good."

As I dressed I wondered if my appearance had changed. Surely such an experience would have left its mark. What would it be like facing him? I promised myself that I should know as soon as I saw him if he was aware of what had happened. But surely such a straightforward man would have said so.

His response had been immediate. It was like a river that had been blocked up for years and had broken its banks.

He was in the dining hall, seated at the table.

"Good day," I said.

He stood up and bowed. I could not see his eyes.

"Good day, Bersaba."

"It is a fine one."

"Indeed, yes."

"Poor Angelet has had a return of her toothache. She is resting."

"That's unfortunate," he said.

I was afraid to meet his eyes. I took a tankard of ale and some cob bread and cold bacon. I was surprised to find that I was hungry.

"I shall have to go to Whitehall this morning," he said. "I shall be leaving within the hour."

"Another summons?" I asked.

"Yes. These are difficult times."

"Will it be a long stay?"

"I think not. I shall soon be making arrangements for Angelet and you to come with me. I think you would enjoy it. It is rather quiet for you here."

"I . . . am happy here," I said. There was a faint tremor in my voice. I could not understand him. His expression was blank. He was not the same man whose bed I had shared such a short while ago.

"He cannot know," I told myself, and I felt sick with disappointment. Could he possibly have thought some change had come over Angelet? I wondered what he thought of her leaving his bed without a word. Perhaps he would reason that she had awakened with her toothache and had quietly slipped away for her dose of Mrs. Cherry's cure. That did not seem unlikely. I was sure that he could not have regarded me so dispassionately if he had had the slightest suspicion. And yet . . . how could it be otherwise? Was I wrong? Was Angelet deceiving me? But why should she? No, I knew enough about these matters and about her to realize that she was frigid and passionless. Then how could he believe a woman would change overnight, and if he had discovered his wife to be so different, how could he tear himself away from her to go to Whitehall? Surely he would have wanted to take her with him?

He was an enigma, and I was no nearer to understanding him than I had been before we had become lovers.

"You say Angelet is sleeping?" he asked.

"Yes. The cure has that effect."

"Then I'll not disturb her. Perhaps you will tell her that I have been called away."

"I will do that."

He rose and bowed to me. "Now if you will excuse me, I have certain preparations to make."

I looked after him in dismay. It was an anticlimax to my passionate adventure.

241

By the time Angelet awoke he had left. I went into her room and she looked at me drowsily.

"What a long sleep you've had!" I said. "There is no doubt about it, Mrs. Cherry's cure is potent. How is the toothache?"

"It's gone."

"It's the sleep that does it. It's so refreshing. By the way, Richard has been called away."

"Oh . . . to Whitehall?"

"Yes. I saw him at breakfast. He said he wouldn't disturb you and asked me to tell you."

"How long will he be away?"

"He wasn't sure. He talked about our going to Whitehall."

She sat up in bed. She looked rested and very young and I noticed that there was no swelling on her cheek now.

"We should, of course," she said. "I want to find a husband for you."

"There speaks the matron," I said. "Are you so pleased with the state of matrimony that you would see everyone else trapped in it?"

I was watching her closely and I saw the faint flush under her skin. I had done her no harm, I promised myself. I had only taken what she did not want.

"You should be married," she said. "Mother will expect it."

"I daresay Mother would rather I married someone near home. She won't want to lose both of us."

"She will not want what is happier for her, but for you. You will make a more suitable match here and I think she would like us to be together."

I wondered if she would if she knew. Dear Mother, whose love had run so smoothly. How horrified she would be if she knew what had happened last night.

"Is that what you want, Angel?"

"You know it is. I feel part of me is missing when you're not here."

"Yes, we are very close together are we not? We are like one person."

"It's true and it's right that we should be together. I hope you will marry someone from the Court. It will have to be a grand marriage for you, Bersaba. You always wanted the best."

"It will have to be as grand as yours."

"Oh, grander. You always had to score, didn't you? You always thought you would marry first."

242

"You had the start while I was laid low." I lifted my fringe. "And look at me now."

"It doesn't detract from your looks, really it doesn't. It makes you more interesting, and when you think how you got them . . ."

"I can't live on that glory forever," I said sharply. "It never matters how one acquires scars. All the world sees is that they are there."

"Richard said we must have a husband worthy of you."

"Did he? When?"

"Some time ago. He has a great regard for you, Bersaba. He said you would be a help to a husband. You're clever, he said. You should marry some official at Court. He said you would be a mistress of intrigue. Yes, that's what he said."

"Did he indeed!"

"Oh, he said it most kindly. He really has great respect for you. I know he wants to get us to Whitehall so that he can find a good husband for you."

"It is kind of him to be so considerate," I said coldly.

And I was thinking, "He didn't know. He couldn't. Yet how could he not?"

He stayed in Whitehall for a week. Was it Army affairs or was it because he knew and did not want to come back to this bizarre situation?

I could not rest. I should go away, of course. It was right that I should. But I longed to see him again. At one stage I almost felt that I would go to him and try to explain what I felt. I must somehow bring an end to this intolerable state of affairs. I was dreadfully uneasy about Angelet and could not bear to contemplate what her horror would be if she knew what had happened. She would never understand. I kept thinking of that smile of relief on her lips as she slept after she had taken her dose and escaped her obligations. Then I could find some consolation in the reminder that I had only taken what she did not want—and indeed had feared. But I could not be truly consoled.

I suggested that Angelet and I ride over to the Longridge Farm. We did and were made very welcome there. Luke took us into his study and read some of his pamphlets to us. I found them interesting because they gave me such an insight into the man's character. He was such a fierce reformer; he was deeply religious and believed that the King in setting himself up as the ruler by divine right was comparing himself with God. He talked with vehemence about the extravagance of the Court and the wickedness of the Queen, whose aim was clearly to introduce Catholicism to the country.

"It is something we shall never have," he cried, striking the table with his clenched fist, and I could imagine his preaching to a crowd.

I was fascinated by his doctrines to a certain extent, but more so by him. He was a Puritan who believed that life should be lived in the utmost simplicity; he scorned our gold and jeweled ornaments, our blue cloaks with their silken lining; yet at the same time I could see that he admired this finery in a way. I knew too that I interested him. When he talked, his eyes never left my face and although my thoughts were full of Richard and yearned for him, I could not help but be pleased by this man's admiration, particularly because it was grudging and he could not help being aware of this innate sensuality of mine even though he fought against recognizing it. It was the essence of femininity in me which appealed to the masculinity in him. It was something nature had given me and which nothing could destroy.

When we rode out from the farmhouse I felt elated.

Angelet said, "There is no doubt that Luke Longridge is taken with you."

"Oh, come," I said, "you are not still husband hunting?"

"Indeed not there," she replied, laughing. "I cannot see you mistress of a farmhouse . . . and a Puritan one. You are far too vain and fond of finery. All the same, he found it hard to take his eyes from you."

"That is because you are a married woman and I am single."

"No, it was something else. I think Ella saw it. She was a little uneasy. She need not have worried, I am sure."

"I too am sure," I said, laughing.

And so we rode back to Far Flamstead, which was dreary and unwelcoming because Richard was not there.

Richard returned to the house and I wondered how I could endure the days when I might come upon him at any moment and the long evenings when Angelet sat with her tapestry frame or her embroidery and he and I sat opposite each other with the small chess table between us. Sometimes I would find his eyes upon me and I would look up quickly to catch him gazing at me, but I could not read his thoughts. He might have been assessing my possibilities in the marriage market.

Once I said to him, "Are you still contemplating marrying me off?"

"Your marriage is a matter to which we must give some thought," he replied.

"And we have, Bersaba," cried Angelet. "I assure you we have. Haven't we, Richard?"

He bowed his head in assent.

"It is good of you to give me so much of your attention. Angelet did not seek a husband. Fate brought him to her. I should like it to happen to me that way."

"That's stupid," said Angelet. "If she stays here she will never meet anyone, will she, Richard?"

I wondered whether he liked the manner in which she referred everything to him. I supposed he did since it showed she was the meek and docile wife.

"I am content here," I said looking at him.

I saw his lips lift slightly, which meant he was pleased.

"Nevertheless, Bersaba, it would not be fair to you. I will arrange something."

I gave my attention to the chess, for I could not bear to hear him talk as though he would not be deeply affected if I went.

I went to my room. I knew I would be unable to sleep for thinking of what I had done. I wondered what my mother would say if she ever heard of it. She would make excuses for me, I did not doubt, but secretly she would be so shocked that she would never recover from it. She loved my father singlemindedly, I knew, but if he had married someone else she would have turned away from him and been prepared to live a life of regret—possibly unmarried, possibly with a second-best.

People like my mother, who were fundamentally good, would never understand the overwhelming temptations which came to people like myself. I could be strong, but this need within me—which I had felt for Bastian—was something which when it was at its full obliterated everything.

I rode over to the Longridge Farm, where I was greeted by Ella. Her brother was out on farm business, she told me.

How neat and prim she looked in her plain gray gown and white apron. I wondered what she would say if she knew of my wickedness. She probably would not receive me here, for Puritans, living such pure lives themselves, were apt to be very harsh on the sins of others.

She talked for a while about the virtues of her brother and how she feared that he might be overbold. Terrible things could happen to those who wrote what was called sedition and was in fact truth.

"I always remember hearing of Dr. Leighton, a Scotsman who wrote *An Appeal to the Parliament; or a Plea against Papacy*. He was publicly whipped on two occasions and stood for two hours in the pillory. His ears were cut off, his nostrils slit, and his cheek was branded with the letters SS, which stood for Sower of Sedition."

I shivered. "Your brother must not run those risks."

"Do you think he will listen to me?"

"I doubt it. It is so with martyrs. They never listen to those who would preserve them."

"Dr. Leighton is out of prison now."

"Perhaps then he can live in peace."

She turned on me fiercely. "What do you think? Ten years the King's prisoner! He has lost his sight, hearing, and the use of his limbs. I suppose that could be called a sort of peace. And all for setting down his thoughts on paper that they might be shared with others!"

"We live in cruel times, Ella."

"It is to change them that Luke and men like him risk their lives."

We were silent for a while. How quiet and peaceful the farmhouse seemed. My mind went back to Far Flamstead and I wondered what Richard was thinking. What if he were to mention the night to Angelet? What would happen then?

Luke Longridge came in and I couldn't help noticing how his eyes lit up at the sight of me. I exerted all my power to attract him because I needed some diversion. I must stop thinking about the half-farcical, half-tragic situation at Far Flamstead which I had created.

"You look somber, sister," he said, but his eyes were on me.

"We were speaking of Dr. Leighton."

"Oh, yes. There is some agitation about him. I am hoping that before long he will regain his health."

"After ten years!" said Ella bitterly. "His life is finished. I doubt he has retained his reason."

I looked straight at Luke and said, "It is a warning to people who would fly in the face of those who have power to harm them."

He sat down at the table, his eyes burning with that fanatical pleasure which talking of these matters gave him.

"Nay!" he cried, "he is an example to us all."

"An example not to follow!" I cried.

"Mistress Landor—"

I interrupted him. "Pray call me Bersaba. We are good friends, are we not?"

"It makes me happy to think so. Bersaba, there is work to be done and if we are made of the stuff that falters when our leaders fall then we are not worthy of the fight."

"Perhaps you are worthy of a peaceful life with your family and children growing up in security."

"There is no security when tyranny prevails."

"Are you sure that when you overcome one tyranny you are not replacing it by another?"

"We must make sure that is not so. There is no tyranny in the humble service of God."

"There is for those who do not wish to serve Him humbly."

"You are an advocate for your kind, Bersaba."

"What kind? I was unaware that I was of any sect. I think as I think. I will be free to form my own opinions and they will not be dictated to by this party or that."

"You would be considered as dangerous as I am."

"Nay, for I would not set my thoughts on paper. I would keep them to myself and not try to force them on others."

Ella brought us refreshments and we went on talking. She leaned her elbows on the table, saying little but watching us. Luke was animated, excited. I said, "Why I do believe you're thinking I am Archbishop Laud himself."

"I could never think you were anyone but who you are. You are too much of an individual to be confused with anyone."

I felt the flush creep into my cheeks and memories—which I was trying so hard to eliminate—came rushing back to me. Then I had successfully—or did I succeed?—attempted to be confused with someone else. I wondered what Luke would say if he knew what I had done. I could imagine all his Puritan feelings rising in disgust.

But my blush did nothing more than to enhance his admiration for me.

I said quickly, "I hate to blush like this. You see, it makes my scar look worse."

"It is no blemish," he said. "Your sister told me how you acquired it."

"In the same way as others have," I answered. "I contracted smallpox."

"She told us how."

"You must not think me a heroine. I should not have gone there had I known."

"There would have been no purpose in going," Ella pointed out.

"The fact that you did so out of anxiety for your maidservant shows that you are good . . . in spite of your efforts to deny it," added Luke, "which, may I tell you, I entirely reject."

"Well, what is going to happen?" I asked.

"This Parliament will be dismissed, and there will be a new one before the year is out. Pym and Hampden will lead it, and then there will be conflict between the King and the Parliament. It will be a question of whether the country will be ruled by those it has elected to rule or by a stubborn man who believes he is on the throne by divine right."

"Be careful, Luke," warned his sister.

"You are rash," I said, and I thought, "We are both rash, and it makes a bond between us."

I said I must go, and they asked why my sister had not come with me.

"She suffers from a toothache."

"Did she not have it before?"

"Yes, it occurs now and then. Mrs. Cherry has a good cure which makes her sleep."

"I trust she will soon be well," said Ella.

"A nagging tooth is often best removed," added Luke.

"I must tell my sister," I said.

Luke took me back. He told me how much he enjoyed my visits, how interesting he found my views.

"In spite of the fact that they do not accord with your own?"

"Partly because of that, and because they are delivered with such lucidity, logic, and reason."

"Perhaps I could bring you to my point of view."

"Nay," he said. "You are a Royalist by nature. I see that. I am a Puritan. I believe that the path to heaven is reached through sacrifice and renunciation of pleasure."

"I would never agree with that. Why should that which is enjoyable be sinful?"

"Simplicity and religious living alone bring the true satisfaction of righteousness."

I did not answer, but I wanted to laugh. I had seen that in his eyes which showed me that he desired me. I did not find him by any means repulsive—even now when there was only one man who could completely satisfy me. There was so much I had to learn about myself. I thought how amusing it would be to prove him wrong.

We had reached Far Flamstead. I said, "You are right, Luke. You are too righteous for me. I'm afraid I am a sinner and always shall be. I find too much pleasure in the good things which the Lord has given us. I can't think why He put them there if he expects us to turn our backs on them. That seems to me churlish. It is like being invited to a banquet and saying to one's host, I will not partake of these good things you offer me because they are too enjoyable and to take pleasure is a sin. Good-bye, Luke. I must return to my sinful life."

"Bersaba—" he said as I turned away.

But I lifted my hand and waved farewell, keeping my back toward him.

I went into the house.

Richard was in the hall.

"You have been riding . . . alone?" he said reproachfully. He looked anxious, which pleased me, but it appeared to be merely a brotherly anxiety.

"I only went to Longridge Farm and Luke Longridge rode back with me."

"You visit them frequently?"

"I like their company."

"You should tell him to take care. There'll be trouble for that man one day if he persists in writing those pamphlets of his."

"I do tell him. He will take no heed of me."

I could not bear to remain there with him, for I was afraid that I would say something reckless. Was it just possible that he did not know?

That afternoon he left Far Flamstead. It was true that there was trouble in the north. One of the reasons there was so much disquiet in the country was that the King was taxing the nobility and the gentry heavily, and the City of London had refused to give the money for which he was asking. Richard said it was desperately needed for the Army and that the King was justified in his demands. Luke, on the other hand, believed that the King had no need of an army and that if he had not tried to interfere with Scotland's religion there would be peace in the north.

I was aware of Angelet's relief at his departure, for much as she admired him and said she loved him, she was happier when he was away and the burden of her duty could be cast aside.

She regretted the fact that she had lost her child which

would, she once said, "have made up for everything." I pinned her down then and boldly said, "Which means that you dread the nights in the big bed, is that it?"

"How crudely you put it, Bersaba," she said, "and considering you are not married yourself and know nothing of these things how can you talk about it?"

"There are some things a spinster can understand," I retorted.

"You won't be a spinster long and then you will know for yourself."

"The point is," I replied, "you want the babies, you'll endure the discomfort of pregnancy, but you dislike the initial necessity."

She blushed and said, "Y-yes. I wish it didn't have to happen like that."

That was enough.

She spent her nights in the Blue Room. Her excuse was that she liked to be near me because it reminded her of old times.

"Why, if we left our doors open we could talk to each other," she said wistfully.

It was an excuse to escape the big four-poster in the room they shared, and she wanted to forget its existence, as she could in the peace of the Blue Room.

So we went on with the dull life, which was so because Richard was not there, and we talked of him now and then and wondered how he was faring.

"There is so much trouble nowadays," said Angelet, secretly hoping that while it did not become awkward it would keep Richard away from Flamstead for a while.

"Let us hope that these matters are soon settled," I replied fervently, meaning it so that he would come back to us.

We went over to Longridge Farm once or twice and were made very welcome. When Luke was there he always singled me out and talked to me. He was always intrigued by my views on any subject, and I had to admit that I enjoyed our talks; they were a substitute in a way for my aching desire for Richard. I was aware that he was falling in love with me and that he was a little disturbed by those longings which I knew so well how to arouse in him. I didn't spare him, either. I wanted to prove his theories wrong. I wanted to show him that he would be as eager to partake of the pleasures of life as I would.

There were days when the rain fell continuously and the house seemed gloomy. Halloween came and we talked of

Carlotta and wondered how she was faring now. I remembered how I had hated her and wanted to kill her—or have someone else kill her for me—and how at the last minute I had saved her. That showed me that I, who thought I knew so much about other people, did not even know myself.

I remember the last day in October very well. Perhaps I felt restless because there was so much mist in the air and it blotted out that landscape so that even I accepted the fact that it would be unwise to go out riding.

In the afternoon I went to the bedchamber and looked at the bed and in a moment of folly I lay on it after having pulled the bedcurtains. I thought then of the night I had spent there and tried to relive every minute of it and to recall what he had said, and what I had replied. We had spoken little. There had been no need for words, and I had to bear constantly in mind that I was supposed to be my sister.

And then suddenly I heard a movement outside the curtains. The slight click of the door, a soft footstep. Someone was in the room.

The first thought which flashed into my mind was: "He has come back."

He would find me lying on this bed and he would know then what he had suspected . . . for suspect he must have.

But there was no escape. If someone was in this room, and that someone pulled aside the bedcurtains, I must be seen.

I could hear my heartbeats. I lay there waiting . . . and then the curtains were pulled back and Angelet was looking down on me.

"Bersaba! What *are* you doing?"

I sat up on one elbow.

"Oh, I was just wondering what it was like to . . . to sleep here."

"Whatever for?"

"Well, you sleep here . . . sometimes, don't you?"

"Well, naturally I do."

"I just wanted to see, that's all."

"I knew someone was here," she said. "For a moment I thought—"

"That Richard had come back?" I asked.

"Y-yes."

"You look relieved."

"Bersaba, what a thing to say!"

"Well, it's true, isn't it?"

I was laughing now—I felt like an observer outside the scene. This was typical of us. I was caught in an awkward situation and I turned the tables promptly and placed my sister in it.

"You've guessed I know that I don't like"—she waved her hands—"all that. . . . I know it goes with marriage and has to be accepted."

I jumped off the bed.

"Well, now I know what it's like to sleep there. Cheer up, Angelet. The Blue Room is very nice . . . and peaceful, and I am in the next room."

She turned to me and hugged me.

"I'm so glad you're here, Bersaba."

"So am I," I answered.

And arm in arm we went out of the room.

This helped to placate my conscience a little. All I had done was save Angelet from what she disliked, and in doing so I had pleased myself and Richard. I had flown in the face of convention; I had committed sins and forced Richard to do the same . . . very well, that was admitted; but it had not brought ill to everyone.

I wasn't easy in my mind, of course. I knew what I had done and it was no use my advising others to face the truth if I didn't face it myself.

That night, when I had said goodnight to my sister and lay in my bed, I could not sleep because I kept going over that moment when Angelet had found me on the bed; and from there my thoughts went to Carlotta and how I had tried to stir up people against her. There was no doubt that I was a very sinful person. Then I wondered what Luke Longridge would say if I ever told him of all the sins I had committed. He would despise me of course and probably forbid me to enter his farmhouse where I might contaminate his sister. I think I should have enjoyed luring him on to some indiscretion to prove that none of us was as good as we thought ourselves to be and that those who wore the cloak of virtue so ostentatiously might well be the ones who had the most to hide.

I don't know why I thought about Luke Longridge. There was only one man who interested me. I wanted to be with him so much; I wanted to make him admit that he knew that I had come to him at night; I wanted him to scheme with me as I used to scheme with Bastian. I wanted to hear his voice saying impatiently, "When, when, where?" as Bastian used to.

And yet I could still think of Luke Longridge.

As I lay there sleepless I fancied I heard strange noises in the house.

"Boards creak," I told myself. "It is nothing."

Suddenly there was a violent noise as though a great caldron had been thrown across the room. I fancied it was coming from the direction of the kitchen. I got out of bed and wrapped a robe around me.

I went to the stairs and listened. That was a sound of scuffling. Someone was in the kitchen. Undoubtedly something was going on down there.

Angelet had come out of her room. She gave a cry of relief when she saw me.

"What is it, Bersaba? I heard . . . noises. . . ."

"Something is happening down there," I said. "Let's go and see."

I called out, "Who's there? What is it?"

Mrs. Cherry appeared. She looked distraught. "Oh, it's nothing at all, mistress. It's just some of the pots as had not been put up right."

I said, "It sounded like a caldron being thrown across the floor."

"These things make a terrible noise."

She stood facing us on the stairs, almost as though she were barring our way.

"It's all right now," she went on, looking at Angelet. "Cherry's putting them up again. Secure this time. One of the men . . . you know. . . . Put up anyhow . . . then we gets this scare in the night."

Cherry appeared. His face was pale, and his eyes looked shifty, I thought. "Begging your pardon, me ladies," he said, "I am that sorry. It was one of them. . . as didn't put the things up right. Mr. Jesson will have something to say about this in the morning."

There was Mr. Jesson and behind him Meg and Grace.

I had the odd impression that they were banding together to stop our advance. It was a stupid notion which had come to me because of all those mock battles. The military tradition was strong in this house.

"I should go back to bed if I were you, my ladies," said Mrs. Cherry. "I'm right down sorry you was disturbed."

Angelet said, "It's all right now then, is it, Mrs. Cherry? They won't fall again?"

"As right as rain," said Mrs. Cherry cheerfully.

"I'll have something to say to somebody in the morning, I promise you," said Jesson.

I turned to Angelet. "On that promise," I said lightly, "I think we should go back to our beds."

"Goodnight, me ladies!" There was almost jubilation in the cry.

"Goodnight," we said.

We went back to the Blue Room first.

"Oh, dear," said Angelet, "I was just getting off."

"Only just? My dear sister, don't you sleep well?"

"I haven't lately. I wish I could. I hate lying awake at night."

"You slept very well on Mrs. Cherry's special cure for toothache," I said.

"Oh, that. Yes, for hours and hours."

"You had such good sleeps then that must have been very refreshing. You know what it was, don't you? The juice of the poppy."

"I wish I could sleep like that every night."

"You would if you took the cure."

"One shouldn't though, should one? It's all right when you have a raging toothache, but you shouldn't take it just because you can't sleep. You wouldn't, would you?"

"I'm not troubled with sleeplessness. I might if I were, perhaps, just now and then when I wanted to be certain of a good night's sleep."

"If it were here now I'd have a dose."

"Shall I ask Mrs. Cherry for it?"

"She's gone to bed now."

"She won't be asleep. I'm sure she would be delighted. She has a bit of conscience about the noise. They all have. Did you notice how uneasy they were?"

"They were worried about waking us."

"I'll ask Mrs. Cherry in the morning . . . if you can get through the night."

"Of course. I'll sleep in time."

"Mind you," I said, "you will have to be cautious with this stuff. It won't do to take it often. Only certain times. I'll be your doctor and prescribe when you need it."

"Oh Bersaba, it is good to have you here!"

"I hope you won't change your mind."

"Change my mind? What do you mean?"

"About having me here. I'm really the bad girl of the family. I'm not like you, Angelet."

I interrupted her as she started on the old story of how I had saved Phoebe's life, and rescued Carlotta from the witch-hunters. I said, "It's time we were in bed. Try to forget all this excitement and sleep. I'll do the same."

I kissed her lightly and she clung to me for a moment.

Then, firmly, I released myself and went into my Lavender Room.

I lay awake for a long time thinking how easy it would be to send Angelet to sleep while I took her place in the marriage bed.

Then I dreamed that Richard came home and that I gave Angelet the dose and when I was on my way to Richard, Mrs. Cherry and Cherry, with Jesson and Meg and Grace, stood on the stairs barring my way.

It was a dream at which I could laugh when I awoke from it because I saw exactly how it had been evolved.

The next afternoon I went down to the kitchen to speak to Mrs. Cherry about her cure. I wanted to make sure that it was safe in small doses.

When I arrived in the kitchen there was no one there. The great fire was burning and there was a smell of baking coming from the oven. A piece of meat was turning on the spit in its early stages of cooking, so that it did not yet need attention.

I looked around and my eyes fell on the caldron whose fall to the ground had awakened us all in the night. And as I looked, I noticed what I had never noticed before, and that was a door which was not shut. Above this door hung aprons and cloths used for cooking and the reason why I had never noticed it before was because it was always hidden. There were things still hung there to hide it, but because the door itself was slightly open, the fact of its existence was betrayed. I went to it. There was a lock on it but that lock had been broken. Quickly I opened the door. Inside was a cupboard in which heavy garments were hanging. Some instinct told me that this was no ordinary cupboard and I drew the coats aside. I was right! A door faced me. The lock on this had been broken but there was a bolt which had been drawn across.

I thought I heard footsteps so I hastily stepped back into the kitchen and shut the cupboard door.

Mrs. Cherry came in.

"I thought I heard someone here," she said.

"I came to have a word with you, Mrs. Cherry."

She was fearful, I could see, and I noticed how her eyes went to the door I had discovered. She would notice that it was not properly shut and that close scrutiny would betray this fact. I wondered why it was important.

She brought up a chair for me and I sat down.

"Your mistress is not sleeping very well," I said, "and I am becoming worried about her."

Apprehension disappeared from Mrs. Cherry's face, which fell into an expression of concern.

"Do you remember when she had a toothache she took some of your special cure?"

"I do indeed, mistress, and she remarked to me that it had stopped the pain."

"It did. You are very clever with your herbs, Mrs. Cherry."

She dimpled. "Oh, it's what you might call a lifelong practice, Mistress Bersaba."

"That's why I've come to you for your help."

"If there's anything I can do . . ."

"There is. I want to ask you if she might have some of the cure to keep in her room so that when she finds it difficult to sleep she might take a dose. Would that be harmful?"

"Well, Mistress Bersaba, as long as she didn't take too much. These things shouldn't be took regular. A little now and then can't do no one no harm. I always say God put them there for our use and it's up to us to make the best of them."

"And people like you who make a study of these things are doing a very useful job for us all."

"Well, mistress, it's my pleasure. I love my little herb garden and if I can find anything new or learn any new recipe . . . well, there's no one happier than Emmy Cherry."

"Emmy Cherry!" I thought. It suited her—so rotund, so eager to serve, and yet with a glint of something in her eyes which made her of interest to me.

"So," I said, "you will let me have the cure?"

"I've been thinking, Mistress Bersaba. The cure is for toothache. You don't need a cure for toothache when you ain't got it, now do you? I've got a little something here which is made mostly of poppy juice and fresh green leaves to give it taste and a spot of juniper to give it a tang. That's not all. But a little nip of this would ensure a good night's rest, I reckon, and do no harm. I'll give it to you."

She went to a cupboard and I followed her. It was like a small room, that cupboard, and I imagined it was an almost exact replica of the one which contained the coats.

This cupboard was lined with shelves, and in it was an array of bottles, neatly labeled. There was no extra door.

She took one of the bottles and gave it to me.

"Here you are, Mistress Bersaba. She'll sleep well on this. Just the one dose will do it. But don't let her take too much. There's always a fear that you'll take a dose, get sleepy, and take another without knowing it. It's been done more than once. Now that's something I wouldn't like to speak for."

"You can trust me, Mrs. Cherry," I said. "I shall see that she only takes it when it is absolutely necessary and I'll keep it in my room."

I took the bottle to my room and put it into a cupboard. When I saw Angelet I told her what I had done.

"Where is it?" she asked.

"I'm keeping it," I told her. "When I think you really need to be put off to sleep, I shall use Mrs. Cherry's soother."

"Let me have it, Bersaba."

"No," I said firmly; and she laughed and was happy in my care for her.

* * *

I couldn't wait to explore that part of the grounds around the kitchens, for I wanted to discover if there was a door there which could be the one in the cupboard.

It was dusk, and no one about when I strolled out in my cloak, for it was chilly. I made my way around the house.

This was where the kitchens would be. There was the window which I knew was there, but I could not find a door. I wondered whether there had been one once and it had been blocked up. If so, there should be some sign of it, but there was nothing.

I looked behind me. The wall of the mock castle was very close and the discovery I did make was that this was its nearest distance from the house. "If it is a ruin, which might crumble at any moment, is it safe to allow it to remain so near the house?" I wondered.

Clearly I could discover nothing there so I went back to my room. But I kept thinking about it.

How long the evening seemed! Angelet sat idly, for she could not see to embroider by the candlelight and I fancied that when Richard was not there she did not feel the need to be busy.

We talked of old times and Trystan Priory and wondered what our mother was doing at that moment. Then, when we mentioned Castle Paling, I was reminded of my exploration that afternoon, and said, "When I went down to the kitchen to speak to Mrs. Cherry I noticed a cupboard I had not seen before. I looked inside and there was a door which was bolted. Where does it lead?"

"I've not idea," replied Angelet.

"You're the mistress of the house. It shouldn't hold any secrets from you."

"I never interfere in the kitchen."

"It's not interfering . . . just to find out why there should be a door in a cupboard."

"Did you ask Mrs. Cherry?"

"No, I didn't."

"Well, if you're curious you could ask her."

"Why don't we go down and see?"

"To ask them, you mean."

"I don't want to ask them. I want to find out for ourselves. It's rather mysterious, I fancy."

"Mysterious? How? Why?"

"How? That's what we have to find out. And why. Well, something tells me it is."

"What do you want to do?"

"Explore."

Her eyes shone. It was almost as though we were children again and I knew that that was what she was thinking. Hadn't I always been the one to lead the way when we did something wild and extraordinary?

"Well," she said, "what do you suggest?"

"We'll wait until they're in bed and then we'll go down to the kitchens and see what's behind the door. . . . If there is anything."

"What if we're discovered?"

"My dear Angelet, what if we are? Are you or are you not the mistress of this house? If you wish to explore your kitchen in the dead of night what right has anyone to stop you?"

She began to laugh.

"You haven't grown up at all," she said accusingly.

"In some ways I may have retained my childishness," I admitted.

The evening passed slowly; we went to our rooms and to our beds because I had said that neither Meg nor Phoebe should suspect anything. This was our adventure.

It was just past midnight when we wrapped our robes about us and took a candle and made our way to the kitchens.

Angelet kept close to me. I sensed that she was a little nervous and I wondered whether I should have suggested she share the adventure. Cautiously I opened the kitchen door and, lifting the candlestick, shone the light over the wall, past the great fireplace to the shelf on which stood the pewter goblets.

"There's the caldron which fell the other night," I said. I lowered the candle. "And there's the door. Come on."

I went to it. It was shut and there was a key in the lock. I turned it and the door opened. I was in the cupboard.

"Hold the candle," I commanded Angelet and when she took it I pushed aside the coats and revealed that other door. The lock had not been mended but the heavy bolt was drawn across it.

"What are you doing?" whispered Angelet.

"I'm going to draw the bolt," I said.

It moved easily, which surprised me, for I had imagined it might be impossible to move if it had not been drawn for a number of years.

I opened the door and as I did so there was a rush of cold air. I looked into darkness.

"Be careful!" cried Angelet.

"Give me the candle."

It was a sort of corridor. On the ground were stones and the walls were of stone, too.

"Come back!" screamed Angelet. "I can hear someone coming."

That brought me out into the cupboard. I too could hear footsteps. I shut the door behind me and drew the bolt. As I did so Mrs. Cherry came into the kitchen.

She gave a little scream and Angelet said, "It's all right, Mrs. Cherry."

"God have mercy," she whispered.

I said quickly, "We thought we heard someone down here—and we came to investigate."

Mrs. Cherry's eyes had lost their bland benignity. She could have been very frightened.

"It's all right though," I went on. "It must have been mice in the wainscot or some bird outside. . . ."

She looked around the room and I noticed that her eyes went to the cupboard.

"I reckon this comes of people not putting up caldrons in their right places, that's what I reckon. People get nervous, that's what, and then they mistake noises in the night."

"I suppose that's what it was. But we have satisfied ourselves, Mrs. Cherry. So there's no need to worry."

"I wouldn't like to think of anything wrong in my kitchen," said Mrs. Cherry.

"There is nothing wrong. We've satisfied ourselves. We'll say goodnight now, and I'm sorry you've been disturbed."

I slipped my left arm through Angelet's right and, holding the candle high in my right hand, I led my sister out of the kitchen.

When we were in the Blue Room I set down the candle, sat on her bed, and laughed.

"Well, that was fun," I said.

"Why did you make up that story about hearing noise? Why didn't you tell her what we were looking for?"

"I felt it would be more fun not to."

"What was it you found, anyway?"

"The door opens onto a sort of alcove with a stone floor."

"Well, what's so interesting about that?"

"My explorations did not go far enough for me to answer."

"Oh, Bersaba, you are mad! You always were. What Mrs. Cherry thought of us I can't imagine."

"She was a little upset. I wonder why?"

"Most people would be after they'd had a fright like that."

"What would you say if I told you I thought that might be a way into the castle?"

"I'd say that you were making it up."

"Well, of course, there is a way to prove it though. And there isn't another way in, is there? I mean, that high wall with the glass on top goes all the way around."

"Richard had the wall put around because it wasn't safe. And there is another door. I found it one day when I was in the copse. Why should there be a way into the castle from the house?"

"I don't know. I just wondered."

"Oh, dear, I shall never sleep tonight. Shall I have a little of the sleeping draught?"

"Well perhaps you are overexcited. It might be a good time to try it."

I went to my room and brought out the bottle.

I gave her the appointed dose and said I would sit with her until she slept.

Within fifteen minutes of taking it she fell into a deep sleep. I sat there for some time thinking about the cupboard and the bolted door. I believed that there was a corridor into the castle and I had discovered it.

I awoke in the night and went into Angelet's room; she was still sleeping. In the morning I asked if she had slept through the night and she assured me that she had.

Civil War

THE NEXT day I made an excuse to go to the kitchen, and then I noticed that the key to the cupboard had been removed, and guessed that Mrs. Cherry or someone had suspected my interest and was determined that my explorations should cease.

I was almost certain that there was a corridor leading from the kitchen into the castle, and since the castle was forbidden as unsafe, naturally the existence of the corridor would be kept a secret.

Then I ceased to think about the matter, for that afternoon Luke Longridge rode over. It was the first time he had called at Far Flamstead, because Richard had never asked him. And in view of the fact that relations must have been rather strained between them after that proposed duel about which Angelet had told me, this was not surprising. He had however raised no objection to our visiting them. True, there had been nothing formal about our visits and we met them more by chance than anything else.

It was Phoebe who came to tell me that Mr. Longridge had called and was asking for me, so I went down to the hall where he waited uneasily. I thought something must be wrong and asked him what.

"No," he said. "I just wanted to talk to you. Could you get a wrap and come out into the gardens?"

"Can't you talk here?" I asked.

"As I am not sure whether General Tolworthy would welcome me in his house, I would prefer it if you would come outside."

I said I would get a wrap and I sent Phoebe for it.

When we were outside, I led him to the enclosed garden. It was too chilly to sit so we walked around as we talked.

"You will wonder at the urgency," he said, "but it is not a hasty matter on my part for I have thought about it continuously for some time. You have been in my thoughts since our first meeting and each day I have hoped that you would ride by."

"You and your sister have always given us a good welcome and both my sister and I have enjoyed our visits," I said.

"No doubt you are aware of my regard for you. I had not thought to marry. There is so much I want to do, but it is natural for a man to take a wife. I hope this does not seem incongruous to you, but I have come to ask you to marry me."

"You can't be serious."

"I am deeply in earnest. I am not a rich man, but I have the farm and some assets. We are not exactly poor."

"I do not assess people by their worldly goods."

"Indeed you do not. You are too wise for that. The rich man of today can be the poor man of tomorrow. The treasures of the heart and mind are those of value."

"Why do you wish to marry me?" I asked.

"Because I love you. I could be happy with you. I could make you happy, and the simple fact is that I shall never know happiness without you."

"I thought you did not believe in happiness."

"You mock me."

"No, I seek to know you."

"There is nothing in the Bible against a man's marrying. It is a worthy action to take."

"But what if you should find pleasure in your marriage?"

"That would find favor in the eyes of God."

"Carnal pleasure?" I said. He was startled. He looked at me in amazement. I said, "We are not children. We must know the reason for our actions. I want to ask you if the thought of carnal pleasure makes you feel you would be happy to live with me."

"How strangely you talk, Bersaba. Hardly like a—"

"Like a Puritan? But I am not a Puritan. I believe you want me as men will want women and offer marriage for that reason. I merely wish to know."

He stepped nearer to me. "You enchant me," he said. "I will admit I want you in this way. I can only be happy with you. Bersaba, you don't answer. Will you marry me?"

"No," I said, almost triumphantly, for I had made him admit to carnal desires; and then that perverse side of my nature was there and I was sorry for him. "I could only marry if I loved . . . as one loves a lover. I make no secret of my

262

needs. I do not love you in that way, though I respect you and like you as my friend. That is the answer, Luke, and I have nothing more to say."

"Bersaba, you will think of this?"

"It would do no good."

"I suppose they will take you to London and there will be balls and banquets. . . ."

"And extravagances," I said.

"And there you will find a man who will make you rich."

"I do not look for riches. I told you that, Luke."

He turned away, and I laid my hand on his arm. "I'm sorry," I said. "But if you really knew me you would not admire me. You want me, yes I know that, but you would not be happy with me. Your conscience would worry you. You would find too much pleasure in me. You are a Puritan . . . I don't know what I am, but it is not that. You will find a wife more suitable, Luke, and you will then thank me and God for this day."

"You are so different from everyone else," he said.

"That is why you should avoid me. You don't know me. I'm not of your kind. Try not to feel too bad. I shall call on your sister as I did before and we'll be friends. We'll talk. We'll fight our verbal battles and enjoy each other's company. Go now, Luke. Don't be downhearted. This is for the best. I know it."

Then I left him and ran into the house.

The next day Richard returned. I heard arrivals and went out into the courtyard to see who had come, and there he was, dismounting, while the groom took charge of his horse.

Forgetting decorum in my pleasure at seeing him, I had run forward holding out my hands. He seized them and held them for a moment looking into my face searchingly, I thought, and I felt my spirits soaring for I believed in that moment that he knew.

"Bersaba," he said and there was something about the way in which he said my name which sounded like a lover speaking to his mistress, but almost immediately he was cool and looking as I had so often seen him look. "I'm back for a brief stay," he said. "Where is Angelet?"

She too had heard and came out into the courtyard.

He took her hands as he had taken mine and kissed her cheek.

"You are well?" he asked solicitously.

"Oh, yes, Richard. And you? How long will you be with us? Are the troubles over?"

"As usual I can't say how long, and the troubles are by no means over. They increase with every day." He slipped his arm through hers and then looked around for me. I went to him and he took my arm and thus linked we went into the hall.

I warned myself that I must not betray this wild excitement which took possession of me. I must overcome it. I must remember that this was my sister's husband.

We supped as usual in the intimate parlor. He seemed almost tender to Angelet.

"Are you sure you are feeling well?" he asked her. "You look a little tired."

"She has not been sleeping very well," I told him.

He was concerned and Angelet murmured that it was nothing.

As the meal progressed he talked a great deal about what was going on. A new Parliament had met and although many of its members had sat with that which had assembled in the previous April and was now known as the Short Parliament, there were some new members. "They are determined," said Richard, "to end all grievances and pull them up by the roots. This bodes ill for men like Wentworth, Earl of Strafford, and Archbishop Laud."

As usual he talked to me of these matters and afterward he said he had work to do and retired to the library.

I went to my room. Angelet was already in the Blue Room. I was excited and she was in fear. I believe that she nourished this aversion to an abnormal proportion. She admired her husband beyond all men; she was proud to be his wife; she would have been completely happy in her marriage if these nightly duties were not part of the contract.

Of course it would seem unnatural if she did not spend the night with him, for he had been away so long and would expect it.

"What's the matter, Angelet?" I asked, knowing full well, and she answered, "I don't know. I feel the toothache coming on." She looked at me appealingly, reminding me of the days of her childhood when she had been afraid of going to some part of the Priory in the dark and would make up all sorts of excuses not to go.

"She does not want him," I thought. "She is afraid of him. That which I long for, she fears." I had been the resourceful one in our childhood and I felt that she was asking me now—as she often had in the past—to find a way out for her.

My heart started to beat fast as I said, "You must have some of the Cherry cure."

"It makes me so sleepy."

"That is what you need."

"Richard has only just come home."

"He will understand."

Her expression lightened and she looked at me adoringly. I was once more the sister on whom she could rely.

"I'll give you a dose," I said quickly. "I'll tuck you in and then I'll go down to the library to tell him. You'll be all right tomorrow. He realizes that."

"Oh, Bersaba, do you think—"

My hands trembled a little as I poured out the dose.

I helped her to bed and sat with her until she slept, which was soon. She looked so happy and relaxed in sleep that my conscience was eased.

"I will go to tell him," I promised myself. "I will confess what I have done and tomorrow I will make plans to go home. I will explain to him that she is afraid and that she needs time to grow accustomed to what is now distasteful to her." I knew that he would understand if I could tell him.

I went to the library. He was not there.

I would find him in the bedchamber. Perhaps he had already gone to Angelet's room to look for her, perhaps he would try to rouse her from her drugged sleep. I had promised her I would explain. So must I, but more than she realized; and then tomorrow I would make plans to leave for Cornwall, and hope that in time they would find happiness together.

I went to the bedchamber and knocked on the door. It was swiftly opened. He took my hand and drew me in.

"Angelet," he said, and there was a note in his voice which I had never heard before when he said her name.

The temptation swept over me. I could impersonate her perfectly. Perhaps once more . . . and then I would explain. My resolutions had crumbled, but I did protest as he embraced me, realizing even as I did so that that would make me even more like Angelet.

"I have to speak to you, Richard," I cried.

"Later," he murmured. "There will be plenty of time to talk. I have been thinking of you, longing for you. . . ."

There was that in his voice, in the touch of his hands, which moved me deeply. More than anything I wanted to please him, to comfort him, to make him happy. If Angelet had suffered from her frigidity, so must he. My love for him overwhelmed me. Why not . . . just for tonight? Then I would go away. And so it was.

He gave no sign that he knew I was not my sister.

I was awakened by strange noises. I started up, horror dawning on me. I was in the four-poster bed and Richard was beside me.

I could not describe the noise, but I knew that someone was in the room. I heard a crash as though a stool were being thrown and there was wild demonical laughter followed by snarling noises such as a wild animal might make.

Richard had thrown back the curtains and was out of bed. I followed.

He had lighted a candle, and I cried out in fear, for something horrible was in the room. In those first seconds I had not thought it human; it was something conjured up in a nightmare. But it *was* human. It was a child, with wild tousled hair and arms so long that they almost reached the ground. The body was bent forward, and the creature shuffled. Its lips were loose, its eyes wild—mad, murderous eyes.

"Cherry!" called Richard, but Cherry was already at the door. Behind him was Mrs. Cherry.

Richard had caught the creature and was holding it while its long arms lashed out in protest. It started to wail like an animal.

Mrs. Cherry murmured, "Mercy on us. I'll get John."

The creature had broken free and had run to a stool. He picked it up, but Richard was there before it could crash through the mirror.

The struggle went on but it was all that both Richard and Cherry could do to hold those thrashing arms.

A man came in. I knew he was Strawberry John because Angelet had mentioned him once and he was immediately recognizable by the scar on his face.

"Now come, my boy," said John. "Now come, my friend. John's here."

The arms stopped thrashing and John seized them suddenly from behind, pinioning the writhing body.

"Now, it doesn't hurt if you're still. You know that. Only if you struggle. Now you come with John. Now . . . now, easy does it. That's better."

The writhing had ceased and the man with the scar gently but firmly led the creature away.

Mrs. Cherry stood trembling in the doorway. "I can't think

how, sir. The bolt had been drawn. Cherry always draws it."

"Never mind now, Mrs. Cherry," said Richard.

I had remained in the shadows but now the violence was over I was aware of the predicament in which I found myself. I was discovered, exposed. I kept telling myself that this was a nightmare from which I would awaken at any moment, but I knew very well it was real.

As the sounds of scuffling died away Richard shut the door and leaned against it.

I shook out my hair to hide the scars on my brow and involuntarily I covered the one on my cheek with my hand.

"That . . . creature is my son," he said. "You will have to know now."

I did not answer. I was afraid to speak because even now I was not sure whether he thought I was Angelet.

I felt there was no need for him to explain. I understood so much. This son was an idiot, a monster; he was shut in the castle with strong man Strawberry John to look after him. The Cherrys knew the secret. He was kept in the castle and the door in the kitchen was the way into that sinister place. I had unbolted the door and it had remained so, which gave this boy-monster, whatever he was, the opportunity to come into the house.

I had set the stage for my own betrayal—which I suppose is what happens to wrongdoers.

I had to think quickly. Could I really deceive him? Could I go on pretending to be Angelet? There were only the scars to betray me.

I said, "I understand, Richard. I understand it all."

He came to me, then he gently lifted the hair from my forehead and kissed my scars. A great joy swept over me. There was no longer need for deception. He knew.

"Did you think I didn't know?" he said. "Oh, Bersaba, why did you do it?"

"Because I am wicked, I suppose."

"Never that," he said. "Afterward I went away. I said it must not happen again and then I came back longing for you to come to me."

"I thought you would hate me if you knew."

"I could never do anything but love you and I shall always remember that you did this for me. Don't you see I shall love you forever?"

I put my head against him and I felt suddenly weak, wanting to be taken care of.

He kissed my hair. Why had I thought he was a cold and

passionless man? I knew that his love for me was as deep and overwhelming as mine for him.

"As soon as you came into this house," he said, stroking my hair, "it was clear to me that I needed you. Every minute with you is an excitement, an adventure. Why did you not come to London in place of—"

He was a man of strict conventions, a man with a sense of righteousness, and he could not bring himself to say Angelet's name.

"You married my sister," I said. "You must have loved her."

"I saw something in her. I thought she was young, fresh, healthy. I thought we might have healthy children. I know it was the shadow of you. You are so alike. Often I have watched you riding out in the gardens and I have not known which was which. It is when you talk, when we are together in love, that there is no similarity whatsoever. There is so much to say to you, I don't know where to begin."

He led me to the bed and we sat down on it with his arm about me while the candle flickering on the dressing table threw an eerie light about the room.

"First my tragedy. Let me tell you about the boy. He is eleven years old . . . my son . . . my only son. His birth killed his mother."

"I think I understand it all. I've pieced it together. You keep him in the castle and that is why you want no one to go near it."

He nodded. "It became obvious that there was something very wrong with him in the first year of his life. Mrs. Cherry nursed him. She insisted and she was good. I owe a great deal to the Cherrys, Jesson, and his daughters. They were all here then. They know the secret and they have helped me to keep it. The other servants are old soldiers, and old soldiers don't talk if they think it would be unwise to do so. There is a strong man—Strawberry John he is called because of a birthmark. He is a man who is thought to be a little strange. He *is* unusual—extraordinary—and of great strength as you have seen tonight. He looks after the boy and has kept him in the castle since he was three years old and began to get violent. No one can control him like Strawberry John. But Mrs. Cherry and Cherry are good with him. The boy's strength is growing. He has the arms of a gorilla and could kill with them."

"Can you keep him there forever?"

"Such people do not live very long, I have heard. I have investigated and learned something of such cases. They usually die in their mid-twenties or thirties. They have the strength of two men, I have been told, and only half their lifespan."

"It is a long way to go."

"We have managed so far. It was thought that he died. Oh, Bersaba, there has been such subterfuge."

"And you are a man who hates subterfuge," I said with meaning.

"I opened the castle, built the wall round it, and he has been there since. A child was buried bearing his name. There have been occasions when he has broken out, but they are rare."

"And this must remain a secret."

"This is my son, Bersaba. I am responsible for him. I want to give him the best life I can and I want children . . . normal children who will grow up in this house and live here through the generations. I fear what effect it would have on . . . Angelet . . . or anyone if they knew. She would be afraid that the children we might have could be similarly tainted. Clearly he has inherited madness from someone."

"His mother . . ."

"She was a gentle girl of good family. There was no madness in her family. I know you will understand. Don't you always understand me? I did not want Angelet to know. If she were to have a child her fears could harm it and herself. You understand that, Bersaba."

He held me against him. "What must we do, Bersaba?" he asked.

"What can we do?"

"We can only part and that means that I shall live sadly all the days that are left to me."

"You have your profession," I said, "and it seems that in the next years you will be occupied with that. And I must go away."

He turned to me and held me close to him. "The moment I was beside you I knew, Bersaba."

"And gave no sign."

"I dared not."

"No," I said, "because you are a righteous man. You were like Adam. The woman tempted me. Oh, don't protest. She did. You see I am not good, Richard. You must realize that. Angelet is like my mother—gentle, kindly, eager to do right. I am not gentle; I'm kind only when I love, and I am anxious to do the right only if it gives me pleasure. You see I will willingly do the wrong for that same reason."

"I never met anyone like you."

"You should pray that you never do again."

"It would be an impossibility and, having known you, I have learned this. If you could have been my wife I would have asked nothing more of life."

I touched his hair with my fingers. "What now, Richard?"

"Oh, God, Bersaba, what are we going to do?"

"There is only one thing to be done. I must go away."

"No." He spoke quietly. "I can't let you go."

"We have to think of Angelet," I went on.

He nodded.

"You must try to understand her. Be patient with her. In time perhaps . . ."

"She will never be you."

"But you married *her*, Richard."

"Why did you not come in the first place?"

"It's no use railing against fate, is it? This has happened to us. We must accept it. She admires you. She loves you. She can't be blamed for her nature any more than we can for ours."

"Having known you, I could not live without you."

"You can and you will. For that is how it must be."

He looked at me desperately. "We might . . . think of some way."

I shook my head. "I am not a good woman, Richard, as you have discovered, but this is my sister . . . my twin sister. This must be an end. I must make some excuse to go."

"You will break her heart and mine."

"Hearts mend quickly when there is someone to apply the healing. You will heal each other."

"I cannot let you go," he said simply.

"And I cannot stay," I answered.

"Please, Bersaba, promise me this. Do not go yet. Wait awhile. Let us think how best to handle this."

"If I stay . . . this can happen again."

There was silence and I knew that he was trying to calm his rising emotions, as I was. I had to be calm. I had to think of Angelet.

"I don't think I could bear to lose you now. You know what my marriage has been like. When you came life changed . . . it became exciting. I was lifted out of my despondency."

"I understand that," I answered. "But now we are overwrought. I must go now."

I saw his face in the candlelight—desperate, yearning, so that he seemed younger and so vulnerable. I longed to com-

270

fort him, to make promises which I knew would be a betrayal of Angelet. God knows I had done her enough injury already. I must stop thinking of myself and Richard.

"Promise you will not go yet," he insisted.

And I gave him my promise. Then I pulled myself away. I almost ran from the room and hastened to my own bed-chamber. I looked in at Angelet. She was sleeping peacefully, with a look of satisfaction and relief on her innocent face.

It was not easy to be natural toward Angelet, but I managed better than he did, and when a messenger came that very afternoon with dispatches from the camp he seemed relieved to go.

I saw him alone before he went. He said, "We will work out a solution." But I knew there was no solution.

Angelet waved farewell and turning to me, said in a voice glowing with pride, "He is in such an important position. He is in constant consultation with the King."

As for myself, I wanted to be alone to think and I walked in the grounds and sat in the pond garden from which I could get a glimpse of the castle wall. I thought of his anguish and that monster child who was incarcerated there, and I wondered what would become of us.

We were in December and Angelet talked a great deal about the coming Christmas and Christmases at home. Our father was still there. Our mother wrote that the setting up of the company offices in Plymouth demanded a great deal of their time and she would be happy to have them with her for Christmas. All that she regretted was the absence of her daughters. I thought of them bringing in the Yule log and the carollers and mummers coming and performing. The family were going to Castle Paling for a week or two. Grandfather Casvellyn was ailing. He was always excited at the end of October because Halloween brought back memories and he used to get so excited about witches and wanted to go out himself to find them and hang them, that he was always weak for some time afterward.

"You see, my darlings," wrote our mother, "nothing is changed. I am so glad that you are together. Angelet must persuade Richard to bring you all here. Of course I know the times are bad and that a soldier has to hold himself in readiness. I do hope all these troubles will dissolve and life be peaceful. We shall be thinking of you on Christmas day."

We should certainly be thinking of them.

It was mid-December when a suspicion which had come to

me some time before was confirmed. I should perhaps not be surprised that I was going to have a child.

I came to the conclusion calmly enough and with a sort of exultation. That was before I would allow myself to contemplate all the difficulties involved. What was I thinking of? I was happy because I was to have Richard's child. But in what position was I to bear it?

Phoebe was watching me closely. I believe she knew more than I realized. She had always watched over me and I had suspected that she was aware that I had not returned to my bed in the early hours of morning on more than one night.

As I lay in my bed I faced the truth. I asked myself what I was going to do. I would tell him and what would his reaction be? In a way he would be delighted, but then the enormity of the difficulties which were before us would rise up and he would, as I was now, search wildly for some way of dealing with the matter.

I could go to my sister and say, "I am to bear your husband's child. You did not want him so I took him and this is the result."

Even for myself, who knew her so well, it was difficult to imagine what Angelet would do.

I knew the solution Richard would offer. He would want to take me away. We would have to think up some reason for my going. He would want me to bear my child in secret and he would come and visit us sometimes.

But how? That would have to be decided.

Why had I not thought of this before? Why had not he? Our passion seemed to have blinded us to everything but the need to satisfy it.

It was characteristic of me that when a possible solution suggested itself I did not hesitate. I had always acted too quickly and my mother had often chided me for it. I was impatient, impulsive by nature. Perhaps it was due to this that my conduct so often brought me into situations from which I found it difficult to extricate myself.

Indeed I should have considered this possibility. Why should not I, a passionate woman, also be a fruitful one? I had not thought beyond the intrigue and immense delight of those occasions, or perhaps I had subconsciously refused to look at a likely result.

The fact remained that I was pregnant and in due course my condition would be known. I had to do something.

I rode over to Longridge Farm. I sat with Ella, talking in the farmhouse, until Luke came in. His pleasure in seeing me was apparent, and I made up my mind that I would speak to him. When he came to take me back to Far Falstead, I did.

I came straight to the point. "You asked me to marry you. Do you still wish it?"

He drew up his horse and looked at me. I returned his gaze unflinchingly. "Because if you do," I went on, "I accept. I will marry you."

"Bersaba!" There was no mistaking the joy in his voice.

I held up my hand to ward him off. "You must know the reason," I said. "I am with child and in the circumstances a husband is rather necessary to me."

I could see that he was finding it difficult to follow my meaning. He clearly did not believe what I was saying could be true.

"It is true," I said. "When you asked me I refused you because I did not know then. I like you. You interest me. I enjoy our discussions, but I want you to know the reason why I will accept your offer. Of course you may change your mind now. You, a gentleman of the Puritan persuasion, would not want a woman such as I am for a wife. I am really most unsuitable and we both know it, but you told me that you loved me and I am now in this somewhat embarrassing position. I have to consider how I can act in a manner calculated to bring the least difficulty to others and of course to myself. Marriage is the obvious answer. That is my proposition."

He was still silent and I went on: "Ah, I have your answer. It is what I expected. Think no more of it. You now know that I am a woman of loose morals and I understand completely—and agree with you—that such a woman is unsuited to be your wife. Your silence answers me. There is no need of words. What I have suggested is preposterous, insulting, and I deserve never to be allowed again to call you my friend. Good-bye."

I turned my horse and was preparing to gallop off when he called my name.

I stopped and looked at him.

"You . . . you bewilder me," he said.

"I realize of course that I have behaved most unconventionally. Good-bye."

"No. Give me time. I want to think."

"The more you think the more you will realize how impossible my suggestion is. I made it because you told me you loved me. You spoke with some vehemence and, as marriage with you would provide a way out for me, I suggested it. But at the same time I see that it is out of the question. Good-bye."

I heard his words as I galloped away.

"Give me . . . time."

That afternoon he came over to Far Flamstead. Phoebe came to tell me that he had called and was asking to speak to me. Once again we went into the garden. It was not the weather for walking and there was a hint of snow to come in the darkening clouds.

"Bersaba," he said, "I want you to marry me."

A warm glow of something I could not understand came over me then. I almost loved him, for I knew how my condition must appear to a man of his Puritan outlook. He must indeed love me, or was it that potent attraction I had which was a kind of promised passion and which I was discovering men were aware of?

"And you would be father to another man's child?"

"I would, since it is yours also."

"Luke," I said, "you are either a very noble man or you love me very much."

"I love you very much," he said.

"Is it a tender love or is it an irresistible desire for me?"

"It is both. Whose child is it?"

"Do you think you should know?"

"I know already. There seems only one whom it could be. Your sister's husband." I saw his lips turn down with anger. "Why?" he cried in anger. "How could you? How could he?"

"For the same reason that you, the Puritan, will go against your principles. You will marry a woman such as I am. Would you have believed it of yourself before you met me?"

He shook his head slowly.

"Then don't question these matters. They are . . . because they are. We are made as we are and for some of us our natural impulses are too great to be resisted. Mine, his, and yours. If I marry you there will be no recrimination. From the day we have taken our vows, this child of mine will be yours and you will think of it as such. Do not think I am not conscious of what you are doing. I love you for it, Luke. I promise you I will be a good and faithful wife and I will give you a son of your own . . . though you must not mind too much if it should be a daughter. . . ."

"I want to marry you," he said. "It shall be as you say. The marriage must take place soon because of the child."

"Secretly?" I said.

"Without delay. It must be thought that we are already married. I shall have to tell Ella, but she will think the child is mine."

"Not only will you marry me but you will tell lies for my sake?"

"Yes," he said, "I will do this. There has come to me that which I longed for and I must not complain of the manner in which it has come."

I held out my hand to him. "You will be a good husband to me, Luke," I said, "and I will do my best to be a good wife to you, I swear it."

It was a simple ceremony in the small parlor of the farmhouse. Ella was a little shocked, for she believed we had forestalled our marriage vows, but the thought of a child was such a delight to her that she was ready to waive her disapproval and I think she was secretly pleased to have another woman in the household, particularly as she knew I was not of the kind to interfere with the management of it.

After the ceremony I rode back to Far Flamstead. It was two days before Christmas.

"I have something to say to you," I told Angelet. "I am married."

She stared at me in disbelief.

"To Luke Longridge," I went on.

She could not believe it. "You're joking. You? Married to a Puritan?"

"Yes, why not? Puritans are good people. I think they make good husbands. However, we shall see."

"When?" she demanded.

"Well, I am already with child."

"So you married secretly! Why did you not go and live at the farm? Your husband was there and you were here. I don't believe it."

"Don't ask too many questions," I said. "I am with child so the marriage must have taken place some time ago."

"A child. . . . When?"

"August perhaps."

"Bersaba!"

"Well, our mother always said I was unpredictable, didn't she?"

"What will Richard say?"

It was my turn to flush. What would he say? I felt floods of misery rushing over me. It was over—that wonderful adventure such as I had never before experienced and never would again.

"It is not his affair," I said coldly.

"He was fond of you. He looked upon himself as a sort of protector. And you married without the consent of our parents . . . or telling us."

"It is done. No one can undo it. And I am going to have a child."

"That will be wonderful." The cloud lifted from her face and she went on. "You will be near me. We shall not be parted. I shall ride over to the farm every day or you will come here. I shall be with you when the baby is born. I shall help you care for it."

"Yes, Angelet," I said, "yes."

Then she embraced and kissed me. "But Luke Longridge . . . the Puritan! Richard won't like it."

"Perhaps not."

"He dislikes the Longridges. He says the Puritans are making trouble in the country. There are too many of them in Parliament and they are always writing those absurd pamphlets. And then they nearly fought that duel."

"What a mercy they didn't, for if they had, one of us might have been without a husband."

"But Richard likes you, Bersaba. I know he does."

"Yes, I think you are right."

"He'll miss talking to you. He loved those battles and the chess and all that. You're so much cleverer at it than I. But you must come here . . . often."

"I shall have to be with my husband, and we mustn't forget the animosity between yours and mine."

"It will make no difference to us."

"None whatever," I said.

Then she kissed me again and talked about the baby.

And I told Phoebe to pack my belongings, for we were going to live at Longridge.

What a strange Christmas day that was. Angelet came to the farm to spend it there. We attended prayers in the morning, when the whole of the household assembled and we all knelt while Luke prayed for our souls.

How different it was from those Christmases celebrated at Trystan and Castle Paling. Here Christmas was not a day for frivolity; we were celebrating the birth of the Lord and simply that; constant references were made to his death, so there was no real rejoicing in his birth.

The table was not loaded with the fancy dishes we had had at home. There was plain pig with some lark pie and we drank the home-brewed ale. Grace was said before the meal and it was all undertaken with a religious solemnity.

Afterward we talked about the meaning of Christmas and I could not resist describing some of the festivities we had indulged in at home. Angelet joined with me explaining how on Twelfth Night, we had elected the Lord of Misrule who had been carried on the shoulders of some of the more stalwart guests to make crosses on the beams in order to ensure good luck in the coming years.

Luke and his sister considered this pagan and insisted that Christmas had one meaning and one only.

I found a certain pleasure in teasing Luke. He knew this and did not dislike it, because he was aware that it was in a measure an indication of my affection for him. For I was fond of him. I could even share a certain passion with him, which might seem strange after my protestations about Richard. Richard was the man for me; he was my love; but so was I made that that did not prevent my dalliance with a man who appealed to me physically as my husband did. There was a certain amount of gratitude in my feelings for him; I could not forget that he had overcome all his scruples in order to possess me and to a woman of my nature that meant a good deal.

I was, too, becoming interested in the child, thinking about it, longing for its birth. I knew its coming would change me in some way. Perhaps I was not the maternal type as my own mother was. Perhaps my mate would always be of more importance to me than the result of our union. That might have been so with Richard but it might not with Luke.

Life and people interested me; and of course I was more interested in myself than anyone else; and when I discovered new traits in my own nature I was tremendously intrigued.

I know that Angelet returned to Far Flamstead quite bewildered, asking herself what I had done.

January came. I was becoming increasingly aware of the life growing within me, and this did much to assuage the pain I felt because I had lost the man I should love best for as long as I lived.

He returned in January. I imagined his riding home thinking of me, wondering how we would contrive to be together. He had shocked me a little when he had admitted knowing of my deception from the first. True, I had often felt he must, but he had made no sign of it when we met afterward and that showed a certain secretiveness in his nature; but then a man must be secretive when he has secrets to hide. And when I had gone to him again he had shown so clearly that the cold man whom Angelet knew was by no means the true one. As thus with Luke—perhaps most of all with Luke, the stern Puritan—who had married me not so much to help me but to make love to me under the protecting cloak of holy matrimony. I thought in the years to come when passion is no longer so insistent he will tell himself that he married me to save me because of the ignominious position into which I had brought myself. I would remind him then of his eagerness to possess me. I would remember these things and make it so that he should not revel in the satisfaction self-righteousness brings to a Puritan.

Life was full of interest, and although I yearned for Richard and deeply mourned his loss, I could think longingly of the child who would be born in August.

Richard sought me out. He rode over to Longridge but did not call on us. I saw him from a window riding by and I got into my riding habit, saddled my horse, and went out to meet him.

Our horses faced each other and I saw the look of shocked bewilderment in Richard's face.

"Bersaba!" he cried. "Married to Luke Longridge! How could you do that? Oh, my God, I understand. Angelet told me you are to have a child."

"It is true, Richard. I saw this as a way out and I took it."

"Because of our child?"

"Yes, because of our child."

"There could have been a solution."

"Oh, yes, you could have set me up in an establishment perhaps. You could have visited me now and then. It was not the life I had planned for myself."

"But what of us?"

"What of us? There was no future for us. You are married to my sister. A madness overtook us . . . me if you like, for I take the blame. You followed when I beckoned. Oh, very willingly, you'll remember. Nevertheless I was the one who led you into the downward slippery path. Then there was Luke. He had asked me to marry him. He would provide the paternity for the child so I married him."

"He will know . . ."

"He already knows. I told him the reason I would marry him."

"Does he know that I am the father of the child?"

"He knows. He must know. He is one of the chief performers in our little piece. He must know what the play is all about."

"And he is willing?"

"He loves me. He is a good husband. I will not let him make a little Puritan of our child. But that is for later."

"Bersaba, you behave so—"

"So immodestly, so different from the manner in which young ladies should? I am myself, Richard, and I make no excuses for it. Our problems will never be faced by trying to push them aside in order to forget them, for they won't be pushed aside. They won't be forgotten. I have sinned. I am to bear a child. Well, I have told Luke that I needed him for a husband and I have promised him that I will be a faithful wife to him and in time bear him children. I shall keep my promises. It would be easier if you and I met as little as possible."

He bowed his head.

"Which will be far from easy."

"It is not easy," I said, "for you are my sister's husband and we shall perforce meet sometimes. We must not allow ourselves to fall into temptation again. We have both been fortunate, and this child will always be there to remind me of what I once shared with you. Nothing can be the same for me again but it is over. Good-bye Richard, my lover. When we meet again you will be only Richard, my sister's husband."

I turned my horse and I did not look at him. My poor beloved, with his unloved Angelet and his sad secret of his mock castle.

In August of 1641 my child was born—a girl—and I called her Arabella. Luke and Ella wished her to be called Patience or Mercy, but I stood out against them and I had my way, as I did over most things in that household.

She was a perfect child and quickly became beautiful. I had refused to consider that my child might be malformed, although the idea had occurred to me. I know it did to Richard. That grim specter must have been hanging over him ever since the monster child was born and he would wonder, I knew, whether some taint in him had made such a child.

As soon as my daughter was put into my arms and I examined her perfect little body I was filled with delight; in a few weeks it became apparent that she was exceptionally bright. I knew very well that all parents think this of their children but at least I could assure myself that, motherly prejudice aside, my Arabella was a normal child.

Ella adored her. Luke eyed her with some suspicion, but that was to be expected; as for myself I was almost idolatrous, so that my little girl was assured of an abundance of love.

When Angelet beheld her she was in ecstasies. She started to discover similarities in the child's features to our mother and to ourselves. My poor dear Angelet. She would, I guessed, have made a better mother than I would, and when I saw her with my child in her arms I felt remorse because this child should have been hers.

I was glad it was a girl. A boy might have shown a stronger resemblance to his father, and I did not want Luke to be reminded. He had done so much for me and I was growing more fond of him. We argued continuously and I had to admit to taking the opposite side of a subject merely to provoke him. He knew this and enjoyed it. Strangely enough, our marriage was a happy one which, considering our opposing natures, was in itself a miracle. But I knew of course that it owed its success to that physical union which he as a Puritan preferred to forget.

That was a momentous year for England. I felt remote from politics in my new domesticity. Even a woman such as myself must change when she bears a child. For the months before and after her birth Arabella was of more importance to me than anything.

One of the first acts of the new Parliament was to demand the impeachment of Thomas Wentworth, Earl of Strafford, who had been the King's chief adviser when the conflict with Scotland had arisen and the victorious Scots had encroached on English soil so that part of the north was in their hands. Strafford had energetically suggested all kinds of unwelcome methods such as loans from abroad, the debasement of the coinage, and bringing in an Irish army to help fight Scotland and to threaten those in England who were showing signs of rebellion. The King and Strafford worked closely together and the Earl had been appointed Lieutenant General of the Army.

I often wished when I heard this that I could have sat in the library with Richard and discussed this matter. I knew that it would cause him grave concern.

So Strafford was impeached, his trial had taken place, and he was found guilty and sentenced to death, for the fact that he had threatened to bring in the Irish to subdue if necessary rebellious Englishmen was construed as treason. The King was in a quandary. He wished to save his friend with whose policies he had been in agreement and when the death warrant was placed before him for some time he prevaricated.

Luke used to pace up and down our bedroom talking of this.

"Strafford must die," he declared. "And the day he does the King is in a very uneasy position."

And finally the King had signed the death warrant and Strafford was executed.

That had been in May, three months before Arabella was born. I was enough aware of what was happening in the country to realize that this event was the most momentous so far and that the cloud which had been on the horizon was now overhead.

But then I was a woman whose child would come into the world in three months time, and that seemed of greater importance to me than anything else.

Events kept Richard away from home. Whether he stayed away more than he needed, I did not know. It seemed that he no longer suggested Angelet should join him in Whitehall. She told me that the situation was too serious for any thought of entertaining there. He was constantly attending conferences with his fellow generals.

Once he came over and rode out to the farm. He must have hung around waiting for me. I saw him and, as on that other occasion, I went out to see him. That was in May of '42. Arabella was nine months old—as healthy a child as any parents could wish to see.

Richard looked at me yearningly and all the old desire was immediately there between us as I leaned over the pales to talk to him.

"I had to see you," he said. "We are on the brink of war. God knows what will become of us all."

"I know. And you and my husband will be on opposing sides."

He waved that aside as though it were unimportant. "The child . . ." he said.

"She is the most beautiful child in the world."

"A perfect child?" he asked anxiously.

"Wait awhile." And I went into the house and brought her out to him.

He looked at her in something like adoration while she regarded him with dignified solemnity.

"A perfect child," he said, and I knew that he was thinking

of that monster shut up in the castle. "It is like you," he went on, "to show me that I could have a perfect child."

"I never doubted that my child would be," I answered.

"Oh, Bersaba, thank you for that brief happiness."

"Was it happiness?" I asked.

"For a few hours, yes," he answered.

"At least it happened," I said. "But it is over now. She will always be here to remind me."

I held her close to me and I thought, "She is my consolation; she is my comfort." And I thought, "Poor Richard, who lacks that comfort."

"You are content in your marriage?" he asked.

"As content as I could be away from you."

"Bersaba . . . you say such words that delight me . . . and yet fill me with hopelessness."

"You have Angelet. She is a part of me. She is good and I am far from good. Try to remember that."

"I try to be kind to her. I would that she did not sometimes remind me of you. Every time I look at her . . ."

"Good-bye, Richard."

"I do not know when we shall meet again. There is about to be a bloody war—the worst kind of war, Bersaba. I can happily fight the Spaniards or the French. It is a different matter when it must be my own countrymen. The country is split. The north and the west, Wales and Cornwall, are for the King, and here in the southeast and the manufacturing districts they are for the Parliament. We shall soon subdue the enemy, never fear, but there will be a violent struggle first."

I left him then and carried my baby into the farmhouse.

I had lost him; I would never know that ecstasy which he alone could give me; and he was a sad and lonely man who was about to be drawn into a conflict distasteful to him. But I should never forget his face as he had looked at our child —our perfect little girl, our Arabella.

At least I had done something for him.

In August of that year, when Arabella was a year old, the King set up his standard at Nottingham. By that time I was pregnant with Luke's child.

Luke was in a state of great excitement. That which he had been preaching against for so long was about to be destroyed. He was as certain of the success of the Parliamentary cause as Richard had been for that of the Royalists.

People were beginning to talk of Cavaliers and Roundheads. The Cavaliers were so called by those people who had attacked the officers of the Court who circled about Whitehall; it was meant to be an abusive epithet implying that these gentlemen were of loose morals and idle. The term Roundhead was said to have come into use during one of the increasingly numerous riots when a certain officer had drawn his sword against the mob. He had shouted that he would cut the throats of those roundheaded dogs who bawled against the bishops.

At this time the Royalists appeared to have everything in their favor. The trained army was Royalist, while the Parliament had only those who went to fight with a great belief in the righteousness of their cause. As Puritans they believed that God must help them, for they saw themselves as His people, but God was not responsive. The battles of Edgehill and Brentford were indecisive and the following spring the Cornish Royalists had claimed the west for the King.

Luke's son was born in February. I called him Lucas. He was like his father but slightly different and my pleasure in my babies absorbed me. Angelet came over to the farmhouse to be with me whenever she could, but she was never sure when Richard would come to Far Flamstead. Not that he often did. He was too much concerned with the fighting.

As with such conflicts the excitement and hopes with which they began soon petered out and the great depression and reality remained, for it had become clear that there was going to be no easy victory for either side. I felt myself torn in this conflict. My instincts were to support the Royalists. I knew the King had acted foolishly; I knew that he was stubborn and that he must be brought to reason; but at the same time I did not wish to see our country ruled by those who thought pleasure sinful. I felt a certain need in me to support Luke, which amazed me. I caught something of his enthusiasm for his cause; there was so much that was good in it. I was torn between the two and felt that I could not have served either side with the zest that was needed for victory.

Luke was depressed by the way things were going. He used to say that the soldiers were untrained and an army was needed which could stand up to the King's disciplined forces. He had the idea of forming his own troop. There were many ready to join. All his farm workers and others from families around came to join. They drilled on our fields and learned the arts of war.

There was much talk now of a man called Oliver Cromwell, who had joined the Army as a captain, and he was clearly one to be reckoned with. Luke spoke of him in glowing terms. He was reorganizing the Army. It was no longer going to be a straggling mob of men who had no weapons and no skills—little but their fervent belief in the right. Belief in the right there must be, but skill too. "Captains must be good honest men," Cromwell was quoted as having said, "and then good honest men will follow them. A plain russet-coated captain who knows what he is fighting for and loves it I would rather have then what you call a gentleman and nothing else." Such words were inspiring, and all over the country those who believed gave themselves up to the task of turning themselves into soldiers.

Luke had gone off with his troop. The months passed and we were at war in earnest, and none of us could guess what the outcome would be.

Those dreary years of war, how sickening they were! What a snare it was, for it could bring little good to either side. Much of the country was laid waste; we lived in a state of agonizing expectation during the first months and then we were lulled to something near indifference. Much of the corn was ruined; the Puritans were destroying many ancient treasures because they believed that beauty in itself was evil and that no man should look on something and find it entrancing—architecture, statuary, paintings—for if it gave pleasure it was evil.

When I heard of such destruction I was ardently Royalist; when I thought of Court extravagances and the stubborn nature of the King I was for the Parliament; but more often I had the inclination to curse them both.

I was thinking of Richard, who was in constant danger. Each day I feared that there would be news of his death or capture. There was Luke, too, who had trained his troop and gone off to fight. It was possible that one day these two would be in the same deadly battle.

"How stupid it is," I cried, "to fight and kill to settle differences."

"What other way is there?" asked Angelet.

"We have words, have we not? Why don't we use them?"

"They would never agree. They have tried words and failed."

Yes, Luke had tried with his pamphlets, but Luke could never see more than one side of this argument. Nor could Richard.

So we waited and lived our lives when the days were long

and there were a few visitors and the talk was all of war—how this side was winning and then shortly after how it was losing. How Cromwell and Fairfax would soon find their heads on London Bridge; how the King would soon have no throne.

And all the time we waited for news.

Angelet and I saw each other frequently. She would come to the farmhouse more often than I went to her because of the children. She adored them. Arabella was growing up to be like me—self-willed and determined to get what she wanted. Lucas was too young to show what he would be like; but he was a sweet cherubic infant.

Poor Angelet! How she would have longed to have had children and would have been a better mother than I suspected. How perverse of nature to have made me, the sensualist, the mother while giving Angelet the qualities needed to rear them.

Strangely enough the children adored me. As soon as Lucas could toddle he would cling to my skirts and look unhappy if his hand were disengaged. They were of course fond of their Aunt Angelet, but I was the center of their lives.

When Lucas was a year old Phoebe came to tell me that Thomas Greer, one of the farm workers, had asked for her and she would marry him if I gave my consent. I said it was ideal and she could still work with me after she was married. The only difference being that she would live in his cottage instead of sleeping in the house. So Phoebe married and almost immediately became pregnant.

Angelet and I were anxious as to what was happening in Cornwall, although there were reports that that part of the country was firmly in the hands of the Royalists. There was no news of course because it was not easy to get messages from one side to another of a country plagued by civil war.

So we waited and hoped for news. Snatches of it came to us from time to time but it went on as before—first one side was victorious and then another; and there was no sign of the end of the war.

It was July of '44. Lucas was a year and five months old and Arabella was three. The day began like any other. The sky, though, was leaden and there was a stillness in the air. I had not seen Angelet that day and I had busied myself with the care of the children and wondered whether what corn there was could be safely brought in. In the days before the war we had been concerned with the weather—now there was a greater enemy—the Royalist Army for us, the Parliamentary one for Angelet. Luke was well known among his enemies as a man who had worked assiduously to further the cause of the Parliament. His writings had done a great deal to inflame opinion. I often reminded myself that he was a marked man and that one day they would take revenge. I used to keep the children with me at night. Now I watched over them myself, for Phoebe was sleeping in the farm cottage with her husband and her time was getting near. I must be ready at any time of the day or night to snatch up my children and escape the vengeance of Luke's enemies.

I had developed a habit of light sleeping, as people will when there may be something to need their attention at a moment's notice. And that night I was awakened suddenly by the sound of whispering voices below my window.

I got out of bed, glanced at the children asleep in their cribs, and went at once to the window.

There were people below.

"Oh, God," I thought. "The Cavaliers have come for their revenge."

I was about to gather up the children when I heard a clanging at the door. I could not escape that way. I would have to face them. I would tell them that General Tolworthy was my brother-in-law, that I was not a Puritan although married to one, and my children were not Puritans. . . .

Boldly I went to the door.

A man was standing there. I recognized him at once by his plain garments and cropped head as a Roundhead.

"You are Mistress Longridge?" said the man.

"I am."

"Your husband is here . . . come all the way from the Moor. He is wounded and would have us bring him to you."

I ran past him. Luke was being held up by two men. There was blood over his doublet and his face was deathly pale.

"Luke!" I cried.

I saw the smile on his terribly pallid features.

"Bersaba . . . " he whispered.

"Carry him in," I commanded. "He is badly wounded."

" 'Tis so indeed, mistress."

I led the way into the farmhouse and they brought him in. They took him to one of the bedrooms.

Ella came out.

I said, "They have brought Luke home. Badly wounded."

They laid him on the bed.

One of the men shook his head and said, "He is sorely tried, mistress."

I said, "There is no time to lose. Wake the servants. We

need hot water . . . bandages . . . I must attend to him."

Ella said to me, "Stay with him. He wants you there. I will see to the rest."

I could trust her. Good calm Ella!

His hand moved toward me and I took it.

"Luke," I whispered. "You're at home. You'll get well. I shall nurse you. You will stay at home, out of this accursed war."

" 'Tis good . . . " he murmured.

"Good to be home, Luke?"

"To be with you," he murmured.

I bent close to him. His skin was clammy and very cold. "We're going to make you well. Ella and I will look after you."

He closed his eyes.

One of the men said to me, "We've come from Marston Moor, mistress. There's many dead up there. But it was victory . . . victory for us . . . and Cromwell."

"Marston Moor!" I cried.

" 'Twas a long journey and he would have us make it. He said he must see you before he died."

"He's not going to die," I said firmly. "We are going to nurse him."

They did not answer. They just looked at me with sorrowing eyes.

Only when we removed his garments did we see the terrible extent of his wounds. Ella looked at me and murmured, "It is the will of God. He fought for what he believed to be right."

But I was angry that men should destroy one another with their deadly weapons when they had been given minds to reason and tongues with which to speak.

"I shall save him!" I cried. "I will."

It was as though I shook my fist at Fate, at God. *I'll not submit to Your will. I'll not let you take him, for it is so stupid for a young life to be taken in this way.*

But it was I who was foolish, for how could I pit myself against the forces of nature?

I stayed with him, for my presence was the only comfort I could give him, and Ella left us because she understood her brother well.

He talked as he died, rambling a little and often incoherent, but I knew what he was telling me.

"We're going to win. . . . This will be remembered. . . . The battle of Marston Moor . . . Cromwell . . . victory

287

. . . the end of evil rule . . . Bersaba . . . my love . . . Bersaba. . . ."

"Yes, Luke. I am here. I shall always be here while you want me."

"It was good . . . was it not . . . ?"

I put my lips close to his ear and said, "It was good."

"There is the boy. Little Lucas. Love him. . . ."

"He is my son, Luke . . . mine and yours. . . ."

"Such happiness. . . . Perhaps it was sinful. . . ."

"Never, never!" I cried vehemently. "How could it be when it brought us Lucas?"

He smiled.

"The cause is won," he said. "It was worthwhile . . . everything . . . and you, Bersaba. . . ."

"Yes, Luke. I am here."

"I loved you. Perhaps it was wrong. . . ."

"It was right . . . absolutely right. And I love you, Luke."

"Stay with me," he said.

And I did until he died.

So I was a widow, and my hatred of the war intensified. It seemed I had deeply cared for him because I was beside myself with grief.

"What do I care who wins if only they will stop."

I mourned for Luke and I was thinking of Richard, who was in the thick of the fight.

Angelet came over to mourn with me.

"My poor, poor Bersaba. I can understand so well. You see, there is Richard."

"Yes," I said ironically, "there is Richard."

"But we must not let the children see our grief."

She was right. They were our salvation.

Poor Ella, this was her greatest tragedy. She had loved her brother and they had always been together. But she had her belief in the rightness of the cause to sustain her.

"He lost his life at Marston Moor," she said, "but he lost it fighting for the right and that battle is going to prove decisive."

"And Richard?" I thought. "What of Richard?"

Angelet wanted us to go to her that Christmas but I would not, for I could not ask Ella to spend Christmas in a Royalist household when her brother had been killed by them.

"And you, Bersaba?" she asked.

"I care not for either side," I answered, "and you are my

sister. I think I care more for people than ideas. I doubt not there are faults on both sides and we cannot expect utopia whoever wins. I don't know what I prefer—the mismanagement of the King or the strictures of the Parliament—perhaps the former, for I am no Puritan. But we cannot say until we have experienced it. No, I care only that they stop this senseless war, this killing of families."

"Oh, Bersaba, you are right. You always are. You are so clever. I would those in high places could take your advice."

I laughed at her. "Nay, I am as foolish as the rest," I said.

I said that she should come to the farm for Christmas so that we could all be together and later on in the year when the spring came I would bring the children over to Far Flamstead for a few days. I said I would bring Phoebe with me and that would mean having her young Thomas, for in these times I could not separate them—even if she had someone to leave him with.

"You should have a new maid now that Phoebe is married and has a baby," said Angelet.

"No one could serve me as Phoebe does. I shall keep her as long as I can. The children will be delighted to come to Flamstead. They are real little Royalists, I believe."

So it was arranged.

Richard came home in May. I purposely did not see him and he stayed only a few days. Angelet came to Longridge after he left. She looked radiant and I supposed that was due to his visit.

"I did not suggest that you come to see him, Bersaba," she told me. "I should have, of course, if he had stayed longer. He is very uneasy. He says that things are not going well for the King's Army. Men like Fairfax and Cromwell are making soldiers of their followers and their religious fervor gives them something which the professional soldier lacks. That's what he said. When are you coming to Flamstead? You promised to bring the children, you know."

So it was arranged and a few days later I with the children and Phoebe went to Far Flamstead.

I was in the enclosed rose garden with the children, Angelet, and Phoebe when one of the servants came running out to us, his face set and tense so that I knew before he spoke that some further calamity had overtaken us.

He cried, "One of the hands from Longridge is here, mistress. He's put out terrible."

I was filled with foreboding. I was still shocked from that

night when they had brought home the dying Luke. I knew that anything could happen, and we must not be surprised how terrible it might be. Now I knew that something was happening at the farm and I secretly thanked God that my children were safe at Flamstead.

I recognized the man at once. He was Jack Treble, one of the farm workers.

When he saw me he shouted, "They have come, mistress. They be at the farm. They have laid it to waste, mistress. I hid myself and got away. It be finished, mistress . . . finished."

I said, "Be calm, Jack. Tell me what happened."

"It was the Cavaliers, mistress. They come and I heard them shouting that it was the home of Luke Longridge, the pamphlet man, and that they would teach him a lesson."

"Oh, God," I cried out involuntarily, "he has already had his lesson."

"Reckon they did know it, mistress. They laid waste the place . . . and they be . . . dead dead, mistress . . . them as tried to stop them."

"Mistress Longridge?" I began.

"I wouldn't know, mistress. I was hid there in the shrubbery . . . close to the ground . . . not daring to move . . . never knowing whether they'd find me like. I dursn't move. I heard 'em. . . . The noise were shocking and the cries, mistress. There be terrible slaughter there of them that tried to protect the farm. They be gone now, though. It happened this morning. I lay there a good half hour, mistress, not daring to come out lest they should see me and put an end of me. Then I came here. I walked. There were no horses left. They took the horses. They took everything they could lay their hands to."

I said, "I shall go back."

Angelet had joined me. "No," she said. "You mustn't go back. What if they're there?"

"I'm going," I said. "I have to find Ella."

They tried to stop me. Poor Phoebe was in a panic. Her Thomas Greer would have been there.

"Why didn't he come with Jack Trebel?" she kept saying, and the tragic answer to that seemed clear enough.

Of one thing I was determined. I was going to Longridge.

Angelet insisted on coming with me and I could not dissuade her, so together we set out, taking with us two of the grooms.

What desolation met our eyes! Was this Longridge Farm?

It stood there, as though boldly defying the intruder, but when one drew near the destruction was obvious. Before the shell of the house lay the bodies of two of the farm workers. I recognized Thomas Greer and I went to him at once. He was dead. My poor, poor Phoebe!

Ella was lying on the farmhouse floor among the wreckage. In her hand was an ax. She must have tried to defend her home. Poor brave Ella! How futile she would be against those soldiers!

The cask of ale was turned on its side and its contents had run all over the kitchen floor. They had broken everything they could—the beams had been torn down—only the walls of the house still stood.

I knelt by Ella and a wild anger filled me. I hated them all—all those who had killed first Luke and then Ella. I wanted no more of this conflict.

"How can anything matter when it is achieved through this?" I cried, and I felt sick with my pain and anger.

I could not mount the stairs, for they had been torn up. There was a hole in the ceiling through which a bedpost hung. This farmhouse, the home of Longridges for generations, had been destroyed in a single day.

Angelet was beside me, tears streaming down her cheeks.

"Bersaba, my dearest sister," she said, sobbing.

I put my arms about her to comfort her, but she went on sobbing while I looked about at the destruction of my home.

I said, "The children are safe. Let us be thankful for that. My husband is dead, my sister in marriage is dead, my home is in ruins, but thank you, oh, merciful God, for leaving me my children."

"You must not blaspheme, Bersaba."

"No!" I cried. "I must stand by and thank God for mercies received. Is that it? My husband is recently dead. Do you understand that?"

She said, "You were always angry in your grief."

"Oh, the cruelty of it," I mourned. "You see, Angelet, I have lost my husband. I have lost my home. . . . I have lost so much that was dear to me."

"You have me, Bersaba," she said, "and while I am here you will always have a home."

I turned to her then and I believe I was weeping too, though I was not conscious of it.

She said, "Come away, my dearest sister, come away with me. I am going to take you back with me. Your home will be my home. We shall never be parted unless it is your wish."

Then she led me away and I returned with her to Far Flamstead.

As we crossed the threshold she said, "Oh, this is cruel . . . cruel."

And I was the one who answered firmly: "It is war."

ANGELET

❖ ❖ ❖

Fear in the House

YESTERDAY Bersaba came back to live at Far Flamstead. I keep thinking of the desolation of the farm and the look in her eyes when she spoke so bitterly of all that had befallen her. My poor Bersaba! So she did indeed love Luke. I often wondered, because the marriage seemed so incongruous.

He loved her deeply. Once he said to me, "When Bersaba comes into a room she lights it up." And I knew what he meant, I don't think he could have told me more clearly how he loved her.

There is nothing entirely bad in life, I believe. Even with all that has happened we have the dear little children here, Arabella, Lucas, and poor Phoebe's Thomas. I love to see them running about in the gardens and listen to their shrieks as they run about. That must be balm to Bersaba's grief.

I am so relieved that she is here. Sometimes the house frightens me. It always did; then Bersaba came and I wasn't afraid. Then she went away, but it was not far and I could go to the farm often. But now she is here again and that at least pleases me.

There has always been something about the house which frightens me. There is the castle, for instance. When I see those walls I start to imagine all sorts of things. I can never forget the nightmare I had once. I believe I did see a man's face there, but as time passes and everyone else thinks it was a nightmare, I begin to believe that too.

I have come to the conclusion, though, that there is something in the castle which has to be hidden, and while these thoughts insist I must be uneasy in my mind. I have asked Richard about it but he becomes so displeased and says that it might be dangerous to go in there and that is why he built the wall. I want to talk about it to him but I dare not.

I have a secret now which I haven't told anyone, not even Bersaba, though I expect now that she is here in the house she will worm it out of me. I think I rather want her to.

It may be that I am going to have a child. When Richard came home last time and we were together, I prayed and prayed then that I might have a child and I really believe my prayers were answered.

If I could, everything would be so worthwhile. When I see Bersaba with her two and Phoebe with hers I am envious of them. I would give anything for a child.

I am sure Richard wants one too. It would make things easier between us perhaps. I have never really understood him. He has never been close to me . . . not as Luke was with Bersaba. She used to tease him about matters which were sacred to him, argue with him, seek to discountenance him—and he seemed to enjoy it, which seemed to me so strange but somehow indicated a closeness between them. Of course I was never able to juggle with words as she could. And then when he said that about the room lighting up it showed me so clearly what she was to him.

It is a terrible tragedy that she has lost him, but then, as I constantly tell her, she has the children.

And now I believe I am to have one.

It's a strange feeling I have that makes me want to keep it secret. I do have strange fancies. I think it's this house because I never had them at Trystan. When I go to the Castle Room I seem to sense Magdalen there and it is as though she is my friend. One doesn't hear voices—that is probably madness—but the conviction comes into the mind and while I was sitting doing my needlework—this was when I first suspected that I might be pregnant—the idea came to me that Magdalen was there with me.

"Keep it a secret," she seemed to be telling me. "Keep it a secret for as long as you can."

I had the same feeling too in the chapel. I have to admit I often go to the chapel. I go there to pray, I tell myself, but it is not only that. I feel drawn there. From the first moment I entered it I felt a repulsion and yet a fascination. It is very cold there. It's because of the stone floor, Meg says. But it seems to me a special sort of coldness. It draws me and repels me.

It was when I was kneeling at the altar that this conviction came to me.

"Wait . . . don't tell," it seemed to say. "Keep your secret for as long as you can."

It is very hard to keep a joyous secret which one wants to shout from the turret tops, yet so strong was the conviction that I have done so . . . so far.

Bersaba has been a week at Far Flamstead. I think Richard will be pleased when he returns. He will realize of course that I had to bring her here, for she had lost her home. But I think he liked her being here. He seemed different when she was. He used to enjoy those games they played before the war and I could see how her battle tactics—which I have no doubt were outrageous—used to amuse him. I don't think he minded her beating him at chess either. I watched him while he was playing and there used to be a faint color under his skin and now and then I would see him lift his eyes and look at her.

We heard from our mother shortly after Bersaba's arrival. The messenger had taken letters to the farm and, finding it destroyed, had come on to Flamstead. I was so glad that I received those letters because I could imagine my mother's distress if the messenger had gone back and told her what he had seen at the farm.

The West Country was fairly quiet, she wrote. She wished that we were with her. At times like this it was good for families to be together. She wanted news of the babies. She longed to see them but she would be terrified if we attempted to cross the country at such a time. We would understand her anxieties and she knew we would seize every opportunity to send news to her.

We wrote at once telling her about the disaster at the farm. She already knew of Luke's death. It would comfort her to know that we were together.

When the messenger had left we talked and talked about

home and our parents, and when we went to our rooms I
found Grace there instead of Meg.

"Meg has a headache, my lady," said Grace. "I said I'
come in her place."

"Poor Meg. She must ask Mrs. Cherry for something."

"She will, my lady, if it gets worse. It is a sorry matter fo
Mistress Longridge, but happy, I said to Meg, that she b
here with you."

"Yes. I am glad that I am able to have her with me. Sh
has suffered terribly."

"And it will be good for you to have her here when you
time comes, my lady."

Grace was watching me intently and I felt the color risin
to my cheeks.

"When . . . my time comes. . . ." I repeated foolishly.

"Well, I could be mistook but I don't think so. I know th
signs. It's being so much with it, you might say."

"You . . . know?"

Grace nodded slowly.

So my secret was out.

I wanted to tell Bersaba first so I did that day. She wa
silent for a while. Then she said, "It was when he came hom
in May."

I nodded and noticed that her mouth turned down mo
mentarily and she looked almost angry. I was filled with sym
pathy, for I guessed she was thinking of Luke.

Then she smiled and said, "You'll have to take care thi
time, Angelet."

"I am determined to."

"I wonder if it will be a boy?" she mused. "He would lik
that."

Then she talked about how she had waited for the births o
Arabella and Lucas and it was very cozy. I was happy becaus
I felt that my state was taking her mind off her own terribl
tragedy.

Because of the war we had very few servants now. Ther
were only the Cherrys, Jesson, Meg, and Grace. Jesson man
aged the stables with two young boys from the village to help
him. They weren't old enough to go to the war, but if it con
tinued I supposed when they were we should lose them.

This had made a different relationship between us. We wer
more intimate, and Mrs. Cherry had become more of a frien
than a servant. It might have been because the Royalist caus
was being undermined and a great many people were predict

ing a Parliamentary victory, which would have an equalizing effect on society.

She came into my room one day and said I was looking peaky and she had a good pick-me-up tonic. "You can't beat herb-twopence," she told me. "I've always said that was a cure for every ailment under the sun."

"I'm afraid of taking tonics, Mrs. Cherry," I said. "I want everything to be natural."

"My patience me!" she cried, her cherry face wrinkling up with mirth. "If herb-twopence ain't the most natural thing on God's earth, my name's not Emmy Cherry. A little dash of it would do you the world of good."

"As a matter of fact I feel very well indeed. If I look a little wan, it's nothing."

"Well, we've got to take care of you. You've got your sister back again. I reckon she'll keep her eye on you."

"I'm sure she will. And she's experienced too."

"Then we've got Grace. We're lucky, I reckon that's what. Does the General know?" Her eyes were sharp suddenly.

"Not yet. It's not possible to reach him. We don't know where he is. This terrible war. . . ."

"So he don't know yet." She shook her head. "If you was to be able to get in touch," she said, "tell him it'll be all right, will you? Tell him that Cherry and me will see everything's all right."

"I will, Mrs. Cherry. You're fond of the General, I know."

"Well, you might say that was putting it mild like. Cherry thinks the world of him. Served with him. Would be with him now if he was fit and well . . . like the rest of them. And all the time I've been here . . . well, I've got to look on him . . . more than a mere master."

"He is a man who inspires great respect."

She lowered her eyes to hide her emotion, I guessed. Then she said brightly, "Well, if you was feeling a bit under the weather you come to me, my lady. I reckon you won't be scorning my herb-twopence once you've felt its effects."

When she left me I went to Bersaba and told her that Mrs. Cherry thought I ought to try some of her cures.

"Do you remember Mrs. Cherry's soothing mixture?" I asked.

"It sent you to sleep, didn't it?"

"I don't sleep very well now," I told her. "Sometimes I have strange dreams. I told you how once I went to the Castle Room and saw a face there—or thought I did. I'm sure I did. It was at night and I took a candle. Mrs. Cherry came and found me there. She thought I was walking in my sleep."

"Were you?" asked Bersaba.

"No. I'm sure I wasn't. I saw a light in the castle from my room and then I went up and saw the face. I thought it was Strawberry John—a man I once saw in the woods. But they didn't believe me any of them and after that I lost the baby."

Bersaba said, "And you think the two incidents were connected?"

"They all said so. I had a fright, you see, and that can bring on a miscarriage, can't it?"

"Tell me exactly what happened," said Bersaba. And I told her.

"Did Richard know?"

"Oh, yes. He thought with the rest that I'd had a nightmare."

"It was all connected with the castle. Did he ever talk to you about the castle?"

"No. There are some things one can't talk about with Richard. He withdraws himself, as it were, so that you know you mustn't talk about it anymore."

"You should not allow yourself to be dominated, Angelet."

"You don't know Richard."

She smiled at me, rather tenderly I thought.

Then she said, "Stop thinking about the castle. Stop thinking about anything but the baby. Just imagine how overjoyed Richard will be when he knows, and how happy you will be when you have your little baby to care for."

"I do try, Bersaba, but then all sorts of thoughts come into my mind. I wonder about Richard, where he is, whether he will ever come back . . . whether like Luke . . . and so many others—"

She gripped my hand so tightly that I winced.

"Don't," she commanded. "He'll come back. I tell you he'll come back."

That was typical of Bersaba. Sometimes she appeared to believe that she could work miracles.

Then she started to talk about babies and she said we would make the clothes ourselves as we should never have a seamstress in these days.

It is wonderful having Bersaba with me.

It was hot that August. The wasps were thick around the plum trees; the children were tanned by the sun; we could always hear Arabella's imperious voice above the rest. When

I watched them at play I would forget the war, forget my fears for Richard, forget everything but that early next year my child would be born.

For days I lived in contentment and then I awoke one night in a state of uneasiness. I couldn't explain what it was, but it was just a strong sense of warning. It was almost as though something were warning me of danger, and the first person I thought of on waking was Magdalen—Richard's first wife.

It may have been because she had been in the house as I had, expecting a child as I was; and then she had died. Deep within me I suppose there was a fear here that because it had happened to her it could happen to me. But why? It was something in the manner of Mrs. Cherry and Cherry (although he was a man of very few words), of Jesson, Grace, and Meg. . . . Yes, the attitude of every one of them had changed toward me since it had become known that I was to have a child. It was almost as though they were watching me, looking for a sign of something.

I got out of bed and went to the window. I couldn't see the castle because I was in the Blue Room. I had not wanted to go to the bedchamber I had shared with Richard; this was more cozy. Bersaba was in the Lavender Room, very close, and all the children slept in a room with Phoebe which was immediately next to hers—so we were all together. I looked out on the peaceful lawns and thought of what had happened to Longridge Farm and how at any moment soldiers could advance and lay waste my home.

But it was not such thoughts which made me uneasy. It was something that overshadowed me alone—it was a personal fear—which, of course, is so much more frightening than those that are shared by others.

I went to the Lavender Room, opened the door, and looked in. Bersaba was asleep. She lay on her back with her hair falling onto the pillow, showing clearly the scars on her forehead. She had always tried to disguise them, but they had not prevented Luke's falling in love with her and loving her in his Puritan way much more fervently than Richard had ever loved me. How odd that Luke, a Puritan, should love like that. But was it something in Bersaba?

I turned away and quietly opened the door of the nursery. Moonlight showed me Arabella and Lucas on their child's pallets and Phoebe sleeping quietly with little Thomas in his crib.

All was well. Why should I have awakened with these fears

on me? But as I stood there I knew that I was being watched and I felt my nerves tingling just as they had that night in the castle room when I had thought a ghost was behind me and had turned to find it was Mrs. Cherry.

I felt limp with terror and afraid to turn around. Then I heard Bersaba laugh softly.

"Angel, what are you doing?"

"Oh!" I turned and there she was, my sister, her eyes wide with something like amusement. "I . . . I couldn't sleep," I stammered.

"You'll catch cold wandering about like that."

"It's a warm night. And what of you?"

"You came and looked at me."

"So you were awake?"

"Not completely. But I looked up and there was my sister looking at me in a very odd sort of manner."

"What do you mean, an odd sort of manner.."

"As if you suspected me of something. Do you?"

"What should I suspect you of?"

"You tell me."

"You say strange things, Bersaba."

"Mrs. Cherry is an old gossip," said Bersaba. "Has she been talking to you?"

"Well, only to offer me herb-twopence. She seems concerned about me."

"Come into my room," said Bersaba. I went in and we sat on her bed.

"Everyone seems concerned about me," I added.

"Well, it's because you're in what they call an interesting condition. They want everything to go well."

She was looking at me intently. "Tell me why you thought it necessary to come looking around at us."

"I woke up."

"Not that old tooth again?" There was a faint hint of mirth in her voice which I didn't understand.

"No. It was withdrawn. I was just unable to sleep."

"You need your sleep now."

"Do you think I ought to take some of Mrs. Cherry's soothing cure? I always remember how you used to give it to me. You were so determined that I was going to sleep."

"Was I?"

"Oh, yes. You used almost to insist that I take it and you poured it out yourself."

"It made you sleep long and deep. You didn't go wandering about in the night when you took it, did you?"

"Of course not."

"Well, it served its purpose. I think you should have a drink at night; warm milk is good for slumber. Ella used to give it to me when I was carrying Arabella and Lucas. I found it good. I'll tell you what—I'm going to see that you have it every night."

"It's nice to have you looking after me."

"And don't listen to any tales the servants might tell you."

"Tales, Bersaba?"

"You know what servants are. Do they ever say anything about . . . the castle?"

"No. They haven't talked of it for a long time."

"Servants get ideas. Don't worry. I'll look after you."

"As you used to over my toothache. I'll never forget how anxious you were for me then, Bersaba."

She rose suddenly and said, "I'm going to take you back to bed. Come on."

And she tucked me in and kissed me lightly on the forehead.

I wished I could get rid of the idea that they were all watching me. It was unnerving in a way. They say that women get strange notions during pregnancies. Was that what was wrong with me? Grace was with me a good deal, for she seized every opportunity to take Meg's place, and she gave me the impression that of all the cases she had attended mine was the extraordinary one, the one which needed extra care.

I used to go up into the Castle Room where Magdalen had sat and stitched at her embroidery. I would look out at the castle turrets and remember the night I had seen the face there. Why should I come here when it was due to what had happened here that I had lost my child before? That must not happen again.

What if I saw that face again looking out at me from the turrets? I wouldn't be frightened this time. I would make sure that it was a real face. The idea came to me that there was someone living in the castle. Was it Strawberry John, who had found a way in and used it as a sort of headquarters for his poaching expeditions? That could well be the answer.

Then there was the occasion when Bersaba and I had explored the kitchens and found that strange cupboard and what was beyond. I thought of that now and then when I was in the kitchen but the door was always hidden by the coats and aprons hanging over it.

I mentioned this to Bersaba and she showed a lack of interest. "It was only a big cupboard," she said. "A very useful one in fact."

I supposed she was right.

She was taking great care of me and I must say she made me feel cherished. She wouldn't allow me to pick up young Lucas because she said he was too heavy and I might strain myself. She watched me all the time, just as they all did, and was always admonishing me to be careful. She used to go down to the kitchens every night and bring up a mug of hot milk. At first I would sip a little and sometimes would leave it by the bed to drink when I awakened, which I invariably did. I had never been a good sleeper and I had often wanted to talk in the old days at Trystan when Bersaba wanted to sleep.

One night I awakened and thought I heard my door close silently. I sat up in bed, startled, and peered about me.

The moon was on the wane and there were several clouds about so it was not very bright. I stared at my door, which was fast shut. Then I got up, opened it, and looked out into the corridor. I went to the door of the Lavender Room. I wondered if Bersaba had looked in at me. Quietly I opened her door. She appeared to be fast asleep so I went back to bed.

It was obviously a dream.

I lay in bed admonishing myself. It was all this watching, all this care of me. Were all women who were expecting a child subjected to such concern? Surely not. It was a fairly commonplace occurrence.

I took up the milk and put it to my lips. Then I decided I didn't want it. It was cold and it didn't really make me sleep. In fact I was growing tired of it.

I tried to lull myself into contentment by wondering about the child and planning the little garments I would start on tomorrow. I had always found comfort in my needle.

I smiled to myself, thinking of Bersaba, who showed quite an interest in the clothes we made. In the past she had always been bored by needlework. What cobbles she used to make, and then I had to unpick her stitches and do it for her! It was wonderful to have her with me. She never forgot to bring me my hot milk, and though I was growing tired of it I couldn't tell her not to bring it because she seemed to enjoy doing it for me and was sure it did me so much good.

Bersaba as nurse! That was amusing and touching.

I would always remember her pouring out the dose of the soothing cure and how she used to watch me while I took it. And now there was this hot milk.

I let her bring it and it stood by my bed all night just in case she came in and in the morning as often as not I would throw it away.

Once a party of Cavaliers came to the house. They were hungry and weary. We fed them and kept them for a night. They had served at one time, they said, with General Tolworthy. They could tell us very little of the war, but they did say it was not easy to know which way it was going. There were defeats in some places, victories in others, but we saw that there was no great hope in them. Bersaba asked if they had encountered the General, but they had not. He had been at Marston Moor but they could not say where he had gone after that, for the forces were so scattered. They themselves could not stay, and their coming had been but a temporary respite.

"We're a danger to you," one of them told us. "If the enemy were to arrive here and find us they would destroy the place."

"They might do that if you are not here," replied Bersaba bitterly.

"Let us hope that even Roundheads would have some respect for defenseless women," one of them answered. "They are supposed to be men of God."

"They have little respect for anything but their own righteousness," retorted Bersaba.

They left us and the days fell into the old pattern. We sewed, we walked, we played with the children; it seemed incredible that so close to us battles were raging and men were killing one another and dying for their cause.

October came. Jesson went into London to buy food and came back with the news that the Parliamentary forces were having successes which must prove vital. It was largely due to General Fairfax and Oliver Cromwell. Cromwell was instituting a New Model Army. He was training them, paying them well, and above all exerting an iron discipline. He never let them forget that their consciences were concerned; he imbued them with the idea that they were fighting for an ideal, an escape from bondage, and that God was on their side. With such an ally they could not fail to succeed.

We talked a great deal after that of Richard and wondered where he was.

"I would give a great deal to know," I said.

"I would he could come home," answered Bersaba fervently.

But nothing happened. The weeks began to pass. The days were long and quiet, overshadowed always by menace.

My condition was beginning to show itself slightly and I rejoiced because I was halfway through my pregnancy. When I was stitching in the Castle Room I felt almost happy because it was so easy to forget the dangers all around and I could lull myself into the belief that I was an ordinary mother expecting her first child.

But it was hardly like that when I did not know from one day to another when the soldiers would come. This was a Royalist household, known as the home of one of the King's most loyal generals, and it would go hard with us if Cromwell's men ever came this way.

Everyone in the household was watching me more than ever. I would often find Mrs. Cherry looking at me with an expression of greatest concern. Grace and Meg, too. "Are you feeling all right, my lady?"

"Yes, of course—don't I look all right?"

"Well, my lady, shouldn't you rest a bit?"

I must escape those watchful eyes.

There was a strangeness about them all—even Bersaba. Sometimes she seemed cautious. She would not discuss the castle, and told me sharply that I must not think about it. Sometimes she wanted to talk about Richard and at others she would abruptly change the subject.

It was rather disquieting and more and more I sought the peace of the Castle Room.

The chapel began to exert a certain influence. I used to find myself wandering down to it. I liked to sit in the pew and think about all the Tolworthys who had worshiped there in happier times and I wondered if Magdalen had come there often to pray for a safe delivery.

That was what I wanted to do now.

I went to the altar. The cloth had been made by several of the ladies of the household one hundred and fifty years ago, Richard had once told me. I touched the stitching reverently. It was so delicately worked, and the colors were exquisite. One day I thought, When my baby is older I will make an altar cloth and I will find just such colors as these. That blue is so beautiful . . . blue for happiness . . . wasn't that a saying? How neatly it was finished off. I wondered how they had done that. . . . I had turned the cloth in my hands and as I did so I must have jerked it forward. There was a clatter as the chalice fell to the floor and in the next second I was hit by one of the vessels, the cloth came away in my hands, I was

304

ing on the chapel floor and at that moment I felt for the
st time the movement of my child and I fainted.

Mrs. Cherry was standing over me. Bersaba was there too.
noticed Mrs. Cherry's face was so pale that the network of
d veins stood out on her cheeks. She was shaking.

Bersaba, kneeling beside me, was saying, "It's all right.
e's better now." She was undoing the collar of my bodice.
All right, Angel. You fainted. It often happens at this
age." Her voice seemed to come from a long way off. "Don't
ove for a bit. Just stay here. You'll feel all right in a mo-
ent. Then I'll get you to your room. But it's nothing. It
appens."

So I lay on the cold floor of the chapel and I remember
eling the life inside me, and I kept repeating Bersaba's
ords: "It often happens at this stage."

Bersaba said, "You should rest for an hour or so. It's noth-
g. Women often faint the first time they feel the movement.
hen you get used to it of course. You've probably got a lively
ild."

It was pleasant lying there. She talked about how she had
en with Arabella and how all these little things were a part
a woman's life during pregnancy.

"It's fortunate for me that you have gone through it all
efore," I said.

"And that I'm here to look after you."

"I hope you always will be," I answered.

"Now you'll have to look after me sometime."

I slept a little and she must have left me, for when I woke
it was to find Mrs. Cherry coming into the room.

"I just had to come in and assure myself you were all right,
y lady."

"It was nothing, Mrs. Cherry. Just a faint when the baby
oved. My sister says it's normal. It often happens the first
me."

"It was the chapel what worried me," said Mrs. Cherry.

"I was looking at the altar cloth. It's so beautifully worked,
d I must have pulled it off."

"And kneeling there at the altar, were you?"

"Yes, I was."

She frowned a little. "Well, my lady, I just wondered.
e're all anxious about you, you know."

"I do know it and I wish you wouldn't be. Everything's per-
ctly all right."

"Oh, I do hope so, my lady!" she said vehemently.

And there I was . . . uneasy again.

I could not sleep. They say women have strange fanci when they are pregnant. I certainly had them that night. began when I thought I heard stealthy footsteps creaking c the stairs. It's nothing, I soothed myself. Just old boards ar my fancy.

I remembered how often I had been afraid of the dai when I was a child and what a comfort it was to know th Bersaba was close. But there was something in the air th night, something that meant danger. But we lived in dange ous times.

Almost without thinking I rose from my bed and, puttir on slippers and a robe, made my way to Bersaba's room.

My heart leaped in fear for she was not there. The be clothes had been thrown back as though she had left hurriedl Then I *had* heard footsteps on the stairs—Bersaba's!

There was a full moon and the room was almost as ligl as day. I went to the window and looked out. I stood the: for a few moments before I saw my sister. She was runnir across the grass as though her life depended on escape.

"Bersaba!" I cried out. "What—" I stopped short, for saw that she was pursued by something—a large, loping, u gainly creature. It had a human shape and yet I was n sure that it was a man.

I started to shout, "The soldiers are here!" as I ran fro the room and sped down the stairs. My one thought was save my sister.

"Bersaba!" I cried again. The creature stopped, halted b the sound of my voice. It turned uncertainly and came lun bering toward me. I could not see its face—perhaps that wa fortunate—but I knew that I was in the presence of som thing not quite natural—something baleful, evil, and that was in acute danger.

I heard Bersaba scream, "Run, Angel!"

Then almost immediately there was the sound of a gu The figure swayed and I saw its huge arms rise as it staggere and fell onto the grass.

Bersaba was beside me. She had her arms about me, hol ing me tightly.

"You're all right now. I thought I saw Richard down her so I came . . . and it was *that*. He saw me and—"

Mr. and Mrs. Cherry were running out of the house and she came to the figure on the grass Mrs. Cherry did a stran thing. She knelt beside it and laid her face on the fallen bod

It was like a nightmare. The coldness of the night and Bersaba and I standing there clinging together as though one feared she would lose the other; the body lying on the grass and Mrs. Cherry rocking back and forth on her heels, incoherently murmuring in obvious uncontrollable grief.

Grace and Meg came out with Jesson, and Grace knelt down and said, "He's dead."

Mrs. Cherry wailed, "Cherry shot him. He shot our son."

Cherry laid his hand on his wife's shoulder and tried to comfort her.

"We ought to get him into the house," said Jesson.

The sight of blood sickened me. Bersaba put her arm about me. "You should go back to bed, Angelet," she said.

I ignored her. I had to know what was happening.

They put him in the weapons room and as he lay there on the floor I caught a glimpse of his face. It was strange and terrifying. Thick and wiry hair grew low on the brow; hair covered the lower part of his face; but there was something evil about that face which had not been put there by death.

Grace took Mrs. Cherry away and we were left with Cherry and Jesson in the hall. I said, "What does this mean? Who is this man? You shot him, Cherry?"

Cherry said, "Yes, I shot him. You heard Mrs. Cherry. It's true. He is our son."

"Where did he come from?" asked Bersaba. "How is it that he has appeared here suddenly?"

"He escaped, my lady. He escaped once before. It has been a great trial to us. He was in a madhouse. He had the strength of two men and he was dangerous. I couldn't have him in the house. He caused such damage before. There didn't seem anything else to do. I knew I'd have to . . . if ever he came back."

Bersaba took control of the situation. She went to the kitchen and brought something from Mrs. Cherry's cupboard, poured it into a goblet, and made Cherry drink it.

"You must control yourself," she said. "What you did you believed to be for the best."

" 'Twas a terrible trial to us all these years, for we never knew when he might break out again."

"There's nothing you can do now," said Bersaba. "He is dead. Tomorrow you must take him out of the house and bury him."

Cherry nodded.

"Jesson shall take you to bed."

"I did it to save you, my lady. I did it to save the house.

307

There's no knowing what he would have done. He goes ma[d]
see. He would have burnt the place down. I had to do it.
had to. Mrs. Cherry must see it. But he's her son and—"

Bersaba turned to Jesson. "Take him to his room, Jesson[,]
she said. "Stay with him and Mrs. Cherry. I'll look after m[y]
sister."

She led me to my room and stayed with me. We talked f[or]
a long time.

"He did right," she said. "You could see that he was mad—
even as he lay there on the grass. If he had got into the hous[e]
he might have murdered us all. Cherry must have known ho[w]
desperate he was."

"To shoot his own son—" I began.

"He is better dead."

Though the children had slept peacefully through the di[s]-
turbance there was no sleep for any of the adults in the hous[e]
that night. In the morning Cherry and Jesson took the bod[y]
away and buried it on the edge of the paddock and they put [a]
stone there on which Cherry engraved the words "Josep[h]
Cherry" and the date.

He talked to us afterward more calmly than he had on th[e]
previous night. Bersaba was wonderful, for she made hi[m]
realize that in sacrificing his son he had saved us all, for th[e]
story Cherry had to tell was horrifying. His son had been bor[n]
abnormal; during his childhood he had become violent. As [a]
boy he had found a special delight in torturing and killi[ng]
animals, and later he had had an uncontrollable urge to d[o]
the same to human beings. He had had to be taken into [a]
madhouse and chained. He had escaped once before and som[e]
instinct had brought him to his parents. So he had come [to]
Far Flamstead. Then his presence had only been discovere[d]
when he had entered the house. He was stopped in tim[e]
before he had set it on fire. Then his father had shot hi[m]
through the leg. That was what he had aimed to do on th[e]
occasion, but the shot had entered his heart.

"You are a brave man, Cherrry," said Bersaba, "and [I]
think everyone in this house should be grateful to you today[!]

Of course the incident had changed the household. Befor[e]
we had been on the alert for soldiers who might destroy o[ur]
home and kill us. Now we had been brought face to face wi[th]
an equally terrifying situation. Both Bersaba and I tremble[d]
at the thought of what might have happened if that madma[n]
had entered the room in which the sleeping children lay, an[d]
we couldn't be grateful enough to Cherry.

Mrs. Cherry had changed. Her grief possessed her; sh[e]

made a wreath of leaves and laid it on her son's grave. I was glad that she bore no resentment against her husband, for he seemed so lost and bewildered that she might well have done.

Her color had changed; the network of veins was more visible. She was more silent than she had been. I thought how strange it was that people harbored secrets of which we were unaware. I couldn't forget her round rosy face, which seemed to match her name, and to discover that all the time she was nursing this bitter secret made me see her in a new light.

As the weeks passed we returned to the wartime pattern. We were alert as ever for approaching enemies but we were all aware that the most ardent Parliamentary soldiers could not have been more terrifying than the madman who could so easily have entered the house while we slept.

It was November—a month of mists and bare trees, green berries on the ivy, and spider webs festooning the hedges.

My baby was due to be born in three months time and I longed for February and the first jasmine and snowdrops. It seemed long in coming.

It was during this month that the terrible conviction came to me that someone was trying to kill me.

There were times when I laughed at my fancies, and I could not bring myself to talk of them, even to Bersaba. I kept telling myself, "Women have strange fancies, don't they, when they are in this condition? They are said to be irrational, to crave strange things, to imagine things are what they are not."

And here was this fancy within me, an eerie conviction that I was being watched and followed. When I went into the quieter places of the house—the Castle Room, the chapel on the spiral stairs, with its steps which were so narrow on one side—I would be aware of danger. "Be careful of that staircase," said Bersaba. "It could be dangerous. If you tripped on that it could be disastrous for the child."

Once, when it was dusk and I was coming down the staircase, I had the feeling that someone was watching me from behind. I fancied I could almost hear the sound of breathing.

I stopped short and said, "Is anyone there?" and I thought I heard a quick intake of breath and then the faint rustle of clothing. I hurried down, though taking care with every step, and went to my room to lie on the bed to recover. I felt my child move within me then and I laid my hands on it reassuringly. I was going to make sure that all was well with it.

Later I admonished myself. What was I thinking of? I believed I knew what had happened to me. The memory of that madman creeping up to the house had unnerved me. I couldn't get it out of my mind. How could I when Mrs. Cherry looked so sad and poor Cherry behaved as though he carried a load of sin on his shoulders? My imagination kept presenting me with pictures of what might have happened. I could imagine myself waking up to find him in my room. I pictured his creeping into the children's room and looking down on those innocent little faces.

I could hear Cherry's voice: "He took a pleasure in torturing and killing animals . . . and later he wanted to do the same to human beings."

He is dead, I reminded myself.

But such an incident was bound to have its effect on anyone as nervous as I had become, and the feeling of being watched persisted. I gave up going to the Castle Room. It was a climb up the stairs and I was getting unwieldy, I told myself. But it was not really that. The place seemed so isolated and I was fearful of being alone.

Then one night I was sure.

Bersaba had brought in my milk. I dozed and then fell into a disturbed sleep. I dreamed that a figure came into my room, stopped by my bed, slipped something into my milk, and then went swiftly and quietly from the room.

I awoke with a start and my hair really did stand up on my head, for as I opened my eyes I saw the door closing.

I called out sharply, "Who's that?"

The door shut. I distinctly heard it. I got out of bed, went to the door and opened it, but there was no one in the corridor.

I returned to my bed and looked at the milk. I could see that something had been put into it, because it had not yet completely dissolved.

I sat on the edge of my bed and thought, "Someone is trying to harm me. It is not my imagination."

I lay on my bed, fighting the impulse to go in to Bersaba.

I had told her how uneasy I felt, and she had brushed that aside. "It's your condition," she had said. "And you were always inclined to be nervous."

She would say that I had dreamed it.

I picked up the milk and smelled it. There was no odor.

For some time I looked at it and then threw it out the window.

I had made up my mind that the next time someone came

310

to my room I was going to be awake and speak to whoever came to tamper with my milk and ask why they wanted to harm me and my child.

It seemed to me that I had lost contact with Bersaba. She was preoccupied. Sometimes she talked about Richard; she wanted to know about our relationship, and that was something I found difficult to discuss with her. There were other times when she did not want to speak of him.

We were all nervous. "I reckon this war's doing something to us all," said Meg. "You never know when soldiers are going to come running over the grass." Then she clapped her hand to her mouth. "Oh, it won't happen, my lady. It couldn't here. They wouldn't dare—not in the General's house."

I knew that she had been warned not to alarm me.

I wasn't sleeping very well. I never drank the milk which was put by my bed, but I did not stop it. I wanted to catch the one whom I suspected of putting something in it. I thought with alarm that if there were no milk they might try some other method. Of course I was wasting milk. We had two cows which Cherry milked each day so there was plenty of fresh milk at that time, but we did not know when the countryside was going to be laid waste, and what we should do for food then.

Then I moved into a phase when I told myself that nothing of this was happening. I had not seen the door close. I had dreamed the whole thing. If I told anyone they would smile and soothingly say I must take care.

Then I began to think about the house and the strangeness of things here, and how different people were from what one had believed them to be. I thought particularly of Mrs. Cherry, who had seemed so rotund and contented when all the time she had had a son who was a dangerous lunatic, who had broken free from his madhouse and come to Far Flamstead and tried to burn the place down. I had discovered that that had happened more than fifteen years ago, and all that time the Cherrys had been watchful lest he should escape again and return.

I began to wonder about the door in the kitchen and whether it was really just an ordinary cupboard in there. It had somehow not looked like one. I was surprised at Bersaba's attitude. She had always been so adventurous, but when once more I tentatively mentioned the cupboard she changed the subject and showed quite clearly that she didn't want to talk about it.

I began to be obsessed by the thought of the cupboard i the kitchen and asked myself why there were always coa hung over the door as though to hide it. It became clear to m that I would go on thinking of it until I had seen inside. thought too about the Cherrys' son and what would ha happened if he had come into the house. It would have bee a good idea to put the children in that cupboard. I almo mentioned this to Bersaba, but she had been so impatie when I talked of it that I had stopped speaking of it.

Why shouldn't I explore my own kitchen? She had sa that to me. Well, why shouldn't I?

It was late afternoon. I had come in for a short wa around the grounds, for I did not go far now and in any ca the weather was getting cold, for we had come into Decen ber and snow was threatened. As I came through the hall noticed how quiet the house was and as I passed the kitchen looked in. There was no one there.

The impulse came suddenly. I went in and, crossing to th cupboard, pushed aside the garments which hung there. Th heavy key was in the door and I opened it. It looked just as had that night when Bersaba and I had explored. I pushe aside the coats. I needed all my strength to draw back th heavy bolt. A rush of cold air caught me and I stepped in what was certainly more than an inner cupboard. It was da and I could see nothing so I went back into the kitchen ar took a candle. I lighted this and went through the cupboard.

It was a carefully made corridor, with an arched ceili some seven feet high. The walls were of stone. I went throug it for what seemed quite a long way and finally I came another door. This also was locked by a heavy bolt.

I pulled it and the door swung open. I was in a courtya and I understood immediately where I was, for toweri above me was the castle.

I was tremendously excited and afraid. I was not to a proach the castle, Richard had said. It was unsafe.

I knew I should not stay, yet I seemed to be fascinated, u able to move. And as I stood there I heard someone shout me.

"Who's that?"

A man came out of the castle. He was tall, with very bro shoulders and a pale face on which was a birthmark, so viv that it was the first thing I noticed about him. Somethi seemed to click in my mind. I had seen him before. He w Strawberry John.

"Get back!" he shouted.

"Wh-Why?" I stammered.

Then I heard strange sounds, and something else lumbered into the courtyard. It was a man, yet somehow different from any other man. Its arms hung to its knees and it walked with a shuffle . . . coming toward me. It was a human, yet not human. My limbs were stiff with terror and would not move. I thought at once of the man I had seen on the lawn.

Strawberry John had leaped on the creature. He had thrown his arms about him and was holding him firmly.

"It's all right, boy," he said in a strangely gentle voice. "We're all right. It's nothing, boy, nothing at all."

The creature was smiling at Strawberry John, who had taken one of its hands. It no longer looked menacing.

Strawberry John waved his arms at me, implying I was to disappear the way I had come, and I stumbled back into the corridor.

With fumbling fingers I drew the bolt. I had dropped my candle in the courtyard and was now in darkness, but I knew where I must go, so I felt my way along those stone walls until I stumbled into the cupboard.

When I came out the first person I saw was Mrs. Cherry. She was standing there, her face ashen.

"You've been in the tunnel! You've been to the castle!" she cried.

"Yes," I said. "I've seen who is there and I want to know what it means."

"It's for the General to tell you," she said, and she sat down at the table and put her head in her hands. She remained thus for a few seconds and then she stood up and came to me.

"In your condition," she said, "this could have caused harm."

I said, "Who is that in there? Who is that . . . boy . . . man . . . ? Who is he?"

"It's not for me to say," she stammered.

"But you know, Mrs. Cherry."

"Oh, my lady. It's our secret—it's what we have to keep." Her eyes lit up suddenly as she said, "I can't keep it no longer. How can I when you've seen? We've looked after him all these years—all of us here and especially Cherry and me and Strawberry John. It's his son, my lady—the General's son."

"No!" I cried. "Magdalen . . . bore that!"

"There," said Mrs. Cherry. "I've told. No one can blame me. I could do no other . . . not after you'd seen. Here,

313

you're all shook up. Let me get you to your room. I'll call your sister."

Yes, I must talk to Bersaba. I had to share this terrible secret with someone. I would never forget the sight of that vapid face.

She led me to my room. "You mustn't be frightened, my lady," she said. "It would be bad for the child. He's quiet most of the time. Just has violent fits now and then. He's not a bad boy. Plays some games. Strawberry John's good with him. He loves him, Strawberry John does. He thinks he'll make something of him one day."

"Bring my sister to me," I said.

And she went away.

Half an hour passed and Bersaba did not come. Then there was a knock on my door. It was Mrs. Cherry again. She had a goblet in her hand.

"I'm so worried about you, my lady. You shouldn't have gone there. I've brought you this. It'll soothe you. A little vervain because you trembled so . . . and pimpernel to cheer you and my dear herb-twopence, which is good for everything. Drink it up."

"I couldn't drink anything, Mrs. Cherry. Leave it there."

She set it down and said, "I couldn't find Mistress Longridge. She's out in the gardens with the children. She had said something about gathering holly and ivy for Christmas. Oh, my lady, 'tis terrible to see you so put out."

"And Strawberry John has always looked after that . . . child?"

"He's a strange man. Some say he's a bit short and some say he has too much. He has a way with animals and the sick. He's always looked after the boy and good to him he's been. The boy would die for him and he for the boy. 'Tas been a great sadness for the General. We knew soon after he was born. And then the castle seemed the place and he was put there for the General couldn't bear to look at him. He'd wanted a child—what man doesn't?—and it was only natural that he should get to wondering what was wrong with him that he should have such as that."

"So he shut him away and wouldn't see him."

"He knew he were safe with Strawberry John."

"And that night when the noise in the kitchen awakened us?"

"That was the boy. The door had been left open and he got through. He was only playful like. He was throwing the pots and pans about. It was like a game to him. He's gentle most times, Strawberry John says. Strawberry John tells me that one day he could be better. He's getting better . . . he doesn't have the violent turns like he did. He'll always be different from others . . . but one day he might be able to live in a nice house like the son of a gentleman."

She paused and then her brow wrinkled. "Didn't he tell you?" she said. "There was that night when he broke in. . . . Didn't he tell you then?"

"He's never told me that he had a son living."

"The General took it bad. We recokned that he wouldn't marry again because he was afraid of himself . . . afraid there might be some taint in him like. He used to shut himself in the library and go through all that had happened to his family. We all knew because Jesson saw the papers when he put them away. Then he brought you here . . . and it seemed as if he might have another son. But when you had that miscarriage—"

She stopped.

"That was because I had a fright in the Castle Room. You all said it was a nightmare. Of course I did really see the lights and the face."

"It was the General's order, my lady. We dursen't go against that." She came close to me and laid her hand on my shoulder. "I hope this hasn't upset you, my lady. I hope it's not going to bring on something."

"I feel all right."

"And now you've seen. You don't think—you don't want—"

"What do you mean, Mrs. Cherry?"

"I was wondering whether you'd feel you wanted to get rid of it."

I stared at her in horror.

"Oh, forgive me, my lady. I shouldn't have said that. But if you was to have another like that—"

"Stop, Mrs. Cherry. *Stop.*"

"Yes, my lady. Drink this. It'll soothe you. I tell you it'll make you sleep and when you've slept you'll begin to see what all this means. You'll begin to make plans and—"

"I don't want to sleep. I want to think about this."

"Yes, you want to think. There are ways. . . . If you was to want to. . . . If you was to feel that you couldn't go on with this. . . ."

"Mrs. Cherry, please, I don't want to hear any more. Please go now."

"Drink up this posset, my lady. I'd like to see you drink that before I go."

"No, later. Not now. I don't want to sleep. I want to think and think."

She went out and I lay on my bed staring wild-eyed at the ceiling.

Bersaba came in. I was so relieved to see her.

"What on earth has happened?" she cried.

I told her that I had been through the tunnel into the castle and that I had seen Richard's son. "He's an idiot," I said. "That's the secret of the castle. That's why we are not to go there."

"Yes," she said.

"You knew?"

"Yes, I knew."

"How did you know?"

"Richard told me."

"He told you, but not me!"

"He was afraid that it would upset you, that you would be worried about having children."

"He was right. I am."

"You must not think of it," she said. "It does not mean that because one was born like that . . . others will be."

"Why should a child be born like that?"

"Something goes wrong."

"But it could be something in the parents."

"Why should it necessarily be in Richard? It might have been some fault in his wife."

"Yet he kept it a secret. How could he have done that to his own son!"

"How can you judge what other people should do? How could he have that boy in this house? He did the next best thing. He put him in the castle, built the wall, and gave him a good guardian. What else could he do?"

"You defend him."

"I'm trying to see his point of view. The boy has been cared for all these years."

"It must be fifteen years," I said.

"What made you go through that cupboard door?"

"Because I was curious."

"So that was why you kept talking about it."

"You wouldn't go with me. I know now why. You knew what was there."

"I wish you hadn't found out now . . . at this stage."

"What worries me, Bersaba, is this: What if my child should be—"

"Put such thoughts out of your mind. It's folly to think like that."

"How can I put thoughts out of my mind when they persist in being there? How would you feel if you were in my place? I keep thinking of that . . . boy. His face haunts me. I'm terrified, Bersaba. If it happened once—"

"It was foolish of you to go exploring now. Why didn't you tell me what you were going to do?"

"The Cherrys have kept the secret. Just think of it. Everyone in this house knew except me. I was the only one in the dark."

"It was important that you should be in the dark."

"I . . . Richard's wife . . . closer to him than any . . . and not to be told!"

"Be reasonable. You were going to bear his child. It was sensible not to tell you. Look at you now. Look at the effect it has had on you. Now, you are going to fret and fume."

"Mrs. Cherry suggested . . . that it could be stopped."

"What!"

"She says that even now—"

"You are mad. Mrs. Cherry is mad. I shall speak to her. How dare she say such a thing!"

"I am mistress of this house, Bersaba, though sometimes I think you fancy that you are."

She turned and went out of the room.

I could not sleep. How long the night seemed. I dared not sleep, for if I did I knew my dreams would be terrible. All the fears of the last months had been nothing compared with those which beset me now. I pictured my child being born. I could hear Richard's saying, "He . . . or she . . . must go to the castle."

There was no hot milk by my bed on this night, but Mrs. Cherry's posset was still there, untouched.

I almost decided to drink it but I knew it would send me to sleep and I did not want to sleep because of those nightmares I feared.

My door was being opened very slowly. I felt my heart begin to pound. Was this the one I was waiting for, the one I had promised myself I would try to catch?

Bersaba came and stood by my bed.

"You are awake, Angelet," she said.

"How can I sleep with so much to think of?"

"You are still worrying about the child?"

"Would you not in my place?"

"You have it in your head that Richard cannot father a normal healthy child."

"If you had seen that . . . creature. He reminded me of the man on the grass."

"Angelet, I have been thinking all day whether I should tell you. It may be a shock to you but I have come to the conclusion that it will be less harmful for you to know than fear for the child. What is important to you now . . . more important than anything . . . is the child. Is that not so, Angel?"

"Of course."

"Richard can have a healthy child. He has."

"I don't understand you."

"Arabella is his daughter."

I lay still, not comprehending. Then I said slowly, "Arabella. Your Arabella. *She* is Richard's daughter?"

"Yes," said Bersaba defiantly.

"You and he—"

"Yes, he and I. Did you ever see a more perfect child? I never did. Nor did anyone."

"Oh, Bersaba," I cried, "*you* and Richard."

"You didn't love him," she accused. "Not really. You were frightened of him."

"And you loved him, I suppose."

"Yes, I did."

"And that was why you married Luke—so that no one would know you were going to have Richard's child. And Luke, what did he think?"

"He knew and helped me."

"You think the world belongs to you, Bersaba. You always did. Other people didn't matter very much, did they?"

"You matter to me now, sister. You are going to be well and your child will be strong and healthy."

"And when Richard comes home," I said, "what then?"

"You will have a healthy child to show him."

"You have already shown him yours."

"That is over, Angelet. When your child is born and Richard comes back I am going home to Trystan Priory."

"Richard won't let you go. He loves you, doesn't he?"

"He is a man who will love his wife and his children. Good night."

She stooped over me and kissed me.

I lay there thinking of them. Lovers in this house . . . and I was here. Why did I not know? Then I remembered. She had insisted on my taking the soothing draught. "This will make you sleep." I pictured her, the sly smile about her mouth. So they put me to sleep while she went to him.

How could she? I remembered my fear of the great four-poster bed and how I could never reconcile myself to that relationship; and she had reveled in it. She was all that I was not. I remembered how Bastian's eyes had followed her and how angry she had been when Carlotta took him from her. Then Bastian had wanted to marry her, she had told me, and she would have none of him. And then she came and took Richard and then Luke wanted her so much that he would take another man's child for her sake.

Oh, Bersaba, my twin sister! What did I know of her? She had become a stranger to me.

A terrible thought came into my mind. She loved Richard; she loved him so much that she could forget that I, who had believed myself to be close and dear to her, was his wife.

Memories stirred. I was back in my room in Pondersby Hall and Ana was standing beside me. What had she said? It was something which had seemed strange at the time. "It would be a mistake to think she had all the good points . . . if the occasion should arise. . . ."

What should Ana have known of Bersaba? But the fact was that she warned me to beware of my sister.

I had imagined someone had put poison into my milk. Who had given me the milk? Who had given me the sleeping draught so that I should not be disturbed while she went to my husband?

I had never been so frightened or so horrified in my life.

Could it really be that my sister wanted my husband so much that she was trying to kill me?

BERSABA

❖ ❖ ❖

In the Tunnel

WAS almost a relief when the soldiers came. It was after
~~C~~ristmas—a travesty of the festive seasons we had known.
~~I~~ made a halfhearted attempt to deck out the house with
~~ho~~lly and ivy for the sake of the children and to make some-
~~thi~~ng of the day for them, but as soon as they had been put to
~~be~~d gloom descended on the house.

~~M~~rs. Cherry had lost her benignity; if ever I went to the
~~kit~~chen I would find her seated at the table staring into space.
~~Ch~~erry said very little; I knew he could not forget the memory
~~of~~ the son he had killed. Nor could Mrs. Cherry. And Cherry's
~~bu~~rden of guilt lay so heavily upon him that it overshadowed
~~th~~e entire household.

~~G~~race and Meg tried to be cheerful. Phoebe sighed for
~~Lo~~ngridge Farm where she had been happy with her husband
~~an~~d I knew she wondered, as we all must, where this was
~~go~~ing to end. Most hard to bear was the restraint which had
~~gr~~own up between Angelet and myself. She could not forgive
~~me~~ for taking her husband and I could not forgive myself.
~~Sh~~e could scarcely bear to be in the room with me and she

had found a key to the door of the Blue Room, which she ha
never thought of locking before. I was afraid that she wou
need something in the night.

I knew that she was suspicious of me and believed that
wanted her to die so that if Richard came back he would l
free to marry me.

Whenever possible I assured her that I was going in
Trystan Priory. I even made preparations.

"This war can't last forever," I used to say. "Somethin
must happen soon."

After that sad Christmas, followed by Twelfth Nigh
which we did not celebrate, Angelet spent a long time
her room with Grace.

I was worried about her because I knew that she was f
from well and I feared that everything that had happene
would be harmful to her. I even played with the idea of askin
my mother to come to us, but I knew that would be ir
possible in view of the state of the country.

It was mid-January and in a month's time Angelet's chi
was due to be born. There was ice on the ponds and a co
wind was blowing from the north. It was not a day to be o
of doors. We burned huge log fires in the main rooms b
there was no comfort in the house. Grace was preparing tl
lying-in chamber although the confinement should be a mon
away and Mrs. Cherry shook her head and said that sl
dreaded the day.

I did not reprove her; as long as Angelet did not hea
Mrs. Cherry's opinion did not matter.

Jesson went out in the afternoon and came riding ba
soon after he left with the news that there were Roundhea
soldiers in the district. They were pillaging the church som
five miles away and destroying the fine ornaments and a
evidence of what they called papistry.

I asked them not to tell my sister. I said, "It may well l
that they won't come this way and her time being so near it
not wise to alarm her unduly."

But I was on the alert. So was Phoebe. I told her not
leave the children and be ready to wrap them in warm thin
at a moment's notice.

Then I went to the kitchen and sent for Jesson and Cherr
I said, "It may be they will not come this way, but if th
do, it is useless to attempt to defend the place against the
That was what happened at Longridge Farm. There is o
thing we can do. We must get everyone down into the tunn
Begin now to take food and drink there and store it. We sha

safe there until they've gone. We're lucky to have such a
deaway."

Both the men agreed that this would be our only chance.

"We'll be ready then," I said.

Darkness had fallen when we heard the shouts of the sol-
rs and I knew then that what we had feared so long had
me to pass.

I quietly commanded Phoebe to tell the children that it was
new game we were playing and bring them down to the
chen. The house must be in darkness, but we would take a
ply of candles into the tunnel. Every one of us must go.

I went to Angelet and said, "The Roundheads may be here
thin five minutes. We are going down to the tunnel."

"You are the mistress of the house already," she replied.

"Don't be foolish," I cried. "You are coming down with me
once."

I wrapped a cloak around her and we had reached the
chen when I heard the shouts not far off.

"Where are the children?" cried Angelet.

"They are here. Everybody is here."

So we entered the tunnel between the castle and the house.

Through the night and the next day we stayed there. The
ildren slept through the night and when they awakened at
t they were excited by the new game, but we knew they
uld soon tire of it. When Lucas began to cry and said he
dn't want to play hideaway anymore, I had to tell him that
must be quiet because it wasn't a game. The soldiers were
the house and we were hiding from them. I saw I had to
ence him even if it meant frightening him a little, for our
es depended on silence at that time.

Arabella kept close to me, more intrigued than fearful; in
candlelight her eyes were luminous with excitement and
ey reminded me of Richard's.

"Soon they'll go away," I whispered, "and then we'll go
ck to the house."

I was more worried about Angelet than anyone. She was
ent and spoke to me only when necessary. I could not
lure this suspicion she had of me, implying that she be-
ved I wanted her to die so that I could marry Richard.

I kept thinking of incidents from our childhood when we
d been together and how important one had been to the
er. The hardest thing I had to bear was her animosity to-
rd me. I wanted her to lean on me, as she always had. Now

323

she leaned away from me. I had shattered the bond betwee
us when I had taken Richard.

I told myself that if we came through this night and day
would go right away. I would never see him again, so the
would not be the temptation to act as I had. I knew tha
could not explain to Angelet, for she would never understa
that overwhelming passion which had beset me.

We spoke in whispers.

Then Mrs. Cherry said suddenly, "What of the boy? W
of Strawberry John? We must get them in here. The soldi
will get into the castle. They'll break down the wall. Wha
happen to the boy? We must go through to the castle. \
must bring them in here."

Cherry said, "Strawberry John will take care of the boy

"But the Roundheads will get him. He's in the cast
Roundheads don't like castles and they'll know whose castle
is. They'll take revenge on one of the King's generals."

Her fingers were plucking at her skirt and her face look
wild in candlelight. I was afraid that she was going to becor
so hysterical that she would endanger us all by screaming
shouting or trying to get out to the boy and Strawberry Joh

Cherry tried to soothe her. "Now, Emmy, don't take c
He'll be all right."

"You don't care. You shot your own son, you did. O
Joseph. You just shot him down."

"I had to, Emmy. Stop it, I say. I had to shoot him. Y
know what happened last time."

"You shot him in the leg then. You could have shot him
the leg again. Couldn't you? But you shot him dead. Our so
He hadn't done anything. Perhaps he wouldn't have. H
just come back to see his mother. That's all he wanted befc
but he saw her in the chapel . . . and he was a natural m
and she was there . . . and he just did what others ha
done before him."

There was silence. Even Mrs. Cherry seemed appalled
what she had said.

Then she started crying. "We'll never get out of he
Those wicked men—they'll burn down the house. The
burn down the castle. What'll happen to us? The entra
will be blocked. We'll be buried alive. I want to get out
here."

"You're frightening the children, Mrs. Cherry," I s
sternly. And to them: "It's nothing . . . nothing. M
Cherry's only playing."

She was silent for a while and we were all straining our ears
t we could only hear muffled sounds.

"We're shut right away here," said Jesson.

Grace said, "Are you feeling all right, my lady?" and Ange-
whispered, "What was she saying about seeing someone in
 chapel?"

"It was nothing, my lady," began Cherry.

Mrs. Cherry said, "Don't try to hold me back, Cherry.
 're not getting out of here. There's that on my mind that
 e got to talk of it."

"Don't say anything, Emmy," said Cherry. "Please don't
 anything."

"It's so long . . . and it's too big a weight on my mind. I
 nt to own him for my own. That boy is mine. Why should I
 own him? I always believed one day he'd get better. He
 sn't bad all the time. He was kind and gentle except when
 turns took him. Joey was never that. He was always cruel
 d wanting to hurt. The boy wasn't. He was gentle. I wanted
 see him well and living like a gentleman in the house. It
 s to have been his. You see how wicked I was."

 was beginning to understand—piecing events and facts
 gether—but I did not want Mrs. Cherry to go on in front of
  children. I was afraid she might frighten them.

The boy in the castle was not the General's son. How could
 be if he were Mrs. Cherry's grandson? The madman had
 me to the house before. He had found Richard's first wife
 the chapel, had raped her, and given her a child—the boy.
Then why had she not denounced him? Why had they not
 own? But then I realized. That young girl—Magdalen was
 r name—was frightened of him, as Angelet had been. She
 d been afraid to tell Richard. But Mrs. Cherry knew and
 erry knew. They had shot him in the leg, but too late for
 agdalen.

Poor girl. What must her months of pregnancy have been
 e, knowing who was the father of the child she was to bear?
 madman.

I was watching Angelet. Was she taking it in? She was just
 ring at Mrs. Cherry as though she were seeing her for the
 st time and was startled by what she saw.

"I only wanted it for him," said Mrs. Cherry sobbing. "I
 ly wanted it for the boy."

"Hush," said her husband.

"It could have been his, couldn't it? I was going to fight for
 When he was eighteen I was going to fight. The son he
 s, or so they thought, and who was to say nay to that? Oh,

my God, and what's happening to him out there? He's
there and the soldiers are there and they hate castles—a
they know this is a General's castle—and my boy's there—
General's son—or so they think."

Then she began to laugh hysterically. "I was going to ma
it come right for him. I wasn't going to have any troubl
She was laughing, beginning to shriek.

I went to her and slapped her face.

She was quiet at once. Then she whispered, "We're go
to die. Like rats in a trap we're going to die. And that's wa
that's what we've been waiting for all these months. Nobod
have anything and the sin lies heavy on me. I would ha
killed her. I got rid of it the first time but that was easy, a
I was going to get rid of it again and make the way easy
my boy. I wasn't going to have anybody standing in his wa

Angelet said quietly, "It's all right, Mrs. Cherry. I und
stand everything now. I'm still here, you know. I've as mi
chance as anyone. I know why you did it all. I know w
happened to Magdalen . . . but it doesn't matter anymor

There was silence, broken by Arabella. "Are you an,
with Mrs. Cherry?" she asked me.

"No, no," I replied.

"She thinks you are. She's crying."

The silence of the tunnel was broken by the stifled sou
of Mrs. Cherry's sobs.

"It'll soon be over," I said to Arabella.

"Is it still a game?" she asked.

"Yes, it's still a game."

"I want to play something else now."

"You'll have to wait until this is finished—then we'll see.'

She snuggled close to me and, seeing that she was satisfi
Lucas and Phoebe's Little Thomas were too.

Jesson crept silently out of the tunnel to investigate.
was soon back.

"They've gone," he said. "The place is deserted, but they
left their mark."

We went back into the house. The tapestries had been t
from the walls and the brass and pewter ornaments w
missing. The chapel had been desecrated. I went up
stairs to our bedrooms. The rich hangings had been pul
down and in some cases torn into shreds and those emb
dered counterpanes which they had left were ruined.

The winery was flooded with wine. I supposed, wryly, t
had thought that was sinful and though they had not drun

mselves they had made sure that we never should. Our
res of food had been taken away. Most of the windows had
n broken. I sat down on a remaining chair and cursed the
pid war.

Then I thought of Angelet and her approaching confine-
nt. Everything we had prepared would be broken or re-
ved. I was trying to think what we were going to do when
eard loud cries and, hurrying down, was confronted by
ace in the kitchen.

"It's Mrs. Cherry. She's going fair mad. The devils have
n in the castle. They've smashed everything to bits."

"And the boy and his keeper?"

"They're dead . . . both of them. It looks as though they
ped from the turret. Strawberry John would never have
e that. It was certain death. I reckon the boy was trying it
John was stopping him. They're both lying out there.
n't go out, mistress, and keep my lady away. 'Tis not a
tty sight."

For a moment I felt limp, unable to plan, unable to think
ond the fact that the secret of the castle was over now and
had moved another step forward.

t was inevitable that all that had happened should have
its effect, and I wasn't completely surprised—nor was
ace—when Angelet's pains began and we knew that the
th was imminent.

The lying-in chamber which had been carefully prepared
s reduced to a shambles and we set about making some-
ng suitable to fit the occasion. It was not easy and Grace
s disturbed. The baby was coming before its time and that
s always somewhat dangerous.

t was good for us in a way to have something so important
do. I kept saying to myself, "We have lost so much but we
all here."

We made Angelet lie on one of the few beds which it was
sible to use and then we went in search of what we would
d. We found a little bed linen which had been overlooked
Jesson made a fire and we heated hot bricks which we
pped in flannel to warm the beds. Everyone was pressed
service. The children were slightly bewildered but I gave
m into the charge of Phoebe and made her impress on
m that we were still playing some extraordinary game
ch was sometimes frightening but sometimes exciting and
y must do as they were told.

Fortunately the soldiers had not harmed the cows and they

327

had failed to penetrate some of the outbuildings such as malting house, where grain and flour were stored, so we w able to get some food. Mrs. Cherry had been too distrau to do anything so Meg took her place in the kitchen and men tried to board up the windows to prevent the cold c ing in and repair the damage as much as possible.

But our great concern was for Angelet, for she looked v ill indeed. The birth was not difficult, though, and withi few hours her son was born. He was puny, being almos month premature, but he was sound in every way. Grace we were going to find the first months difficult in rearing h but once he'd got through them, established himself a were, there should be nothing wrong with him. It was A let who gave us cause for alarm. She was very weak and lacked so much that we needed.

I left the baby to Grace and made my sister my concer would sit by her through the day and night. Now and the would doze out of very exhaustion but I wanted her to kn that I was close. This seemed to give her some comfort an gave me a great deal. My sins weighed heavily on me they were nonetheless heavy because I knew that if I h been in the same position again I should have acted in exa the same way.

I wished I could have explained to Angelet.

She lay still, exhausted by her ordeal, but sometimes would smile at me and if I moved away I would see anxious look in her face.

Four days passed.

The baby was making some progress, and Grace said, ' ought to be baptized and christened. I could send Cherry my father for a priest."

I said she should do that.

I asked Angelet if she would like to call the baby Rich and she nodded, well pleased. So the child was christened I called him by the endearing diminutive of Dickon.

Grace talked to me seriously: "Our Dickon will live. H gaining weight . . . he's getting interested in life. But lady—it's been hard times for her. I don't know if we pull her through. There's so much we lack. The house de have what it should. I knew it was going to be difficult, bu we could have got it over before them Roundheads came—'

I said firmly, "We're going to get her well again. Sh live, Grace."

Grace looked at me as Angelet herself had so many tin suggesting that I was pitting my strength against that of G

But it did seem as though Angelet were getting stronger. She was talking more.

She said, "I like to have you here, Bersaba."

"Of course," I answered. "My place is here."

"It all went wrong didn't it? You should have been the one who came to London. You should have met him. That would have made him happy, wouldn't it?"

I said, "He is happy."

"You used to pride yourself on telling the truth. You always used to say, 'What's the good of pretending?' You must remember that now, Bersaba. I'm glad it wasn't you who was trying to kill me. I thought it was."

"You couldn't have thought that."

"Yes, I did. Because I knew someone was. I ought to have remembered that first time. But I thought that was due to the shock. They convinced me that it was. But I remember now Mrs. Cherry gave me some posset. There must have been something in that to bring on my miscarriage. She knew a great deal about herbs. She loved that boy. She wanted everything for him. She was afraid if I had a healthy child it would be his father's heir and she was going to fight with everything she had for that boy."

"Don't think about it now. It's past and done with. You have your baby. He's doing well, Angel. He's going to be a bonny boy. Grace says so, and Grace knows."

"I want to think about it. I want there to be complete understanding between us. I can see it all so clearly. Poor Magdalen! What a terrible experience for her, and it happened in the chapel, and for nine months she kept that secret from him."

"She should have told him."

"She couldn't, Bersaba. I understand. She was afraid of him, afraid it would turn him from her. I understand. I might have been the same. You are strong and so sure of yourself. You would have known what to do. But I understand. And then she died having that . . . creature . . . and he was Mrs. Cherry's grandson and she wanted everything for him. We mustn't be hard on Mrs. Cherry. It was all for love, Bersaba. We have to remember that."

"She was endangering your life for that—"

"For her grandson, and I don't think she wanted to kill me. She just wanted my child not to be born. Try to understand her, Bersaba. Let's try to understand everything."

"Angel," I said, "do you remember we used to say the

329

qualities—good and bad—were divided among us? You took all the good ones and left the bad to me."

"That's not true. You're so much more worthwhile than I am. Richard thought so . . . so did Luke . . . so will the children. Let's be truthful. I want you to marry Richard . . . if he comes out of this."

"Richard's wife is going to be well and when he comes back she is going to show him their beautiful child, young Dickon, and he will then be different. Don't forget this grim secret has been hanging over him all these years. Secrets like that warp people's natures."

"Will he ever come back?"

"This foolish war is not going to last forever."

"And if the Roundheads win?"

"There'll be some way out of it."

"If he comes back—"

"When he comes back," I said firmly, "you will be here waiting for him."

"In his house, which is little more than a ruin."

"You'll stay here somehow. It can't be long now and Richard will know what to do."

"And you, Bersaba?"

"I have made up my mind. I am going home. I shall take the children with me—Arabella and Lucas—and Phoebe will bring her Thomas. We shall ride down to Cornwall to our mother. Do you doubt she will be glad to see us?"

"She will rejoice to see you, Bersaba."

"And I shall tell her that you are waiting for your husband. It will relieve her mind."

"And when he comes back?"

"I shall be far away. As soon as you are strong I am going. You will have Grace to look after you and the servants here. You will manage until he returns. The soldiers will not come back. They have paid their call and left their mark on this beautiful house so that it is beautiful no longer and that should please them. Now rest, Angelet. I'm going to bring you some milk."

She smiled wryly. "You always wanted to bring me milk."

"I still do. We have two perfectly good cows which our Roundhead friends were considerate enough to leave us."

I leaned over the bed and kissed her.

"You are going to get well," I said, "and that makes me happy."

"Is that a command?" she asked.

"Of course."

Two days later her condition deteriorated and Grace talked darkly of fever.

I was with her all the time. She could not rest unless she had her hand in mine.

"It's strange, Bersaba," she said, "there's only going to be one of us."

"No, no. That's not so."

"It is. I know it. Now I want to talk to you seriously, Bersaba. Care for Dickon."

"I promise."

"Marry Richard . . . if he comes back. You can make him happy. I never could. I'm not clever enough. You amused him and were what he needed. Do you think I didn't know? I think I saw it when you were in the library playing your games. He came alive with you. You'll be happy. There's no secret now, is there? No ghosts . . . no specter . . . no living skeletons of the past. It's all clear now. So please, Bersaba, do this."

I kept saying, "You are going to get well. How could life be the same for me without you? Haven't there always been two of us?"

"It's better for there to be one sometimes. I'm happy that we are together now . . . in understanding. I have been so foolish. When I knew about you and Richard I thought you were trying to kill me. I deserve to die for that."

"I never heard such nonsense. Richard loves you. I am going away . . . I am going to leave you to be happy. You have your beautiful son. And I have my children."

"We both have his children, Bersaba. It seems that was meant. Of course we both loved the same man. We were as one person. I can be happy, Bersaba, if I think you are going to be and there is some purpose in my going."

I tried to reason with her, for I could not bear to hear her talk like that. I blamed myself for so much that had happened and there was small comfort in the knowledge that she did not blame me.

I sat by her bed through the night and in the early hours of the morning, she died.

I had never felt so alone in all my life.

Over the Sea

I STAYED at Far Flamstead for three months until I considered young Richard was old enough to travel; then I set out for Trystan Priory with my children, Angelet's son, and Phoebe and her child.

Traveling at such times was hazardous but it seemed hardly likely that either side would attack two women and a band of children. We took two of the young boys from the stable who were too young to be in either army and we set out.

It took us many weeks to travel, for we had to make many detours. Many of the inns we had known were no longer there. Sometimes we would sleep in the shell of a building to protect us from the night air. But it was by that time May and the weather was good. There was spring in the air and my spirits rose a little as I listened to the sound of the sedge warblers in the reeds and the call of the peewits and whitethroats. The hawthorns were weighed down with bud and blossom as I smelled their scent on the air and it was like a promise that life was ready to burst into flower again.

We had not been able to warn my parents of our coming and I shall never forget the moment when we rode into the courtyard. There was shouting and tumult throughout the house. There were my mother and father embracing first me and then the children; and that agonizing moment when they looked around for Angelet.

It was terrible to have to tell them. I feared my mother would never get over it. Secretly I believed that the balance of her affection had always tipped in Angelet's favor but that was because she was the complete mother and her concern went to the one she instinctively knew was in greater need of her protection.

I signed to Phoebe and she came forward and put young Dickon into my mother's arms; and I believe then that something happened to soothe the pain.

The child was hers from that moment. She was going to rear him, nurture him, make him strong and healthy, and she declared that he had a look of her beloved Angelet.

So I returned to Trystan Priory.

What happened is common knowledge.

There was the defeat at Naseby when the King lost half his army.

The news came slowly to Cornwall, but we knew in spite of our loyalty the Royalist cause was lost. The Parliament was demanding the control of the militia and the establishment of Presbyterianism throughout England and when this was refused the King became a fugitive and took refuge in the Isle of Wight. He was seized at Carisbrooke and brought to London.

There came that sad January day in the year of 1649 when our King was executed on the scaffold in front of the Banqueting House in Whitehall.

"Nothing will ever be the same again," said my father.

Indeed, everything was different. We must dress with somber propriety; we must go regularly to church; we must all conform to the standard set to us.

Grandfather Casvellyn, who was a very old man, had shouted his wrath with such vehemence that he had been seized with apoplexy and died. So life at Castle Paling was very different too. The girls had married, but Bastian had not.

As soon as he had known that I was home he had come riding to Trystan. Since then he has asked me to marry him on three occasions. On each one I have refused, but I have a notion that one day I might accept.

My mother wished me to. The children needed a father, she believed. It was becoming a new rather drab world, and a family could be a great comfort. I knew that Trystan was home for as long as I wanted, but I believe she secretly hoped I would become mistress of Castle Paling.

She would miss me. We used to sit in the evenings and talk about the days when Angelet and I were children. "You are so like her," she said, "that sometimes I feel that she lives on in you."

Phoebe was courted by Jim Stallick, who looked after the Priory horses; she married him but still continued to work for me, and I was glad to see her happy again.

It was a year after the death of the King. The war was not completely over, for the new King, Charles II, had come from the Continent to Scotland and was trying to raise his

333

standard. But Cromwell was too strong and the Royalists had little hope.

I was in the garden one day when a traveler came to the Priory.

He had asked for me and one of the servants brought him out to the garden. I took one look at him and knew.

Richard!

He had aged. How many years was it since I had seen him? Six . . . seven . . . seven hard years of hiding, secret planning . . . escaping from his enemies.

He took my hands and looked at me.

He said, "I went to Flamstead. They told me you were here."

"Are you well? You look exhausted."

"I have ridden far," he said.

"Then you must come into the house."

"It is not safe for you to entertain a fugitive from the King's Army."

"You would always find refuge here."

He shook his head. "I could not allow you to endanger yourself and your family. The news is bad. The King has been defeated and forced to flee the country. We must all go . . . and plan from someplace other than England. We shall not rest until Charles II is on the throne. I am going across the sea to plan for that day."

"You must come in. You need food and rest."

He said, "What I need is a boat that will take me to France."

"So you have come only to go away again."

"I came to see you."

"They told you what had happened at Flamstead?"

He nodded.

"Your beautiful house . . ." I said.

"But you were safe. I have come to ask you something. Perhaps it is too much. It could be dangerous."

I said, "Life is dull here. I hate the Puritan rule. I have realized that I am an ardent Royalist."

"It will not be easy in France."

"No?" I said excitedly. "But there would be a cause . . . something to fight for. I should have to bring the children— Arabella and Lucas. Dickon must stay with my mother. She would never let him go."

"Bersaba," he said, "you are the one thing in this world that hasn't changed."

I took his hands and looked into his face.

"I always knew what I wanted," I said. "It is as though the world has started to turn again."

"Then," he said, "you will come with me?"

"I'm surprised that you ask questions to which you know the answer. That's not like you."

"I couldn't believe it. I thought you might have changed."

"Never," I said. "Never."

We were married in the church yesterday. My father was able to provide us with a boat. We are going to sail tomorrow with the tide. I, Arabella, Lucas, and Richard. This is my last night in Trystan Priory, and I write here in the room I once shared with Angelet, and as I write I feel she is standing over me and that she is content.

I look out across the scene so familiar to me during my childhood. Somewhere beyond is the sea and tomorrow before it is light I with my husband and children will cross to France and there we will build a new future.

The Best in Gothic Romance